The Sweet Gum Tree

Katherine Allred

CERRIDWEN PRESS

What the critics are saying...

છ

5 Hearts "The Sweet Gum Tree will linger in my mind for weeks to come, and I'll be lucky if I can resist reading it again immediately." ~ *Tara Black, The Romance Studio*

"Once you start reading this narrative piece, you will not want to stop until the very end." ~ *Chantay, Euro-Reviews*

"THE SWEET GUM TREE is a well-written page turner, and the best book I have read this year. Very highly recommended and a Perfect 10."~ *Marilyn Heyman, Romance Reviews Today*

"Ms. Allred has proven her talent by writing an emotionally gripping and awe-inspiring novel destined to be read again and again." ~ *Joletta , Fallen Angel Reviews*

A Cerridwen Press Publication

www.cerridwenpress.com

The Sweet Gum Tree

ISBN 9781419953248
ALL RIGHTS RESERVED.
The Sweet Gum Tree Copyright © 2005 Katherine Allred
Edited by Pamela Campbell.
Cover art by Syneca.

This book printed in the U.S.A. by Jasmine-Jade Enterprises, LLC.

Electronic book Publication May 2005
Trade paperback Publication November 2005

Cerridwen Press is an imprint of Ellora's Cave Publishing, Inc.®

Also by Katherine Allred

ଽ

Second Time Around
What Price Paradise

About the Author

ଽ

In real life, I'm Kathy to those who know me, since Katherine has always sounded snooty to my ears. Physically, I'm 5'5" with brown eyes. The rest of me is subject to change at the whim of my caloric intake, exercise regimen (or lack thereof), and Miss Clairol. I've worked at everything from killing bugs to telephone operator. I have a degree in journalism that is stuffed in a drawer somewhere. I've been writing for seven years now and have sold seven novels, five most recently to Cerridwen Press. The Sweet Gum Tree won the PASIC Book of Your Heart contest in 2002 in the single title category. I've been a member of Romance Writers of America since the day I started writing, and serve as judge for numerous chapter contests. I've been married to the same man for thirty-eight years now. We got married when I was two. That's my story, I'm sticking to it.

Katherine welcomes comments from readers. You can find her website and email address on her author bio page at www.cerridwenpress.com.

THE SWEET GUM TREE

න

Dedication

જ

*For my grandfather, Cecil R. Sandefer, who not only
instilled in me a love for books and showed me how to
dream, he taught me everything I know about Wowzer
Cats. Miss you, Daddy.*

*And for Amy, Justin, and Jeremy. I can only hope we
gave you a childhood with as many good memories as I
have of mine.*

Chapter One

Growing up in the Crowley Ridge area of Arkansas, I paid little attention to the sweet gum trees except to admire their brilliant colors during the fall. And maybe to laugh when the Judge cursed each time he ran the lawn mower over the hard burs they produce, the tiny missiles banging against the house or car with a loud thunk and denting the mower blades he kept so carefully honed.

It wasn't until I was a grown woman that I realized the true nature of the tree. A sweet gum is the chameleon of wood, its corky exterior hiding its inner ability to imitate anything from cherry to mahogany. But its real value, one unrealized by most people, is its deep red heart, steady and strong. They see only the pale fibrous wood, easily warped, that surrounds the core.

Like the town of Morganville saw Nick Anderson.

As with most small town southerners, respectability was as much a part of my DNA as was my hair and eye color. It was the goal everyone strived for, the standard by which every citizen of Morganville was judged. And while my family, the Frenchs, weren't the richest–that honor going to Ian and Helena Morgan–we were one of the most respected. Thanks mostly to the Judge, my grandfather.

His name was Carl, but no one, including his daughters, had ever called him anything but Judge. He retired from the bench when I was five, and since my own father pulled a vanishing act shortly before my birth, the Judge stepped forward to fill that role for me. I thought the man walked on water and took every word from his lips as gospel.

"Alix," he told me. "Stay away from the railroad tracks. A wowzer cat lives under the trestle, and you don't want to get tangled up with one of those."

"What's a wowzer cat?" I asked, enthralled.

"It's a fifty pound cat with eight legs and nine bung holes, and it's meaner than a gar."

The Judge had an odd sense of humor.

The summer I was eight I'd spent most of my free time stretched out in the high grass near the trestle, trying my best to catch a glimpse of this elusive animal. I felt sorry for it and thought if anyone could tame it, I was that person. After all, hadn't I tamed the half-wild kittens in the barn?

I remained a believer until my first close encounter with Nick Anderson that fall.

Everyone knew who the Andersons were. Frank, Nick's father, owned the salvage yard on the outskirts of town. It was five square acres filled with the rusting, twisted corpses of dead vehicles, most of them shrouded in weeds or covered by wild morning glory vines. In between the rows lay pools of stagnant water, their surfaces multicolored with the iridescent hues from leaked oil. At the very back of the lot sat a tiny trailer, in little better shape than the vehicles surrounding it, where the Andersons, father and son, lived.

Frank Anderson was the only person in town who cared nothing about respectability. He was a large man, well over six feet, and his weight showed his propensity to strong drink. I never saw him dressed in anything but khaki pants, soiled with stains of unknown origin, his huge stomach, covered in a badly stretched T-shirt, sagging over his belt.

It wasn't uncommon to find him sitting on the bench in front of the general store or staggering down Main Street, a bottle gripped in his right hand, mumbling about the sons of bitches who all thought they were better than he was, and how he'd show them someday. Every kid in Morganville knew to give him a wide berth when he was in that condition. Frank

Anderson wasn't exactly what you'd call friendly even when he was sober. Drunk, he was downright dangerous.

Apparently, the only one who could stand him was Liz Swanner. Jenna Howard, my best friend since kindergarten, told me Mr. Anderson paid Liz to let him "do it" to her. I don't think either of us was exactly sure what that meant, but I thought Liz could probably use whatever money he gave her. After all, she had six kids to feed and no job to support them. The whole family was on welfare, although they barely got enough to survive.

The Swanner house was the last one between the salvage yard and town. It sat alone, an outcast from its neighbors, a single-story shotgun house with flakes of paint clinging here and there to its weathered boards. Several mangy dogs graced the bare dirt in front like living lawn ornaments, the southern equivalent of pink flamingos.

I stared out the truck window as the Judge drove by the Swanner's house, my curiosity boundless toward a life so different from my own, but there was no sign of human habitation. Lindsey, the youngest of the Swanner brood was in my class at school, but no one really knew her. She always kept to herself, seeming to shrink into invisibility in spite of her white-blonde hair and blue eyes. No one was ever cruel to her. Most of the kids simply forgot she was around.

That particular day, my mother and my aunts had run me out of the house while they prepared for the church social to take place the next day. It would be the last hurrah before school started and they were going all out for the event. Mounds of food already filled the refrigerator and both the Judge and I had been threatened with Dire Consequences if we were to touch it.

I was sitting on the swing that the Judge had made for me in the backyard; a logging chain with the ends wrapped around a sturdy branch of the sweet gum tree and nailed in place, with a notched board seat. Years of use had worn away the grass beneath it and left a deep groove where my feet dragged. Bored, I was contemplating enlisting Jenna to help me corner the wowzer cat when the Judge appeared from the shed and headed for his truck.

In stature, the Judge was one of the biggest men I've ever known, but physically, he was short without an ounce of fat on him. A pair of black glasses with thick lenses were constantly perched on his nose and his crew-cut hair was dark gray on the sides, blending into a lighter gray strip down the center of his head. His manner of dress was always the same; a brown work shirt and jeans on weekdays, a suit on Sunday.

As soon as I realized he was leaving, I leaped to my feet and followed. The Judge never offered to take me with him, and I never asked permission. It was understood by everyone concerned that where he went, I went too.

The truck passed the Swanner house and I shifted my gaze forward as we turned in at Anderson's Salvage Yard. The Judge pulled to a stop at the end of a row and we climbed out. The main focus of the salvage yard was the big tin building sitting in front of the gate, heat waves shimmering from the top and the scent of stale oil and gasoline permeating the air.

I could feel Frank Anderson's glare as soon as we stepped inside. He was sitting behind a dirty counter, his feet propped up on top of it. "Judge. What brings you out this way?" His voice was surly, like he was doing us a favor by acknowledging our presence.

"I'm looking for a fuel pump that'll fit the '52 Chevy I'm rebuilding. Think you might have something?"

The Judge had bought that car the day he retired and spent most of his time working on it. At first, he'd let me sit inside while he tinkered, until the day I accidentally blew the horn while his head was under the hood. Now I was banished to standing beside him, handing over tools as he needed them.

"I might." Mr. Anderson turned his head. "Hey, boy!"

The rustling sound from the back of the building was the first indication I had that Nick was present. Partially hidden by the shadows, he rose from the engine parts that were scattered around him like chickens around my mother's skirt at feeding time. Silently, he moved through the debris and stopped at the counter, waiting.

"Go take the fuel pump off that '52 Chevy pickup in the back of the lot." Mr. Anderson turned his glare back on the Judge. "It'll probably work."

When Nick grabbed a toolbox off the counter, I decided to go with him. The town being small, I knew who he was, but I'd never talked to him before. I was eight, he was ten, and even if there hadn't been a gap in our ages, Nick didn't frequent the same circles I did. As far as I knew, he didn't frequent any circles at all. The few times I'd seen him at school, he had always been alone, leaning against a tree or the building, watching but never participating in the play. The only difference between him and Lindsey Swanner was that everyone knew Nick was there. Even at ten he was hard to ignore.

"Don't get dirty, Alix," the Judge called as I skipped out the door.

"No, Sir. I won't." I was well aware of the repercussions from Aunt Darla, the oldest of my mother's sisters, if I got dirty. The woman considered dirt of any type her mortal enemy and searched it out with a diligence that was both frightening and awe-inspiring. When I was little she had me convinced that one speck of dirt on my person had the potential to kill me on the spot. It wasn't until I had a few bouts of hysteria that my mother forced Aunt Darla to retract her previous statements and assure me that I wasn't going to die. These days I repaid the favor by getting dirty at every opportunity, thereby sending Aunt Darla into a few hysterics of her own.

The Judge says what goes around, comes around, and we both understood his warning was mostly for show. At least if Aunt Darla yelled at him, he could honestly say he'd told me to stay clean.

Since Nick's legs were twice the length of mine, I had to run to catch up with him. When I did, I watched him from the corners of my eyes. He was tall for his age and thin, his body all sinew and bones that seemed to protrude in every direction. His black hair was thick and long, even for a world that used the Beatles and the Rolling Stones as the current fashion trend.

"You must know a lot about motors," I ventured when the silence became too much for me.

"I guess."

A thrill of excitement shot through my stomach. He was going to talk to me! "I help the Judge work on his car sometimes."

He glanced in my direction, his gray eyes skeptical. "You're too short to reach the engine."

My nose promptly went out of joint. "I am not short. My mother says I just have a delicate bone structure. Besides, I don't work on the engine, I hand him the stuff he needs."

When he didn't answer, I decided to forgive him for the insult. "My name is Alix."

His lips curved upward a bit. "I know who you are. Everybody in town knows who you are."

I was mortified by this news. Sure, I'd done some things that tended to get me noticed, like waltzing up the center aisle at church and stretching out on my stomach with my chin propped on my hands as I listened to Reverend Green's sermon. But that had been years ago and I was hoping people would quit bringing it up every chance they got. Having a reputation can be tough when you're eight. It was time to change the subject.

"I'm going to catch a wowzer cat this afternoon," I bragged. "It lives under the trestle down at the railroad tracks."

One of his eyebrows shot up. "What's a wowzer cat?"

"It's a fifty pound cat with eight legs and nine bung holes, and it's meaner than a gar. But I'm going to tame it and take it home with me."

This time his teeth showed when he grinned. "Even if it was real, why would you want to take something like that home?"

I wasn't about to admit I felt sorry for it. "To scare my Aunt Darla." I hesitated. "You don't think there really is a wowzer cat?"

He stopped at a battered blue pickup and took out a crowbar to pry up the hood. "Who told you there was?"

"The Judge."

One of his shoulders lifted in a shrug. "Maybe he was trying to scare you into staying off the tracks. They're too dangerous for a kid to play on."

He moved around the truck to lean over the fender well, his too-small shirt riding up his back with the movement, and suddenly I forgot all about wowzer cats and my reputation as I stared at the raw welt he'd exposed.

The only time I'd ever been hit by an adult was when Mama swatted my bottom for saying a cuss word that I'd heard the Judge use, in front of a church elder, and then I cried for two hours. Mama felt so guilty she cried with me and promised to never spank me again. Next time I cussed, she'd just wash my mouth out with soap and have done with it. But I knew instinctively what the mark on Nick's back was. It was two inches wide and curved around his side, the edges of the strip laced with cuts, most of it dark blue in color.

Lifting one finger, I touched the mark gently. "Does it still hurt?"

His body jerked and stiffened as he spun to stare at me, his eyes going the same shade of black-gray as the sky when it's going to storm. I stared right back, not willing to give an inch, but inside a mixture of horror and sympathy filled me. None of it showed on my face, though. I understood pride.

"Why did he hit you?"

Nick's hand tightened around the wrench he was holding. "He doesn't need a reason." He glanced toward the tin building. "Look, don't say anything to anybody, okay? Most of the time I stay out of his way."

"I won't tell, I promise. But you need some medicine on it." For once I was willing to take Aunt Darla at her word. Uneasy visions of gangrene, tetanus, and infection bounced inside my head.

"Don't have any. Besides, it's getting better."

Maybe, but I wasn't taking any chances. "I'll be right back." I headed for the truck at a run, and once there, rummaged frantically through the glove box until I found the small round tin I was searching for. Bee balm.

Wherever the Judge went, there was sure to be bee balm nearby. He bought it in bulk, twelve tins to the box, and swore the salve could cure anything. I knew from firsthand experience that its powers were nothing short of miraculous. The Judge had slathered it on me for everything from a splinter wound to a skinned knee, and each time I had healed with no permanent damage. The only unhappy incident connected to the salve was the time I thought it must be a balm to soothe bees and applied it to the back of a honey bee gathering nectar from the clover in our yard. Unfortunately, the salve stuck the bee and me together, and I wound up getting stung. Obviously, it was not meant to soothe bees, because that one was pretty ticked off by the experience.

Nick had one end of the fuel pump off by the time I slid to a stop beside him. "Hold up your shirt."

He paused, eyeing the tin in my hand. "What's that?"

"Bee balm. It will keep you from getting an infection." I ignored the gleam of amusement in his eyes as he straightened and lifted his shirt just enough to expose the welt.

Keeping the honeybee in mind, I dipped out a tiny bit of salve and went to work on his back. His skin was hot under my hand, and in spite of his scruffy, worn clothes I could smell the clean scent of soap coming from him. He watched me, his expression hooded as I moved around his side and finished where the welt ended on his stomach.

"There. All done." I put the lid back on the tin and held it out. "You can keep it. We've got lots more."

Still watching me, he slid it into his shirt pocket. "Are you gonna be a nurse or something?"

"Nope. I'm going to be a writer."

His expression turned to one of intense interest. "It takes someone special to write books."

"Well, I'm special, then, 'cause that's what I'm going to do."

"You may be right, Peewee." He lifted a hand and tugged on one of my dark pigtails. His tone was so warm that I couldn't take offense at the nickname. Coming from him, it sounded more like an endearment than another slur on my size.

"Do you like to read?" I asked, leaning on the fender as he went back to work.

"When I can. The old man thinks reading is a waste of time. He'd rather spend his money on liquor than books."

This attitude boggled my mind even more than his wounded back. Everyone in my family read. Books were as necessary to us as food or sleep. I don't know how old I was when I started reading, but I know my mother accidentally discovered my talent when I was four. She had bought me a new fairy tale, promising to read it to me that night when I went to bed. Unwilling to wait that long, I was reading it aloud to my dolls when she came into the room. From the amount of excitement this feat generated, you'd have thought I'd found the cure for cancer. I couldn't imagine anyone who thought reading was a waste of time.

I was still thinking about this weird □avourite when I caught a movement from the corner of my eye. Lindsey Swanner was standing a few cars down from us, one finger in her mouth as she watched Nick. Her hair was tangled around her shoulders, and she was barefoot.

"What's she doing here?"

"Waiting on me." He finally freed the fuel pump and pulled it out from under the hood.

"Why?"

He shrugged one shoulder and wiped an arm across his sweaty forehead. "I take care of her."

"Why?"

"Because nobody else does."

"Is she your sister?" I asked, my curiosity growing.

He gave me a wary look, but shook his head. "No, her daddy was Paul Nyland. He died in an accident at the lumber mill before she was born. They moved here right after that."

A sudden surge of pity hit me and I turned and marched up to Lindsey. Nick followed, his stance suddenly restrained and defensive. I should have paid more attention to his attitude. If I had, I might have saved myself a lot pain further down the road. But at eight, I only knew one thing. Mother said God put each of us on this earth for a purpose, and that day I decided mine was to save Nick Anderson. If that meant helping Lindsey at the same time, I was more than willing.

Lindsey cowered as I faced her, her blue eyes huge.

"We're having a church social tomorrow," I told her. "There's going to be lots of food, and singing and games. You don't have to get dressed up, and you don't even have to go to church first if you don't want to. It's going to be at the park. You make Nick bring you. I'll be waiting."

At the time, I was unaware the Judge had watched the entire thing through the small grime-encrusted window of the tin building. He remained thoughtful as we drove back through town.

"You like that Anderson kid?"

I was sitting on my knees, wondering if I could talk him into stopping at the Mercantile for a soda when he asked me the question. "He's okay, for a boy."

"You may be right, Honey pie." He rubbed a hand over his crew-cut. "But you be careful with him. Don't let your soft heart overrule your common sense."

I sighed as we passed the store without slowing. "I asked him and Lindsey to the church social tomorrow. Was that all right?"

"I reckon. But you best tell your mother about it, and don't be disappointed if they don't come."

"Yes, sir."

My mother, Ellie, was the youngest of the Judge's daughters, and the only one who'd gotten married. Aunt Darla was the oldest, with Aunt Jane, the quiet one, falling somewhere in the middle. They all lived with the Judge in the big old two-story house that sprawled on our small farm about a mile from town.

I knew they had an older brother, my Uncle Vern, but I'd never met him. He'd moved away a long time before I was born and married a woman the family didn't approve of. When he was spoken of at all, it was in hushed whispers, by everyone but my mother. She had no problem bringing his name up on a regular basis, to Aunt Darla's irritation.

"He's my brother and I'll talk about him when I want to," I heard my mother calmly pronounce as I bounced through the kitchen door. She was at the table, putting the finishing touches on a lemon icebox pie. Aunt Darla was at the sink, washing vegetables. Being wise, Aunt Jane had already fled the area.

"Whether you like it or not, Sister," my mother continued, "Vern is still part of this family. I think it's a shame we never get to see him and his children."

"Shame is right," Aunt Darla retorted. "Vern's ashamed of that woman he married, as he well should be. Imagine, marrying someone who danced in a bar."

These discussions were nothing new to me. Trying to keep a low profile, I took a glass from the cabinet and edged toward the pitcher of lemonade on the table. I didn't get far before Aunt Darla paused in her tirade and sniffed suspiciously.

"Is that gasoline I smell?" She leaned closer to me and sniffed again. "It is! Alix, where have you been?"

"I went to the salvage yard with the Judge. He had to get a fuel pump for his car."

"I swear, the Judge should have better sense than to take a little girl to a place like that. Ellie, are you going to let him keep this up?"

Mama smiled at me, her blue-green eyes that were so like my own, sparkling. "It looks like she survived the trip."

I made it to the lemonade and poured a glass before sitting down. "Mama, I invited Nick Anderson and Lindsey Swanner to the church social. The Judge said I should tell you."

To her credit, she barely blinked. "That was very kind of you, Alix. We should have thought of inviting them a long time ago." She shot a glare in Aunt Darla's direction and I glanced over my shoulder in time to see my aunt's mouth snap closed.

Not only was Aunt Darla our first line of defense against dirt, she was also the staunch protector of our respectability. Any indication that our position in society might be threatened sent her into a quivering fit of righteous indignation and a lecture on the rules of proper ☐avourite.

While nothing was ever said in my presence, I knew my mother's divorce and her insistence that both she and I use her maiden name had caused something of a scandal in the family. But although she was the youngest, my mother was the only person alive who could quell Aunt Darla with a single look.

I turned back to my mother. "Is it okay if I give Nick some of my books? His daddy won't let him buy any."

From behind me Aunt Darla snorted, but I paid no attention.

"They're your books, Alix. You can do whatever you want with them."

"Thank you, Mama." I jumped up. "I'm going to pick some out right now."

As soon as I reached the stairs, I stopped and turned to listen. I'd found out that the really interesting conversations always happened shortly after I left the room. Nor was I to be disappointed this time.

"You're making a mistake, letting her get involved with that boy." My aunt's voice floated through the door. "You know what Frank Anderson is like."

"Yes, I do." Mother's voice was calm. "I also know it's not the boy's fault. Would you visit the sins of the father on the son, Sister?"

My aunt sniffed. "The apple doesn't fall far from the tree. Give him another year or two and he'll end up just like his daddy."

"And if he does, who will be to blame? We've known from the beginning that Frank Anderson wasn't fit to raise a child, but we've all looked the other way. So who's doing the right thing? Us by ignoring that boy, or Alix by caring enough to try and reach him? If he does show up tomorrow, I fully intend to invite him to this house whenever he wants to come."

"You wouldn't!"

"Yes, I would. I'm not turning my head anymore. Maybe we can show that young man there's more to life than what he's learning from Frank."

Oh, sweet bliss. I shut my eyes as vindication rolled over me. Mama was on my side. She was going to help me save Nick. Together, how could we fail?

I paused with a guilty jump on the bottom step. Aunt Jane was standing at the top of the stairs, arms crossed over chest as she watched me. Lifting a finger to her lips, she tilted her head toward the bedroom.

Next to Mama and the Judge, Aunt Jane was my avourite person in the whole world. I often wondered where her looks came from. The rest of us all had dark hair and light eyes, but Aunt Jane's hair was a warm honey color, her expressive eyes dark as night. Mama said she was the spitting image of her great-grandmother, but since there were no pictures of the lady, I had to take her word for it.

I had picked up snippets of conversations that led me to believe Aunt Jane had once been deeply in love, but, through circumstances over which she had no control, had lost the man of her dreams. This made her a tragic figure in my eyes, a Sleeping Beauty waiting for the awakening kiss of her prince.

As soon as we were out of earshot from the kitchen she put a hand on my shoulder. "Alix, you know it's not polite to listen to other people's conversations."

"Yes, Ma'am." I hung my head.

She put her finger under my chin and tilted my head back up until I looked at her. "Tell me, why this sudden interest in the Anderson boy?"

"I don't know. I guess I feel sorry for him."

"You're sure that's what it is?"

"Not just that. I like him. He's not like his daddy," I said with a touch of defiance.

A smile lifted her lips. "Good. Helping someone because you feel sorry for them is one thing, but doing it because you like them and care about what happens to them is better. That means you aren't doing it for yourself."

"Aunt Darla says her charity work with the children's home makes her feel good."

"I know, but that's different, Alix. The home is an institution. They depend on people's charity to help them care for a lot of kids that wouldn't have a place to live without them. Nick Anderson isn't an institution. He's a person. How do you think he'd feel if he thought you looked on him as a charity case?"

I knew how I'd feel. Insulted, indignant, mad, hurt. "It's not like that, Aunt Jane. I swear."

She nodded. "I didn't think so, but I wanted to make sure you knew the difference. Be his friend, Sweetie, but don't insult him by feeling sorry for him. No one wants pity."

"Yes, Ma'am."

So I gained another ally in my mission to save Nick. And while I didn't know it yet, the Judge would prove the greatest attraction of all for this lonely boy with the strong, steady heart.

Chapter Two

ಬ

Morganville has one city park, a well-manicured ten acres that sits on the side of a hill and offers a fine view of the town below. A few years ago the community built a restroom, a jogging track and added another, more modern playground. But the day my family met Nick, there were only numerous picnic tables, a few blackened iron grills on pipe stands, one swing set and a slide, all grouped under the shade of stately oaks, elms, and sweet gum trees.

Church, never my favorite way to spend a warm summer morning at the best of times, had been pure torture for me. I was anxious and fidgety, unable to muster even a pretense of interest as I sat on the wooden pew, squeezed between Mama and the Judge. Mama told me twice to be still, and the Judge kept offering me gum. I had to stop accepting after five pieces. My teeth were sticking together and I could barely open my mouth to chew.

When the last amen was said, I made a run for the bathroom, dodging through the parishioners like a steel bearing in a pinball machine, to skin out of my good dress and into my denim shorts and red top. By the time I got back outside, most of the women, including my mother and aunts had left for the park and I knew they would be pushing tables together, setting the food out, and laying claim to each family's eating area. Most of the men were gathered in knots outside the church, smoking, talking and laughing.

I located the Judge under a cloud of pipe smoke and shifted from foot to foot, waiting for a break in the conversation. What if Nick and Lindsey showed up, then left because I wasn't there? That thought was enough to have me tugging on the Judge's hand, and a surge of relief filled me when he headed for the truck.

Our church socials could have done justice to a presidential gala as far as the food was concerned. Six tables were shoved together, their worn tops covered with an assortment of multicolored linen tablecloths. They groaned from the weight of bowls and dishes, huddling together without an inch to spare between them. Women bustled around the food, removing foil coverings and plastic lids, sneaking surreptitious looks at the offerings of others, secretly comparing it to their own.

As soon as the truck slowed to a stop, I bolted out the door, winding my way to Mother. She was laughing with Helena Morgan when I reached her. "Have you seen them?" I whispered urgently.

Leaning over, she put her lips near my ear. "Over by the woods. You make sure he stays, Alix."

"I will." My gaze was already scanning the shaded area at the edge of the park. It took me a while to find him. His dark shirt and pants blended in with the shadows and he stood so still he seemed part of them. He was alone.

Reaching down deep for a dignity I was far from feeling, I forced myself to stroll casually in his direction. Even though I could only see his outline, I could feel him watching me.

"Hi." I stopped in front of him and he straightened, looking down at me as if I were a mystery he had to solve. "I'm glad you came."

"I'm not staying. I only showed up to tell you not to wait. Lindsey doesn't like to be around strangers." His clothes were cleaner than normal, his shirt neatly ironed and no stains decorated the worn jeans. If he hadn't wanted to stay, why go to the trouble? That insight made me even more determined to keep him there.

"You can't leave." I took his hand. If I'd thought it would help, I'd have wrapped my arms around his legs and hung on for dear life to keep him at the park. How was I going to save him if he wouldn't cooperate? "I have something for you."

"What?" He tried to shake me loose, but I refused to let go. His hand felt good in mine. Strong and warm.

"I brought you some of my books."

Longing flowed from him even as he denied it. "I don't take charity."

"It's not charity. I'm not giving you the books, I'm loaning them to you. Just like a library does. Besides, I've already read them, so they were sitting there gathering dust."

That wasn't exactly the truth, but I was hoping God understood the deception. After two hours of anxiety-ridden deliberation, I had made up my mind to give him the most treasured jewels on my bookshelves, Tolkien's *Lord of the Rings* trilogy. I didn't understand back then that most kids weren't at my advanced reading level, but even if I had, I would have trusted Nick to grasp the concept behind the stories. I'm not sure why I believed in him so strongly. I only know that I did.

He hesitated, his gray eyes moving over the crowd of people filling the park. I could almost read his mind. *I don't belong here*, he was thinking. *They'll make me leave.*

"Mama said to make sure you stayed," I tempted him. "Her feelings will be hurt if you don't eat with us. She and my aunts have been cooking for days." In the south, we absorb polite manipulation and velvet-edged diplomacy with our mother's milk.

"You told her you invited me?"

"Yes. And she said you're welcome in our house any time you want to come."

"You wouldn't be lying just to get me down there, would you, Peewee?" His eyes were as soft as his voice when he looked at me.

"I don't lie." My free hand behind my back, I crossed my fingers. Just in case God had been listening when I'd told Nick about the books. "You go to hell for lying."

"She really said that?"

"Yes. And the Judge said it was okay for you to come, too."

Visibly, he braced himself, then nodded.

When I stepped out of the trees, tugging Nick along behind me, every kid in the park stopped what they were doing and gaped at us. There was no doubt my reputation had just risen another couple of notches, or dropped, depending on your point of view, but for once I didn't care. The only thing I cared about was his grip, getting tighter and tighter on mine the nearer we got to the picnic tables. Part of him couldn't believe he would be accepted as easily as I made it sound, and he was waiting for the axe to fall.

The hum of adult conversation rippled to a halt as I led Nick to my mother. A dull red flush tinted the skin on his face and neck, and sweat made his hand slick on mine.

"See, Mama? I told you he'd stay."

"So you did." She smiled at Nick. My mother was always beautiful, but when she smiled you could almost hear a heavenly choir break into song. "Nick, I'm glad you made it. Our table is right over there and I expect you to join us, you hear?"

"Yes, Ma'am."

He must have heard the choir too, because he was looking at my mother as through he'd seen an angel. Behind Mama, Helena Morgan's lips thinned to a tight line and she shared a disgusted look with Gretchen Treece, the mayor's wife. I hoped Nick hadn't seen them.

The two women, along with my mother and aunts, were the core of high society in Morganville. The town had been named after one of Ian Morgan's ancestors, and they owned the lumber industry that employed most of the people in the area. Mr. Howard, my best friend Jenna's father, worked for them. Hugh, the Morgan's only child, was the same age as me and because our mothers were friends, we had been forced to endure each other's company since we were in diapers. Hugh was always pulling my hair or taking advantage of my competitive nature by challenging me to feats both dangerous and stupid. Most of my scars were the result of dares I couldn't resist. But I never looked on Hugh as malicious. He was only a boy who liked to tease me, and while it was aggravating, I could live with it.

Piggy Treece, known to everyone but Jenna and me as Peggy, was a different story. The overweight blonde daughter of Mayor Tim and Gretchen was spoiled rotten. If ever a child was born hateful, it was Peggy. She hung around Hugh constantly, making snide remarks about the other kids in general and me in particular. We hated each other with the fervor of born enemies. At the moment, she was standing near Hugh, hands on her chunky hips as she smirked in my direction. I turned my back on them.

"Mama, where did you put the books?"

"They're in the basket on our table."

I tugged on Nick's hand. "Come on. Wait until you see what I brought." If I'd known the pain those books would cause him before the week was out, I doubt I would have given them to him. But then, if I'd been able to see the future I might have done a lot of things differently where Nick was concerned.

Handing them over one at a time, I explained they were about Hobbits, little people from a place called Middle Earth. Nick took each book as though it were made of a rare and precious glass that could break if he touched it wrong.

"You've read these?" He looked from the thick books to me and back again.

"Sure. They're my favorites, but I like all kinds of science fiction and fantasy. I've got tons. When you finish these, you can bring them back and pick out some more you like."

"Why are you doing this?" One of his hands caressed the books.

"Because books are made to be read," I told him. "And you like to read."

"A church picnic is one thing, but your folks aren't going to want me hanging around your house."

"I told you, Mama said you're welcome anytime you want to come."

"She was being polite."

"Mama is always polite, but she wouldn't have said it if she didn't mean it."

He didn't start believing me until later that day, while we were eating. It was the Judge who convinced him.

Our picnics have a strict hierarchy when it comes to serving food. One of the men says grace, then the chaos begins. Children's plates were fixed first, and when they were settled and busy eating, the men lined up, women fussing around them, making sure they found everything. The women went last, being careful to sample every dish on the tables so no one would have hurt feelings.

When the children were called, Nick followed me reluctantly. We were an island of two in a sea of kids as we made our way down the table, everyone giving us a wide berth. When it became clear to me that he wasn't going to dig in, I did it for him, piling his plate high with everything I thought he might like. Heaps of potato salad, baked beans, corn on the cob, and deviled eggs were topped by slices of ham, fried chicken, and yeast rolls. Our paper plates threatened to fold and collapse as we carried them to our table.

I left Nick staring between the food and the books, an inscrutable expression on his face, and darted back into the fray to snag two sodas from a cooler of ice. By the time I made it back, the Judge had taken a seat across from Nick and was quizzing him about engines. One of the best things about the Judge was that he never talked to you like you were a kid.

"You like working on engines?" I heard as I plunked a soda in front of Nick.

"Yes, sir. Engines make sense, like a big jigsaw puzzle. Each part has one place where it fits and the motor won't work unless that part is where it's supposed to be."

The Judge nodded. "Problem is trying to figure out which parts are the bad ones. I'm hoping the fuel pump I bought yesterday helps. I've been working on that Chevy for three years now and still haven't managed to start it."

"What does it do when you try?"

And just like that, Nick was lost. He and the Judge talked engines the rest of the afternoon. I don't think he even realized that he'd cleaned his plate, one hand staying possessively on the books while they mulled over possible mechanical failures and how to rectify the trouble. Not even the presence of my mother and aunts slowed the discussion. I stayed with them, forgoing a chance to whip some butt in the softball game after dinner, happy to simply watch Nick. I'd never seen him so animated before, so enthusiastic, and it fascinated me. He was beautiful in a way I'd never considered. His black hair shot blue-white highlights when he moved. His gray eyes sparkled with interest. And when he laughed, dimples appeared in his cheeks, giving him a mischievous look. Once I caught my mother and both aunts staring at him with a bemused expression before they gave each other meaningful glances.

In hindsight, I suspect that was the day my crush on Nick started. I was only eight and I didn't understand love and desire, would have thought it was disgusting if anyone had told me about it, but watching him made me feel warm and content inside. Somehow, my mission had gone from saving him to keeping him close enough that I could see him every day. My brain whirled with schemes and plans, but the Judge solved my dilemma before I could put any of them into action. By the time the picnic ended and everyone was packing to go home, Nick had agreed to help the Judge work on the Chevy whenever he had some free time.

* * * * *

School was due to start the Friday after the picnic, which gave me only a few more days to savor my freedom. On Wednesday, Jenna received permission from Droogin the Dragon, a neighbor her father paid to take care of her while he worked, to visit me for the day. We were starting fourth grade that year and we did an in-depth analysis of everything from the teacher, and the clothes we'd bought, to the other kids in our class. Somehow, I managed to restrain myself from talking about Nick. He was mine, and I didn't want to share him even with my best friend.

Jenna reminded me a lot of Little Orphan Annie. She didn't have the funny eyes, but she sure had the hair. It was bright red, a tangled mass of fiery corkscrews that defied any attempt to tame it. Her personality went right along with her hair. She was a live wire, never still, always talking. Small doses of Jenna usually went a long way, but for me she was perfect. While I didn't have a shy bone in my body, I enjoyed listening more than talking, which suited Jenna to a tee. There was nothing I liked better than curling up with a book for hours on end. Jenna thought books were a form of torture inflicted on us by sadistic teachers who wanted to make our lives miserable. I'd done my best to change her attitude, but truthfully, I think she couldn't sit still long enough to read.

We were in the barn that day, playing with the newest batch of kittens to arrive. They were three weeks old, tottering on weak legs as they explored us and their surroundings. The mother, still half-wild, sat on the other side of the barn keeping a watchful eye on her babies.

"Hugh likes you," Jenna stated.

"Yuck! He does not." I ran a hand over the soft fur of a black kitten attached to my shirt like Velcro.

"That's why he's always teasing you."

"He teases everyone. That's just Hugh."

"Well, I think he's cute."

"You think all boys are cute." Jenna was light-years ahead of me when it came to the opposite sex. She had passed the point where all males were nuisances in the third grade.

I caught a movement out of the corner of my eye and glanced toward the open barn doors. Nick's gaze met mine and he smiled a little before vanishing in the direction of the shed. During the last few days, he seemed to have developed an uncanny knack for knowing when the Judge was going to be working on the Chevy. As soon as the Judge raised the hood, Nick would appear. They would huddle over the engine like doctors trying to save the life of a patient on the operating table, mumbling to each other as they poked this and prodded that. Usually I stood nearby, the nurse waiting to slap the appropriate tool into an outstretched hand.

"Wrench." *Whack.*

"Screwdriver." *Whack.*

But today, I had company. They would have to get along without me.

"What's he doing here?" Jenna's blue eyes narrowed as she watched me.

"Helping the Judge work on his car."

She tugged a straw over the ground, letting one of the kittens make tentative swipes at it. "Piggy is telling everyone you're in love with him because you brought him to the picnic Sunday. She calls him Nasty Nicky."

Instantly, I bristled. "He is not nasty. He's a lot cleaner than Piggy. She sweats all the time." Jenna and her father hadn't been at the picnic. When they went at all, they attended the Methodist church near their house.

"I know." Her turned-up nose wrinkled. "I had to sit next to her in art last year. So why did you take him to the picnic?"

I shrugged. "Because he's nice, once you get him to talk to you. I like him. And he's not like his father. He reads books."

She lifted her blue eyes heavenward. "Well, that explains it. Anyone who reads is a saint to you. He's probably your soul mate."

"What's a soul mate?"

"The person you're supposed to marry when you grow up."

"I'm not getting married," I insisted. "I'm going to be a writer."

"Don't you want to have kids?"

I thought about the question for a second or two. There were several babies in our church and I always enjoyed playing with them. "Maybe."

"Well, you have to be married if you want kids."

"Liz Swanner isn't married and she has six."

We stared at each other as we pondered this mystery.

"Maybe if she were married she wouldn't have had that many," Jenna ventured. "Let's go ask your mother."

"Okay."

My mother solved the dilemma very simply. She told us we thought too much and then shoved a handful of warm cookies at us.

Jenna had to leave shortly after that so the topic was dropped, but I couldn't stop wondering. Nick would surely know. After all, he lived next door to the Swanners. The problem was getting him away from the Judge long enough to ask. Instinctively, I knew the Judge wouldn't approve of my discussing the situation with Nick.

I didn't get the opportunity to ask him that day. By the time I got to the shed, he had already left. I didn't see him again until the next night, and my first glimpse of him then scared all the questions right out of my head.

* * * * *

"Alix? Take the scraps from supper out to the barn for the cats," my mother called from the kitchen.

"Yes, Ma'am." I had been lying on my stomach on the living room floor, reading and listening to the cicadas singing through the open windows as dusk fell. The Judge, pipe stem gripped between his teeth, was sitting in the recliner reading the newspaper.

Even though it had been years since the barn housed any horses or cows, it was still the home of many smaller animals. Not only did it serve as a refuge and nursery for a large cat population, we got an occasional stray dog, a few barn owls, some pigeons, squirrels, a possum or two, and of course, the mice. Once I had even surprised a small gray fox. All of which is probably why I wasn't alarmed when I heard a rustling from the back of the building.

There were a couple of tin plates set out and I dumped half the contents of the bowl into each one, using a spoon to scrape the last drops off. Some of the friendlier cats had come running as soon as I stepped into the barn. The others waited until I straightened and stepped away from the food.

The rustling came again, followed by a low moan. The hair on my neck and arms popped erect as I stared into the darkness. No animal was making that noise. "Who's there?"

When no one answered, I edged toward the door and reached for the light switch. The Judge had installed electricity in the barn at the same time he'd converted the tack and feed rooms into living quarters for Mr. Bob, our handyman. No one had used the room since Mr. Bob died, although it was still kept furnished, and cleaned on a regular basis.

Taking a deep breath, I hit the switch, a gasp escaping my lips as I saw where the noise came from. Nick was lying on his side, curled protectively around something clenched to his stomach. The bowl I was holding slid from my fingers and I darted across the building, falling to my knees beside him. "Nick? What's wrong?" He was so still I was terrified, afraid he was dead. "Nick?" When I touched his shoulder to shake him, he groaned again and opened his eyes, their gray depths glazed with pain.

"Your books," he whispered. "I tried to hide them, but he found them, was going to burn them. Couldn't let him do it. I had to bring them back." Slowly, he uncurled one arm to expose the books he held so tightly.

It wasn't until I reached for them that I realized my hand was wet. I stared in horror at the red coating my fingers. "You're bleeding!"

"I'm okay. Have to go."

He struggled to rise, but I held him down. How he'd walked the three miles from the salvage yard to our farm I'll never know. But one look at his shredded back convinced me all the bee balm in the world wasn't going to fix this. His shirt was in tatters, blood oozing from dozen of wounds. I had to get help, fast.

"Don't move. I'm going to get Mama."

"No." His hand closed around my arm. "You promised you wouldn't tell anyone. If they find out, they'll put me in a home."

Tears filled my eyes as he tried again to stand. I couldn't let him leave. He'd never make it home. "Wait. Please. Let me get the Judge. I'll make him promise not to do anything before I tell him. He'll know what to do."

A shiver racked his slim frame and he settled back to the floor like a deflated balloon. Nick's world contained no shades of gray. Everything was black and white. Either you were a good guy who could be trusted, or you weren't. He had already decided the Judge and I were part of the good guys.

"Make him promise," he whispered, his eyes closing.

I shot out of the barn faster than I'd ever moved, only slowing when I reached the kitchen, half-afraid he'd change his mind and try to leave again before I got help. My mother and my aunts were still cleaning up after supper, and I held my hand behind my back so they wouldn't see the blood.

"Alix? Where's the bowl?"

"I'm sorry. I forgot and left it in the barn. I'll get it in just a second."

The Judge looked up as I leaned over the arm of his chair. "Come outside with me, please? It's an emergency," I whispered.

One of his eyebrows went up, but he folded the paper, stood and followed me into the night. "What's wrong, Alix?"

A lone lightning bug drifted between us as I stared up at him. "Before I tell you, he said you have to promise not to tell anyone else."

"Who said I have to promise?"

"Nick. Please, Judge. He's afraid if you know you'll send him to a home."

I think he must have heard the desperation in my voice because he nodded. "Okay, I promise no one is going to send him to a home."

"He's in the barn and he's hurt really bad." I held out my hand to show him the blood. "I don't know what to do."

He headed toward the barn, his jaw clenched. "Stay here."

"I can't. He'll leave if I'm not with you."

When he didn't answer, I took it as permission to go with him. As far as I was concerned, Nick was my responsibility and if I had to risk punishment to stay with him, I would.

I'd heard more than one person in town say the Judge was like an avenging angel when he'd sat on the bench, that justice and honor meant more to him than his own life, but I didn't understand what they meant until that night. I'd never even seen the Judge mad before, but I saw it now.

Nick had managed to sit up. His head hung limply and he was breathing heavily when the Judge reached him. My grandfather's entire body went stiff and I swear his eyes blazed fire. A string of words I'd never heard before issued from his lips, but when he spoke to Nick his voice was soft.

"I'm gonna help you stand up, son. Alix, open the door to Mr. Bob's room. We'll put him in there."

I hurried to obey, turning the light on and rushing to pull the blankets down on the twin-sized bed that sat in one corner. Mr. Bob's needs had been simple. A bed, an easy chair with a table beside it, an electric heater for cold winter nights, and a bathroom. Since he'd taken all his meals with the family, there wasn't even a kitchen.

Nick's face was white as the Judge lowered him to the bed, but he didn't make a sound.

"You're already running a fever," the Judge said, gently removing the remnants of Nick's shirt. "Lie down on your stomach. Alix, get the first aid kit out of the bathroom, and find something clean to put warm water in."

The first aid kit was easy. We kept it in the medicine cabinet over the bathroom sink. There was also a bottle of aspirin and I grabbed that, too. Something to put water in was a little harder unless I wanted to go explain what was happening to my mother. There weren't any dishes or even buckets in the barn. Wait. The bowl I'd carried scraps in.

I darted into the barn and grabbed it, taking it back to the sink. There, I scrubbed it out with hand soap and rinsed it clean. When it was full of warm water, I dropped in a washcloth from the closet and carried it to the Judge.

"I'll try to take it easy, son, but this is going to hurt some." The Judge lifted the washcloth out and began bathing the blood from Nick's back. In an agony of sympathy, I sat on the floor by the bed and held his hand.

"Did your daddy do this?" Under the circumstances, it was amazing how calm the Judge sounded.

Nick didn't answer.

"You should be seeing a doctor."

"No. You promised. He just got drunk is all."

The Judge's teeth ground together so loudly I could hear them. "From now on, when he starts drinking, you come over here. This is your room now, hear me?"

"I can't. He'd come looking for me and cause you problems."

"You let me worry about that. I made you a promise, now I want one from you. When he starts drinking, you come over here."

Nick hesitated, then nodded weakly. "I promise."

Once his back was cleaned and medicine applied, the Judge found one of Mr. Bob's T-shirts for Nick to wear, then tucked him under the blankets and turned to me. "Alix, you stay here and keep an eye on him until I get back. I've got some business to take care of."

"What should I do?"

"Just keep him in bed and give him water if he's thirsty."

"Yes, sir."

It wasn't until years later that I discovered where he went that night. After a quick swing by the sheriff's house, they confronted Frank Anderson. Not only did they threaten to take Nick away from him, the Judge promised him a healthy jail term if he ever touched Nick again. The sheriff got into the act by informing him that Nick had permission to stay at our house any time he wanted to, and if Frank knew what was good for him he'd accept the situation.

And while no one ever actually admitted it, I was pretty sure the female contingent of my family also knew what had happened. The barn cats suddenly became the recipients of three square meals a day, all nicely arranged on our good dishes with a fork and a glass of milk included. For once, even Aunt Darla kept her mouth shut.

I sat with Nick that night, never letting go of his hand, and we talked when he could.

"You won't be able to go to school tomorrow."

"I have to." He shifted restlessly, wincing as the movement hurt his back.

"No, you don't. We never do anything the first day. I'll find out who your teacher is and get the list of school supplies for you."

"I don't care about that." He watched me from under drooping eyelids. "But I have to be there for Lindsey. She'll be scared if I don't go."

"I'll tell her you're okay. I'll even play with her so she won't be worried."

"She won't play." He hesitated. "She's not like you, Peewee. She doesn't talk to anybody except me, and only then when she has to."

"Is she retarded?"

"No. Maybe a little slow, but it's not her fault. Nobody's ever cared about her or tried to help her." His voice was little more than a whisper, and I could see he was barely awake.

"Go to sleep," I told him. "I'll make sure Lindsey is fine tomorrow and I won't scare her." I was still sitting on the floor, but I leaned over until my head was on the pillow beside his, our foreheads almost touching.

"You're something special, Peewee," he murmured.

"So are you," I answered.

I must have fallen asleep there, because when I next woke it was morning and I was in my own bed.

Chapter Three

Nick couldn't have gone to school the next day no matter how determined he was. It was all he could do to lift his head from the bed, and he still ran a fever off and on. I did what I told him I would, getting the list of school supplies from his teacher and keeping watch on Lindsey. Her big owl-eyes brimmed with tears when I told her Nick wouldn't be there, so I sat with her each recess, assuring her he was fine and would be back in school as soon as he could. She never said a word, just stared at the ground like I wasn't there.

Normally, I piddled my way home after school, stopping to play or talk to the other kids who walked with me, but that day, I ran all the way.

"How is he?" I asked the Judge.

"Sore, but he's going to be okay."

Relief flowed through me. "Can I go see him?"

"I reckon. He'd probably like some company besides mine."

So I spent the whole evening in Nick's room, telling him about the first day of school, about Lindsey, feeding him supper when he couldn't move his arms without gasping from pain. I even retrieved the books I'd loaned him, found the place he'd marked, and read to him until he dozed off. I would have stayed there all night if the Judge hadn't shown up and sent me to the house.

The next morning Mama halted my headlong rush to the barn and hustled me into the car for our annual trip to buy school supplies. I took both my list and Nick's. If Mama noticed that our basket was quite a bit fuller than usual, she didn't protest.

To my surprise, our second stop that morning was at the used clothing store. Mama went through it in a very business-like manner, picking out jeans, shirts, underwear, and shoes. All of the items were obviously used but still in excellent condition. She even bought a warm winter jacket. When we got home she cut all the string tags off the garments, folded them neatly, and looking me straight in the eye, held the pile out.

"I cleaned the closets this morning, Alix, and found a bunch of your Uncle Vern's old clothes. Would you take them out to Mr. Bob's room and put them in the chest for me?"

I think I loved my mother more at that minute than I ever had before. "Thank you," I whispered, hugging her hard.

It was a week before Nick recovered enough to do more than sit up. During that week the bare room was transformed into a cozy nest. First an old desk appeared, then a bookshelf which I promptly filled for him. Next a braided rug covered the bare floor and the single window was adorned with new plaid curtains.

According to the Judge, my mother and aunts had gone into one of their cleaning frenzies and were tossing out everything in the attic. Since he hated to throw away anything still useful, he put it in Nick's room. I doubt we fooled Nick for a minute, but he never said anything, and I lost count of the times I'd catch him touching the books or clothes with an expression of wonder on his face. No one had ever cared about him before either, except maybe Lindsey, and he wasn't sure how to take it.

We never heard a word from Frank Anderson while Nick recuperated, and I don't think he ever hit Nick again, but Nick kept his promise to the Judge. The room in the barn was undisputedly his. Many nights over the next ten years I'd look out and see the gently glowing light spilling from the window and know he was there, safe. Sometimes, if it wasn't too late, I'd sneak down and we'd talk or read together. And I finally got to ask Nick my question about babies.

It was late in the evening on a Friday, about two weeks after Nick's return to school. I'd seen the light come on in his room and, taking the new copy of *Dune* I was reading, went down to join him. While our school housed all the grades from kindergarten to senior high, I rarely had a chance to talk with him during the day. During recess, he would stand behind Lindsey, arms crossed, glaring at anyone who came too close. I had been admitted to this closed circle, but Nick didn't talk much when other people were around. He would acknowledge me with a small nod, then return to his "on guard" position.

We were sitting on his bed that night, legs crossed as we used the wall for a back support, our shoulders touching companionably as we read. He had finished all of *Lord of the Rings*, and was working his way through *The Chronicles of Amber*.

I put my finger under an unfamiliar word and looked up. "What's a concubine?" Maybe I should mention here that my mother monitored my reading very carefully, so while I was advanced in reading skills, I was also incredibly naïve and overprotected. I now suspect that she steered my interest toward science fiction because it had so little in the way of sexual references. She hadn't discovered my copy of *Dune* yet. I'd slipped it into the basket on my last trip to town with the Judge, and since he was so used to my hunger for books, he'd never commented on it.

Nick glanced up from his book at my question. "I think it's a woman who's kind of like a wife, but isn't really married."

Aha! Had I inadvertently stumbled on the answer that would explain Liz Swanner's six kids? "Can concubines have babies?"

"Sure."

That had to be it, but I wanted to make sure I got this right before I reported back to Jenna. "Is Liz Swanner a concubine?"

His eyes narrowed. "No."

Drat. I'd been so sure. "Well, then how come she has six kids? Jenna says you have to be married to have babies."

"Jenna is wrong."

A vague tingle of alarm went through me. If you didn't have to be married, that meant any female could have babies. Including me. And I darn sure wasn't ready to be a mother yet. When I told Nick as much, he shook his head.

"You can't have one alone. It takes a man and a woman together to make a baby. Besides, you aren't old enough."

Now this was getting interesting. "How old do you have to be?"

"I think it's different for everybody. You'll know when you're old enough."

"How?"

His chest lifted in a long-suffering sigh. "You just will."

"Are you old enough?"

Red tinted his cheeks. "Boys aren't the same as girls."

Well, even I knew that. I'd been around enough mothers who were in the process of changing diapers to determine the plumbing on boys wasn't like my own. I had even checked once, after my first glimpse of a baby boy, to make sure there weren't any surprises lurking down there. "But are you old enough?"

"It doesn't matter. I'm not gonna make any woman have a baby."

"You mean you don't ever want to have any kids?"

"It's not that." He hesitated, staring across the room. "It's just that it's better for the kid to have two parents who are married and who love them. I won't have a kid unless I'm married to its mother, and I don't think that's gonna happen."

"Why not?"

His shoulder lifted in a shrug. "I'm Frank Anderson's son and I live in a junkyard. Who'd want to marry me?"

"I'll marry you," I told him decisively. "That way, we can both have kids someday."

He grinned, those dimples emerging in a blaze of glory. "Yeah, you probably would. But I don't think you should go around telling people you're going to marry me. They might get the wrong idea." Draping an arm around my shoulders, he gave me a little shake. "Now shut up and read. I just got to a good part."

I snuggled down next to him, happily sure that our future had been settled. There were still some blank areas in my knowledge of where babies came from, but I knew that together we could work it out. How hard could it be when Liz Swanner had managed it six times?

Of course, I didn't pay much attention to Nick's admonition about telling people I was going to marry him. It was almost a week later when I was sitting at the kitchen table doing my homework while Mama and my aunts cooked. Nick hadn't used his room since the weekend before and I was constantly jumping up to look out the back door, hoping he'd show up.

After the last check with no sign of him, I sighed mightily and resumed my seat.

"Alix, you're going to wear that chair out if you don't sit still," Mama said.

"She's watching for that boy." Leave it to Aunt Darla to point out the obvious. "She spends entirely too much time holed up in that room alone with him. Aren't you the least bit worried, Ellie?"

"Why should I be?" Mama stirred a pot of soup beans on the stove, then opened the oven door to check the cornbread. "There are no other children in the family for Alix to play with. I imagine he's like an older brother to her."

"No, he's not," I told her earnestly. "I'm gonna marry him and we're going to have kids together."

All three women stopped what they were doing and gaped at me. Aunt Darla's hand went to her heart, her face turned red, and sputtering sounds came from her lips. Aunt Jane was the first to find her voice.

"Whose idea was that, Alix?"

"Mine."

"And just how did the subject come up?" Mama's face was nearly as red as Aunt Darla's.

"I asked him what a concubine was."

Mama lowered herself weakly into the chair across from me. "I think you better tell me the whole thing. From the beginning."

I have an excellent memory. I repeated the conversation verbatim. Mama took it pretty good, except for the parts about Liz Swanner, then she did some sputtering that put Aunt Darla to shame. When I finished the tale, her lips thinned to a straight line.

"I want to see that book."

"Okay." I'd already read it, anyway.

As I was leaving the room to get it, I heard Mama tell Aunt Darla, "At least Nick behaved like a gentleman. That child is too curious for her own good sometimes."

I wanted to stop and listen to the rest of what they said, but I suspected Aunt Jane would be checking to see if I were doing just that. Instead, I trudged upstairs, got the book, and trudged back down. I'd always thought being curious was a *good* thing. How else was I going to learn if I couldn't ask questions? At least Mama didn't seem to be blaming Nick.

She took the book from me and thumbed through it, reading a passage here and there before looking up at me, a puzzled frown wrinkling her forehead. "Alix, did you understand this story?"

"Sure. It was really good. Especially the parts about the giant sandworms."

Mama shook her head and rubbed a hand over her cheek. "Maybe I should have listened to Mr. Viders and let them move you up a grade," she murmured.

This was news to me. Mr. Viders was the school principal and I hadn't known he'd talked to Mama, much less wanted to move me up a grade. The thought didn't thrill me. Leave Jenna and all my friends? Not if I could help it.

"I don't want to move up, Mama. I like my grade. Mrs. Wade is my best teacher yet. She's real nice and smart, too. She always answers my questions and never tells me to be quiet."

Mama's gaze sharpened. "Have your other teachers told you that?"

"Sometimes."

Her chest lifted in a sigh. "Okay, you can stay in Mrs. Wade's class. But from now on, Alix, I want to see your books before you read them, and if you have any questions about what you read, come ask me."

"Yes, Ma'am."

"And as for marrying Nick..." She hesitated. "You're only eight. You'll change your mind a dozen times before you're old enough to get married. It wouldn't do to get Nick's hopes up and then have to hurt his feelings, would it?"

"No, Ma'am."

Mama could be tricky when she wanted to, but her tactics failed this time. I knew I would never change my mind about marrying Nick. But from now on I was going to take his advice and keep that tidbit to myself.

* * * * *

Things settled into a routine that first year. Nick would stay in his room on the weekends, with occasional weeknights thrown in when Frank went on a binge. At first, he refused to go anywhere near the house, but eventually I coaxed him into joining us for meals. My mother and aunts fussed over him until it got downright embarrassing, and I knew he was uncomfortable with the attention. Nick was not a herd animal. Whether by choice or by the hard lessons forced on him though life, he was a lone wolf determined to make his own way in the world.

I finally had a long talk with my mother, and the next time Nick ate with us he was treated as any other family member would be. Nick and I were both relieved.

Once, I asked him about his room in the trailer that sat at the back of the salvage yard.

"I don't have a room." He was concentrating on the cards in his hand. I had taught him to play gin rummy the night before, and he was determined to beat me this time.

"Where do you sleep?" I surveyed my cards, then discarded a seven. I was trying to form a picture of what he did when he wasn't with me, but I'd never been in a trailer before.

Nick pounced on the seven, then spread his cards triumphantly on the blanket. "I sleep on the couch. Gin!" He counted both our totals and added it to the neat line of figures on the notepad beside him. One thing I'd discovered was that he was a whiz with math. You could ask him to multiply long strings of numbers and he'd pop the answer right back like he'd pulled it out of thin air. And he didn't even need paper to do it. I was more than a bit envious of this talent. My grades came easy to me, always high without much effort on my part, but math was one subject I had to work at.

"Aren't you afraid to stay in the trailer when it storms?"

We have terrible storms here. It's not unusual to get two or three tornadoes touching down every spring, and sometimes more than that. Nearly everyone has a storm cellar, and those who don't feel no qualms about running to a ☐ishonour's when things start to get hairy. One memorable year a twister took out the huge sycamore tree that grew behind our shed, and sucked the chickens right out of the chicken house without damaging a single board. There were feathers scattered over a two-mile area, but we never found a chicken, naked or otherwise.

"You get used to it." Nick shuffled the cards and dealt the next hand.

"I don't think I would."

"If it gets really bad we go over to the Swanner's. They've got a root cellar, but it's only a dirt hole in the ground. I'd rather stay outside."

The thought of Frank Anderson huddling in a hole with the Swanner's brought another image to my mind. "Does your father pay Liz Swanner to let him 'do it' to her?"

Nick's head shot up and he glared at me. "Where did you hear that?"

"From kids at school." I wasn't about to implicate Jenna yet again. If nothing else, I was loyal.

"People should mind their own business. Besides, you don't even know what it means."

"What does it mean?" I asked, ever hopeful.

"Nothing. And I'm not talking about this with you." He looked back down at his cards.

"Are you mad at me?"

"No."

Maybe he wasn't mad, but I had upset him. His eyes had gone from gray to molten and his body was tensed. "The only reason I asked was because I figured she could use the money."

He didn't answer.

"I'm sorry."

A sigh lifted his chest and he looked up at me. "It's not your fault. I just don't want to talk about it, okay?"

"Okay."

It was years before I realized he was embarrassed by what his father did, that he hated watching Liz Swanner's tired acceptance when his father pulled her into the bedroom. Even worse for Nick was listening to the sounds coming from that room, knowing all her kids were listening, too. If it hadn't been for Lindsey, he never would have set foot on the place.

Liz wasn't the only woman Frank used, she was simply the closest. Nick told me once that his father thought nothing of bringing home some two-bit hooker he'd found and taking her, knowing Nick could see everything he did because there was no door on the bedroom in the trailer. When Nick was old enough, he would leave the second his father showed up with a woman, sometimes spending the entire night huddled in the cold tin building that served as an office for the salvage yard. So Nick learned the facts of life earlier than most and in a particularly ugly way, a way that affected most of his teenage years. While other boys his age spent ninety-eight percent of their time figuring out how to get girls into bed, Nick avoided them like the plague, something that was destined to cause a real rift in our friendship when I hit puberty. But ignorance is bliss, and for right then, I was happy. Especially after I discovered that while I was vowing to save Nick, he had taken on the job of being my protector and staunchest defender. The incident that enlightened me occurred right before Christmas.

The fourth grade class at Morganville School didn't have the luxury of individual desks. The students were assigned seats at numerous long tables designed to hold four people, two on each side. It was my misfortune to share my side of the table with Mooney Orr.

Mooney was the class bully, a boy who had already failed two grades by the time he landed in mine. He was fat, sweaty and loud, and all the kids were scared of him. With good reason. If Mooney wanted something he took it, and woe to the child who tried to stop him. But Mooney was also crafty and sly. He never retaliated when an adult was near, preferring to ambush his prey when he could catch them off-guard, knowing it would be his word against the victims if the kid were stupid enough to tell.

Sitting next to him was torture. I always carried extra pencils because I knew Mooney would confiscate the one I was using. And I considered myself lucky that pencils were all he'd taken so far. At least, I was lucky until the week before our midterm tests.

Because the weather was nasty that Monday, our recess was taken in the gym. I was sitting on the bleachers taking a breather, watching Jenna chase Hugh in a game of tag, when Mooney confronted me.

"You're gonna let me copy off your paper when we take our tests next week," he said. "If you don't, I'll stomp you into the ground."

He swaggered off, secure in the thought that I'd comply with his demand. I watched him in shock. Cheat? He wanted me to cheat on the tests? The Judge would disown me. I would never be able to look my grandfather in the eye again. There was no way I could let Mooney copy, even knowing he would kill me when it was over. Death before ☐ishonour was my family motto.

But that didn't stop me from being scared spitless. By the end of the week my life was in shambles. I couldn't eat because my stomach stayed clenched in a tight ball of tension. I couldn't sleep because when I did, I'd have screaming nightmares. I couldn't even read because all my energy was focused on my impending demise.

It never occurred to me to seek help. Frenchs weren't tattletales. Mooney was my problem and I had to take care of him on my own. My family knew something was wrong from my unnatural silence and obvious loss of appetite. At different times, each of them asked me if I was coming down with something. I even avoided Nick that hellish week, although I knew he frowned at me in puzzlement from his post behind Lindsey on the school steps.

The day of the tests dawned bright and sunny, if somewhat chilly. I gave Mama an extra-tight hug goodbye, hoping she wouldn't cry too much at my funeral, and trudged off to meet my doom.

A small miracle occurred when I reached the school. For the first time ever, Nick left Lindsey and cornered me before I could go inside.

"You ain't said boo to me in over a week. Are you mad at me for something?"

"No." I fought hard to hold back the tears threatening to spill over. My teeth were chattering so hard I could barely speak, and nausea turned my stomach in circles. "But you probably shouldn't plan on marrying me anymore."

With that cryptic statement, I ran into the building, leaving him staring after me.

The trouble started immediately. Mooney glared a warning at me when I took my seat. Mrs. Wade handed out the first test. Swallowing hard, I picked up my pencil and curved my left arm protectively around the paper before I started writing.

Mooney's foot shot out and hit my calf under the table. Hard. "Move your arm," he hissed.

"No." My voice quivered, but I held steady.

"Mooney, Alix, is there a problem?" Mrs. Wade watched us with an eagle eye.

"No, Ma'am," Mooney answered before I had a chance. "I just had a cramp in my leg." He bent over his test as though he were busy being a good little student. But from the corner of his mouth he said, "You're gonna be sorry, you little bitch."

The rest of that day was a blur to me. I don't know how I got through it, or actually managed to pass the tests myself. When it was time to go home I lingered in the hall until I had no choice. I had to leave, not knowing when or where the attack would come, only certain that it would happen. I wasn't going to make it easy for him, though. I'd fight to my last breath.

But Mooney made a mistake. Apparently he was so enraged by my refusal to give in that he couldn't wait until I was off the school grounds to attack. I hadn't even made it to the front sidewalk when someone grabbed my pigtail and threw me to the ground. My books flew in all directions and the air went out of my lungs with a whoosh.

I never had a chance. Before my screaming lungs could draw another breath, Mooney was on top of me, his ham-like fist swinging. The first one hit my left eye and I saw stars. For a second, everything went black and I didn't feel the second blow. There was no third because suddenly Nick was there. He ripped Mooney off me and plowed into him with a determination that was fearsome to behold.

Someone screamed. Teachers came running from all directions, grabbing both boys and pulling them apart. Still Nick struggled to reach Mooney. I could vaguely hear Mrs. Wade, who was kneeling beside me, ask me where I hurt, but I couldn't answer. All my attention was focused on Nick.

"If you ever touch her again, I'll kill you," he snarled.

Mooney, like all bullies, changed his tune when he was on the receiving end. "They started it," he whined, making sure he stayed out of Nick's reach. "I wasn't doing anything." Blood poured from his nose.

There wasn't a scratch on Nick, but his shirt was torn and I saw how he protected his right side.

"You stop your lying right now, Mooney Orr," Mrs. Wade said. "I saw the entire thing. You should be ashamed of yourself, jumping on a little girl like Alix."

All three of us were hauled to the nurse's office and our parents called. Nick refused to leave my side, hovering over me protectively until Miss Sams, the nurse, made him stand on the other side of the cot so she could check me for injuries. I had skinned elbows, a busted lip, and a black eye. Nick had a large bruise on his ribs and some raw knuckles. But Mooney had lost two teeth and gained a busted nose.

When Miss Sams moved away to work on Mooney, I gazed up at Nick with my one good eye, tears streaming down and filling my ear. If there were tears coming from my other eye, the bag of ice currently resting on it froze them.

"You saved my life," I sobbed.

Nick squatted beside me, awkwardly patting my shoulder. "Hey, you didn't think I was gonna let you get out of marrying me that easy, did you?"

"Oh, Nick!" I sat up and wrapped my arms around him. The bag of ice dropped to my lap, and my lip started bleeding again, but I didn't care. "I thought I was gonna die."

And that's how Mama, the Judge, and Mr. Viders found us. Me crying and bleeding all over Nick, him trying to soothe me without much success.

"My baby!" Mama wailed when she saw my face. She yanked me away from Nick and rocked me, so I cried and bled all over her until Mr. Viders took control of the situation. The Judge simply clenched his jaw and glared daggers at Mooney.

They made me tell them the whole story, even though I didn't want to. Nick and I were praised and fussed over; me for maintaining my honor under cruel and unusual circumstances, him for coming to my rescue. Mooney was towed out of the building, his mother's hand twisting his ear, presumably on the way to see the doctor. From then on, he was banished to a seat all by himself at the back of the class. I guess he learned his lesson 'cause he never bothered me again.

Frank Anderson never showed up at the school, but then, no one had really expected him to. Nick went home with us, and after I was tucked into bed Mama allowed him to come up and sit with me.

By this time, my eye was swelled shut and he touched it gently, looking mad all over again. "You should have told me. I'll never let nobody hurt you again, Alix, I swear."

But there are more kinds of hurt than physical ones, hurts that run ever deeper and leave bigger scars, and not even Nick could protect me from himself.

Chapter Four

ᔛ

When I was twelve, my normally unflappable mother stuttered and stammered her way through a rather muddled explanation of the facts of life, then shoved a book called *Becoming a Woman* into my hand and ran. By then, of course, Jenna and I had pretty much figured out the basics, thanks to a couple of dogs and a lot of gossip from the other girls in school.

My family kept a close eye on me for a few days after Mama gave me "the talk", waiting to see if I'd been traumatized beyond repair. Personally, I think the only one traumatized was Mama. Every time I'd look at her she'd turn beet-red.

Sex was a four-letter word in our family. When its use was required, it was always spelled, as if actually saying it would bring down the fiery wrath of God on our heads. The age of free love might have come and gone in the rest of the world, but in Morganville girls who got pregnant without the benefit of matrimony were still talked about in whispers, behind shielding hands.

Even the women's liberation movement was viewed as a rather puzzling oddity by our female population. They had always thought they were partners, not slaves, and to them a glass ceiling was just something that was apt to break in a hailstorm. It was the combined goal of all our women to see their daughters happily married to a Good Man, raising a houseful of kids. A career to them was working as a volunteer at the library or hospital, or at the local five-and-dime in the makeup department for minimum wage.

And because no one around me paid much attention to those things, I didn't either. My main concern was my body. As usual, Jenna had beaten me to the punch yet again, starting her periods when we were twelve. I had to wait another whole year and I was beginning to wonder if something was wrong with me. With every twinge or unusual sensation I'd run to the bathroom, hope warring with anxiety.

The year I turned thirteen was a momentous one for me in more ways than one. My body finally started to change, hard painful knots forming on my chest, and hair sprouting in places it had never been before. Mama took me shopping for my first training bras, and my monthlies started, which thrilled me for all of two months, and then I was sick of them. My hairstyle went from pigtails in fourth grade, to a ponytail in fifth, then to a braid in sixth. By ninth grade I was leaving it loose to hang down my back.

Mama wasn't Mama anymore, she was Mother, usually followed by a "pallease!" when she wanted me to do something I considered beneath me. Like wear a frilly dress instead of my strategically torn, stone-washed, designer blue jeans.

That was also the year I discovered Boys. Or maybe I should say they discovered me. By then I knew what they wanted and I wasn't buying it, although I will admit I was flattered by the attention and not above a little flirting. After all, I was southern, and southern woman are selectively bred for their ability to flirt. How else were we going to catch us a man and raise us a brood of kids?

The bane of my existence was that Nick didn't seem to notice all the changes I'd undergone. He still treated me the same way he had when I was eight, with casual warmth and humor. But I sure noted the changes in him.

At fifteen, he was nearly six feet tall. His voice had deepened into a rich baritone that did funny things to my stomach and made my heart race. His body, while still slim, had grown some muscular bulges that I couldn't help but admire. And I wasn't the only one. If boys had discovered me, girls thought they'd hit the jackpot with Nick. The fact that he was Frank Anderson's son and a lone wolf only increased their interest, added a bit of danger to the mix. They didn't view him as marriage material, but his looks made him desirable as a trophy.

I'd been forced to watch during the last school year while they strutted by his position on the steps, tossing their hair and sending inviting smiles his way. His expression remained stoic, but I saw the way his eyes moved over them and I wanted to yank out their hair, one fistful at a time. Strange, but I was never jealous of Lindsey, even though she'd filled out nicely, too. Maybe because I was used to seeing them together, and she was so quiet that I simply forgot she was there.

When my friends talked for hours about hunky rock stars, I smiled but didn't participate. There was only one boy I wanted, and I lived for the times when I could be alone with him. It was simple. When I was with Nick, I was happy. When I wasn't, I was restless and miserable. I became adept at finding excuses to touch him. A hand on his arm, innocently brushing a strand of hair away from his face, legs touching as we sat side by side.

He did nothing to encourage these feelings except be himself. For me, that was enough. But the biggest reaction I'd ever gotten out of him was a puzzled frown directed at the boys flirting with me, like he couldn't figure out what all the fuss was about.

That was also the year my Uncle Vern moved back, looking tired and old, the traumatized survivor of a messy divorce, and brought his twin sons, Casey and Cody, with him. There were only two weeks of school left when I came home one afternoon and found these three strangers in our living room. I smiled politely while I was introduced and tried not to notice that my newly found, seventeen-year-old cousins were staring at me like I was some species of alien that had suddenly appeared in their garden. Sort of shocked, curious, and eager, all at the same time.

Both boys had a more masculine version of our family looks. Dark hair, blue-green eyes, medium height. Their northern accents sounded funny to my ears, sharp and staccato, and I felt a bit overwhelmed by so many males in my predominantly female household. But my family was ecstatic to have them back. Even Aunt Darla was excited now that my uncle had come to his senses and rid himself of "that woman". The noise level in the house was giving me a headache and I'd smiled until the muscles around my mouth hurt by the time we'd finished supper. At the first opportunity I slipped out the back door into the warm spring night.

I was surprised to see a light in the shed since I hadn't been expecting Nick that night. He and the Judge had long since finished restoring the Chevy. It sat in the garage, covered by a tarp which protected the beige and brick-colored paint job. The Judge only drove it on special occasions, like the day he'd taken Nick to get his learner's permit. He'd been offered a small fortune for the car, but he always refused to sell.

Thrilled that I was going to see Nick tonight, I stopped in the shed door, my gaze going from him to the mangled Ford pickup that occupied the spot where the Chevy had once sat.

Nick grinned when he saw me. "What do you think of my truck?"

"I think you need to jack it up and run another one under it." The truck was in horrible shape, one door completely gone and the other bashed in. Jagged pieces of metal curled up around the fenders. It was impossible to tell what color it had once been. Now it was just rusty.

"Where did you get it?" I leaned beside him and peered under the hood, making sure my arm rested against his.

"Someone brought it to the salvage yard last week. It's not as bad as it looks. The motor is in pretty good condition and the body can be fixed. The Judge said if I'd bring it over, he'd help me work on it. I'd like to get it finished before I get my license."

"Are you going to take me to the Star-Vu to see a movie when you do?" The Star-Vu was our local drive-in. On the weekends it was taken over by teenagers, being one of the few places in town to take a date.

"Sure thing, Peewee." He slid a finger playfully down my nose, then glanced toward the house as a burst of laughter reached us. "Sounds like they're having a party."

"I guess they are, kind of. My Uncle Vern is back, and he brought his sons with him. They'll be seniors when school starts in the fall."

Nick frowned. "Are they going to move in with you?"

He wasn't comfortable around other males, except for the Judge, and I realized he was afraid he'd have to stop coming over so often. I hurried to reassure him.

"No. Uncle Vern already has a job at the Morgan's lumber mill, and he rented that small house of Mrs. Thompson's on the edge of town. They'll only stay here until it's ready to live in, a few nights at most."

"So why aren't you in there celebrating?" He leaned back over the motor and removed the air filter.

"They were giving me a headache."

"You don't like them?"

I shrugged. "That's just it. I don't know them well enough to decide, but everyone expects me to treat them like I've known them forever. And the boys keep looking at me funny."

He straightened, his gaze piercing as he stared at me. "Funny how?"

"I don't know, just funny. It makes me uncomfortable."

"Stay away from them," he growled. "Don't let them get you alone."

"Why not?" Maybe I was older, but my curiosity was still intact.

He looked away before he answered me. "Because they're guys and you're a girl, and you said yourself you don't know them."

Hallelujah! He'd noticed I was a girl! I was gloating over that when what he'd said sank in. Nervously, I chewed my bottom lip. "They're my cousins, Nick. You don't really think they'd...well, you know, hurt me, do you?"

"Trust your instincts. If those guys make you uncomfortable, there's a reason."

A shiver ran over me. What if he was right? At least I knew Nick had my best interests at heart, and I wasn't too sure about my new relatives. "Okay."

A sound from the front of the shed had both of us turning in that direction as my cousins came to an abrupt stop, identical expressions of surprise on their faces when they saw Nick.

The boys eyed each other warily while I stammered my way through the introductions. Although he was two years younger, Nick was three inches taller than Casey and Cody, and he didn't look like the kind of person you wanted to mess with. I was extremely glad he was there.

"Are you Alix's boyfriend?"

Casey was the one who asked. They were identical twins, but I'd discovered that Casey had a small scar nearly hidden in his eyebrow that Cody lacked.

Nick hesitated and glanced down at me. "You could say that."

It was all I could do to keep from gaping at him. Lord, I wished I had a tape recorder in my pocket, because by tomorrow I'd be doubting my own ears. He gave me a half-smile, then looked back at Casey.

"You got a problem with it?"

Casey held up a hand. "No skin off my nose. She's all yours."

The twins didn't stay long after that. As soon as I was sure they were gone, I turned on Nick. "You lied." I was standing with my feet apart, hands on my hips.

His gaze ran over me and to my absolute shock, his face turned red. "Not exactly."

"You told them I was your girlfriend."

As though he couldn't help himself, his eyes wandered over my body yet again, like he was really seeing me for the first time. "Well, you are a girl, and we are friends." He cleared his throat. "Besides, your feelings were right about them. Now that they think you have a boyfriend they'll leave you alone."

"Oh." All the wind went out of my sails and disappointment left a hollow place in my chest as he picked up a wrench and went back to work on the truck motor.

"You're not old enough to have a real boyfriend," he muttered.

I stiffened. "If I'm old enough to have babies, then I'm damn well old enough to have a boyfriend," I ground out. "And just as soon as I decide on who it's going to be, I'll let you know so you can stop lying to people."

The wrench he was holding hit the engine with a stunned clang, but I wasn't waiting around to hear what he had to say about my pronouncement. I ran all the way back to the house, up the stairs, and into my room, locking the door behind me. It was two days before I deigned to talk to him again, or even acknowledge his existence, but I did notice he was paying more attention to the boys who flocked around me, and he wasn't frowning anymore. He was downright scowling. But the real problems didn't start until a month after school was out for the summer.

For once, I was home alone, something that didn't happen often in a family like mine. The Judge had gone to some kind of civic meeting, Aunt Darla was at the Children's Home, and Mother and Aunt Jane were grocery shopping, something I hated and avoided whenever possible. I'd finished my chores, then read for a while, but I was too restless to sit still for long.

Grabbing a soda from the fridge, I went outside to sit on my swing. The seat had been replaced a few times over the years, and I knew I was too old for it now, but I couldn't bring myself to give it up yet.

The heat outside was miserable, the humidity so high it was like breathing underwater. Not a breath of air stirred the leaves on the tree above, and for once, the robins weren't fighting over nesting space. There wasn't a sound anywhere, I realized abruptly.

I lifted my gaze to the line of thick black clouds rolling in from the southwest. I've never been afraid of storms, but when you live in an area prone to tornados, you learn to respect them. You also learn the warning signs pretty early in life, and this one looked like it was going to be bad. Maybe it would be smart to check the local TV station and see if any warnings had been issued.

Before I could suit action to thought, Nick captured my attention. He'd stepped out of the woods behind the barn and was heading in my direction, pausing now and then to look up. I went to meet him and we converged at the corner of the yard, both of us staring at the sky like two old farmers anxious for their crops.

"What do you think?" I asked him. The world around us was turning a sickly green color and the wind was picking up.

"It doesn't look good. Where's your family?"

We watched a streak of neon purple lightning flash across the sky while my nervousness increased. "They aren't here. I'm getting worried, Nick."

"Come on. Let's head for the cellar." He put his hand on my back and herded me toward our concrete hole in the ground.

"But what if they don't make it home in time?"

"There's nothing we can do about it, and they would want you out of danger." He lifted the metal lid and laid it back against the ground, then descended the steps. There was the scrape of a match and the dim glow of the hurricane lamp filled the cellar before he rejoined me.

Together, we stood and watched the clouds roll and tumble across the sky. The wind began to howl, nearly lifting me off my feet with its violence, and the thunder was a constant, angry rumble, low and menacing. I was wiping the first splatter of rain off my arm when I saw the slender tail drop down, form a funnel and stretch toward the ground.

"Oh, my God," I whispered.

Nick's head whipped around and the next thing I knew, his arm was around my waist and he was dragging me down the stairs. The cellar door slammed shut and he shot the lock into place with a frantic push.

"Down in the corner! Hurry!"

We had both grown up hearing stories about twisters driving two-by-fours through concrete cellar walls, so I obeyed automatically. Nick crouched beside me, his arms wrapping around me protectively. I had always sworn that if I were ever interviewed on TV after a storm, I *would not* be one of those people who say things like, "It sounded just like a freight train running through my house." But now I knew why they said it. There wasn't another way to describe the sound that came anywhere close to what I was hearing. It seemed to go on forever, getting louder and louder with every second that passed. When the cellar door started banging and shimmying in its frame, I screamed and did my level best to crawl inside Nick.

He was holding me so tightly that, if I hadn't been scared out of my mind, I'd have worried about my ribs.

"It's okay," he murmured in my ear. "You're gonna be alright. It's almost over." But I could feel him trembling against me.

The metal door stopped its dancing and settled back into place, and the noise faded away into the distance.

I raised my head and looked up at him, not quite ready to believe the nightmare had ended and we were still alive. He wiped my tear-damp cheek with his thumb.

"It's okay," he whispered again. An odd look lingered in his gray eyes as he gazed down at me, but I didn't know he was going to kiss me until his lips touched mine.

I'd never been kissed before, and I doubted Nick had ever kissed anyone. At first, it was hesitant and clumsy, eager and endearing. It was a spontaneous reaction to our brush with danger, and while neither of us was experienced, we had instinct on our side.

My arms slid up until they curved around his neck, and when I felt his tongue touch my lips, it never occurred to me to resist. This was Nick. My Nick. A low, agonized sound came from somewhere deep inside him as I returned the kiss, and his hand moved over my back, under my shirt.

I don't know how long it lasted. It could have been hours and still not been enough to suit me. But suddenly he went still.

"No."

The word ripped from his throat with more pain than I'd ever heard from someone his age, and I found myself alone on the cold, damp floor. Confused, my senses spinning from so many different emotions in such a short space of time, I clambered to my feet.

"Nick?"

He didn't answer me. He was fumbling desperately with the lock on the door. When it finally opened, he bolted. By the time I stepped outside, he was vanishing into the woods. He'd left me all alone, something the Nick I knew would never have done under circumstances such as these.

Upset, uneasy, and scared all over again, I turned on my shaky legs to look around me. The house still stood, but the windows were shattered and bare patches of plywood showed through missing shingles. Debris littered the yard; downed tree limbs, rocks, and some boards that looked as if they might have come from the front wall of the barn, were nearly covered by a million leaves. And the tree that had held my swing was gone, the twisted remains of its stump lying beside a huge gaping hole, roots exposed like skeletal arms unearthed from the grave. The rain fell in a fine mist now, and in the west the sun was already breaking through the clouds.

I stood there, frozen with shock, as Mama's car peeled into the driveway on two wheels, followed hard by the Judge's truck, then Aunt Darla's sedan. I was passed around and hugged and fussed over until neighbors started to arrive and everyone went to check out the damage. The general consensus was that we were lucky the tornado had never reached the ground. It had only hovered in the air above the farm before being sucked back into the clouds.

Someone noticed I was shaking and a blanket was located and draped around my shoulders. Bobby Donovan, a local contractor and our nearest neighbor, had been one of the first on the scene. He was busily writing up repair estimates, conferring occasionally with Pete Townsend, our insurance agent, until they reached a mutually satisfying dollar amount, and Pete wrote the Judge a check. The repair work would start first thing in the morning.

But no amount of repair was going to fix the hollow feeling inside me. Something was desperately wrong for Nick to abandon me the way he had, and I was afraid of what he'd say the next time I saw him. I didn't know it would be two weeks before he set foot on the farm again, or that he'd ignore me so completely when he finally did. It was as though I'd ceased to exist for him, and nothing in my life had ever hurt me as much as that did.

June faded into the hottest July on record. The windows in the house were replaced, the roof reshingled, and new carpets were put down to replace the water-soaked ones. The hole where the sweet gum tree had been was filled in and smoothed over, and grass was already growing over the scar. The Judge even made me a new swing in another tree, but it was never the same and I only used it enough to keep from hurting his feelings.

Nick started using his room in the barn again, but he waited until all the lights were out in the house before he'd show up. The first time I slipped out to talk to him I found the door locked, and he wouldn't answer me when I called to him.

It was right after that painful discovery when I began keeping a journal. Somewhere in my mind, I thought that if I got the entire thing down on paper, maybe I could figure out what I'd done wrong and fix it so Nick would talk to me again. But I'd filled half the leather-bound notebook and was no closer to understanding than I'd been when I started.

I was miserable. My whole world had been turned upside down and a huge chunk torn out of it. Weepy and depressed, I pushed my hair behind my ear and stared down at the journal pages lying on the kitchen table.

"I bought some of those cookies you like," my mother said. She was standing at the kitchen sink, hands buried in suds as she washed the lunch dishes.

"I'm not hungry."

"You're never hungry anymore. If you don't start eating, you'll dry up and blow away."

I could feel her gaze on me when I didn't answer.

"Did you and Nick have a fight?"

"No."

"Then what's going on? He never comes to the house anymore, and you're acting like someone kicked your favorite cat."

"I don't know, Mama. Why don't you ask Nick?" And if she got an answer, I hoped she'd share it with me. I glanced out the back door in time to see him disappear into the shed. Every part of me surged with the longing to join him, make him talk to me, but I knew at the first sight of me he'd leave. The only time he tolerated my presence in the shed these days was when the Judge was helping him, and even then he acted like I wasn't there.

"I'm going to my room." I closed the journal and went upstairs, determined not to cry again. It would only make Mama give me the third degree and there was nothing I could tell her.

And so it continued for the rest of the summer. It was worse than the week before midterms in fourth grade. At least I'd known that week would end when Mooney killed me. Now I had no hope at all. Nick hated me and he didn't show any signs of getting over it in the near future.

It was almost time for school to start when the entire thing came to a head. The resulting emotional explosion came damn near to making both Nick and me casualties of my stupidity. But something had to give. I just didn't know it was going to be me.

Chapter Five

Over the summer, Uncle Vern and the twins had acquired the habit of having dinner with us every Friday evening. After the meal, everyone would adjourn to the front porch for a little conversation. We all relished that brief period of time when the sun was low enough to cool things off, but full dark with its hordes of bloodthirsty mosquitoes hadn't yet arrived.

The more I was around Uncle Vern, the better I liked him. The way he listened to me and took everything I said seriously reminded me of the Judge. And when I told a joke, he laughed in all the right places.

The twins I still wasn't sure about. Until that night, I'd always taken Nick's advice, never letting them catch me alone. But I was in a funky mood that particular Friday. For the last few days, my anger had built until I was in danger of being consumed from the inside out. I was tired of mooning around, worrying about Nick when he'd made it so clear that he didn't care a flip about me.

That's why, when the twins asked if I wanted to go to the Burger Zone with them, I turned pleading eyes on my mother. "Can I?"

She hesitated, warring emotions speeding across her face. She didn't approve of kids hanging out at the Burger Zone, thought it was asking for trouble. But on the other hand, this was the first time I'd shown any interest in life since the tornado.

"Please?" I added, for good measure.

"Well, I suppose it would be okay this once." She glanced at the boys. "You two watch out for her and don't keep her out too late."

"Yes, Ma'am. We won't."

Casey grinned at me and held out his hand. "Let's go, Squirt."

The Judge's jaw clenched, and from the way he glared at Mother I knew he would give her what-for when they were alone. He didn't approve one bit of her letting me go.

I shoved my uneasiness aside and took Casey's hand. Cody climbed into the driver's seat and they squeezed me into the front between them.

"Where's your boyfriend these days?" Casey asked.

"He's not my boyfriend."

"You two have a fight?"

"No. He's just not my boyfriend."

We were barely out of the driveway when he reached under the seat and lifted a bottle from the floor. "Drink?"

I eyed the whiskey. Once upon a time, Nick would've had a fit if he'd known what I was doing. That was enough to make me reach for the bottle, defiance lifting my chin. Nick didn't rule my life anymore.

"Sure. Why not?" I held the rim to my lips and took a big slug. Both boys laughed when I choked, tears filling my eyes as I gasped for breath. From my throat to my stomach, it felt like I'd swallowed liquid fire.

"You'll get used to it," Cody said. "Take another one."

The second time, I discovered that if I held my breath and swallowed like I was taking medicine, I could keep from gagging. The flames in my stomach settled into a pleasant pool of warmth that spread to my arms and legs. This wasn't so bad, after all.

The boys passed the bottle around a few more times before we got to the Burger Zone, and I was feeling a bit lightheaded as they parked.

The Burger Zone was *the* place for kids to hang out in Morganville on the weekends. It was a small, seedy dive, with a few tables inside that no one ever used. All the action went on outside, in the parking lot. Jenna was going to be green with envy when she found out I'd been there with Casey and Cody. She'd been nagging her father to let her hang out at the Zone for the last year. So far, he hadn't given in.

The place was cram-packed with cars when we arrived, and several had their doors open, the radios turned up full blast. The roar of conversation died away for a second when I climbed out of the car behind Casey, but I was too busy trying to control my rubbery legs to pay much attention. Cody put his arm around my waist to steady me.

Apparently the twins had been here often enough to develop a lot of friends, because they surrounded us now, boys and girls both, mostly seniors.

"What did you bring Miss Prim and Proper for?" Devon Garner gestured at me.

"She's okay."

I didn't check to see which of my cousins had given me that ringing accolade. "What's wrong with me?" I glared at Devon.

He grinned, his gaze skimming down my body. "Maybe nothing. You gonna share that bottle, Miss Priss?"

Devon was a good-looking kid, blond hair, dark brown eyes, and the star player on our basketball team. And he'd never so much as glanced in my direction before.

"Nope," I told him. "It's mine." I took another long drink and his grin widened. The world was spinning around me, but for the first time since Nick had kissed me, I was relaxed and semi-happy. So much so that a giggle escaped my lips. This'll show him, I thought.

Devon pried me out from under Cody's arm. "Tell you what, Miss Priss. Dance with me and maybe I'll share my bottle with you."

I squinted at the green bottle he was holding, trying to focus on the label. "What is it?"

"Wine."

Hadn't I heard somewhere that wine wasn't as strong as whiskey? From the way I felt, it might be a good idea to cut back a bit.

"Okay." I shoved the whiskey at Cody and reached for the wine.

"Not so fast. Dance first, drink later."

"You're stooping kind of low on the food chain these days, aren't you, Dev?" The question came from a chunky blonde girl. Oh, lord. Piggy Treece. I might as well take an ad out in the local paper and save her the trouble of running her mouth about my drinking.

"It has its advantages," he shot back. "As you should know."

That sounded a bit odd to me, but then, everything sounded odd, and I couldn't seem to stop giggling. Devon pulled me right up against his body, and I wondered why we were slow dancing when it was a fast song. Oh, well. One was as good as another.

I dropped my head onto his chest and closed my eyes. Then promptly opened them again, wide, when bright lights spun behind my eyelids in a mad circle.

"Whoa," I murmured. Couldn't make that mistake again. I pushed away from Devon and yanked the bottle from his hand. Now this stuff wasn't half-bad. At least, not compared to the whiskey. I raised the bottle and took another long drink.

"Hey, save some for the rest of us." He retrieved his wine from my limp hand.

"I think I need to sit down," I confided.

"Sure thing." His hands went to my waist and he lifted me onto the hood of a car, then stepped closer. He seemed to loom in front of me, and I blinked several times to see if he'd go back to normal size. He didn't.

"You ever been kissed before, Miss Priss?"

My chin went up. "Of course I have."

"Show me."

I leaned forward and bumped into his head. Oh, my! That's why he looked so big. He'd only been an inch away. I adjusted for distance and plastered my mouth to his.

I was only dimly aware that he'd pried my lips open, that his hands had slid under my shirt. I felt my bra loosen, but couldn't muster the energy to protest.

"Let's get in the car," Devon murmured, his mouth moving down my neck.

I gazed around blurrily, the other kids seeming to blend together and then apart in a manner I'd never experienced before. "Where are my cousins?"

"They're busy." He opened the car door.

"Why are we getting in the back?"

"It'll be more comfortable."

Something was wrong here. I wasn't sure what, I only knew I didn't want to get in that car. "The wine," I hedged.

"Got it." He waved the bottle.

"I really should find my cousins."

His grip tightened on my arm. "Later. Now get in the car."

"No. Let go of me." I struggled desperately to free myself, fear overcoming some of the effects of the liquor.

"You heard her, Garner. Let go."

Nick! I spun to face him when Devon released me, my heart pounding so hard I could hear the blood rushing through my veins. "What are you doing here?"

His expression could have frozen the flames on a welding torch. "What do you think I'm doing? Go get in the truck, Alix."

I suddenly remembered why I'd come to the Burger Zone in the first place, and I didn't like his tone. "No. I'm having fun."

Devon slipped his arm around my waist. "Beat it, Anderson. She's staying with me."

"I don't think so." Nick's eyes narrowed and danger radiated from him like a miasma.

Smelling blood, the other kids surrounded us like sharks in a feeding frenzy. Casey and Cody appeared from the crowd and took up positions on either side of Devon and me.

"You heard her, kid. She doesn't want to hang around with trash like you anymore."

Oh, now that was going a little too far. Maybe I was mad at him, but nobody called Nick trash when I was around. I put my hands on Casey's chest and shoved with all my strength. His arms windmilled and he sat down hard. "You shut up," I snarled. "The only trash around here is you!"

While everyone was off balance from my unexpected attack, Nick grabbed me and shoved me behind him. "Get in the truck," he hissed.

And leave him alone with these animals? Not a chance. I dodged around him, closed my fist, and swung at Devon, yelping when I connected with his chin. All hell broke loose. I have a vague memory of crawling between someone's legs, over the rough gravel of the parking lot, and sinking my teeth into a thigh. Everyone was fighting, swinging indiscriminately at whomever was closest. I don't know how it would have ended if someone hadn't seen the cops tearing down the road toward us. Kids scattered like puffs of smoke in a high wind.

I spit a piece of material from my mouth as Nick scooped me up, tossed me over his shoulder and ran for his truck. "Did we win?" I inquired from my upside down location.

"Just shut up, Alix."

He threw me onto the seat, scrambled over me, and peeled out of the parking lot, gravel spraying from beneath his tires.

"How about that," I commented weakly, eyeing his cut, bloody lip. "You got new doors on the truck."

"Are you out of your mind?" he roared. "I tell you not to be alone with your cousins and what do you do? You crawl in a car with them, get drunk, nearly get raped, and start a brawl."

Miserably, I scrunched down by the door. "Why do you care what happens to me? You hate me."

"I don't hate you."

At least he wasn't snarling now. "Yes, you do. You never talk to me anymore. You won't even look at me." A tear oozed from my eye and dribbled down my cheek. When he didn't answer, I swiped it away, getting mad all over again. "See? You won't even talk to me now. Well I've got news for you. You don't own me and you can't stop me from coming to the Burger Zone every night if I want to. I don't need you around to take care of me. I'm not some damn baby!" My voice kept getting louder until I was yelling the last few words.

"That's the problem," he muttered, without looking at me.

But right then I developed a new difficulty. "Stop the truck."

He took one look at my face and whipped the truck over, slamming it into park. We were out in the country somewhere, on a gravel back road beside a field. I stumbled out and bent double as my stomach went into open rebellion. After what felt like thirty minutes of violent heaving on my part, Nick thrust an orange shop towel into my hand.

"Maybe you'll feel better now."

Better? The only way I'd feel better was if I died. "Where are we?"

"I don't have my license yet. I'm taking you home, but we have to stay off the main streets." He reached back into the truck, retrieved a bottle of soda, and handed it to me. "Rinse your mouth out with that."

I did, then leaned weakly against a rusty fender and pushed my hair away from my face. The moon was big and full, and a whippoorwill called from off to our right. "How did you know where I was?"

"I heard the Judge yelling at your mother for letting you go."

"So you decided to come after me?" I glanced at him from under my eyelashes. He was leaning next to me, his hands shoved into his pockets.

"Yeah."

If I hadn't been half-drunk, I'd never have said what I did then. "I've missed you."

He looked down at his feet. "I've missed you, too."

I turned toward him, tears streaming down my cheeks again. "Then why are you treating me like this? What did I do wrong? If you'll tell me, I promise, I'll never do it again."

Awkwardly, he put his arms around me and pulled me close. "It wasn't you," he rasped. "You didn't do anything wrong. It was me."

"I don't understand!"

"I know you don't, and I should have explained before." With a lot of false starts and hesitation, he told me about his father, how he brought women home with him all the time, how he treated them. His chin rested on top of my head as he talked.

"I promised myself I'd never do that to any woman, act like she was a piece of meat, just someone to use and then forget about. But I started getting all these strange...feelings whenever you touched me. I kept telling myself you were only a kid, and as long as I believed it, everything was okay. I could control it."

He took a deep, shaky breath. "That day in the cellar, I wanted…" His words halted. "I didn't want to stop. It scared me. You're the best thing that's ever happened to me, Alix. I'm not going to let anything hurt you, not even me. I figured I had to stay away from you for your own good."

I leaned back and stared up at him in amazement. "You mean to tell me you put me through hell because you got horny?" Okay, so I was a little more than half-drunk. And still mad. I stepped back and took a swing at his head. He stepped under it and grabbed my arms.

"Damn it, let me go!"

"Not until you settle down."

"I can't believe this," I yelled. "Did it ever occur to you that I might have something to say about it if I thought you were going too far? Or were *you* planning on raping me?" From the expression on his face, it *hadn't* occurred to him that I might not simply fall over and spread my legs. "What kind of person do you think I am? I thought we were friends, I thought you knew me."

"So did I," he mumbled. "But I'd have sworn you'd never do anything like you did tonight, so maybe I don't."

"That was your fault." I glared at him. "I only went because I was mad at you."

"You've got a weird way of looking at things, Alix."

"I do not."

He finally let go of my arms. "Okay, you're right. I'm sorry. I've been acting like an asshole."

I studied his face. "Are you going to stop ignoring me?"

For the first time that night, he smiled. "Yes."

"And you'll start talking to me again?"

"Yes."

He staggered when I threw myself into his arms. "Then I forgive you," I whispered.

"Just promise me one thing."

"What?" I'd have done almost anything at that point, I was so happy to discover he didn't hate me.

"Don't drink anymore. 'Cause I got to tell you, Alix, you are one mean drunk."

"Deal." I laughed.

Nick took me home right after that, and I managed to make it to my room without rousing my family. I was still awake when Mama opened the door and tiptoed to the side of the bed, gazed down at me, and sighed with relief, but I pretended to be asleep. When she left, I sent up a silent prayer that she'd never find out what had happened, and promised to be good from now on.

My relationship with Nick settled into an uneasy pattern after that night. We were still friends, but something had changed. Now I knew that while I was dreaming about him, he was dreaming about me, and we couldn't go back to the way we'd been before. Every time we were together, awareness crackled between us like static electricity. Our touches were no longer innocent, but done deliberately and at every opportunity. One of us would be talking, then suddenly stop and we'd stare at each other in silence.

Things were different at school, too. Rumors about my rapid degeneration and subsequent rescue by Nick flew over the grapevine faster than a brush fire after a ten year drought. My classmates looked on me with a respect bordering on awe. The seniors glared at me every time we met. Most of them still sported bruises and various injuries when school started, and Devon had a limp that kept him out of basketball practice for a month.

The first break between classes, Jenna dragged me outside and demanded all the details. I gave her an abbreviated version, after which she did a lot of glaring at Devon and my cousins.

"Bastards," she declared.

She'd gotten a short haircut that did wonders for her face, making her eyes look big and gorgeous, the way it curled softly on her cheeks. And she was wearing makeup. Looked like I needed to have another talk with Mother.

"So what's up with you and Nick? I heard you two were an item."

"We're just friends, you know that." Whatever was going on between Nick and me was too strong, too personal to talk about, even with my best friend.

"Yeah? Well, he sure isn't looking at you like a friend. Let me put it this way. If you were a rabbit and he were a wolf, you'd be dead meat right now. Lord, I wish a guy would look at me that way."

I glanced over my shoulder to see what she was talking about. Nick was standing fifty feet away, propping up a tree while he stared in my direction. There was something strange about this picture, but it took me a second to figure out what it was. He wasn't on the steps guarding Lindsey. He returned my gaze steadily until I turned back to Jenna.

"Wonder where Lindsey is?"

"I heard she quit."

"Why would she do that?"

Jenna shrugged. "Liz dropped number seven a few weeks ago. She needed Lindsey to stay home and take care of it while she worked."

"She got a job?"

"Yep, out at the roadhouse, waiting tables. Lots of folks think the kid might be Frank Anderson's."

Why hadn't Nick mentioned any of this to me? He must be upset about something like that. I sure would have been. But Nick wasn't the kind to talk about his problems. It was nothing short of a miracle that he'd told me as much as he had about Frank the night of the brawl, and I suspect that if I'd been stone cold sober, he wouldn't have.

"So, what's it like to get drunk?" Jenna asked, as though she'd read my mind.

I shuddered and she laughed. "That bad?"

"Worse. I wasn't that sick when I had my tonsils taken out. I'll never touch liquor again."

Several boys arrived then, Hugh Morgan among them, and we dropped the subject. Hugh didn't pull my hair anymore, or egg me on to feats both reckless and dangerous. Now he only teased me unmercifully and dogged my steps like a lost puppy. But I wasn't interested in Hugh or any of the other boys, and I didn't feel like flirting. I pasted on a smile and edged around until I could watch Nick without being too obvious about it. When it was time to go back in, I made sure I walked right by him. Neither of us said a word, but our hands skimmed, clung for a moment, and then let go. For now, it was enough.

A few days later I finally got to ask him about Lindsey and the new baby. We were in his room, me in the easy chair, and Nick on the bed.

"Did you know Lindsey was going to quit school?" I asked.

"I didn't know for sure until the day before we started back, but I figured she would."

"Because of her mom's new baby?"

He shrugged. "Partly. But mostly because she hated school. Being around people always scares her."

I got up and went to the bed. Nick scooted over to make room for me, and I sat down and put my hand on his arm. "People are saying the new baby might be your father's."

An inscrutable expression filled his eyes. "He's not."

"How can you be sure?"

"Take my word for it, he's not."

Not long after that talk, I ran into Liz at the drugstore. She was holding the baby in front of her like a sack of potatoes, so I got a good look at him. His hair was a mass of fiery red corkscrew curls, and he had huge blue eyes. In short, he looked enough like Jenna to be her twin. Nick knew the first time I saw that little boy I'd realize the truth. And it didn't take the rest of the town long to figure it out, either.

Jenna became pale and withdrawn, and cried on my shoulder a lot. I gave her what comfort I could, which wasn't much. For a while she nearly lived at my house, and Aunt Jane finally had a long talk with her. Things started to get better after that, but Jenna could never look at a Swanner again without flinching.

My fourteenth birthday came and went, and then my fifteenth. Casey and Cody graduated and left for the university in Little Rock. Nick and I continued to tiptoe around each other, both of us longing for more, but neither willing to risk what we had by pushing it too hard. Until the year I turned seventeen and my life took a direct hit from the hands of fate. If I'd thought Uncle Vern coming home was a shock, it was nothing compared to the turmoil my father brought with him.

Chapter Six

❧

On my sixteenth birthday, the Judge put me behind the wheel of the Chevy and took me to the police station for my driver's test, just like he'd done with Nick. When I passed with flying colors, he handed over the Chevy's keys and the title as my present from him. I was ecstatic.

"At least I know you'll survive if you have a wreck in this one," he told me. The Judge put no faith in the fiberglass bodies on new cars, said they offered about as much protection as an eggshell.

Nick had graduated from high school that spring and now worked full-time as a mechanic at Paul Hawkins' garage. On the evening of my birthday, he took me out to his room and gave me my present. It was one of those necklaces that look like half of a broken heart. His name was on the back, and while I was trying not to cry, he pulled the other half out from under his shirt and showed me where my name was etched. I couldn't help myself. I kissed him. And I knew right away that I might have bitten off more than I could chew.

It was the first time we'd really kissed since that day in the cellar, but Nick had been a boy then. Now he was, at least physically, a man. And he was hungry. There was no hesitation when he returned the kiss, and it washed every other thought out of my head. I felt like I was being devoured. Heat like I'd never known slammed into me and I wanted to melt into him and never come out again.

But while Nick's body tensed and his hands moved over me restlessly, a tiny fear grew in my mind. I wanted him, but I knew it was going to hurt the first time. And that fear was all tied up with the small town morality I'd grown up with. Good girls didn't, not until they had a ring on their finger. Bad girls did, and they always paid for their mistakes.

"Nick..."

His hands went still on my back and he lifted his head to look at me. A shudder ran over him and he closed his eyes, dropping his forehead to mine. "I know." His voice was husky. "Just give me a second." His arms tightened around me and I rested my head on his chest.

"I love you."

I could hear the wry smile in his words when he answered. "Now is not the best time in the world to tell me that."

"I know."

We were silent for a few minutes as he got himself under control.

"Nick? Have you ever..."

"No." He lifted his head again, studied me. "I've thought about it, but it never seemed right."

The idea of him making love to anyone else sent a shaft of pain straight through my middle. "You better wait on me, damn it."

"I don't think I have much choice." He brushed my hair back. "You're the only one I've ever wanted, Alix, the only one I'll ever want. That's a promise." He smiled. "But I don't want to push you into anything you're not ready for."

I nodded. "Maybe we could...practice sometimes?" Okay, so I liked the way he'd made me feel and wanted more of it.

His chuckle was low and deep. "God, you're going to kill me, aren't you? Now, turn around and I'll put the necklace on for you."

When he'd fastened it, I picked it up and slid it under my shirt, swearing never to take it off. And for the next year we did "practice" occasionally, but Nick was always very careful to keep things on an even keel. It was one of the happiest years of my life.

Looking back, I wonder why we were so secretive about our relationship. We never let on how we felt about each other in front of others, almost as though we'd made a pact. I think Aunt Jane knew. A few times when Nick was eating dinner with us I'd catch her looking from him to me, a sadness in her gaze that sent chills over my skin.

I'd been catching a lot of grief from Mama and Aunt Darla after my seventeenth birthday because I didn't appear interested in dating.

"It's just not natural for a girl your age to ignore boys," Aunt Darla declared.

The whole family, Nick included, was sitting on the front porch that evening, and of course, everyone had an opinion.

"I don't ignore them," I told her. "I just don't date them."

"Sweetheart, surely there's someone you like?" Mama said. "What about Hugh? Helena told me he's asked you to the movies."

"I didn't like what was playing." I glanced at Nick and rolled my eyes. He gave me a brooding look in return.

"Leave her alone, Ellie." The Judge spoke in my defense. "You should be thankful the girl's got too much sense to be boy crazy."

"She's only seventeen," Aunt Jane added. "She has plenty of time."

Later, I got Nick's input on the subject.

"Maybe they're right," he told me. That brooding expression was still on his face. "Maybe you should be dating."

My mouth dropped open. "You actually want me to date other guys?"

He sighed. "No. I'd probably go nuts if you did. But it might be better for you." He hesitated. "Alix, I'm always going to be Frank Anderson's kid. The only future I've got is working at Hawkins' garage. You deserve better than that. Somebody like Hugh could give you a good life."

"I don't love Hugh," I said, hurt that he'd even suggest such a thing. "And I wish everyone would find something else to occupy their time and stop nagging me."

Be careful what you wish for might be clichéd, but there's usually a reason why those old sayings have lasted so long. The next day, my father came home.

* * * * *

"Are you going to the garden?" I watched as Mama gathered a knife and a large tin wash pan.

"Yes. The snap beans need picking, and so do the cucumbers and tomatoes. And I want to check the corn. It was almost ready a few days ago."

"I'll go with you." I tossed aside the magazine I'd been thumbing through and got another knife. The garden was one of my favorite places on earth. The feel of the soft, moist dirt under my bare feet and the scent of growing plants was something I looked forward to every year. Almost as much as I looked forward to the first taste of a ripe, red tomato, warm from the sun, the juice dribbling down my chin as I sank my teeth through the tender skin.

When the garden was producing, it was rare for anyone to go grocery shopping. About once a month someone would go for the staples—flour, sugar, coffee, and tea—things we couldn't grow ourselves. Our meals were typically southern and no one ever worried about cholesterol or antioxidants. Even meat was no problem because the Judge paid to a have a calf and a pig slaughtered every year, and the white-wrapped packages with red stamps proclaiming the contents filled one entire freezer.

A typical supper for us consisted of meat, usually fried, cornbread, fried or mashed potatoes, green beans, sliced ripe tomatoes, green onions, and cucumbers in vinegar, salted and peppered. If you'd offered anyone in my family tofu, they wouldn't have had a clue what you were talking about, and wouldn't have eaten it if they had. To them, we ate healthy. It was the junk and fast food that could kill you.

The garden was an acre plot behind the barn, and I was dreaming about fresh corn-on-the-cob for supper that evening as I followed Mama down the back steps. We both paused as a shiny black car pulled into the drive.

"Who in the world..." Mama muttered, one hand cupped above her eyes to block the sun's glare.

The car wasn't familiar to me either, so I figured it was probably a salesman or the Jehovah's Witnesses. We get a lot of both around here. Most folks simply sent the Witnesses on their way or didn't answer the door at all, but heaven help them if Aunt Darla was around. She'd usher the Witnesses right into the living room, pour them a glass of tea, and set about converting them to the Southern Baptist faith. I've known her to keep the poor victims hostage for up to three hours at a whack while she quoted verse and scripture faster than they could come up with answers. She said it was her Christian duty to show them the error of their ways.

But the man climbing out of the car didn't look like a salesman or a Witness, in spite of being well dressed. He wasn't carrying a briefcase or a handful of pamphlets. He was tall and slim, with dark hair that curled gently around his nape, and warm, dark brown eyes that smiled hesitantly as he walked toward us.

The first indication I had that all was not well was the sound of Mama's tin pan hitting the gravel of the driveway. It was so loud I nearly jumped out of my skin.

"Oh, God," she whispered, her face white as new cotton on the boll.

"Mama?" This wasn't like her at all, and I was suddenly worried. "What's wrong?"

"Go in the house, Alix."

"No. I'm not leaving you here alone."

"Please," she whispered.

By then he'd reached us, and when he spoke, his voice held both apology and determination. "I'm sorry it has to be this way, Ellie, but you haven't left me much choice. She's seventeen. It's time you let her make up her own mind."

Mama stepped in front of me, her back tense. "She's too young. Now get out of here before I call the police."

"You can call them if it will make you feel better, but I'm not leaving until I have a chance to talk to Alix." His gaze fastened on me over Mama's shoulder.

I was on the verge of panic. I didn't know what was going on, but I knew Mama felt threatened by this man, and that set all my protective alarms screaming on high volume. Before I had time to react, Aunt Darla and Aunt Jane charged out of the house like angry mother bears. Aunt Jane put her arm around Mama's shoulder while Aunt Darla grabbed me and tried to tow me back inside. I dug in my heels and refused to budge. They had been talking about me like I wasn't there, and I wanted to know what was going on.

"This is the wrong way to go about this, James." Aunt Jane's face was almost as white as Mama's, but her voice was calm. "You're only going to upset everyone."

Mama was crying softly, hands over her face, and I broke loose from Aunt Darla to move closer to her.

"I've tried calling, Jane, but Ellie always hangs up on me. Alix is my daughter. I've got a right to see her."

My father? I stared at the stranger, frozen with shock as a wave of dizziness hit me. When I was five, I had developed a curiosity about the man who was my father. After all, the other kids I knew had one and I wasn't quite sure why I didn't. Mama told me they hadn't gotten along so he'd joined the navy. But I sensed my questions bothered her and soon dropped the line of inquisition. I had the Judge, so I didn't miss not having a real father. I'd never even seen a picture of him before. The only thing I knew about my father was his name. James Tipton.

"You're my father?" I blurted the words before I could stop myself, and both Mama and Aunt Jane shot me horrified looks, as if they only that second realized I was still there.

He took a step closer to me and lifted a shaky hand to my cheek. "Yes, I am. God, you're so beautiful, Alix, so grown up. I've been waiting to meet you for a long time now."

"No." Aunt Darla shoved me behind her and swatted his hand away. "Please, James. Give us a few days to talk to her, to try and sort this mess out."

Tiredly, he rubbed his forehead. "Fine. You've got two days. But if I don't hear from you by then, I'll be back." His gaze fastened on me again. "We need to talk."

I didn't move, simply stood and watched as he climbed into his car and drove off, then numbly followed my mother and aunts back to the kitchen. They settled Mama into a chair like she was an invalid.

"Alix, go wet a washcloth with cold water," Aunt Jane directed.

Knowing she only wanted me out of the room, I left, then stopped and leaned against the wall outside the kitchen. It says a lot about their state of mind that Aunt Jane never thought to see if I was listening.

"What am I going to do?" Mama sobbed.

"You have to tell her the truth, Ellie. If you don't, James will."

"I can't. She'll hate me, Jane."

"Alix is an intelligent girl," Aunt Darla said. "She'll understand."

"No, she won't. All her life we've told her to respect herself, that truth and honesty are the most important things in life, and at the same time we've been lying to her. How is she going to understand that? What can I say that will make her accept that her mother was never married to her father?"

I had heard enough. My breath was coming in labored gasps and spots swam before my eyes. The only thing I could think about was getting away. Grabbing the Chevy's key, I ran out the front door, my mother's frantic voice following me when they realized I'd been listening.

Sick to my stomach, I drove blindly, paying no attention to where I was going. My whole life had been one big lie and I didn't know what to do, how to react. I was a bastard, no better than any of the Swanner kids. But at least Liz hadn't put on a big act, tried to be something she wasn't. She'd survived the only way she knew how, and I'd always respected her for that.

How could I forgive my family for what they'd done to me? How could I ever face them again now that I knew the truth?

I don't remember where I went that night, but I wound up at the Star-Vu Drive-In. It was closed, the concession stand and playground ghostly in the pale moonlight. I pulled the Chevy behind the screen and got out, walking barefoot to the picnic table. I was still there when Nick found me.

Without a word, he sat down and pulled me onto his lap. I curled into him and buried my face against his neck, shaking in spite of the warm night air.

"Want to talk about it?" he murmured.

I shook my head.

"Do you want to go home?"

Another shake, more violent this time.

"Okay, we'll just sit here." One hand stroked my hair in a soothing, repetitive motion.

"It doesn't change who you are, you know," he said.

"They told you?" I was humiliated and disbelieving. My family couldn't tell me the truth, but now they told Nick?

"I don't think they meant to. Everyone went kind of nuts when you ran off. Your mom called me at work, nearly hysterical, to see if you were there, and it sort of came out. Half the county is looking for you, but they only told people you were upset."

"I can't go home, Nick. Not yet."

"So, what do you want to do?"

I thought about it. There really was only one option. "I'll go to Jenna's."

He stood, letting my feet slide to the ground. "I'll follow you."

"You don't have to do that."

"Yes, I do." He leaned down and kissed me gently, then took my hand. "Come on. After you're settled, I'll go let your folks know you aren't lying in a ditch somewhere."

Jenna wasn't surprised to see me. Mama had called her earlier, hoping I'd gone to her house. I told her what had happened, and as I had once done for her, she tried her best to comfort me. At first, I was a little surprised my family didn't come rushing over the second they knew where I was, but Nick had told them to give me time, that I was in no shape to hash things out just yet.

The next morning the Judge brought some of my clothes by, and when he was ready to leave he asked me to walk him to the truck.

"How are you?" he asked quietly.

I shrugged and looked down at the ground. I couldn't tell him I was fine when I wasn't.

"Your Mama is hurting, too, Alix. Maybe she was wrong to lie to you, but she did it because she loves you." He reached into his shirt pocket, pulled out a slip of paper, and handed it to me. The only thing on it was a phone number. "I know you aren't ready to talk to Ellie yet, but you need to talk to someone. Someone who can tell you the truth. Call him, Alix."

I stared at the number. I didn't have to ask who it belonged to. "Does Mama know you're giving me this?"

"We talked it over. She's willing to try anything that might help."

"I'll think about it." I stuck the paper in my pocket.

I stayed at Jenna's for over a week, trying to pull myself together. Nick came by almost every evening, never coming in the house, and staying only a few minutes before he'd leave again. But I suppose it was enough for Jenna to put two and two together.

"You're in love with him, aren't you?" she asked me. "Don't deny it. I can see it on your face every time you look at him."

I was too tired to argue. "And you don't approve, right?" We knew each other almost too well.

"It's not that, exactly." She hesitated. "Alix, it scares me. Nick isn't like us. He's not like *any* of the other boys we know. I don't want to see you hurt."

"Nick would never do anything to hurt me."

She dropped the subject, but I knew she hadn't forgotten it. Jenna could be almost as bad as my family when it came to worrying about me.

Nick wasn't the only one who came by to check on me. Hugh began coming over, too. He didn't know what was wrong, only that something traumatic had happened to me, and neither Jenna nor I enlightened him as to what. Jenna took over the duty of entertaining him when it became obvious I couldn't, and they would talk and laugh while I sat silently, lost in my own thoughts.

Things couldn't go on the way they had been, and I finally called the number the Judge had given me. He was right. I needed to know the truth and I wasn't sure anymore that I'd get it from Mama. My hands were shaky when I lifted the phone, and I had no idea what I was going to say.

He answered on the first ring, almost as though he'd been waiting for my call.

"This is Alix," I said, my grip on the receiver so tight I was surprised it didn't crack.

"I'm glad you called. We need to talk, Alix. Can I come over?"

I shook my head, then realized he couldn't see me. "Maybe I could meet you somewhere?"

"Anywhere you want."

"The city park." It was the first place that popped into my mind, and at least I knew we wouldn't be interrupted this time of day.

"I'll be there in twenty minutes."

"Okay." I returned the phone to the cradle.

Jenna had been listening and her eyes reflected her concern. "Do you want me to go with you?"

"No. I think this is something I have to do on my own."

She nodded. "You know I'm here if you need me."

I was waiting on a picnic table twenty minutes later when my father's black car pulled to a stop beside the Chevy. He was dressed more casually this time, as though he hadn't wanted to take time to change, and he looked as nervous as I felt. Gingerly, he sat down beside me.

"Hi."

I returned the greeting.

"You know, I've wanted to meet you for so long and been so afraid you'd hate me, that now I don't know what to say."

"Did you love my mother?" I hadn't intended to be so blunt, but the words slipped out on their own.

"Yes, I did."

"Then why didn't you marry her?"

He took a deep breath and rubbed his forehead. "I should have. I was going to, but—" He shook his head and started again. "Alix, none of this is your mother's fault. We weren't much older than you are now when we met, and I was engaged to another woman. But the first time I saw Ellie I knew I'd made a mistake. It was love at first sight, and she felt the same way about me, but my fiancée was a very special person and neither of us wanted to hurt her. We started meeting in private. It was wrong and stupid, and we tried to stop. Every time we'd sneak off to be alone, we'd tell each other it couldn't happen again. But we waited too long. When she told me she was pregnant, I didn't know how to handle it. I told her we'd get married, but we were both afraid, Alix. Afraid of what everyone would say, afraid of how your family would react, and most of all, ashamed of what we'd done to…my fiancée."

I think I knew before I asked. It was the only logical explanation given what he'd told me and the snippets of information I'd gathered growing up. "Who was she, this fiancée of yours?"

He propped his elbows on his knees and looked down. "Your Aunt Jane."

I nodded. "So you what? Just took off and left Mama to straighten the mess out alone?"

"Pretty much. I know, I was a son of a bitch. I'm not trying to make excuses. It was too much for me and I panicked and ran. You don't know how many times since then I've regretted it. A few years later I called your mother, but by then she'd made up the story of our fake marriage and divorce, and she wouldn't talk to me. Not that I blame her. After what I'd done, I didn't deserve her forgiveness. But I did deserve the chance to get to know my daughter, Alix. In spite of everything, I loved you. I still do. All I'm asking is that you try not to hate me, that you'll give me—us—the time to work this out together."

"I don't know what to call you," I whispered.

"Dad would be nice, but if you're not ready for that, Jim will do."

"Where have you been all this time?"

"In the navy until a few years ago. Now I live in Jonesboro and work for an accounting firm. I wanted to be as close to you as possible."

"You never got married?"

"No. I guess part of me still loves your mother and always will."

"And Aunt Jane?"

He hesitated again. "I cared about her, Alix, but I don't think I ever really loved her. If we'd gotten married it would have been a disaster. I think she understands that now, and she's obviously forgiven your mother and loves you. They all do. Your mother is waiting to hear from you. She's nearly sick with worry."

"You've talked to her?"

"Yes. Several times in the last week. It's not going to be easy for either of us, but I believe she's willing to work around her feelings toward me for your sake. Everything she did was to protect you, Alix. Don't you think it's time to go home now?"

"I don't know." Part of me longed to, felt only half-alive without my family. But the other part still hesitated, unsure of how to behave now that everything I'd believed in had come crashing down.

"You don't have to do it alone," he said. "I'll go with you."

I couldn't move in with Jenna permanently. Sooner or later I had to face my mother. It might as well be now. Slowly, I slid off the wooden seat. "Okay."

My father was a stranger to me. I don't know why his presence seemed so comforting at that moment. Maybe it was *because* he was a stranger, someone who could take a neutral stance in the emotional upheaval I knew was coming. If he'd blamed my mother, or tried to excuse what he'd done, things would have been different. But he hadn't, and for that if nothing else, I thought I might come to like him.

Mama was watching for us at the back door. She met me halfway, her step hesitant as her eyes searched mine. And suddenly, I was three years old again, depending on her to fix all my injuries, to make my world safe. "I'm sorry, Mama," I whispered, tears choking my throat until it hurt.

Without a word, she held her arms open and I stumbled into them, both of us crying and apologizing, each tripping over the words in our rush to make amends, then laughing through our tears. My father stood quietly beside us, a bit of moisture in his eyes as well.

Eventually the waterworks dried up and the three of us spent a long time talking that night. Mama refused to let Jim take all the blame for what had happened. She said if she'd handled the situation differently, been honest with herself and Jane from the start, things would have worked out better for all of us. She also agreed that I should get to know my father, spend some time with him occasionally.

But while I gained a father, in the long run I lost an element of closeness with my mother that we could never get back. I was changed by the experience I'd gone through, as was she. We still loved each other and always would, but I wasn't a naïve little girl anymore. I had found the hidden closet in our lives and dragged the skeletons out into the bright light of day. We could never put them back again.

If our relationship hadn't changed, maybe I could have talked to her later when I needed to so desperately. But it had, and I didn't, and a hundred wishes won't change the past. Mama had found that out the hard way. My lesson was still coming, and it would be the most grueling thing I'd experienced up to that point. But maybe I needed it. Maybe I couldn't have gotten through what came afterwards if I hadn't been tempered by the flames of Nick's leaving.

Chapter Seven

❧

Another year went by. Life gradually settled back to its normal routine after my father's first appearance, and if I was a little quieter no one seemed to notice, not even Nick. But then, I hadn't seen much of Nick lately. When he'd first gone to work at the garage, he'd lived almost exclusively in his room in the barn. That continued through the winter I was in eleventh grade and on into the summer. Now, inexplicably, he began staying at the salvage yard again and rarely showed up at the farm.

I didn't think too much about it at first. Other things occupied my mind. My eighteenth birthday had come and gone, I had a father I was trying to become accustomed to, and I was a senior that year. On top of that, Hugh had stepped up his campaign to get me to go out with him.

Hugh was a nice looking young man, tall and well-built with his mother's thick, light brown hair and his father's green eyes. He was popular, too, and could have had his choice of any of the girls in town even without his family's money backing him up. Although she'd never admitted it, I think Jenna had a mad crush on him during most of our school years. But I suspected that his family, like mine, was pushing him to date me. Helena Morgan had very definite ideas about who was suitable for her son, and I was on the top of her list. If she'd known the circumstances of my birth she might have changed her mind, but as far as anyone but a handful of people knew, my father was merely my mother's ex-husband.

All in all, I was simply tired of telling Hugh "no" every thirty minutes. That's why, a month into my final year of school, I decided it was time for Nick and me to bring our relationship into the open. I didn't want to hide anymore. I wanted the entire world to know I loved him.

It had been two weeks since I'd last seen him and I didn't know when he'd be back in his room. Not willing to wait, I headed for the garage as soon as school was out that afternoon. I parked the Chevy on the far side of the air pump so it wouldn't be in anyone's way and headed for the work bay. I never made it.

I had only taken a few steps when I saw him. He was in back of the building, old worn-out tires scattered around him in haphazard piles, and he wasn't alone. Lindsey was with him. I could have ignored that if it weren't for their postures, but the way they were standing brought me to a sudden halt.

Lindsey's face was lifted to his, and Nick was looking down at her, his expression intense while he talked to her in a low gentle voice I could hear, but not understand. His hand curled around her nape in a possessive way that even I couldn't miss, his thumb moving over her cheek. Lindsey's body curved toward his as if drawn by magnetic forces beyond her control. And just like that, I knew why he hadn't been coming to the farm. I was only surprised I hadn't realized it until now.

Coming as it did, while I was still wrestling with having a father in my life and dealing with the changes in my relationship with Mama, it was too much for me to take. I didn't get mad, or jealous, or throw a fit. My emotions simply shut down until all I felt was blessed numbness. I can only imagine that's what Nick saw when he looked up abruptly, his eyes meeting mine.

I turned around, got back in the car, and left. If Nick made any attempt to stop me, I didn't hear it and wouldn't have listened if I had. Couldn't listen. But I don't think he did.

Once home, I went straight to the phone and dialed Hugh's number. Still reacting, not thinking. Anything to keep from thinking.

My voice was calm when he answered. "Hugh? It's Alix. Do you still want to go to the movies tomorrow night?" I listened while he said yes. "Great. Pick me up about six-thirty."

If Nick thought I'd confront him about what I'd seen, demand an explanation like I would have a year ago, he was wrong. I couldn't seem to make myself care enough to bother. For the next three months I moved on autopilot. I ate, I went to school, I studied like I never had before, and I dated Hugh every time he asked me. Gradually, people began to link our names together like they always do with couples. It was Alix and Hugh, never simply Alix alone, or Hugh alone. People started to take it for granted that we'd be married as soon as we graduated, and the only one who wasn't thrilled was Piggy Treece. She'd always thought she and Hugh were meant for each other and she didn't appreciate my interference. She and her friends did their best to start nasty rumors about me, but it's hard to wound someone who doesn't care, and they finally gave it up.

Hugh never took more liberties than a goodnight kiss while we were together. He was a friend, first and foremost, and I think he suspected that something wasn't quite right. He treated me like I was some rare and fragile egg that might shatter if he held me wrong. Who knows? Maybe he was right.

On Christmas, we spent most of the day together, first with my family for dinner, then with his for supper. He gave me a beautiful charm bracelet adorned with a multitude of tiny, delicate charms. I gave him a plaque with his name embossed on the front and the words "Vice President" etched underneath to put on his desk when he started working with his father. His family got a big kick out of it, but I think they were all secretly pleased at my faith in Hugh.

It had been a nice day, one more day I'd managed to get through without collapsing. And if I'd had to shove aside the memory of a necklace with a broken heart dangling from the end when Hugh gave me my gift, I managed that, too.

It was late when he took me home, and colder than usual for that time of year. This far south we rarely had a white Christmas, but the taste of snow drifted on the air. Hugh put his arm around me as he walked me to the door, then kissed me, a long, slow kiss that left me totally unmoved. When it was over he lifted a hand to my cheek.

"I'll call you tomorrow."

"Okay."

"Goodnight, Alix."

"Goodnight." I stood with my hand on the door, watching as he pulled out of the drive, his taillights flaring red in the steam from the car's exhaust as he slowed for a curve. Not until he was out of sight did I glance at the silent figure hidden by the deep shadows of a corner porch post.

"What do you want, Nick?"

He shifted restlessly before he spoke. "Do you love him?" His voice sounded raw, as if he hadn't used it in a long time.

"I don't think that's any of your business."

I wasn't expecting him to move so fast, or to grab me so desperately. "It is my business, damn it, and you know it! For God's sake, Alix, scream at me, cuss me out, take a swing at me, but don't ignore me anymore."

"Ignore you?" I tilted my head and studied him. "Let me see. The last time I saw you, you were practically making love to Lindsey in broad daylight, right out in public. No, I'm pretty sure I didn't ignore you."

"It wasn't what it looked like, I swear."

"Right. That's why you tried so hard to find me and explain what you were really doing." His hands gripped my arms, fingers flexing in an unconscious rhythm.

"Would you have believed me?"

"No, and I don't believe you now."

"Have I ever lied to you before?"

"For all I know, everything you've ever told me was a lie." I tried to pull away from him, but he hung on tighter.

"It wasn't a lie."

"Why did you wait until now if it weren't true?"

At least he had the grace to look down. "I didn't plan on talking to you tonight, but I had to make sure you were all right. God, Alix, I've been going crazy. I know you don't love him, no matter what you say, but everyone's talking about how you're going to marry him after you graduate. Please, hate me if you have to, never speak to me again, but don't settle for someone you don't love because I hurt you."

The pain on his face was etched starkly in the moonlight, and I couldn't help myself. God help me, I started to doubt what I'd seen with my own eyes and something inside me that had been frozen began to melt.

"Why were you with her like that, Nick?"

He took a deep, shaky breath. "She's been having some problems. I've been helping her. That's all it is."

"What kind of problems?"

"Personal ones." He hesitated. "I can't tell you what they are, Alix, any more than I'd talk about what you tell me to her." He released me and stepped back. "I shouldn't have come. I can't expect you to believe me when it's something I can't explain."

"Wait." I followed him to the steps. "I asked you once if you'd ever made love to anyone before. You said no. Can you still tell me that, Nick?"

He turned, his lower position on the stairs putting us at eye level. "Yes."

I searched his face for any sign that he was telling me the truth, and I thought I saw it. I wanted to see it because it hurt too much to keep believing he had betrayed me. When I closed the distance between us, all the pain and anger I'd been bottling up inside flooded into the kiss I gave him. All the long months of wanting him and thinking I'd never have him again. All the love I'd tried so hard to kill without a shred of success.

And we both went up in flames.

His arms fastened around me convulsively and his voice held a frantic note when he moaned my name.

"Your room," I whispered.

Neither of us was quite sane as his mouth came down on mine again, and I was barely aware that he'd lifted me into his arms and was moving around the house toward the barn. He must have been in there earlier because the electric stove was still on, the room warm and comfortable. In its glow, Nick put me on the narrow bed and followed me down, his body covering mine, and for the first time in three long months, I felt alive again.

Our movements were rapid and jerky as we rid ourselves of the hindering barriers presented by our clothes, punctuated by more kisses and desperate caresses. But when we were finally bare, our movements slowed. Now that the moment was here, we wanted to take our time and savor it.

Nick's eyes turned to molten lead when he leaned on an elbow and gazed down at me. "So beautiful," he whispered. "So damn beautiful." He ran a hand softly down my body and I arched under his touch like a cat. "Please, don't be afraid."

"I'm not," I said, realizing it was true. I'd been doing some looking of my own and was mildly surprised at his size and a bit curious to see if his erection felt as hard as it appeared, but I wasn't afraid.

Ours was a voyage of sweet discovery that night, and we spent endless hours exploring all the secret, foreign places we'd longed to visit. And we taught each other what pleased us, hands guiding hands, then returning to tease the last place they'd found. By the time Nick's weight pressed me into the bed we were mindless with shared pleasure. He entered me with one hard lunge and then froze, his lips raining kisses of apology over my face. But the pain, while sharp, wasn't as bad as I'd thought it would be, gone before I had more than registered it, and then forgotten when he began to move again. Immediately an indefinable something began to build inside me and I clutched Nick tightly, surging toward a goal I'd never known existed. When I reached it, I cried out, shattering into a million splinters of light. Nick's groan of pleasure sounded hard on the heels of my own, his body going stiff as he found release.

For a few minutes neither of us moved while our breathing returned to normal. I felt drugged, my entire body heavy with a delicious lassitude I didn't want to end. But suddenly Nick began to shake. Tremor after tremor rippled over him. Alarmed, I shifted, trying to see what was happening, but he rolled to the side and clutched me tightly, his face buried in my hair.

"I'm sorry," he whispered, his voice harsh and full of pain. "Oh, God, I'm so sorry. I never meant for this to happen, to hurt you this way."

"Stop it," I ordered softly, my fingers moving through his hair. "You didn't hurt me. What happened tonight happened because I wanted it every bit as much as you did. It was beautiful, Nick. Don't turn it into something ugly. You aren't your father. You could never do the things he does."

"But I don't have anything to offer you. I don't even have my own place to live."

"Someday you will. And for now, I've got you. That's all that matters to me."

"I thought I'd lost you," he murmured. "I've never been so afraid in my life. I felt hollow, like part of me had been ripped out." His shaking finally eased to periodic spasms. "I swear, Alix, someday I'll make you proud to be seen with me."

"I already am. And I'm tired of hiding. I'm going to tell Hugh that I can't see him anymore, that I love you."

It was so long before he answered that I wondered if he'd fallen asleep. Abruptly, he sat up on the edge of the bed.

Elbows on his knees, he rubbed his face with both hands. "You can't."

"Why not?" I was confused and a little hurt by his refusal.

He dropped his hands and turned to look at me, his gaze running over my face as though he wanted to memorize every detail. "Because the mess with Lindsey isn't over yet, and until it is…"

"Until it is, you don't want anyone to know about us."

"Yes. I have an idea but she's fighting it, and I don't know how long it will take to convince her."

"I don't understand why this is your problem, Nick."

His expression turned grim. "Believe me, it is. I know it's asking a lot, and if you don't think you can handle it, I'll try to understand. But I don't have any choice in this, Alix." He took a deep breath. "It's important that people…think I'm seeing Lindsey."

"You want me to keep dating Hugh." It wasn't a question. I knew that's what he was getting at in his round-about way.

"Yes."

"That's not fair, Nick. Not to us or Hugh."

"God, don't you think I know that? It's why I tried so hard to stay away from you."

"What about us?"

His hand moved to my cheek, traced it gently. "I can't give you up again. It would kill me."

Because I loved him so much, I had to trust him. "How long will it take?"

"I wish I knew, but I can't give you a time frame. It could be a week, or it could be months. Can you live with that?"

I caught his hand and pressed it more tightly to my cheek. "I'll have to, because I can't give you up either. We'll work it out somehow."

"I don't know I got lucky enough to have someone like you," he whispered. "But I'm so glad I did."

We made love again after that, then fell asleep in each other's arms. Nick woke me before daylight so I could slip up to my bed unnoticed, but I almost didn't make it. We couldn't seem to let go of each other after our night together and ended up making love yet again.

When we were both dressed, he shut off the heater and walked me to the door, lingering for a long, tender kiss as the first pale echo of light tinged the horizon. I had just settled into my bed when I heard Aunt Darla, always an early riser, make her way to the bathroom. With a sigh of relief at the near miss, I snuggled down and went to sleep, dreaming about the next time I'd be alone with Nick.

In retrospect, I'm amazed no one noticed the change in me. I started laughing again, and I stayed in a rosy fog of happiness that made me absent-minded and forgetful. On the nights I had a date with Hugh, I'd come home to find Nick waiting, leaning against the side of the house in the shadows. Together we'd walk to his room, so eager to be alone again that we'd barely make it through the door before we were tugging each other's clothes off.

On the nights I didn't have a date, I'd wait impatiently by my window, watching for the light to come on in his room. He never showed up before midnight, and I never asked him what he'd been doing. I just accepted that he was here now, more than likely lying on the bed naked and ready for me. The thought of his glorious body, so strong and well muscled, was enough to have me sneaking down the stairs, running through the darkness to be with him, excitement making my heart race. Every time, he'd smile at me and hold out his arms.

"What took you so long?" he'd ask.

We were like two children who had discovered a new and exotic toy. One second we'd be serious and intent, the next, laughing and giggling helplessly. And we loved each other.

God, how we loved each other. There were times when we'd do nothing but kiss for hours on end, wallowing in our feelings.

There were only a few flies in the ointment during those wonderful months. One was Hugh. While I'd never love him the way I did Nick, I had come to care about him a great deal. I didn't want to hurt him and I felt guilty for using him.

The other was Lindsey. I hated seeing her with Nick. It didn't happen often, but it did happen. The first time was on a Friday evening. Hugh had picked me up for our regular date, but that particular night he stopped at Hawkins for gas on our way to the movies.

Nick was still there, and Mr. Viders, our school principal, was in the office, waiting on him to finish changing the oil in his car. And while Nick worked, Lindsey sat on a stack of tires behind him, her gaze locked on his every movement. Her little brother was on her lap, as silent as she was.

"Want a soda?"

I jerked my attention back to Hugh and smiled. "Sure."

We climbed out of the car as Nick headed in our direction, but I stopped. The gas cap was on my side and I was hoping to get a moment alone with Nick.

"Hey, Nick." Hugh greeted him as they met. "How's it going?"

"Fine. Fill it up?"

"Please." Hugh went into the office and I could see him talking to Mr. Viders.

My gaze went back to Lindsey. She was still watching Nick as though her life depended on keeping him in sight. And it hurt. As much as I tried to fight it, it hurt.

The rattle of the gas nozzle drew me, and I glanced around. He was standing as close to me as possible without making it too obvious.

"Don't look like that," he begged, his voice low.

"It's hard seeing you with her, Nick."

"I know." Beneath the window where no one could see, his fingers curled around mine and squeezed. "Every time he kisses you goodnight I want to strangle him."

We shared a long look full of sympathy and understanding. "Are you coming over tonight?" I finally asked.

"Yes."

"Okay." I slipped my hand from his when the bell over the office door rang.

Hugh gave me an odd look as he paid Nick for the gas, and I braced myself for questions. But he didn't ask any, merely handed me my soda and opened the car door for me before climbing in on the driver's side.

Later that night, after Nick and I made love, I broached the subject of Lindsey again. Nick looked so tired that it suddenly hit me how little sleep he must be getting. He worked all day, then spent the evenings with Lindsey until he came to me after midnight. He didn't show up every night, but he was there enough to make me worry about him. On those nights he was lucky to get a few hours sleep.

"How much longer is this going to last?" I asked.

"I don't know." His fingers traced an absentminded path down my arm. "Sometimes I think I'm making progress, then she'll just clam up and refuse to talk about it. I feel like I'm beating my head against a brick wall. And...the situation...seems to be getting worse. It's reached the point where I'm afraid to leave her alone for a single minute."

It was the closest he'd ever come to telling me what was going on, and I realized he wouldn't have said that much if he hadn't been so tired he couldn't think straight. He must have known the same thing, because instantly he shut up.

I snuggled closer and wrapped my arms around him. "Go to sleep," I whispered.

With a yawn, he did just that, but I stayed awake the rest of the night, driving myself crazy wondering why he was afraid for Lindsey. What could possibly happen to her when she rarely left her home? And from what I'd seen, when she did go out it was always with Nick.

Of course, I solved nothing that night. I only prayed that Nick would feel enough confidence in me to tell me everything when it was over. Neither of us knew that it wouldn't be over for many long years, or that Frank Anderson would wind up dead, lying in a pool of blood on the grimy floor of his trailer.

I did, however, realize I might have a big problem of my own when I walked into the kitchen a few weeks later and found my mother and Helena Morgan huddled over a spring catalogue. They were talking in excited whispers that came to a screeching halt when I strolled through the door. Both of them looked up and gave me patently fake smiles of pure innocence.

"Okay, where is it?" I demanded.

Mama arched an eyebrow. "Where's what, dear?"

"The body. When two people look like you two do, there has to be a body involved."

"Nonsense. We were just...um, looking at the new fashions."

"That's right." Helena nodded eagerly.

"Uh–huh." I went to the fridge and poured a glass of tea, trying to ignore the fact that they'd decided I was blind and were signaling each other frantically. "Isn't it a little early in the season to be thinking about spring clothes?" I carried my drink to the table and sat down.

"It's never too early, Darling." Helena beamed at me. "And I do so love spring. It makes me think of weddings."

Uh-oh. This was trouble with a capital T. I forced myself to stay calm. "Really? It makes me think of mosquitoes and storms."

Right then Aunt Darla came skidding into the room. "It just hit me," she started excitedly. "Lilacs...oh, Alix. I didn't know you were here." The three of them went through another round of facial contortions while my heart sank.

It was even worse than I'd thought. They were already planning my wedding. To Hugh.

"So tell me, Alix, what's your favorite time of the year?" Helena inquired.

"Christmas," I spit out, hoping I could head them off at the pass and buy some time.

"Oh." Their faces fell, but I knew Nick and I couldn't put things off much longer without hurting a lot of people.

I did try later that day to prepare Mama. After Helena left I curled up on the couch with a copy of *The Heart of Midlothian* that I was reading for my honors lit class. It wasn't long before Mama joined me, picking up a magazine and thumbing through it casually. She stopped on a lipstick ad and studied it as if world peace depended on her picking out the right shade.

"So many choices," she murmured. "Tell me, Alix, is red still your favorite color?"

Carefully, I closed my book and put it on my lap. "Mama, I know what you're doing."

"What do you mean? I'm looking at makeup."

"No, you aren't. You're making wedding plans." I took a deep breath. "Hugh hasn't asked me to marry him, Mama. And even if he does, I might not say yes. I'm not sure I feel that way about him."

She looked honestly puzzled. "Of course you'd say yes. Hugh is the only boy you've ever dated. Who else would you marry? And Helena says he's crazy about you. There's no doubt he'll ask."

I tried a different track. "Did you ever think I would rather go to college than tie myself down with a husband?"

"Well, I suppose if you really wanted to go, you could do both. I'm sure Hugh wouldn't mind, and it would give you something to occupy your time until the first baby is on the way."

Mothers. Can't live with them, can't hit them over the head with a board. I picked up my book and went back to reading.

The episode may not have reached my mother, but it did have one enormous effect on me. I was scared out of my mind that Hugh was going to pop the question at any second. It reached the point where all he had to do was walk up behind me in the hall at school, and I nearly crawled out of my skin.

Naturally, he noticed my sudden case of nerves. "Is something wrong, Alix?"

"No, of course not. Why would you think anything was wrong?"

"I don't know." He arched his eyebrows and noted my position half-in and half-out of my locker, no mean feat, let me tell you. "Call it a hunch," he said.

I extracted myself and tried on one of those innocent smiles for size. "Honestly, Hugh. Nothing is wrong."

"No problems at home?"

"Not a one."

His eyes narrowed. "Has my mother been bothering you?"

Which, of course, let me know she'd been bothering him. I turned my back and gathered the books for my next class. "No."

"You're sure?"

"Positive." I faced him.

"Okay." He leaned down and kissed my cheek. "See you tonight? I thought we could go to the basketball game."

"That'll be great." It would also be fairly safe since I couldn't see him dropping to one knee in the middle of a crowd. Hugh wasn't an introvert like Nick was, but he wasn't a showoff either. He would never ask me to marry him in the hall at school, I realized with a spurt of relief. If he ever proposed, it would be in a quietly romantic way.

That thought cheered me somewhat and calmed me down, but it also made me sad. Lucky me, I'd have to break his heart after he'd gone through elaborate preparations to make me happy.

Or so I thought.

Chapter Eight

Graduation day drew ever nearer and my whole class was abuzz with plans for the prom. As the person with the highest grade point average, I had been named valedictorian. Hugh was salutatorian, and our parents were convinced it was another sign we belonged together. Even worse, Hugh started dropping hints about the future.

"Where would you like to live after graduation?" he asked me.

Nome, Alaska, I thought glumly. But I didn't say it. "I haven't given it much thought."

"They're building some really nice houses out at Fair Oaks. You should drive over and look at a few."

I stared at him. Fair Oaks was a new subdivision just outside of town, some big city contractor's idea of genteel southern living. The houses were rambling modern structures, all single-story and set on a five acre plot. I knew they cost a fortune.

I also knew I couldn't take much more of this.

Mama still wouldn't listen to my protests about marrying Hugh, and I didn't dare talk to the Judge, even though he'd be on my side. I was too afraid he'd suspect what was going on between me and Nick, and I didn't know how he'd react. The Judge tended to be a tad bit overprotective where I was concerned, and I didn't want him going after Nick with the shotgun for impugning my honor.

My father had been hanging around a lot, casting wistful looks at Mama while he chatted with the Judge. In a strange way, I think he filled the gap in the Judge's life that Nick had once occupied. My whole family missed Nick. They knew he spent the night in the barn occasionally, but they rarely saw him anymore since he arrived so late and left so early.

One evening, after the weather turned warm, I asked my father to take a walk with me. Mama smiled on us benignly as we left. One thing about Mama. She still looked like an angel when she smiled, but by now I knew how deceiving looks could be. The woman had a stubborn streak that would put a Missouri mule to shame, and she wasn't above using guilt to get her way.

Dad put his arm around my shoulders while we strolled in the direction of the woods, but he didn't say much. I could feel curiosity coming off him in waves. While we had spent time alone together, going out to eat and such, I'd never really confided in him the way daughters do with fathers.

Well, he was about to get his money's worth in one fell swoop, I decided ruefully. I only hoped he was up to the challenge.

"Okay, let's have it." He arched an eyebrow. The man was no dummy.

I plopped down on a log, the remains of an oak tree that had fallen years ago during one of our winter ice storms, and he sat beside me. "It's Mama. She's driving me crazy."

"About what?"

"Hugh." I hesitated. "Dad, she's bound and determined I'm going to marry him, and she won't listen to a word I say on the subject."

"Do you love him?"

I shrugged. "I suppose so, in a way. I just don't want to marry him."

"Then don't let your mother push you into it. It's your life, Alix. You have to do what makes you happy." He studied me with a more intense scrutiny than usual. "It's Nick, isn't it?"

Like I said, the man was no dummy. He'd met Nick, and had listened to all the family stories about how I'd adopted him and our exploits over the years. Once he had even come looking for me and caught me in the barn with Nick. Luckily, we weren't doing anything but talking that time, but we must have given ourselves away to someone who wasn't as close to the situation as the rest of my family.

I was tired of denying my feelings for Nick, so I nodded. "Yes. I've loved him for a long time."

"Does he feel the same way about you?"

It suddenly occurred to me that Nick had never told me loved me. I'd only assumed he did from the way he acted. I still believed he loved me, but my self-confidence was a bit shaken. "I think so."

"Then why hasn't he done something about it?"

Good question. I wished I had a logical answer. "There are some problems," I said vaguely.

He was silent for a moment, thinking that over. "Nick didn't strike me as the type that would let the woman he loves marry someone else. Have you told him what your mother is doing?"

"No." I hadn't wanted to make him feel any worse than he already did. And deep down, I was afraid that if he thought our relationship was giving me trouble, he'd stop seeing me.

"Maybe you should."

He was right. I'd only needed to hear someone say it. It was time to face the music. I'd been more than patient over the last few months. If Nick really loved me, it was time to do something about it. And if he didn't, if Lindsey was more important to him than I was, well, it was better to find out now.

So that's how I set in motion the events that culminated in Frank Anderson's death.

It was Wednesday evening when I had my talk with Dad. That night I didn't wait in my room for Nick as I usually did. I went down to the barn and waited, moving restlessly through the long hours before his arrival, playing out different scenarios in my head. No matter how he reacted, I had to be prepared.

His surprise at finding me there faded fast when he saw my face. "What's wrong?" he asked, closing and locking the door behind him.

"I can't do this anymore," I told him in an anguished whisper. "Things are getting completely out of hand. Mama has done everything but set the actual date for Hugh's and my wedding, and she won't listen to me when I try to talk to her."

With my first words, the blood drained from his face. "She really thinks you're going to marry him?"

"Of course she does! I've been dating him for almost a year now, and she doesn't know I've been seeing anyone else. Whenever I tell her I don't want to marry him, she decides it's only a case of wedding jitters and I'll get over it. And Hugh's mother isn't helping any. She's over nearly every day, bringing magazines and catalogues."

"Christ." He dropped onto the bed, his shoulders slumped. "Why haven't you said anything before now?"

"I didn't want to worry you, and I thought I could handle it. But no one is paying attention to what I'm telling them. It's like trying to stop a runaway train with one hand tied behind my back."

"Has Hugh..."

"Asked me to marry him?" I shook my head and sat down next to him. "Not yet, but he's going to. Soon. The other day he suggested I drive out to Fair Oaks and see if I liked the houses they're building."

I picked up his hand and gripped it tightly. "We have to tell them about us, Nick. It's the only option. Unless you *want* me to marry Hugh," I added quietly.

He went still. "I guess I deserved that, didn't I? I sure haven't done much to make you think otherwise." When he turned to face me his voice was low. "I don't want you to marry Hugh. It kills me every time I know you're with him. But I don't know what else to do, Alix. There's still Lindsey's...problem to worry about." He stood and started pacing.

"Are things getting any better?"

"No."

"Do you have any reason to think they will?"

He ran a hand through his dark hair in frustration. "No. She still won't listen to me."

"So how long are we going to put our lives on hold? Another six months? A year? Two?" I stood slowly. "You can't have us both, Nick. You need to decide who you want."

"You'd really marry him?" His expression was one of shock mixed with despair.

I paused with my hand on the lock and looked over my shoulder. "No. But the only other solution I can come up with is for me to leave. Eventually, they'll get the message. Either way, I need to know what your decision is soon. If I'm leaving, I have some plans to make."

There was no manipulation intended in my ultimatum. I meant every word I'd uttered. I'd given it a lot of thought while I was pacing the room in the barn and didn't feel like I had much choice. Part of me was so sure he'd choose Lindsey that I'd half-settled on a destination for my relocation. Tucson, Arizona. Something about the red bluffs I'd seen in pictures appealed to me, and the city was big enough that I should be able to support myself while I went to college, without completely intimidating me like New York or Dallas would. Because if he chose Lindsey, there was no way I could stay, see them together every day.

I waited for his answer, then waited a little longer, my heart sinking as the silence deepened. I couldn't stand it anymore. Just the fact that he wasn't saying anything was answer enough for me. "Goodbye, Nick." I opened the door.

"Stop."

I hovered on the threshold, afraid to turn around.

"For God's sake, Alix, don't go."

"I don't think God cares one way or the other. He pretty much lets me make my own decisions."

"For my sake, then." He moved up behind me and put his hands on my shoulders. "You're right. About everything. I can't force Lindsey to accept my help, and as long as I keep protecting her, she doesn't have to do anything on her own."

His lips touched my hair. "Christ, I'm sorry, Alix. Sorry I've put you through this for so long. I'll do whatever you want. Just don't leave me."

I turned, hope nearly choking me. "We can tell everyone?"

"Yes." His hands caressed my neck, moved up to cradle my cheeks.

"When?"

He took a deep breath. "Tomorrow evening. Give me a chance to talk to Lindsey after work, then I'll come straight over."

"You're sure?"

There was a brief hesitation, a flash of uncertainty in his eyes, but he nodded. "I'm sure."

"Oh, Nick." I went into his arms and our lovemaking that night was all the sweeter for knowing how close we'd come to losing each other. We lingered for hours, one minute tender, the next frantic. Nick especially seemed insatiable. We'd barely finish before he'd start again. Not that I complained. I was more than willing to spend the rest of my life in his bed, doing nothing else.

"They're going to throw a fit, you know," he murmured after the last time. "Are you ready for that?"

I stretched and turned onto my side, snuggling up to him with my head on his shoulder. "I think they'll be shocked, but Aunt Darla is the only one who'll really fight it. You know how she is. She's like a snapping turtle. When she latches onto an idea she won't let go until it thunders. But once Mama realizes we're serious, she'll give in. Deep down she only wants what's best for me." I ran a hand over his chest and down the hard planes of his stomach. "You're what's best for me. And Daddy is on our side. He'll help us convince Mama and the others."

"He knows?" Nick caught my hand and brought it to his lips.

"Yes. I think he's suspected for a while now. We had a long talk this afternoon and he wasn't a bit surprised. He likes you."

He rolled until he'd pinned me to the bed, his elbows taking most of his weight while his hands cradled my face. "Are you sure, Alix? I can't give you a big house like Hugh could. It will take me a few months to even save enough for a small apartment."

I held his intent gaze steadily. "I've never asked for a big house. That was Hugh's idea. And you won't have to do it alone. Mrs. Lucas, Doctor Mansfield's office manager, offered me a receptionist job after I graduate."

"You shouldn't have to work." His fingers threaded gently through my hair.

"Oh? What should I do? Sit around all day on a satin pillow twiddling my thumbs? Nick, I'd go crazy in a week with nothing to do. I want to work."

"You should go to college. You're too smart not to."

I shrugged. "I can do both. It might take me a little longer to finish, but I'm not in a hurry."

He got quiet for a second. "I can't believe we're actually talking about a future together. I'm almost afraid to hope, like

116

the powers that be will know and do something to screw it up."

"They wouldn't dare."

He gave me a long, deep kiss, then rolled to a sitting position and checked his watch. "I'm not taking any chances. It'll be dawn in another thirty minutes. We better get you back in the house."

"Just promise me you won't back out tomorrow."

"I promise, I won't back out."

How different things might have been if he had, but at the time, I was so sure we were doing the right thing.

* * * * *

Thursday was sweet agony for me. I couldn't concentrate on anything except the evening ahead. Jenna kept giving me strange looks, once asking if I was okay when I didn't hear what she'd said.

Finally, during lunch, she cornered me. We were standing outside the school store, a small building behind the classrooms that sold everything from paper and pencils to sodas and candy. "I know something is going on. You might as well 'fess up."

She knew me too well. If I didn't give her an answer that satisfied her, she'd keep picking at me until I did. Still, I hesitated. It wasn't that I thought Jenna would tell anyone. We'd kept each other's confidences too often for that. It was more that I understood how she felt about me and Nick, and I didn't want anything to spoil this day.

"I'll tell you tomorrow night, I promise." I figured that would give me time to tell Hugh first.

She leaned against the wall beside me and stared down at the ground. "This has something to do with Nick, doesn't it?"

"What makes you say that?"

She shook her head. "Everything you do involves Nick in one way or another. After all this time, you're still in love with him."

I couldn't deny it so I remained silent.

"There are dozens of rumors about him and Lindsey Swanner, you know."

"I know."

"But you still love him."

"Yes."

"Are you sleeping with him?" She shifted to see me better, and one look at my fiery face was all she needed. "Oh, my God. You are. Alix, how could you do that to Hugh? He loves you."

I kept my voice low, afraid someone would overhear us. "No, Jenna. He doesn't love me. He and I care about each other, but not that way. His mother is pushing him into asking me to marry him the same way mine is pushing me to say yes. Giving in is the path of least resistance, and as long as he isn't in love with anyone else, he'll do what she wants."

"He'd probably do what she wants even if he were in love with someone else," she said. If the trace of misery in her voice puzzled me, I chalked it up to her failing relationship with Scott Hastings. They'd been dating for most of the year, but things were cooling off rapidly as graduation approached. Scott had big plans to attend a prestigious college in the east while Jenna had already lined up a job with the Mid-Delta Real Estate Company here in town.

"Hey, cheer up. You and Scott can still write to each other."

She looked at me as though I'd suddenly sprouted a horn in the middle of my forehead. "I don't think so. We both agree it's better if we don't see each other again after the prom."

"I'm sorry."

One shoulder lifted in a shrug. "No big deal. I don't love him anymore than you love Hugh. He was only someone to have fun with." She pushed away from the wall. "When are you going to tell Hugh?"

"I'm not sure yet," I hedged. "I have to break the news to my family first and they're going to be in shock."

"Want to borrow a roll of duct tape?" She smiled wanly. "You'll need it for Aunt Darla's mouth."

We headed back inside, but she stopped me as we reached the door. "I know Nick is gorgeous, Alix, and that you've loved him forever, but please be careful. I've got a bad feeling about this."

Maybe she had a touch of the second sight. Or maybe she was simply a pessimist, although she'd never shown signs of being one before. More than likely it was Hugh she was worried about. I just didn't know it back then.

That evening I made a pure nuisance of myself, getting in everyone's way while they cooked supper, trying to help rush things along. And I watched the clock on the stove like a hawk, imagining Nick's every move. Right about the time we sat down to eat, he was getting off work. He'd go straight to Lindsey's, I knew, and I pushed the food around on my plate restlessly. How long would it take? An hour? Surely not two.

Forty-five minutes later I was wearing a groove in the front porch when his truck finally pulled into the driveway. Dashing down the steps, I met him as he climbed out. "You made it."

"Of course I did." He pulled me close and kissed me, right there in full sight of the whole world, and I knew everything was going to be all right.

"Come on." I took his hand and tugged. "Everyone is still in the kitchen."

"Hold your horses." He laughed. "At least give me time to take a shower and change clothes before we face the music."

I paused to check him over. He was wearing the dark blue uniform he worked in, and oil stains spotted it here and there. He looked wonderful to me, but I realized he'd never get past Aunt Darla in that condition.

"Okay. I'll go with you."

Once in his room with the door locked, he stripped while I got his clean clothes out and put them on the bed. The sound of running water drew me to the open bathroom door. Odd, but as many times as we'd made love I'd never watched him take a shower, and being there with him created a sense of intimacy I'd never experienced before.

The curtain around the tub was a clear plastic and I had no trouble seeing his every move as he lathered up the soap and scrubbed his body. I only wished it were my hands doing the honors, but I knew if I offered we wouldn't make it back to the house for hours. Casually, I put the lid down on the toilet and sat so we could talk without yelling.

"Jenna gave me the third degree at school today."

"Did you tell her?"

"Not in so many words, but I guess she figured it out. I don't think she's real happy about it."

"A lot of people are going to be shocked, Alix. You might as well get ready for it."

"I'm ready." I watched as he ducked his head under the water and rinsed off the shampoo. "How did Lindsey take it?"

He used both hands to wipe the water from his face, hesitated, then shook his head. "I don't think she believed me." Turning the water off, he shoved the curtain back and reached for the towel I held out, a frown on his face.

"You're still worried about her."

"I can't help it, Peewee," he said softly. "I've been taking care of her since she was a little kid." He paused in the act of drying, his gaze fixed on some distant point only he could see. "Telling her was terrible, one of the hardest thing I've ever done. She just sat there staring at me, like she was waiting for the punch line. I kept asking her if she understood, and she'd nod, but I could see she didn't understand anything."

I stood and put my hand on his chest. "I'm sorry."

His gaze focused on me and he dropped his forehead to mine. "It's not your fault, Alix. It's mine. I could have forced her to do what I wanted months ago. She wouldn't have liked it, but she'd have done it."

"Done what?" I whispered, half afraid of his answer.

"Leave town." He pulled back and looked down at me, his eyes dark.

Surprise rippled through me, and a bit of elation. Of all the things I'd imagined he was doing, trying to get Lindsey to leave town hadn't been among them. "Oh," I murmured.

As though he'd read my mind, his lips curved in a smile and he kissed the end of my nose. "I'd better get dressed while I still can."

I should have asked him why he wanted Lindsey to leave. Maybe at that point he would have told me. But I knew from experience that getting information out of Nick was like trying to pull a hen's teeth, and I didn't want anything to delay our confrontation with my family.

When he finished dressing, we walked toward the house holding hands, and I couldn't help but remember that first church social when his hand gripped mine tighter and tighter. So much had changed since then, and so much remained the same. He wasn't afraid anymore, but he was still mine.

We went in through the back door, expecting to find Mama and my aunts around the table. Instead, the only one there was my father. He was leaning against a cabinet, eating a piece of the apple pie Aunt Jane had fixed for supper. He looked up when we came in and then arched an eyebrow at me. I gave him a slight nod, and he smiled.

"Nick, nice to see you again."

"Thanks. You too, sir."

"Where is everyone?" I asked.

Before he could answer, Mama darted into the room. She'd changed into a good dress and my eyes narrowed as I watched her rummage through a stack of papers on the countertop.

"Now where did I leave those estimates?" She glanced up then gave Nick a sunny smile, apparently missing our linked hands. "Nick, Dear! We haven't seen you in ages. Have you had supper?" She hurried over and gave him a peck on the cheek.

"No, ma'am."

"Alix, fix him a plate while the food is still warm."

"Are you going somewhere, Mama?"

"Of course. You know the Ladies' Decoration Committee meets at church tonight."

I nearly groaned. I'd totally forgotten about that committee. "Do you think you could miss it this one time?"

"Don't be silly, Alix. There's no reason to miss it."

When I shot my father a pleading look, he hastily put his pie down. "Maybe you could be a bit late tonight, Ellie. Alix wants to talk to you."

"It can wait, can't it, dear?" She tossed the reply over her shoulder without looking at me. Pushing my father gently aside, she pounced on a pile of papers. "There they are! Darla, Jane? It's time to go!"

My aunts bustled into the room, fussed over Nick for a second, then they were gone. I sighed in frustration and Nick put his arm around me.

"Don't get upset. We can do it tomorrow when everyone is here."

"He's right," my father added. "Why don't you two go to a movie or something? Your mother's attention would have been split even if she'd stayed."

Disappointment was a sharp sting after the day's anticipation, but I made myself smile. "I guess you're right." I went to fix Nick's food. "What are you doing here tonight?"

"The Judge and I are going to a tractor pull in town." He rinsed his plate and left it in the sink. "And we'd better get going."

"Have fun."

"We will." He gave me a quick kiss on the cheek. "Now stop fretting. You've got all the time in the world."

As soon as he left the room, Nick pulled me down on his lap and brushed the hair away from my face. "We do have all the time in the world." He smiled. "And I still owe you a trip to the Star-Vu. Let's go have some fun tonight and I'll come over first thing in the morning, before work, and we'll catch them at breakfast."

"Okay." I returned his smile.

We did go to the movie that night, and since it was a Thursday, nearly had the place to ourselves. It was to be the first and last time we'd ever go on a real date together. The movie was boring, but we weren't watching it anyway, too caught up in each other. And we discovered what millions of teenagers before us had discovered. Making love in a bed was a lot more comfortable than on a truck seat, even though we managed nicely.

It was around ten when we got home, and Nick walked me to the door. I wanted to ask him to stay, but I couldn't. I didn't want to hear him tell me that he had to go check on Lindsey, even though I knew that's what he'd do.

We should have had some premonition that disaster was about to strike, some primitive intuition that warned us, but we didn't. Our entire lives were about to change, and yet neither of us had so much as an inkling that by this same time tomorrow night he'd be gone, from Morganville and from my life. And so we kissed goodbye as usual and he left. I watched him go, waiting until his truck was out of sight before going inside. If I'd known what he was walking into, I never would have let him leave.

Chapter Nine

№

Even from my position in the far distant future, every detail of that next day still stands out in sharp relief. The normal actions I undertook every morning gained an importance that's etched them into my mind permanently. Why didn't I know something was wrong? How could I have missed the silence in our usually noisy house while I went about preparing for another day of school in ignorance? How could I have spent twenty minutes fussing with my hair and trying to pick out the perfect outfit for Nick's arrival and our revelation to my family?

Oh, God. How could I have been so happy? I was even singing under my breath as I jogged down the stairs. The first hint I had that all was not well didn't occur until I entered the kitchen. My whole family was gathered around the table nursing cups of coffee and there was no sign that anyone had attempted to cook breakfast. It was most unusual in a home where breakfast is always done in a big way, with eggs, bacon or sausage, biscuits, gravy, homemade jelly, and butter. I don't remember a box of cereal ever entering our cabinets.

I stopped in the door and eyed my father, puzzled as to why he would be there so early, and wearing what looked suspiciously like the same clothes he'd had on the night before. For that matter, the Judge was wearing the same clothes, too, and he appeared haggard and tired, as though he'd been up all night. Mama really should have a talk with my father about keeping the Judge out so late, I decided. After all, he wasn't a young man anymore.

"Good morning." I glanced at the clock before grabbing a glass and filling it with orange juice. Nick should be here any second. He was already a bit late.

"Alix," my mother's voice was hesitant and there was a funny little catch in it. "You'd better sit down, Sweetheart. We've got some bad news."

"Bad news?" I frowned at her over my shoulder, wondering why she looked so pale.

"There's no easy way to do this, Ellie." Grim-faced, my father stood and put his hands on my shoulders. He knew, better than anyone else, what this was going to do to me. His voice was gentle when he spoke, but he gave it to me straight.

"Alix, Frank Anderson was killed last night and the police have arrested Nick for shooting him."

"What?" The glass slid from my fingers and shattered on the floor, filling the room with the scent of oranges. "That's impossible. Nick couldn't kill anyone. Why are you doing this?" My voice was rising, but I couldn't help it. Their expressions were suddenly making me very afraid.

Anguish filled my father's eyes and he pulled me close, holding me tightly. "It's true, Sweetheart. God, I'm so sorry. Nick called the police himself. The Judge and I have been at the jail all night. Nick says it was self-defense and I think we've convinced them he's telling the truth."

Mama and Aunt Jane flanked us as I pushed away, doing their best to comfort me. But there was no comfort, only shock and confusion. The reality of what they were telling me hadn't kicked in yet, but it was barreling toward me at the speed of light.

Aunt Darla, ever the practical one, was down on her hands and knees, mopping up broken glass and juice. Tears streamed down her cheeks. Part of me hadn't believed any of this until I saw her reaction. "Stop it," I whispered. "Stop crying. It's going to be okay. If they believe him, they'll let him go."

I took a step toward the Judge. "They're going to let him go, aren't they? They have to let him go if it was self-defense."

"Alix, it's not that easy." He ran a hand over his forehead, dislodging his glasses. "A man was killed."

"Oh, God." My legs shook and the room spun around me dizzily. Someone pushed me onto a chair. "How, please tell me how?"

The Judge took a deep breath. "Nick said Frank was drunk when he got home last night, and in a mean mood. Did a lot of screaming and yelling about how Nick had let him down, turned against him. Nick said he was trying to leave when Frank picked up a knife and swung at him." He shook his head. "After all the beatings Frank gave him when he was growing up, it's no surprise Nick snapped. He says the next thing he remembers, Frank was on the floor dead, and he was standing there holding the gun Frank kept."

"But there'll be a trial, won't there? He'll never be convicted, especially after we tell them about that night in the barn."

"The sheriff knows about that night, too. That's one of the things that helped me convince them..." He paused. "There's not going to be a trial, Alix. They gave Nick a choice. Either he could join the army and leave town for good, or take his chances on a manslaughter charge. He's leaving today, as soon as the recruiter can get his paperwork filled out."

"No." My hands gripped the table so hard my fingers were numb. "He wouldn't leave me."

"He doesn't have a choice, Alix." My father stood beside me while my mother and aunts sniffled and wiped their eyes. "If he doesn't go, he could spend the next five years in prison."

"I have to see him. Where is he?"

"He's still at the jail," the Judge said. "The police aren't letting him out of their sight until he's on a bus. Jim and I will take you."

"Maybe I should go with you." My mother started for the door.

"No." As much as I hate to admit it now, somewhere in the back of my mind I partially blamed her for everything that was happening. If it hadn't been for her stubborn insistence that I marry Hugh, if she'd stayed last night and listened to us instead of rushing off to her silly meeting, Nick might not have gone home so early. It wasn't rational, I know, but nothing about that morning was quite sane.

She stopped. "Alix—"

"No," I repeated. "I'll be fine." Pushing away from the table, I stood, swaying as another wave of dizziness washed over me.

My father gripped my arm tightly. "Hang on," he murmured, his voice for my ears alone. "You have to be strong for Nick. He's in bad shape, Sweetheart."

I closed my eyes, straightened my spine, took a deep breath, and nodded. For Nick, I could do anything. "I'm ready."

The jail in Morganville was a tiny thing, four grungy, dank cells attached to the back of City Hall where the police station was located. They served mainly as holding cells until the person incarcerated could be transported to the larger jail in Jonesboro, where the county and federal courts were located. I prayed I wouldn't have to see Nick in one of those cells, and apparently God was listening this time. They had him in a small conference room, a burly deputy standing guard outside the door.

Nick sat slumped at the long table, elbows propped on the surface, face buried in his hands. A handcuff stretched from his right wrist to fasten around the table leg, giving him just enough room to move freely without allowing him more than a foot from the table. The pain that had been building inside me settled in my throat and chest, expanded until I struggled for breath as I closed the door quietly behind me.

A second passed before he lifted his head and looked at me, another one before recognition dawned in his eyes. In the space of one night he'd aged ten years, his face ravaged with grief and weary resignation, his beautiful eyes bloodshot and filled with a hopelessness that tore at me.

He stood slowly, and without being conscious of moving, I found myself holding him, his left arm pressing me tightly to his body. Neither of us spoke, we simply clung together, trying to comfort each other in the only way we could, though simple human touch.

"They shouldn't have let you come," he choked, his voice trembling. "But, God, I'm glad they did. I was so afraid I wouldn't get to see you again."

"It's not that bad," I whispered. "You can write to me, and I'll write back. In four years you'll be out of the army and you can come home. I'll wait, Nick. For as long as it takes. I love you."

He shook his head then pushed me away gently. "You don't understand, Alix. I can't come back here. Not for a long time. If I do, they can throw me in jail."

"Then I'll come to you, wherever you are."

"No." He lifted a hand to my cheek. "I won't let you do that. Your family is here, your roots. You can't destroy your life for me."

"I don't have a life without you." I was desperate, frantic with fear as I realized what he was doing.

"Yes, you do." He took a deep breath. "As much as I wanted to believe it, dreamed about it, it was stupid to think people would accept our being together. Now, it would be even worse. I'm not just trash, I'm a murderer, and they'll always see me that way. I can't do that to you. You have to forget about me, Peewee."

"Can you forget about me?"

His eyes shimmered with tears. "No. Not if I live to be a hundred."

"Then don't ask me to do what you can't."

He caught me close again, buried his face in my hair. "Do it for me, Alix. I need to know you'll be happy if I'm going to have any chance of getting through this. Promise me. Please."

"I promise you this. I'll love you until the day I die even if I have to live without you. And if it's fifty years from now, you come home, Nick Anderson. Do you hear me? I'll be waiting on you."

He wiped away the tears streaming down my cheeks, and forced himself to smile. "This isn't a church social, Sweetheart. You aren't going to be able to save me this time."

"You knew?"

"I knew."

Behind us the door opened and the sheriff came in, his gaze going from me to Nick. "The recruiter is here and ready to go, Nick."

While the sheriff unfastened the handcuffs, Nick kept his gaze on my face. "Stay here until I'm gone."

I nodded, knowing it would only be harder for him if I watched him leave. "I love you." I mouthed the words as the sheriff took him by the arm and led him toward the door.

Abruptly, Nick stopped. "Wait. Just another second, please."

The sheriff glanced at me and nodded. To my surprise, Nick reached under his shirt and pulled out the half-heart pendant. With his gaze fixed on mine, he slid the chain over my head. "No one should have to go through life with only half a heart," he whispered.

I'm not sure I said anything out loud, but he saw the understanding in my eyes. With one final, heartbreaking smile, he was gone, and it felt like my life was over. He may never have said the words, but with that one last gesture, Nick had given me my heart back while letting me know he wouldn't have one without me, and the thought almost destroyed me.

I didn't know then what the Judge had gone through to give Nick this chance, and it was probably a good thing I didn't. I was in no shape to appreciate his efforts. You see, the Judge still had a lot of influence with our law enforcement officials, and he'd exerted a lot of pressure and called in a lot of favors to keep Nick out of jail. If I had known, I probably would have hated him, blamed him for taking Nick away from me.

Clutching the pendant in one hand, I let the darkness that had been threatening at the edges of my vision creep in and cover me, and for a while I didn't have to think, didn't have to feel.

* * * * *

They took me home and put me to bed, Mama and my aunts fluttering around me like beautiful, useless butterflies. They mopped my forehead with cold clothes when the thought of never seeing Nick again made me nauseous, and they brought me bowls of soup that sat on the nightstand untouched until a skim formed over the top. They watched me with worried eyes and urged me to sleep, but sleep wouldn't come. I lay awake through the long hours of Friday and Saturday, staring at nothing, replaying every moment of the last few weeks with Nick over and over in my mind, like a video tape stuck on a loop.

Finally, late Sunday night, I slipped out of the house, weak as a newborn kitten, and made my way to the barn on shaky legs. Once in his room, I wrapped his shirt around me and curled up on the bed that still held his scent, and at last I was able to sleep. It was the deep, dreamless sleep of emotional exhaustion, and though part of me was aware of someone coming and going, I didn't wake fully until Monday night.

When I opened my eyes it was to find Aunt Jane sitting in the rocking chair, her head against the back as she watched me. She looked as tired as I felt.

"Do you think Nick would want to see you like this?" she asked quietly.

"He's gone and he's never coming back, Aunt Jane."

She straightened and arched her back until it popped. "So you're going to curl up and die? Wake up, Alix. Life isn't kind, and we rarely get what we want out of it. We do the best we can, and we keep putting one foot in front of the other. You may not have Nick, but you've got a lot of other people who love you and are worried about you. It's time you thought about them."

"Does Mama know?"

"About you and Nick?" She shook her head. "Your mother is a kind, loving woman who cares about you more than life, but she only sees what she wants to see. She's convinced herself, Darla and the Judge that you've got a virus, and the shock of what happened to Nick made it worse." She stood. "I left you a sandwich and some soup. Eat it before you come back to the house." When she reached the door, she stopped. "You might be interested to know Frank Anderson's funeral is tomorrow morning. The state is burying him in the county cemetery."

My head was spinning as I swung my feet to the floor, and I reached automatically for the tray of food. It hit me with staggering force that I hadn't thought about Frank being dead a single time. But I thought about it while I ate, and the more I did, the angrier I got. I was going to that funeral tomorrow come hell or high water. There were a few things I needed to get off my chest.

* * * * *

It was a dismal day for a funeral, the sky overcast with periodic burst of a fine, soaking drizzle, but I was glad it was raining. It wouldn't have been fair for the sun to shine on Frank Anderson's last day above ground.

Aunt Jane went with me. Neither of us dressed up, we simply climbed into the car and left. Everyone was so happy to see me up and moving that they didn't think to ask questions.

I sat staring at the green tent when we reached the cemetery. It stood far back in one corner, with a bright yellow backhoe was parked a discreet distance away. Chairs lined the area, but no one sat in them. A pile of dirt was mounded to one side, covered by green cloth, but there were no flowers. A restless-looking minister I had never seen before stood shifting from one foot to the other as we got out. He looked at us hopefully when we reached the tent.

"Are you relatives of the deceased?"

"No." I pointed to the coffin. "Would you open it, please, and give me a few minutes alone?"

"Of course."

He motioned to one of the workers who stood waiting nearby, and together they lifted the lid on the top half. Frank Anderson looked better in death than he'd ever looked in life, which only stoked my anger higher. Someone had dressed him in a cheap blue suit and a white shirt, with a red and gray tie knotted around his neck. His hands were folded peacefully on his chest, and his black hair was neatly combed. Hate like I'd never known filled me, spilled over.

"You bastard," I whispered. "I'm glad you're dead, glad he killed you. You didn't deserve a son like him. All you ever did was make his life miserable. And now everyone thinks he's just like you. But he's not. He could never be like you. He's more of a man at twenty than you've ever been in your life, and even if he never comes back, he'll make something of himself. You wait and see."

Aunt Jane put her arm around my shoulders and I nodded at the minister. When the lid was closed again, I cast one last look at it. "I hope you rot in hell, you son of a bitch."

We left the poor minister standing there in shock, and I never shed another tear. There was something cathartic about telling Frank what I thought of him.

The next day I went back to school. There was a lot of gossip about the killing, but I refused to listen. Hugh was solicitous and concerned, thinking I was still getting over my "virus". Jenna knew the truth and stayed by my side constantly, watching me closely as though she were afraid I might do something drastic. Not once did she tell me, "I told you so," and for that I was grateful. I couldn't have made it though the next few weeks without her. When my mother insisted I buy a prom dress, Jenna went with me and chose the dress. I couldn't force any interest in a silly dance.

My stupor lasted until prom night, when I finally came to my senses enough to realize there might be another reason for my continuing bouts of nausea and dizzy spells. A reason that was going to bring me back to life and change me forever.

* * * * *

Hugh picked me up right on schedule in his new Mercedes, a graduation present from his parents. Mama took pictures of us while he pinned white roses onto my shimmering red gown, then kissed my cheek. "You look like a fairy tale princess with her prince," she said, wiping a tear away.

I smiled wanly. "Thank you, Mama."

"Now, you two have fun tonight."

"We will." Hugh took my hand, escorted me to the car, and helped me inside while Mama waved from the porch. I felt like I was moving through thick water. Nothing seemed real or right, and all I really wanted to do was go curl up on the bed in Nick's room. For Hugh's sake, and for Mama's, I couldn't.

The prom was being held at the fanciest hotel in Jonesboro, and the ballroom had been decorated to a fare-thee-well with live flowers in every shade of white imaginable, all trimmed in metallic gold and silver ribbons. They adorned every table and lined the walls, creating the illusion of a snowy garden. I had to hold my breath against the cloying sweetness that filled the room.

Jenna was there with Scott, who wasn't scheduled to leave until after the graduation ceremony Monday evening.

"You look like hell," she whispered as the guys left to get drinks. "At least try to smile."

I bared my teeth. "Is that better?"

"Only if you plan on biting someone."

"God, Jenna. I don't know what I'm doing here. I should have made some excuse." The music was loud and noisy and couples brushed by us as they danced. The heat level in the room was rising by the minute, emanating from the tightly packed bodies.

"Alix, you can't keep going like this. You've lost weight and you look like you're going to pass out any second."

"It's the heat in here. Why doesn't someone turn the air up?"

She gave me an odd look. "Are you sure you aren't really sick? It's not that warm in here."

"Maybe I got carsick on the ride over."

The guys made their way back through the crowd and Hugh handed me a glass of punch. Thank heavens it wasn't the sugary stuff, I thought, downing the contents of the crystal glass. The tart taste of pineapple juice mixed with other fruits and ginger ale settled my stomach a bit, and I smiled at him. "Thanks."

"More?" He arched a brow in question.

"No, I'm fine."

"Then how about a dance?"

"Sure." It was a slow one, and I had to admit, we moved well together. I couldn't imagine Nick on a dance floor like this. He was too private, too introverted, to ever do anything so public. I doubted he even knew how to dance, or would have cared to learn if given the chance.

Hugh's sudden turn brought me crashing back to the here and now as a wave of dizziness hit me. "Whoa." I staggered, and he stopped, a look of concern on his face.

"Alix, you need to see a doctor. This virus is hanging on way too long."

"I'll be okay. I think it's the heat."

He gave me the same look Jenna had and I knew I needed to escape for a while. "Excuse me. I'll be right back."

Without waiting for an answer, I headed for the nearest bathroom. A light sheen of sweat coated my skin and I wet a paper towel with cold water and patted my face, trying not to disturb my makeup as I listened to the other girls making use of the facility.

One of them deposited several coins into the tampon machine on the wall and turned the knob. "Boy, it's just my luck to start tonight. Now I'll be bloated and cramping all evening."

"Well, at least you caught it before it ruined your dress," her friend replied.

Idly, I did some mental calculations. It seemed like it had been quite a while since I'd had my monthly. Hadn't it been due the day I'd talked to my father about Nick? But that was a little over two weeks ago, and I was never late. Slowly, I lowered the hand holding the paper towel and stared at my reflection in the mirror.

Nick hadn't left me alone after all, I thought, stunned. I was pregnant. His child was growing inside me. A slow-building excitement gripped me. I was going to have Nick's baby, a baby that would be mine forever, a part of him no one could take away.

Dazed, I wandered out of the restroom and sat down on the first chair I came to. I don't know how long I was there before Hugh found me. When he waved a hand in front of me, I blinked, then focused on his face. Oh, God. I'd forgotten about Hugh.

"You okay?" he asked.

"Yes, but we need to talk." It was way past time to put this charade to an end. I didn't want to hurt him, but he would know the truth soon anyway. Everyone would know, I realized. My chin went up. Well, they could think what they wanted, but they better not let me hear any of their gossip. No one was going to treat our child the way people had treated Nick.

Hugh took my hand and helped me stand. "Where do you want to talk?"

"Outside."

The night air was much warmer than the ballroom had been, but I wasn't hot anymore. I felt better than I had since Nick left. I had a reason to go on now.

We walked to Hugh's car in silence and leaned against the side. It was beautiful out, the moon big and full. I glanced at Hugh, trying not to remember a similar night, a rusty pickup, a dirt-covered country road, and a fifteen-year-old boy.

"We can't keep going like this, Hugh," I told him softly. "You don't love me. Both of us have been letting our parents push us along. We should have stopped it a long time ago."

He was staring down at the ground, hands tucked into his pockets. "Why now?"

I took a deep breath and faced him. "Because now I'm pregnant. Everyone will know it soon."

His gaze lifted, his face expressionless as he studied me. "Is it Nick's?"

"You knew about us?"

A wry smile turned up the corners of his lips. "Yeah. I saw the way you looked at each other that night at the gas station."

"I'm sorry. Why didn't you say something?"

He shrugged. "I guess I kept hoping things would change. Can you reach him, let him know?"

"No." I turned away. I'd already tried to find out where he was stationed, but the sheriff was the only one who knew where Nick had been sent and he wasn't talking. "He made it pretty clear he wasn't coming back and told me to forget about him."

"What are you going to do?"

"I don't know yet. Maybe leave town. I can't put my family through this again. It would kill them. But I won't give up my baby either."

"How far along are you?"

"About a month, I think." I wasn't sure why he wanted to know, but I owed him the answers to any questions he asked.

It got quiet again, the only sound coming from the traffic out on the highway.

"You're wrong about one thing, you know," Hugh said finally. "It might not be the kind of grand, world-stopping passion you want, but I do love you. I have since we were kids." Slowly, he pulled his hand out of his pocket and opened it. In his palm rested a blue velvet box, and my eyes filled with tears when he showed me the sparkling diamond ring inside.

"I was going to do this later, but there's no sense in waiting."

"Hugh..." My tears spilled over and ran freely down my cheeks.

"Please, let me finish." He took a deep breath. "You need a husband and the baby will need a father. I'm asking you to let me be both. Alix, will you do me the honor of agreeing to be my wife?"

I couldn't believe this was happening. "But the baby isn't yours," I stuttered.

"It will be if you let it." He shrugged. "And everyone will think it is, anyway. Let them think it, Alix. I swear, I'll love it like it was mine." He wiped the tears from my cheeks. "Think about it. We can get married tonight and no would ever have to know the truth. Your family won't be disgraced, you won't have to leave, and the baby will never have people looking down on it. We can even have the justice of the peace backdate the marriage certificate so everyone will think we were married secretly months ago."

"A J.P. would do that?"

This time his smile was full-fledged. "I know one who will. My family spends a lot of money on his campaigns."

"I don't know what to say."

"Do you care about me at all, Alix?"

"Of course I do. You're one of the best friends I've ever had."

He nodded. "Then say yes. We can make this work."

Maybe I was in shock, or maybe I was simply a coward, but what he was offering was more than I was capable of refusing right then. Respectability for myself and my child, a loving, safe home to raise it in, and someone who honestly cared about me. If I'd had a week or two to think about it, my answer might have been different, but I didn't have that long. Hugh was waiting and I couldn't hurt him again.

"Yes," I whispered, trembling as he slid the diamond on my finger.

The justice of the peace never batted an eye when we showed up on his doorstep. He merely complied with Hugh's request, accepted an undisclosed amount of money, and told us to bring him copies of our birth certificates next week. All the forms were filled out and the ceremony performed in his den with his wife and housekeeper as witnesses. According to our marriage license, we had been married since February second.

Back in the car, I turned to my new husband. "Now what?"

"Now, we go pick up something to eat, and then I've got a surprise for you."

He went to the drive-through window of a fast food joint and ordered burgers and fries for both of us, a soda for him and milk for me. When the food arrived, he put the car in gear, and headed back toward Morganville. Just outside of town, he turned right and I stared at him in surprise. The road he'd turned onto led to Fair Oaks, the new subdivision.

"Hugh, what are you doing?"

"You'll see." He steered the car into a long, sweeping driveway that ended at a darkened house. One of the newest, I realized. It was long and sprawling, with curving flower beds along the front, empty now, but waiting for someone to fill them.

"What do you think?" He waved a hand at the house.

"I think it's beautiful, but won't we get in trouble for being here?"

"No, it's ours. We closed on it last week. All you and I have to do is buy some furniture and move in." He opened the car door and gathered up the food. "Come on, Mrs. Morgan. Let's go look at our new home and do some talking."

And that's what we did. Hugh took me on a tour of the house that lasted half an hour. It was undoubtedly a dream home, even if it wasn't exactly what I would have chosen for myself. Wide open spaces graced with huge floor-to-ceiling windows made the rooms flow into each other. The kitchen was an ultramodern fantasy come true, and there was even a swimming pool and hot tub on the patio behind the house.

After the tour was completed we sat on the floor in the dining room, facing each other as we ate and talked. I can't say

I was happy, but being honest with Hugh had brought such relief that combined with my knowledge of the baby, I was almost euphoric. After all the past months of pretending, I could finally be myself with him again. Together, we got our stories straight and decided we'd tell our parents Monday night after the graduation ceremony. Our marriage was going to cause enough chaos. The news about the baby would have to wait another month.

It felt good to laugh with Hugh like we'd done when we were children, and it gradually began to dawn on me that if it hadn't been for Nick, I would probably have fallen in love with Hugh, would have married him happily. Was it possible fate was righting itself? I didn't know. I only knew that I intended to work as hard as I could to make Hugh happy. He deserved no less.

It never occurred to me that night that Hugh and I would have to share a bed, and if it occurred to him, he didn't mention it. We talked until the sun began to peek over the horizon, and then he took me home, walking me to the door and kissing me goodnight just like he'd always done.

"I'm sorry, Nick," I whispered, slipping his pendant from my neck. "I didn't know what else to do."

Chapter Ten

🔊

Resentment is a funny thing. It can sneak up on you for some of the craziest reasons. I suppose its human nature, our way of protecting ourselves emotionally. I'd read enough to know that one of the symptoms of grief was a deep anger at the loved one who'd died, anger that impaired your judgment, made you want to scream and curse because they'd left you. But Nick hadn't died, and I didn't realize that I was suffering the symptoms of grief.

Over the weekend it gradually soaked in that I'd married Hugh, that even if Nick showed up at that very second, it would be too late. And as I began to think about that day at the police station, I started to believe a lie. Maybe I had to believe it in order to keep going, to put one foot in front of the other as Aunt Jane had said I must.

Because there was no real reason for Nick and me to be apart. He knew, and I knew, that I would have followed him happily to the ends of the earth and back. But he hadn't wanted me. The more I thought about it, the deeper my sense of resentment became. It turned into a slow, simmering anger that colored everything I did.

Graduation day dawned bright and sunny, the sky a deep cerulean blue with fluffy cotton-ball clouds decorating the heavens. The temperatures were already hitting the nineties during the day. I'd spent most of Saturday sleeping after the all-nighter Hugh and I had pulled. Sunday, Hugh spent the day with us, and we practiced our graduation speeches on each other. When I asked him where he'd been the day before, he smiled mysteriously and told me, "Making plans for Monday night."

I slipped him my birth certificate so he could take it to the justice of the peace the next day. He gave it back to me Monday when he arrived, and I returned it to Mama's drawer with no one the wiser.

The ceremony that night went off without a hitch, my family and Hugh's applauding wildly after our speeches, and again when we were called to receive our diplomas. Afterward, we spent a tearful thirty minutes saying goodbye to our classmates who were leaving, promising to stay in touch. And once again, a sense of unreality descended on me. I'd always envisioned this day with Nick sitting beside my family on the bleachers, smiling down at me proudly. But he'd made it clear he didn't want me, and I convinced myself he wouldn't want the baby either.

It's okay, I promised silently, one hand on my stomach. *I want you. We'll always have each other.*

Ian and Helena invited my whole family out to eat at the country club after the ceremony, and I managed to talk Jenna into coming along. I knew her father well enough to understand his idea of a celebration was to park himself in front of the TV for the evening with lots of beer on hand. Besides, I wanted her with me when Hugh and I broke the news.

We were a noisy bunch that evening as we found our places around the linen covered table. Several different conversations were going on at once, everyone laughing and talking. Hugh had asked me to put my rings on during the drive over, and my stomach was in a knot waiting for someone to notice them. So far, it hadn't happened, and I tried to keep them hidden under the edge of the table.

My father inadvertently brought on the announcement. He had positioned himself beside my mother, directly across the table from Hugh and me, and the way it happened, I would have sworn he and Hugh arranged it beforehand.

"So, Hugh. Are you going to start work right away, or take a few days off first?" Daddy was surveying the menu when he asked the question.

Hugh casually draped his arm across my shoulders. "I'm going to be taking a few weeks off."

From the end of the table, Ian's head came up. "I thought you were going to start tomorrow?"

"No, there are a few more important things I have to take care of first."

Both Ian and Helena frowned, and Ian carefully put his menu down on the table. "What could be more important than the business?"

Hugh glanced at me and smiled. "A honeymoon. We're leaving later tonight." He reached into his shirt pocket and pulled out an airline folder. Stunned, I took it and glanced at the destination. Hawaii. "I promised Alix we'd go as soon as school was over."

You could have heard a pin drop from fifty feet away, it got so quiet.

"A honeymoon?" my mother said weakly, one hand covering her heart as she stared at my rings. "You're already married?"

My stomach knotted at her expression, and regret filled me. I knew how much she'd wanted me to have the big wedding she had never had. "I'm sorry, Mama. We wanted to tell you, but you were so busy planning everything we didn't have the heart."

"But when?" Helena stammered.

"February second," Hugh told her. "We didn't really want a big wedding, and we didn't want to wait."

My father was staring at me as if I'd suddenly developed huge purple spots all over my face, and there was no doubt he'd demand an explanation the first chance he got. He knew only too well how I felt about Nick, and he wasn't buying the elopement story for a second.

For that matter, neither was Jenna. To my surprise, her blue eyes were swimming with tears when I glanced at her. Before I could say anything, she jumped to her feet, mumbled an "excuse me", and darted toward the bathroom.

Hastily, I shoved my chair back and went after her. She was locked in a stall when I got there. I checked to make sure we were alone.

"Jenna, I'm sorry I didn't tell you."

There was the sound of toilet paper tearing away from the roll and a sniff, but no answer.

"Please, I know you're upset with me, but can't you be happy for us?"

"Happy?" She half-laughed, half-choked the word out. "Does Hugh know it's Nick you love?"

"He knows," I said quietly. "He knows everything."

There was the click of a lock turning and the stall door opened. Jenna faced me. "Are you really married?"

"Yes. We got married prom night."

"But why? Why did you marry him when you don't love him?"

I took a deep breath and checked the room once more. "I'm pregnant. Hugh and I had a long talk and I told him the truth about everything. He wanted to marry me anyway, Jenna. He even wants the baby."

Her face whitened as she stared at me. "You're using him to give Nick's bastard a name."

I stiffened as equal measures of pain and anger ripped through me. I might have expected that sort of reaction from people who didn't know me well, but not from my best friend.

"Yes, Jenna. That's exactly what I'm doing. I set the entire thing up to trap Hugh. And since you so obviously disapprove, don't feel obligated to continue the pretense of being my friend." I turned and marched out of the bathroom, my head held high.

Mama, Aunt Darla, and Helena had their heads together, excitedly making plans for a big reception to announce our marriage when I slid into my chair. Hugh arched an eyebrow at me.

"Where's Jenna?"

"She wasn't feeling well. I think she went home."

I sat numbly through the rest of the meal, letting Hugh handle our respective families. He managed to convince them not to schedule the party for another few weeks, and insisted that he and I preferred picking out our own furniture when it appeared the families were going to take over that area, too.

Afterward, we barely had enough time to run home and throw some clothes in a suitcase. I was happy I'd avoided Daddy for a while. I didn't think I could stand another scene like the one with Jenna. Not right now.

Mama dug out a bag of rice while I was packing, and when we left, they pelted us with the white grains. Everyone hugged, Mama cried a little, and the Judge squeezed me a bit tighter than normal, his eyes damp. When Daddy hugged me I promised him quietly that we'd talk when I got back and told him not to worry.

Once in Hugh's car, I relaxed a little. "I think they bought it." I shifted to look at him. "When did you come up with the idea of the trip?"

"Saturday." He smiled and closed his fingers around my hand. "I figured it would give them a week to calm down and get used to the idea without driving us crazy. I hope Hawaii is okay with you?"

"It sounds wonderful. I've never been out of the state before."

"We went a few times for vacations. It's a beautiful place." He glanced at me again. "Are you going to tell me what really happened with Jenna?"

I sighed. "She said I only married you to give Nick's bastard a name."

His hand tightened on mine. "I'm sorry. You two have been friends for a long time. She was probably hurt because you didn't tell her sooner. I'm sure she'll come around when she has time to think about it."

"Maybe." I wasn't sure I could ever forgive her, though. Calling me names was one thing. Calling my baby a bastard was something I couldn't and wouldn't tolerate.

The airport at Jonesboro was a small one, mostly flying commuter planes to bigger cities like Little Rock and Memphis. Ours went to Memphis, where we caught a jet for the islands after a short delay.

We were somewhere over the ocean, Hugh dozing beside me, when it finally hit me exactly what a honeymoon was for. Dear Lord, Hugh wasn't simply my friend anymore, he was my husband and this was not a game we were playing. For better or worse, we were married and that gave him the right to make love to me.

I'd never wanted anyone but Nick before and the idea of doing with Hugh what I'd only done with the man I loved sent me teetering on the edge of panic. Could I do it? I had to, somehow.

I think that was when I began to delude myself about my new husband, forcing myself to see only what I wanted to see, not what he really was. It was safer that way, and it allowed me to get through the honeymoon with my sanity intact.

In the dim light of the plane, I studied Hugh's profile. He didn't look eighteen, I realized. He looked older, maybe mid-twenties. And he was ruggedly handsome, his skin a deep bronze with tiny smile lines around his eyes and mouth. His light brown hair was streaked abundantly with strands of gold.

No, he wasn't Nick, but Nick was gone and he wasn't coming back. I had no right to deny Hugh when he'd taken on so readily the responsibility that Nick hadn't wanted.

Hugh's eyes opened and he smiled when he realized I was watching him. "What? Was I snoring?"

"No. I was only thinking about how handsome you are."

The lines around his eyes deepened when his smile turned into a grin. "I thought you'd never notice." Carefully, he pulled me into his arms and settled my head on his chest. "Try to get some sleep," he murmured into my hair. "We won't land until early in the morning."

Maybe he really does love me, I thought, amazed. And while I knew I would never experience the all-consuming passion with him that I'd had with Nick, there are more kinds of love than one. I convinced myself that eventually a steady, warm, comforting love would grow between Hugh and me. A love that had the potential to last forever. And so, without a second thought or a quiver of anxiety, I fell head-first into a fantasy trap of my own making.

When I went to him our first night in Hawaii, I had suppressed all my nervousness and buried my misgivings beneath a veneer of calm. He was lying on the bed in our hotel room, wearing only his jeans, watching TV while I showered. There hadn't been time to buy any sexy lingerie so I had to make do with my best cotton gown. It didn't seem to matter to him that I wasn't dressed in silk and lace, though. His gaze locked on me as soon as I stepped into the room.

"Make love to me," I whispered.

He swung his feet to the floor and walked across the room to meet me. "Alix, are you sure? I don't want to rush you."

"I'm sure."

Picking me up, he carried me to the bed and made love to me with a skill that left me feeling warm and cared for, if unsatisfied. It was more than I'd expected, and at the time, I believed it would be enough.

That night also let me know that I wasn't the first person he'd made love to. In a way, that relieved some of my own guilt. I don't think I could have stood thinking he'd waited for me.

The rest of that week passed in a blur of sand, sun, water and getting to know each other all over again. Hugh always seemed to know when thoughts of Nick would make me sad or upset me. He'd tease me out of my moods until I was laughing with him. He even bought an outrageous flowered shirt for the baby, surprising me with it one evening while we ate dinner in our suite. I think we both hated to board a plane for home and the real world, but it was inevitable.

We went straight to our new house from the airport and discovered our families had been pretty busy in our absence. While they had taken Hugh at his word about the furniture and decorations, they had done everything else. The refrigerator and pantry was stocked to the brim with food, flowers sat on every flat surface, and the phones and utilities had all been turned on. The Judge had even brought over his tiller and plowed up a garden spot at the back of the five acres.

In the master bedroom we found they had disobeyed us in one respect. A large bedroom suite now occupied the space that had been empty the last time we were there, the bed neatly made. There was a note on the pillow and Hugh picked it up.

It's better than sleeping on the floor, and if you don't like it, you can bring it back when you buy a new one.

Love,

Mother

"What do you think?" Hugh asked me. "It was my grandparents'."

"I love it, Hugh." I ran a hand over the knotty pine headboard. "It fits the space perfectly."

"Then we'll keep it."

The next few weeks flew by even faster than our honeymoon had. We went a little wild buying things for the house, but Hugh told me not to worry about the money. His grandparents had left him independently wealthy. Both of our families were constant visitors, helping, inspecting and generally offering opinions on everything we did.

My father was first. He showed up at the door bright and early the day after we got back. Hugh took one look at him and excused himself, claiming he had to take a shower. I refrained from mentioning that his hair was still wet from the one he'd just taken.

"Come in, Daddy." I headed for the kitchen. "I don't have anything to cook with yet, but we've got donuts and instant coffee."

"I don't want anything." He leaned against the counter. "Alix, what's going on? How could you marry Hugh when we both know it's Nick you love?"

I braced myself and took a deep breath. "Nick is gone, Daddy, and I'm pregnant."

"What?" The blood drained from his face.

I faced him. "I'm pregnant."

"Christ." He ran a shaky hand over his face. "Does Hugh know?"

"He knows. It was his idea for us to get married. He wants the baby, Daddy."

"But Nick—"

"Nick didn't want me," I interrupted. "He made that pretty clear. He even refused to write."

"Maybe if he knew about the baby…"

Angrily, I shook my head. "Do you think I'd want to spend the rest of my life knowing he was only with me because I got pregnant?"

"He has the right to know."

I went to him and put my arms around him. "Don't equate this with what happened to you, Daddy. It's not the same situation. I did what I had to do, what was right for me and the baby. Hugh has been wonderful to me, and I really do care about him. Nick is gone and he's never coming back."

With a sigh, he rested his chin on the top of my head and hugged me. "I think you're making a big mistake, Baby, but I guess the decision has to be yours. I will say this. Hugh is a hell of a man, taking on something like this. I hope for both your sakes it doesn't blow up in your faces."

"It won't," I promised. "Everything will work out fine."

He left shortly after that, and Hugh came out of the bedroom. If he'd heard the conversation with my father, and I didn't see how he could have missed it, he never mentioned it.

By the day of our party, the house was finished except for the bright corner room. We had reserved that one for a nursery. It was early that afternoon when Jenna paid us a visit.

I was in the dinning room with Hugh, unwrapping the last of the china we had bought and placing it in the cherry cabinet, when the doorbell chimed.

"I'll get it." He vanished into the living room.

I heard the door open and then the low murmur of voices. It seemed to go on for a long time. Curious, I was about to join him when he reappeared.

"Look who's here."

One glimpse of that red hair was enough to have my spine stiffening and my chin going up. Hugh crossed the room, kissed me, and then stuffed his wallet in his back pocket. "I told Dad I'd run by the office for a while today."

I nodded. "Don't stay too long. We have to get ready for tonight." I turned back to the china, pretending to ignore Jenna. She had hurt me and I wasn't going to let it go easily.

She hovered in the doorway until Hugh was gone, then hesitantly crossed the room. "Alix, I'm sorry. I've been miserable these last few weeks. Hate me if you want to, but at least talk to me."

"Why? So you can call my baby a bastard again?"

"I didn't mean it. You know I could never feel that way. I was hurt and upset and it just slipped out. That whole day was terrible for me. Scott was leaving, my father acted like he couldn't care less that I'd graduated with honors, and then you and Hugh sprang the news that you'd gotten married and hadn't bothered to tell me. I overreacted. You don't have to beat me up, because I've been doing it myself every single day since then."

She put her hand on my arm. "I've missed you. You're the only real friend I've ever had and I don't want to lose you. We always promised each other that if one of us had kids, the other one would be their aunt. Please, Alix. Don't shut me out because of one mistake. Let me be the baby's aunt."

Tears filled my eyes and clogged my throat. It couldn't have been easy for her to come to me and apologize, and the truth was, I'd missed her too. Badly.

"Okay," I choked. Then we were both crying, hugging each other while we tried to wipe the tears away. She kept apologizing until I finally threatened to hurt her if she didn't stop, and that brought on the laughter. After we calmed down, I showed her around the house and she oohed and ahhed over everything and promised to help me with the nursery.

But something else was bothering her, and I knew her well enough to sense she wanted to tell me but was reluctant to bring it up.

"You might as well get it off your chest," I told her when we got back to the kitchen. She sighed and took the glasses of tea from my hands.

"I'll carry these. You better sit down."

"That bad, huh?"

"Yes, I think it's going to be."

"Okay, I'm sitting." I plunked myself down on a chair and she took the one across from me.

"If there was any way I could keep you from finding this out, I wouldn't tell you. But everyone will know soon and I'd rather you heard it now, from me."

My heart quivered. "Jenna, you're scaring me."

She toyed with the condensation on her glass for a second. "You know Sheriff McAbee plays poker with my dad occasionally?"

"Yes."

"Well, he was there last night and I heard them talking." She looked up and met my gaze. "Liz Swanner reported Lindsey missing yesterday morning. The sheriff told Dad it took him about an hour to discover what had happened to her. Lindsey caught a bus out of town." Jenna took a deep breath. "Alix, she went to join Nick."

I stared at her as nausea roiled in my stomach. "He's positive?"

"As much as he can be without talking to Lindsey. She went to the same town, and Liz said she didn't have any money. The only way she could have gotten a ticket was if Nick sent it to her."

I barely made it to the bathroom before my stomach emptied.

"Oh, God. I knew you were going to be upset." Jenna rushed around frantically, wetting a washcloth and putting it on the back of my neck. "Maybe I better call Hugh and tell him to come home."

"No." I sank weakly to the floor and rested my head against the cold tub. "There's nothing he can do."

She lowered herself to the floor in front of me and rubbed my wrist. "I shouldn't have blurted it out like that. I've never been good at this kind of thing."

"It isn't your fault." A hysterical laugh bubbled out of me. "I told him he couldn't have me and Lindsey both, that he had to choose. Looks like he finally did."

"Maybe there's a good reason. We have no way of knowing what's going on."

"Oh, there's a reason all right. He loves Lindsey. God, Jenna, I can't believe how stupid I've been."

"You love him."

I shifted enough to see her. "Not anymore. I'm not wasting another second of my time on him."

"What are you going to do?"

By sheer determination I pushed myself to my feet. "I'm going to forget that Nick Anderson ever lived. I'm going to that party tonight and I'm never looking back. And I'm going to be the best damn wife in Morganville."

"But the baby is Nick's."

"No," I told her, my voice cold. "The baby is mine. Mine and Hugh's. Nick will never touch it."

And so my simmering anger began its slow journey toward hatred. That day at the cemetery I had told Frank Anderson that Nick would never be like him. Now I knew the truth. Nick was worse.

Chapter Eleven

✍

With Hugh and Jenna's support, I made it through the party that night. Jenna had been right about the whole town knowing where Lindsey had gone. Gossip and speculation flew in every direction, fueling my anger with every word.

"I don't know why everyone is so surprised," Gretchen Treece commented to Helena. "They were two of a kind. Peggy told me she saw them at the drive-in quite a few times in that old truck of his, and the windows were always fogged up. It's disgusting the way some people carry on."

I ground my teeth together, smiled, and moved away, but I never doubted the truth of her statement. Why should I? Nick himself had told me he wanted everyone to think he was dating Lindsey. I was simply so stupid and trusting that I believed his reasons were innocent.

The next afternoon, I went to the beauty shop and had my hair cut off. I told Hugh it was because it would be easier to care for during my pregnancy, but the real reason was because every time I went by a mirror, I remembered how much Nick had loved my long hair. Sometimes revenge takes simple outlets.

Surprisingly, the new, shorter style suited me. I had topped out at a whopping five feet, two inches, and with my small bone structure, the feathery cut gave me a pixyish appearance that made my eyes seem huge and mysterious.

There was one last chore I had to take care of before I could I get on with my life. The pendant Nick had given me had to be disposed of. I sat in my bedroom for a long time that afternoon, staring at it. And in the end, I couldn't bring myself to throw it away. Instead, I put it carefully into a box and drove out to the farm.

Once there, I went to the barn, to Nick's room. It was the first time I'd been back in weeks, and it was as if all traces of Nick had been erased from the earth. His clothes were gone and the sheets and blankets on the narrow bed had been washed and replaced, leaving no trace of his scent.

For the last time I allowed myself to cry, and even as my tears fell I cursed Nick with every breath. When it was over, I put the box containing the pendant into the linen closet, shoving it all the way to the back on the top shelf. Then I shut the door, on the closet and on Nick.

After that, life settled into a routine I welcomed. Hugh joined his father fulltime at the mill and I took on the role of wife with a vengeance. Even Aunt Darla could find no speck of dirt in my house, and she did look.

The Judge found an excuse to come by almost every day, and I welcomed his visits. Together, we planted my first vegetable garden, each row laid out with mathematical precision. The once empty flower beds around the house now bloomed with shrubs and flowers; Azaleas, Japanese Holly, and Spirea backed geraniums, petunias, sweet peas, and hosta, with several colors of crepe myrtle thrown in for height and contrast.

When Hugh and I judged the time was right, we gathered our families and broke the news about the baby. Everyone was ecstatic, and I entered an entire new world I'd never paid much attention to before; the southern tradition of educating first-time mothers by passing on bits of wisdom gathered from the generations of women who'd gone before.

"Alix!" My mother yelped when she caught me reaching for a bowl on the top shelf of the cabinets. "Stop that this instant. Don't you know you'll wrap the cord around the baby's neck?"

When I was plagued with heartburn, Aunt Darla told me that it meant the baby would have a lot of hair.

Helena got into the act by warning me not to let anything frighten me because it would "mark" the baby. It seemed everyone had examples of this type of phenomena, and they regaled me with them at every opportunity. I laughed the stories off, but my poor obstetrician, a transplanted New Yorker, was horrified when I repeated the tales to her, and ordered me not to listen to a thing my family said. I don't think she ever quite grasped the concept of southern tradition, and a few years later she moved her practice back to "civilization".

Everything seemed rosy and perfect on the surface, but nothing could have been farther from the truth. In spite of the act I was putting on, I was in more pain than I'd ever experienced before. You can't turn love on and off like a light switch, no matter how hard you try. All you can do is wall it off, one brick at a time, until you've created an impenetrable fortress around your emotions. And once that fortress is built, you camouflage it so well that even you can't see it anymore. That's what I did with my love for Nick, and hate became my camouflage. It affected everything in my life. For the first time, I lost sight of the core of the sweet gum tree and now saw only the pale fibrous wood, warped and untrustworthy.

One major consequence of this change was my sudden inability to trust Hugh. I'd been stupid once and believed everything Nick told me. It wasn't going to happen again, and if Hugh seemed too good to be true, then he must have an ulterior motive. My fantasy ended with a resounding crash as I tore the blinders from my eyes.

I spent a lot of time watching Hugh, wondering why a man would seem so happy about a baby that wasn't his. If he'd ever exhibited the slightest interest in children before, I might have understood. But he hadn't. Now he was suddenly playing the expectant father to the hilt and my suspicions were running rampant.

There was only one conclusion I could reach. I'd been right about Hugh from the beginning. He didn't love me. He had pursued me only because it was what his family wanted and expected. And while he had plenty of money, if he kept his parents happy he stood to inherit an industry that controlled an entire town and the area surrounding it. Maybe he did care about me in a way, but our relationship was more like that of a brother and sister than husband and wife. I was his trophy, the most suitable candidate to help him get what he really wanted, respectability and power, both precious commodities in our small southern town. The baby was simply window dressing, something that would complete the picture of a happy family he was trying to project.

I knew deep inside that his happiness, like mine, was merely an act, albeit a convincing one. He helped Jenna and me with the nursery, doing most of the manual labor. We teased him unmercifully when he put the rails of the crib on upside down and had to redo them. And as my girth expanded he became more solicitous, insisting I stop working so hard around the house, making sure I had something to prop my swollen ankles on. He would rest his hand on my stomach, laughing when the baby kicked vigorously. Toward the end of the pregnancy, he even attended Lamaze classes with me.

It didn't take me long to figure out that these warm exhibitions occurred for the most part when others were around. Not that Hugh was ever anything but kind. But as my pregnancy progressed, he seemed to lapse into brooding silences more often when we were alone, and I couldn't help but wonder if he'd reached the same conclusion I had. Because I finally realized just how big a mistake we had made in marrying for the wrong reasons. A mistake I now had to live with and handle alone. Jenna thought Hugh had wings and a halo, and my family had their own small crisis to deal with.

A week before Christmas my mother came over to help me decorate our tree. My normally effusive mother remained silent as we strung lights, her brow furrowed. I waited, knowing she'd get around to what was on her mind sooner or later. Finally, with a sigh, she sank onto the couch.

"Your father asked me to marry him."

This news came as no surprise to me and I smiled. I'd wondered how long it would take him to get up the nerve.

"What did you tell him?"

"That I had to think about it." She nibbled her bottom lip. "It would mean moving to Jonesboro and leaving the Judge."

"Mama, it's not like the Judge will be alone. Aunt Darla and Aunt Jane will still be there to take care of him, and Jonesboro is only twenty minutes away."

She looked up at me, her eyes pleading. "What would Jane think, Alix? I can't hurt her again."

I sat down and took her hand. "Do you love him, Mama?"

"Yes," she whispered. "I think I always have."

"Then marry him. Aunt Jane will understand. She wants you to be happy."

"Do you really think so?"

"Talk to her."

I guess Daddy wasn't taking any chances on her backing out once she said yes. The wedding took place on Christmas day, and my mother was as giddy as a teenager. If Aunt Jane felt any lingering sadness, she hid it well, and the day was wonderful for all of us. The next week was spent in a flurry of getting Mama moved to Daddy's house in Jonesboro, although for the most part I was relegated to sitting in a chair, watching.

A few days later, on a cold January night, I went into labor. We hadn't been in bed long, maybe a few hours, when a nightmare woke me. Drenched in sweat, I swung my feet over the side of the bed, pulled on a robe, and waddled into the kitchen to warm a cup of milk. The first pain hit as I finished pouring milk from the pan. Gripping the edge of the counter, I held my breath until it ended, then dumped the milk down the drain and rinsed out the pan and cup.

Some deep, instinctive need to be alone kept me from waking Hugh. I sat in the dimly lit room at the table, keeping an eye on the clock as the pains came closer together, each one lasting a little longer than the one before. I was still there four hours later when Hugh stumbled sleepily from the bedroom, his hair rumpled and his eyes partially closed.

"Alix? What are you doing?"

"Having a baby," I told him calmly.

His eyes flew open. "Now?"

"Pretty much."

"Why didn't you wake me?"

"There wasn't much sense in both of us staying awake this early in the labor." I couldn't tell him the real reason. At the time, I don't think I understood it myself. Hugh wasn't the father of my baby, and way down inside I didn't trust him, didn't trust any male anymore.

He squatted beside me. "How far apart are the pains?"

I glanced at the clock. "Every fifteen minutes."

"Okay, I'll call the doctor and then we'll get you dressed."

I offered no objection as he took over. Another pain hit and all my energy focused inward. And that's where it stayed for the next eight hours as I worked to give birth to my daughter.

Katie came into the world with a loud protest, her tiny face screwed into a mask of fury as she screamed her displeasure at being shoved from her warm nest, only quieting when they wrapped her in a blanket and put her in my arms. Tears filled my eyes as I inspected her. She looked so much like Nick that I didn't see how anyone could miss it. Her small head was covered in thick black hair that showed an immediate tendency to curl on the ends, and even when she was finally quiet, the indication of dimples showed clearly on her plump baby cheeks.

Hugh stayed with me through the whole thing, coaching me, rubbing my back and stomach when the pains became intense, happily cutting the cord when the doctor handed him the scissors, and later, filling my room with pink flowers and handing out cigars.

But by then I didn't care if it was all an act. I had Katie, and in the space of a single instant my life changed. She was my world, the reason I lived and breathed, and nothing else mattered to me.

Katie wasn't what people call a "good" child. From the beginning she was bright and intelligent and constantly moving. Her smiles and laughter lit up our lives, and her gray eyes always sparkled with joy. We all spoiled her shamelessly, and she soaked it up like it was her right, then demanded more.

Even Hugh wasn't immune to her charms. One afternoon, when she was three months old, I caught him in the nursery. Katie's chubby fists were buried in his hair, and she was laughing hysterically while Hugh blew raspberries on her tummy. I slipped away quietly before they saw me, and at that moment I really and truly loved Hugh. It was destined to be both the first and last time I harbored any real emotion toward him.

Three months later, when Katie was six months old, she died. The doctors said it was SIDS, but I only knew that one second I had my beautiful, warm child in my arms, and the next she was gone and I had nothing. When they buried her, they should have buried me too. The only thing left was an empty shell that breathed in and out, that ate because she was forced into it, and refused to talk to anyone. I locked myself in the nursery and stayed there until my family, sick with grief and worry, threw me out and packed all of Katie's things into boxes before forcing me to go to the doctor. But there was no pill known to man that could help me get through the trauma of losing my child.

I would wake in the middle of the night, Katie's desolate cries echoing in my ears, and drive to the cemetery, staying there in the dark with one hand on her grave, singing lullabies until Hugh would show up and take me home.

And somehow, in my pain and anguish, it was Nick I blamed. Nick I raged at during those lonely, empty hours by Katie's grave. None of this would have happened if he hadn't left us. If it had been me he sent for instead of Lindsey, Katie would be alive now. He should have been there, should have found a way to keep her safe. But he hadn't, and I hated him even more because of it.

Strangely enough, it was Ian, Hugh's father, who brought me back to some semblance of life. One morning he showed up at our house, marched into our room, and ordered me out of bed.

"Get dressed," he told me. "You're going to work."

He gave me a job as his "assistant", a position obviously created to keep me busy. I only went along with his tyranny because it was easier to comply than to resist. But gradually, the work caught my interest and I began pouring myself into the lumber industry. After two years, I knew more about the business than Hugh did. A year after that I went to the bank and used the Morgan name to secure a loan. When I got it, I opened my own building supply company, Morganville's first. I deliberately made it as big as the chain stores in Jonesboro, and every minute of my time, night and day, went into making it a success. Southern Supply became my life, the only thing I cared about.

And so, the first time I became aware that Hugh was having an affair, I ignored it. In a way, it was almost a relief. For a while I didn't have to deal with him myself. I never knew who the woman was and didn't want to know. The only thing I wanted was to bury my head in the sand and forget the past, forget that my arms and heart still ached for the daughter I'd had such a short time. And I was succeeding admirably. As time went on, I became numb inside, a condition I welcomed and struggled to maintain. I felt nothing, not anger, or joy, or sadness. Life was easier that way.

Then, fifteen years after he left, Nick came home.

Part Two

&

Chapter Twelve

છ

All hell broke loose in Morganville when I left Hugh. The gossip zipped back and forth like a hummingbird on amphetamines, and the entire town was at war over its differing opinions. Part of them thought I'd lost my mind, and the other part, the part that knew about Hugh's continued affairs, applauded my good sense. Not that any of it bothered me. I moved through the storm of rumors calm and unruffled, offering no explanations or apologies, ignoring the whispers that followed me wherever I went.

Both my family and Hugh's were frantic, and after two months of attempted brow-beatings, wailing, and guilt trips, had resorted to giving me the cold shoulder. Even my mother barely spoke to me. For a while, the silence was a relief. I still had the Judge, who thought anything I did was just fine and dandy, and my father, who'd never approved of my marriage to Hugh anyway. And, much to my surprise, Jenna. She'd always seemed to think Hugh walked on water, but when she found out I was divorcing him, her only comment was, "It's about time."

The truth was, Hugh and I hadn't had a marriage since Katie died. We lived together like strangers, each going our own way, barely speaking when we were in the same room. I'd simply made the separation official. Leaving had finally become easier than pretending to be happy with each other when we weren't.

Hugh, of course, played the wounded spouse, the man whose wife had dumped him with no warning and for no apparent reason, but I knew he was relieved. He'd signed the divorce papers with no hesitation at all, especially since I was asking nothing from him, not even his name. In one more month I would be Alix French again.

I felt neither relieved nor depressed. It was only one more event that had no impact on me. I moved back to the farm, into the room in the barn, and at best, I was content.

In a sense, the place had changed. The single twin bed was the same, as was the blue and green plaid curtain on the window, faded now with time and strong sunlight. The same chair still sat in a corner. But the large room hadn't stayed empty all this time. Cody, my cousin, had used it for several years when he'd first returned from college, and he'd added an apartment-sized stove and refrigerator, and a four-foot-long section of cabinets, the base holding a kitchen sink. He'd also had a phone line installed.

Cody had turned out to be something of a surprise. He'd majored in criminology and as soon as his degree was in his hand, he'd moved back to Morganville and went to work as a deputy. Now he was the sheriff and one of my very best friends.

Once, he'd tried to apologize for that night at the Burger Zone when I was a kid, but I cut him off. I refused to think about Nick, or remember that night. I refused to feel anything. People who felt got hurt. Hadn't I learned that the hard way? I wasn't going to let it happen again. Which is why I took the news of Nick's return without so much as an increase in my heartbeat. Oh, yes. I had learned.

It was an early spring day, the first green shoots beginning to push their way out of the ground. I locked the doors of Southern Supply and climbed into the Chevy, piling the sheaf of papers I carried on the seat beside me. Kenny Millsap, my general manager, ran the store on Saturdays, but I always took paperwork home with me on Friday nights. It gave me something to do on my days off.

I was a bit puzzled to find Jenna's Lincoln parked in front of the barn when I got home. Five years ago she'd bought out

Mid-Delta Real Estate and I knew she'd had an appointment scheduled early this evening. If it was already over, it probably hadn't gone well.

"Hi. What's up?" I asked, as I caught sight of her pacing the length of the aisle in front of the empty stalls. She looked agitated and upset, and the horde of cats that normally hung around had all found cover.

She followed me to the door of my room before answering. "Alix, you aren't going to believe who my appointment turned out to be."

"Who?" I put the papers on a small table against the back wall and pulled a pair of jeans and a shirt out of the closet. I wanted to take a walk in the woods behind the barn before supper, get a little exercise and fresh air.

"Will you stop and look at me? This is important."

Still holding my clothes, I turned to her. "Okay, you have my complete attention. Now, who was it?"

"Nick Anderson."

I remained silent, didn't even blink. If her news startled me, I let none of it show in my face.

"Well, aren't you going to say something?"

"What do you expect me to say?" I draped the clothes over a chair and stripped off my dark blue tailored suit, balancing myself with one hand on the chair back.

"I expect you to be upset, or mad, or something!" She waved her hands in the air. "He's back, Alix, and he's staying. He's buying the twenty acres next to the farm. He's going to be your neighbor. Hell, he's planning on building a house five feet from your property line. You'll be tripping over him every time you walk outside."

I shrugged as I stepped into the jeans. "It's a free country."

With an air of disgust, she plopped onto the easy chair. "Now I'm really worried. I thought for sure this would get a reaction out of you. You loved him, Alix. How can you be so calm after what he did to you?"

I pulled a T-shirt over my head, then raked a hand through my short hair to fix it. "That was a long time ago. Nick means nothing to me."

"Does anything?" Her gaze was piercing. "You walk and talk, you breathe and eat, you work and sleep, but you aren't alive anymore. I thought once you got away from Hugh things might be different, but they aren't. You've only changed location. Do you have any idea how long it's been since I've heard you laugh?"

I knew exactly. The last time I'd laughed, the last time I'd cared about anything except my business, was the day before Katie died.

As usual, she seemed to read my mind. "You're going to see Nick sooner or later. Will you tell him about Katie?"

I stiffened, then forced my tense shoulders to relax. No one had mentioned Katie in my presence for years. It was as though she'd never existed for anyone but me, and her name sounded alien on Jenna's lips.

"No. Katie is none of his business."

But Jenna had discovered the chink in my armor and she prodded it unmercifully. "Katie was his daughter, too. Don't you think he has the right to know about her?"

"No." I threw my suit onto a hanger and slammed it into the closet. "She was never his child and she never will be."

"Ah-ha! Is that a bit of anger I detect? Maybe there's some life in you after all."

"Drop it, Jenna."

With a sigh, she watched me take out a sweater and tie the arms around my waist. "Okay, okay. It's just that you're scaring me, Alix. You act like that damn robot on Star Trek. No, I take that back. At least Data wants to feel human."

"Jenna, I'm fine, really."

"Where are you going?"

"For a walk. I've been sitting at my desk all day."

"Loan me a pair of jeans and I'll go with you. And if you're a good girl, I'll even treat you to a hamburger later."

"Deal."

We walked in silence for a while, the leftover leaves from last fall crunching under our feet. All around us, wild plum and redbud trees were in full bloom. The buzzing of bees, busily collecting nectar, filled the air.

"How does your mother like her new house?"

"Fine, I suppose." About six months ago, Daddy had retired. He and Mother had sold their house in Jonesboro and bought a smaller one down the street from the farm so she could be closer to the Judge.

"Don't tell me she's still not talking to you?"

My smile contained no humor. "Only when she has to. You know how close she and Helena are. They're feeding each other's indignation. I'm hoping they'll get over it when they realize this isn't a game, that I really am divorcing Hugh and they can't change my mind."

"They probably will. What about Darla?"

"You know Aunt Darla. She couldn't stop talking if someone held a gun to her head. There's not a week goes by that I don't get at least one lecture on how I'm putting my immortal soul in danger. According to her, I'm going to hell in a handbasket."

I hadn't set foot in a church since Katie's funeral, much to Aunt Darla's dismay. The problems with Hugh, plus my sudden accessibility after I moved back to the farm, had simply escalated her tirades. I'd passed the point where I listened anymore. She seemed happy enough if I merely nodded once in a while as though agreeing with her statements.

"Aunt Jane is the only one who doesn't seem to have an opinion one way or the other. She still treats me the same way she did before I got married and left home."

"Do you think it's ever crossed her mind that if your father had married her, you'd be her daughter?"

"I don't know. Maybe."

Jenna gave me a sideways, speculative look. "Nick asked me about you. He knows you and Hugh are getting a divorce."

"Everyone knows about Hugh and me. I hear they have a betting pool at the barbershop and the odds are five to one I'll call off the divorce."

"Yeah?" She perked up. "Maybe I should stop by tomorrow."

"Don't. Everyone will figure you've got inside information and it'll ruin their fun."

"I suppose you're right. Of course, when everyone discovers that Nick is back, the odds may change."

"What are you talking about?"

"Oh, come on, Alix. You honestly don't think you were that good at hiding the way you felt about each other, do you? Every kid in school knew. Well, except Piggy. She was so busy being jealous of you and Hugh, she couldn't see anything else."

While I'd never really cared who Hugh's women were, I knew for a fact that one of them had been Piggy. Shortly before I left him, she'd made it a point to let me know, hanging on him, touching him in ways only a lover would.

She wasn't exactly overweight now, she was more — abundant. Not to mention married with two kids, a boy and girl, both as mean and spoiled as Piggy. The oldest had been born approximately six months after she had married Devon Garner, the star basketball player who had nearly raped me that night at the Burger Zone. She'd always claimed the baby

171

was premature even though he weighted in at nine pounds, six ounces.

I was in no position to throw stones as far as the baby went, but it was apparent to everyone Devon had been trapped into the marriage because he was second best to Hugh. These days, there was little sign of the old Devon left. He worked for an insurance company in town and had a quiet, beaten look about him. In spite of our past, I felt sorry for him. No one deserved Piggy.

But something else was bothering me, and I couldn't stop thinking about it. Hesitantly, I cleared my throat. "So, how does Nick look?"

"Hot damn! I knew you were interested."

Heat flushed my cheeks. "I'm not interested, merely curious. I hope he's fat and bald."

"Well, you can get over that hope real fast. God, Alix, he's even more gorgeous now than when we were kids. Wait until you see him. He could be a movie star, one of those manly men who play the tough guys in westerns. I expected to see a six-shooter strapped on his hips. And he sure doesn't look like he's hurting for money anymore. I swear, he says he's paying cash for that land, and it's not cheap."

I turned abruptly, not wanting to hear another word about Nick, and headed back toward the barn. "Come on. Let's go get that burger."

* * * * *

Staying calm when Jenna told me about Nick was one thing. Actually seeing him again was something else entirely, and I fretted about the possibility for the rest of the weekend. Southern Supply generated enough paperwork to keep me in my room and occupied, but I had trouble concentrating.

At one point Sunday afternoon, I heard the distant echo of hammering coming from the direction of the twenty acres Nick was buying, but I wouldn't allow myself to look.

Shortly after the noise started, the Judge appeared in the open door leading to the barn. "You hear that hammering?"

"Yes, Sir." I stayed focused on the invoices in front of me.

"Know who it is?"

"Nick," I answered.

"Okay, just wanted to make sure you knew he was back. Think I'll go over and say hello."

I finally looked up. "Don't you dare do anything to exert yourself."

We were all a little worried about the Judge. He didn't seem to have much energy anymore, and he barely ate enough to keep a bird alive. He'd been on medication for his blood pressure for two years now.

"Stop fussing at me. You're getting as bad as Darla. She watches me like a damn vulture. Can't even go to the bathroom without her standing at the door checking on me. I know what I can do and what I can't."

"Knowing and doing are two different things, you stubborn old coot. And we only fuss because we love you."

He used one finger to push his glasses back up his nose, then peered at me over the rims. "You want to walk over there and keep an eye on me?"

"Thanks, but I'll have to trust you this time. I've got too much work left to do."

I wouldn't be able to avoid Nick forever, not in a town the size of Morganville, but I sure wasn't going to look for him. I didn't even wonder why he hadn't tried to find me yet. It was obvious. He hadn't wanted me fifteen years ago; I had no reason to think he'd changed his mind now. No doubt he was happily married to Lindsey. I only wished they'd found somewhere else to settle down. I wasn't sure Morganville was big enough for the three of us.

Late Monday afternoon, my time ran out. I was on the loading dock at Southern Supply, chewing my bottom lip while I tried to figure out if the custom-cut countertop a contractor had ordered could be salvaged. The inside corners had been cut and joined at the wrong angle and it was looking hopeless.

"Alix?" The intercom crackled with static as Kenny paged me.

"Yes, Kenny?" I was still distracted. It looked like we were going to take a loss on the countertop. "Reorder it," I told Doug, my dock manager. "And tell them they better get it right or I'll find someone else to do my cabinet work. This is the second time they've messed up this month."

He jogged to the phone as Kenny spoke again. "Got a customer at the front desk who wants to open an account."

"Okay, I'll be right there."

I was proud of what Southern Supply had become. It was the biggest store in Morganville and second only to the lumber mill in employing the people in the area. We had building contractors from all over the northeast part of the state who used us exclusively for their material. Hardly a day went by when several new customers didn't apply for accounts, so I wasn't expecting anything out of the ordinary as I walked to the front desk.

Reaching under the counter, I picked up a credit application form and straightened, facing the man now standing casually in front of me.

"Hello, Peewee." Nick's soft voice rolled over me like molasses over a hot biscuit.

I stood there frozen, my heart pounding an erratic rhythm that made it hard to breathe, while my subconscious automatically catalogued his appearance. If anything, Jenna had understated the facts. He was taller, at least six-two, maybe more. No silver marred his thick hair, but it was shorter than I'd ever seen it before.

When he'd left fifteen years ago, his body, while well-developed, still retained boyish overtones, lanky and lean like the healthy young animal he was. Nothing about the man standing here now was boyish. He was dressed in black slacks, a black pullover shirt, and a black linen jacket that hit him just above the knees, the dark color serving to emphasize the deep bronze of his skin. And not even his clothing could hide the long thick muscles of his legs, the broad shoulders or the flat stomach.

His face had changed, too. All the roundness was gone, leaving hard lines and chiseled planes that loudly proclaimed here was a man who knew what he wanted and wasn't afraid to go after it. A five o'clock shadow darkened his jaw. Only the dimples and the gray eyes were the same, and those I would have recognized anywhere.

The smile curving his lips faded a bit as I continued to stare at him silently, and he took a step closer. He held a set of rolled-up plans in one hand.

"Alix? Don't tell me you've forgotten me?"

By some miracle my voice came out cool and steady, even though inside I was trembling with a dozen conflicting emotions. "Nick. Jenna told me you were back." I put the papers down and shoved them toward him. "If you'll fill these out, we can see about getting your account opened."

A puzzled expression filled his eyes as he reached inside his jacket for a pen. "You look great, Alix."

"Thanks." I forced a smile. I'd gotten real good at pretending. I could do it even when I wanted to scream.

He pulled the forms closer and studied them a second before glancing back up. "How have you been?"

"Fine."

His gaze searched mine as he hesitated. "And Hugh? I heard the two of you are separated."

"You heard right." I pointed to the form. "Just fill in your address, phone number, social security number, and the name of your loan officer. We'll do the rest."

"I don't have a loan officer."

"Then the name and address of your bank will do."

He put down the information I'd requested, shooting glances at me the entire time. When he finished, he handed it across the counter.

"It was great seeing the Judge yesterday. He looks just like he always did."

"Yes, he does. I take it you're building a house on the land you're buying?"

"Alix, is something wrong?" His brows were lowered, mouth curving downward in a worried frown.

"Of course not." I refused to meet his eyes. He's simply another customer, I told myself. Ruthlessly, I ground my building anger under my heel and reached for the plans. I couldn't believe he was acting as though no time had passed, as though we could take up right where we'd left off. "It usually takes the bank a few days to get back to us on the applications, but if you'd like, we can make up a material list for you and have it ready to go."

"That will be fine."

Nick's gaze burned into me while I unrolled the plans, but I ignored him. "Have you decided on a contractor yet? If you haven't, we keep a list..." My voice trailed off as I stared down at the blueprint, and everything in me went still.

The year I was eighteen, when Hugh had been after me to go look at the houses in Fair Oaks, I'd come across a picture in a magazine. It was of an old farmhouse that had been restored, and I'd fallen instantly in love with the sweeping porches, wide expanses of glass, the half-dozen gables, and the old-fashioned flower beds full of hollyhocks, roses and honeysuckle. It hadn't been just a house to me; it was what a home should be.

Cutting it carefully from the magazine, I'd clipped it to a blank sheet of paper and then spent hours designing the inside. It was my dream house, the one I would have built if I'd had any choice in the matter. And now it stared back at me from Nick's blueprints, every detail exactly as I'd drawn it.

"What do you think?" he asked, his voice soft, hopeful.

"Where did you get this?" My hands were shaking so hard the paper rattled.

"From you. You left it in my room one night, and I've been carrying it around with me for the last fifteen years. When I knew we were coming back, I had the plans drawn up from your sketches. I wasn't sure you'd remember it."

Not only did I remember it, I remembered the night I left it. We'd made love, one of the last times we'd spent together in his room, and I hadn't thought to take my drawings with me when I'd left. By the time I did think about them again, Nick was gone and I'd married Hugh. I had assumed the plans were thrown away when Aunt Darla cleaned out the room.

Now Nick was going to build it. For him and Lindsey. My anger boiled, seethed until I could barely speak. "I see." The plans rolled up with a snap as I released them. "Kenny can figure it up for you. When you get the foundation down, just call him and he'll get the material delivered out to you."

"Alix..." He reached for my hand, but I pulled away just as movement from his left caught my attention. I never found out what he intended to say because my legs went rubbery and I couldn't breathe. All I could do was stare at the boy who'd stopped beside him. It was like seeing Nick again as he'd been at fifteen, like seeing a male version of what Katie would be if she'd lived.

"Hey, Dad. Bowie is taking Lindsey and me to Jonesboro for supper and to do some shopping. He wants to know if we should wait on you."

The expression on Nick's face when he looked at the boy screamed love and pride. Casually, he slung an arm around the young man's shoulders. "Daniel, this is Alix French. Alix, this is my son, Daniel."

Twin dimples popped out when Daniel grinned and my heart stuttered to a standstill. Agonizing pain ripped through me as he extended a hand.

"Hi. It's a pleasure. Dad's told me all about you."

Somehow, I managed to shake his hand and welcome him to Morganville, all while my brain chanted over and over, "*he's Katie's brother—he's Katie's brother.*"

It had honestly never occurred to me that Nick might have other children. Maybe because I hadn't *wanted* to think about it. Stupid of me, in retrospect, but I now felt doubly betrayed and was even more determined that he'd never find out about Katie.

"You go ahead," Nick was telling Daniel. "I'll see you guys later."

Dear Lord. Even Nick's accent was gone. He didn't exactly sound northern, but he didn't sound southern anymore either.

As Daniel headed for the door, I waved Kenny over. "Kenny, this is Mr. Anderson. You'll be taking care of his account from now on." Picking up the form Nick had filled out, I shoved it in Kenny's hand and turned, fully intending to leave Nick standing there.

"Alix, wait. How about letting me buy you dinner tonight? We can talk over old times, catch up with what's been happening."

I suspect my hair was standing on end when I rounded furiously on Nick. My anger and pain had finally reached the point of no return.

"Old times? Listen to me, you bastard. The only thing I want to do is forget you ever existed. And if that's not clear enough for you, let me spell it out. I will not have dinner with you, ever. Not only do I *not* want to 'catch up', I don't give a damn what you've been doing all this time. In other words, leave me the hell alone!" *Jenna would be proud of me*, I thought a bit hysterically. I certainly wasn't reacting like an unemotional robot now.

The blood drained from Nick's face, and poor Kenny's eyes were the size of dinner plates. "Kenny, you're in charge," I snarled, grabbing my purse from beneath the counter. "I'm leaving early."

But I'd forgotten how stubborn and determined Nick could be. He caught up with me as I reached the Chevy and grabbed my arm. All over the parking lot, customers stopped what they were doing to watch.

His eyes narrowed as he stared at me. "Do you want to tell me what that was all about?"

"Think about it." I struggled to retake possession of my arm, but he hung on, his grip firm yet gentle.

"I've thought about a lot of things the last fifteen years, things we need to talk about."

"Well, I don't want to talk to you." Oh, God. I sounded like a spoiled four-year-old, and the situation was deteriorating rapidly. I had to get away from him. "Please let go of me."

He hesitated, then released my arm. But he didn't back off. Instead, he cupped my cheek with one hand, his thumb caressing my skin. "I've missed you, Peewee. I don't know why you hate me now, but I'm going to find out, and I'm not going to leave you alone. I came home thinking you were happily married to Hugh, but even then I hoped at the very least we could still be friends."

"Oh, is that what we were? Friends?" I jerked away from him, climbed into the Chevy, and slammed the door shut. "You know something, Nick? That may just be the only truthful thing you've ever said to me. And you know something else? I don't need or want friends like you." I started the car and put it in gear. "Say hello to Lindsey for me," I snapped as the car shot backward out of the parking space.

It was a miracle I didn't hit someone. When I glanced back at the store, Nick was standing there watching me leave, his hands knotted into fists at his sides. *Take that, you asshole,* I thought.

Morganville had changed drastically since my childhood. The old general store had been converted into an IGA, the benches adorned with old men in deep conversations were gone from the front sidewalk now. The one-room plank post office with the rickety steps had been hauled to the middle of a field where it sat alone, falling into more disrepair every year. The new one was a modern brick building on Main Street and the old site now held the barbershop and a laundromat.

The streets were paved instead of the gravel I had once scampered over barefoot, and city hall had been moved to a newer building with more office space, the old one sitting empty, used only for meetings of the senior citizens' group. At the traffic light that had been installed on the highway, a convenience store sat on the corner to the right, and what had once been Hawkins' Gas Station on the left was now an auto parts store. But I saw none of the changes as I drove through town this time. Anger blurred my vision.

By the time I made it home, I was shaking. What the hell was wrong with me? I never reacted like that, never. The last time I'd lost control of my temper had been that night at the Burger Zone, and I figured being drunk was a pretty good excuse for that episode.

This time I had no excuse. I'd done exactly what I'd promised myself I wouldn't do. I had let Nick get to me. He'd have to be pretty stupid not to figure out how I felt about Lindsey after that fit I threw, and Nick had never been stupid.

Taking the picture of Katie from my wallet, I curled up on the bed and ran my finger over her tiny face. It was the last picture I'd had made of her, one of the few I kept with me.

"Your father's back, baby," I whispered. "And you've got a brother. Oh, Katie, he looks so much like you that it hurts to see him. But don't you worry. We're going to be just fine, I promise. I don't care how mad he makes me, he'll never find out about you. He doesn't deserve to know. Not after he abandoned us. Not after he let you die."

The phone rang, but I ignored it. I was too busy repairing the crack Nick had put in my protective walls to deal with anyone right now. Brick by brick, I reinforced each section, making myself remember why I hated him, why I couldn't go through this again.

It took me over an hour, but when it was finished, I was calm and cool, sure that nothing could endanger my emotional stability ever again. Especially not Nick.

Famous last words, or a premonition? Because Nick had meant it when he'd said he wasn't going to leave me alone.

Chapter Thirteen

ಸ

After changing into a pair of shorts and a T-shirt, I slapped a couple of ham sandwiches together and carried my plate and a glass of tea to the bench in front of the barn. For someone who didn't normally have much of an appetite, I was amazingly starved. It didn't help that I could smell the mouthwatering scent of pork chops drifting from the house.

Finding a spot in the sunshine, I closed my eyes and pictured the supper being prepared. Fried potatoes and probably greens, I decided. With a sigh, I opened my eyes and took a bite from my own supper. I hadn't felt welcome in the house since I'd left Hugh, especially not when Mama was there, like she was this evening.

The newest batch of kittens swarmed around my feet. They hadn't learned the cool disdain of their elders yet, and begged pitifully for food, their tiny eyes nearly crossing with the effort they put into their cries. Needless to say, they wound up polishing off my second sandwich. I always had been a sucker for the underdog, or in this case, the undercat.

"Looks like it's just you and me, fellows," I told them, tearing the sandwich into bite-sized pieces they could handle, and making sure it was distributed equitably.

While miniature growls and paw-slapping erupted around me, I picked up my tea and stared toward Nick's property. Curiosity was killing me, but hell would freeze over before I'd go over there. Apparently, the hammering yesterday had been due to driving in stakes that laid out the foundation of the house, and I could see small mounds of dirt that indicated the footing had been dug sometime today.

Nick certainly wasn't wasting any time. And what made it even worse, he'd chosen the exact spot for the house that I would have. When finished, the house would be surrounded by trees. The huge mimosa I'd climbed as a child would be situated near the back porch, allowing the fragrance from its pink hula-skirt blooms to wash over anyone who sat there during the summer.

If he'd planned for years, he couldn't have come up with a better way to drive his betrayal home. He was building my house, in my spot, and he was building it for Lindsey. The very thought made me so sick I was glad I hadn't eaten that second sandwich.

I looked around hopefully when I heard the back door of the house close, but it was only Daddy. Taking a sip of tea, I leaned my head back against the barn wall and watched him approach. He sat beside me, dodging cats, and stretched his long legs out in front of him. A kitten promptly began crawling upward, using him for a ladder. *Why couldn't I have inherited his height?* I thought irritably. Being short, with everything out of reach, was a pain in the rear.

"You look tired," he said.

"Not really. The sun is making me sleepy."

"Why don't you come to the house and have supper with us?"

The kitten reached his knee and I scooped it up, cuddling it close, feeling it vibrate against me as it purred. "I can't, Daddy."

"Alix, cutting yourself off isn't going to help. Your mother loves you."

"Does she?" I turned my head to look at him. "I haven't seen much sign of it lately. All she cares about is her status, about how people will treat her now that I've left Hugh. It doesn't matter to her that I was miserable being married to him."

"Have you told her that?"

"No. The only thing she wants me to say is that I'm going back to Hugh."

He rubbed the bridge of his nose. "Talking works both ways, Alix. You have to give her a chance to understand. Right now, all she's hearing is Helena's side of the story, and the woman has your mother fit to be tied. She's just about convinced Ellie that you need therapy, that you're suffering from depression and once you get help things will go back to the way they were." He hesitated. "That episode today isn't going to help matters any."

"Episode?" I arched a brow at him.

"Kenny called. It seems you scared him right out of his socks, and then when you didn't answer the phone, he really got worried. He's never seen you blow up at a customer before."

"Christ." My head started to pound. "The whole family knows?"

"Alix, half the town witnessed it firsthand. Everyone knows. They probably have a couple more betting pools going by now." He grinned. "You're getting rather notorious lately."

This was going from bad to worse. "And what is so humorous about that?"

"Honestly?" He chuckled. "I'm thrilled something finally happened to shake you up a bit. If it took Nick coming back, then I'm grateful to him."

"So you think I'm depressed, too?"

"Depressed, no." His smile faded as he studied me. "But for a long time now I've watched you slowly shut your emotions away where no one can touch them. It's not healthy, Alix, and I admit it's worried me more than a little. That stunt you pulled today gives me hope. Anger is an honest emotion and you showed it in spades. Maybe you're finally starting to come to life again."

Jenna had called me a robot, Mama thought I need a shrink, then Daddy got all proud because I'd made a fool of myself. I needed some aspirin.

He glanced toward the house, then got to his feet. "There's one more thing you should probably know. I've heard some rumors that a few people aren't happy about Nick being back. They don't like having a murderer running loose."

I may have convinced myself that I hated Nick, but that didn't mean I wanted lies spread about him. "That's silly. It was self-defense. Nick is no more a murderer than I am."

"I know. But the town has a long memory, and gossips don't discriminate in their choice of victims. You should know that better than most."

"Well, even if it's true, there's not much I can do about it. I can't even get them to stop talking about me."

He nodded. "That's because you're still a Morgan, the closest thing to royalty this town has, and that makes you fair game. It's different with Nick. Some of what I've heard is just plain vicious. Think about it, Sweetheart." He leaned down and kissed my forehead. "I better get to the house before your mother sends the troops after me. The girls are in the midst of planning a trip."

"To where?"

"Hardy. I've been nominated to take them Friday morning so they can spend the weekend buying out the craft stores. We'll probably stay with your Uncle Vern, so you'll have to keep an eye on the Judge."

Uncle Vern had moved to Hardy after he'd retired. He said his social security check went further there, and he could spend his time hunting and fishing.

"I will." I didn't add that as little as three months ago, it would have been a given that I'd go along with them. I loved Hardy, an old town on Spring River, in the Ozark foothills, that catered to tourists. Its single main street was lined with ancient buildings that now held craft shops of every shape and variety. Camping and canoeing on the river was also a big draw.

A dull ache settled around my heart as I watched my father walk away. I'd never felt so lonely in my life, so alienated from the women in my family. It was as if the supports had been knocked out from under me, leaving me teetering on the edge of a void I hadn't known was there. I had Jenna, of course, but it wasn't the same, and she had her own busy life to lead. Mentally, I made a note to do something to thank her, maybe send her a nice bunch of flowers.

I looked down at the black and white kitten sprawled across my arm, sound asleep, and thought about what my father had said. I knew exactly what he'd implied. I may have left Hugh, but the town still regarded me as a Morgan. Plus I was the owner of Southern Supply, a store quite a few people made their living from. A few well-chosen words from me in the right places could probably stop, or at least slow, the gossip about Nick.

Depositing the limp kitten on the bench, I went back into my room. I didn't know what to do. If it had only been Nick and Lindsey, I wouldn't give a flip what people were saying. They were adults, they should be able to handle it the same way I did. But there was also Daniel, and I couldn't bring myself to hate him, even though that small, mean spirit that lives in all of us wanted me to, kept whispering that he was the product of Nick's betrayal. And yet the saner, rational part of me knew that none of what had happened was the boy's fault. Plus, he looked too much like Katie for me to ignore.

There was one thing I could do, and that was talk to Cody. As the sheriff, he would know if anything could be done legally to Nick, and he knew when to keep his mouth shut. At least that would tell me what I'd be up against and give me a few more days to think about it.

But deep down, I already knew. I couldn't let Daniel be treated the same way Nick had been treated growing up. He was Katie's brother, and even though I'd only discovered his existence a few hours ago, in my heart, I felt getting to know him would somehow bring me closer to her. If that meant saving Nick from the good people of Morganville in the process, so be it. In a strange way, we'd come full circle and were right back where we'd started. The thought didn't thrill me.

God, how do I get myself into these messes? I thought, taking the aspirin bottle out of the medicine cabinet.

* * * * *

Cody looked at me inquiringly from across my desk as I handed him a cup of coffee. I had to admit, he'd turned out pretty darn good. He'd even lost his northern accent, speaking now like a native son.

Why he'd never married was a mystery to me. The way he looked in his uniform caused normally respectable women to act like a gaggle of giggling school girls when he walked into a room. It was disgusting, but Cody seemed to take it all in stride, never failing to be polite even while he remained uninterested. I knew he dated occasionally, but it always seemed to be women from out of town, and it never got serious.

I'd called him first thing that morning and asked him to stop by when he had a chance.

"What's up?" he asked, one eyebrow arched.

"You know Nick Anderson is back?" I relaxed in my chair, trying to look casual.

"Sure." He took a sip from the cup, his eyes narrowed against the steam as he watched me over the rim. Unlike Sheriff McAbee, his predecessor, Cody made it a point to know everything that went on in the county.

"And you know what happened fifteen years ago?"

"I've read the file." His voice remained noncommittal.

"So, what do you think?" I waved a hand nervously in the air.

He set his cup down carefully and tipped the brim of his hat back with one finger. "You mean, does Nick have a legal right to come back?" He crossed an ankle over his knee, settling deeper into the chair. "Alix, Sheriff McAbee had no legal right to force him to leave. I haven't seen anything that would lead me to believe Frank Anderson's killing was anything but self-defense. If Nick had put up a fuss, there wasn't much McAbee could have done about it. Too many people knew Frank was abusive." He hesitated. "McAbee was from the 'good old boy' school of law enforcement. If he didn't want to honor a law, he just did an end-run around it. By all rights, there should have been an arraignment. I've always figured the Judge twisted his arm a little that night because he didn't want to put Nick through all that."

That news left a bitter taste in my mouth. Had Nick known they couldn't force him to leave and chosen to go anyway? It wouldn't surprise me.

I took a deep breath. "Could the case be reopened? Could he be tried for murder after all this time?"

"There's no statute of limitations on murder, so hypothetically, yes, it could be reopened. But there would have to be some pretty solid evidence for me to consider it, and I don't see it happening. Why the sudden concern about Anderson?"

My shoulders tensed. "I'm not concerned about him. But there's been some talk, and I don't want to see his son get hurt."

"Uh-huh." He picked the coffee up and took another sip. "You and Anderson used to be pretty close."

"That was a long time ago."

"Not that long." He finished the coffee and stood. "Be careful, Alix. Your marriage just ended and you don't need to rush into anything else. I'd hate to see you get hurt again. As for the talk, that's all it is. People will forget about Nick as soon as something new comes along to gossip about."

"Believe me. You have nothing to worry about." I stood and came around the desk. "Heard from Casey lately?"

"Naw. But you know how he is."

I did. Casey had gone on to law school at the University of Arkansas at Little Rock after college. It was there he'd met his high-priced wife, and together they'd set up a ritzy practice in our capitol city. We rarely saw him these days and suspected he had his eye on a career in politics. It seemed he was always too busy for family.

"Well, when you do, tell him hello for me." I kissed his cheek. "And thanks for coming by."

* * * * *

I got my first chance to make some headway on the gossip about Nick a lot faster than I'd wanted or expected, and in a way that rendered a few repercussions I hadn't planned on.

The sky was a uniform gray when I left Southern Supply that evening, the clouds low and slow moving, and a fine rain misted my windshield as I drove through town. It wasn't heavy enough to soak, just enough to make me feel damp and uncomfortable. I knew from experience that in a few hours fog would cover everything like a fluffy white blanket, and I decided to stop at the IGA on my way home instead of waiting until I changed out of my work clothes.

The IGA was owned and run by Mr. and Mrs. Burgess, lifetime residents of Morganville. Their prices were a bit higher than the big chain grocery stores in Jonesboro, but I'd always figured the convenience and the savings in gas made up the difference. Besides, their son, Neil, worked for me. He was a nice young man with a sweet wife and two babies, and he worked hard at his job.

The store was full of people who had the same idea I did. I ignored them for the most part, merely giving a nod and a smile when someone spoke to me. It had been a long day. I only wanted to get the items I needed, go home, take a hot shower, and curl up with a book for the evening.

There were two checkout counters, situated so close together there was barely room to walk between them. Mrs. Burgess manned one, Mr. Burgess the other. Mrs. Burgess was currently busy checking Gretchen Treece's groceries, although it looked like they were doing more talking than checking. I went to Mr. Burgess' lane. I'd always liked him better anyway.

We exchanged perfunctory greetings as I placed the handbasket holding my items on the counter, then reached into my purse for my checkbook. Mr. Burgess' fingers flew over the cash register keys as he tallied up my items. By the time he finished, both lines had filled up with customers waiting their turn.

Gretchen chose that moment to notice me. "Why, Alix. I swear, I haven't seen you at the club in ages."

No, and if I had anything to say about it, I'd never set foot in the place again. But I made myself smile. "Really?"

"I suppose you heard that Nick Anderson is back?" Her eyes were avid with curiosity. Immediately, I tensed, but before I had a chance to respond, Mrs. Burgess jumped into the conversation.

"Well, I think it's just awful, letting a murderer run around loose like decent folk. I can promise you he won't be doing any business here. We don't need his money."

Without thinking, I snatched back the check I'd handed Mr. Burgess. "Well, since you obviously don't need any more business, I'll just take mine elsewhere. And while I'm at it, I'll spread the word that people should find another place to shop. I know Acres will appreciate the extra business."

Acres was a store out on the highway and the bane of Mrs. Burgess' existence. While smaller than the IGA, they carried much the same stock and she constantly complained about the competition.

Mr. Burgess took my check back and glared at his wife. "Ain't nobody ever been refused service in this store, and there ain't never going to be. Do I make myself clear?"

Mrs. Burgess' face reddened, but she kept her mouth shut, probably remembering suddenly that her son worked for me. Unfortunately, Gretchen was only getting warmed up.

"Now, Mr. Burgess, you know we have to set a high standard for this town. If we don't, degenerates and perverts will overrun our streets, corrupt our children. And it all starts with people of low moral standing. They're the ones we need to keep out of Morganville."

I swear, I don't know what hit me. Maybe it was all those years of watching Piggy throw herself at anything in pants, doing her best to make my life miserable. Whatever the reason, a fierce elation welled up inside me as I spoke.

"Oh, really?" I purred. "I wasn't aware that Peggy was leaving town, but since we don't allow people of low morals to live here, I guess it is for the best."

You could have heard a pin drop, the silence behind me was so deep. I could almost feel the other customers leaning forward, ears straining to catch every word.

The blood drained from Gretchen's face, but her nose went up in the air and she sniffed. "I don't know what you're talking about."

"Then allow me to enlighten you." I braced both hands on the counter. No doubt I was a fearsome sight to behold right then, because Gretchen took a hurried step back.

"Since Peggy turned thirteen years old, every woman in this town has known to lock their husbands up when she was around. Not that it did them much good. Your daughter seems to have no qualms about climbing any man in her vicinity. Including my husband." I lifted one hand and examined my nails casually.

"I will admit, though, she must not be that good. That was one of the shortest affairs Hugh ever had." I lowered my hand and looked her right in the eye. "Of course, I *had* to divorce him after that. There was no way I could sleep with him knowing where he'd been. I'd have had to boil him first. What if he picked up some disease from her?" A shudder I didn't have to fake ran through me.

Gretchen sputtered furiously and looked like she was ready to faint, but I had one more point to make. "People who live in glass houses shouldn't throw stones, Gretchen. You might want to remember that before you start trying to run someone out of town."

Calmly, I picked up the bags Mr. Burgess had packed for me, then paused to let my gaze sweep the crowd. Most of the women were smiling, as if they were tempted to let loose with a spontaneous cheer. The men were a different story. The majority of them looked worried, their gazes skittering away from mine, guilt written all over their expressions. Probably wondering how much I knew, I decided. And after those looks, I knew quite a lot. In sheer numbers alone, Piggy had managed to put Liz Swanner to shame.

My adrenaline rush lasted long enough to get me home, but as soon as I put my groceries away, I collapsed on the edge of the bed and buried my face in my hands. "Oh, God, oh, God, oh, God," I chanted, rocking back and forth. I couldn't believe what I'd done. Maybe Helena was right and I really did need a shrink.

Until this evening, I'd never shared any aspect of my personal life with anyone. Now I'd told half the damn town that I knew about Hugh's affairs. Well, if nothing else came of it, maybe they'd stop looking at me as the poor, deluded little woman who didn't have a clue what her husband was up to.

The image of a volcano popped into my mind, one with small steam vents on its side to release the pressure, and a shaky laugh tore its way from my throat, the first honest amusement I'd felt in years. That volcano was exactly what I felt like. It was so wonderful, so freeing, to finally turn loose and say exactly what I was thinking. And while I normally wasn't a hurtful person, if anyone had deserved it, it was Gretchen with her holier-than-thou attitude.

The problem with volcanoes, I mused, was that eventually the big explosion was going to happen no matter how much steam was let off. I was wondering what would set mine off, and who would get caught in the pyroclastic debris, when someone knocked on the door.

I had known Nick was working next door with a crew of men when I'd left that morning, and I'd seen him again when I'd unloaded my bags from the car that evening, but for once my mind was on other things. He was the last person I expected to find on the other side of the door, and my anger did a slow burn all over again.

"What do you want?" I blocked the threshold with my body, ignoring the fact that he could pick me up and set me aside with one finger if he wanted to. I was also trying real hard not to notice how his damp black T-shirt clung to his upper body, or the way he looked in tight, faded jeans, or the way beads of moisture sparkled in his dark hair.

"Only some first aid. You don't have to bite my head off." He held up his right hand to show me a small puncture wound oozing blood from the base of his thumb. "I don't have the water hooked up next door yet and I figured it needed to be cleaned out."

His expression was suspiciously innocent. I put my hands on my hips as I glared at him. "It doesn't look to me like you'll risk bleeding to death if you try to make it home."

The dimples in his cheeks deepened when he grinned. "Ah, but you see, I don't have any bee balm at home."

I spit out the dirtiest word I knew, one I'd never said in mixed company before, and stalked to the bathroom. The yank I gave the door of the medicine cabinet nearly tore it out of the wall. Still mumbling under my breath, I grabbed a tin of bee balm, spun, and then came to a dead stop.

Nick had closed the door behind him and now stood at my sink, washing the blood from his hand. His presence seemed to fill the room, suck the oxygen right out of it until I couldn't breathe.

When he was through, he turned the water off and pulled a couple of paper towels from the roll before turning. Leaning his rear against the sink, he gazed around the room while he dried his hands. "It still feels like home, in spite of the changes. Same chair, same rug, same curtains—" His glance swung in my direction. "Same bed."

Spine stiff, I thrust the tin at him. "Here. Keep it."

Instead of taking it, he held out his hand. "Would you mind doing the honors? Kind of hard to reach with my left hand."

Damn right I minded. I didn't even want him in my room, much less to actually touch him. "I'm sure your wife will be happy to do it for you," I snarled.

He didn't even blink. His gaze stayed locked on mine like the sights from a sniper's gun. "I don't have a wife. I've never been married."

If he thought that's what I wanted to hear, he was dead wrong. "Oh? Well, I have to say, Nick, I didn't think it was possible for you to drop any lower in my esteem, but you just managed it. Let me see. What was it you said?" I continued in a mocking voice. "I'll never have a kid unless I'm married to its mother. A kid should have two parents who love it."

His head lowered and he stared at the floor for a second. "Some things are out of our control, Alix."

"Don't be stupid," I snapped. "Or is it possible you've still never heard of condoms? You know what those are, Nick? Some people call them rubbers. One of their functions is to prevent pregnancy. Don't you dare stand there and tell me it was out of your control." I was so mad I was vibrating.

"I know what they are." He ran a hand through his hair in a gesture that was so familiar I wanted to scream. "Alix, don't—"

For the second time that evening, someone knocked on the door, cutting off whatever Nick had been about to say. Had it only been yesterday I was bemoaning my loneliness? Right now I'd give a month's wages if everyone would simply leave me the hell alone.

Braced for a battle, hair still on end, I grabbed the knob and pulled. Apparently I wasn't the only one ready for a fight. I barely registered Hugh's face before he started yelling at me.

"Have you lost your mind?" His hands fisted on his hips, and he glared at me like he'd never seen me before. Then again, maybe he hadn't.

"There is that possibility," I said. "I take it you heard about the events at the IGA?"

"Heard about it?" He was so agitated he hadn't even noticed Nick. "Gretchen was so hysterical they had to sedate her to get her out of the store! Everybody in town now thinks I'm the scum of the earth. Goddamn it, Alix, I agreed to your divorce and now you're trying to ruin me. Do you know what this is going to do to my reputation?"

This entire thing was turning into a slapstick comedy, and my lips twitched. *Now* he was worried about his reputation?

Choking on laughter, I patted his chest. "Don't worry about it, Hugh. If your reputation is ruined, you aren't alone. About two-thirds of the men in town are right there with you. Besides, it's not like your affairs were a big dark secret. Even your mother knew about them."

"I didn't have any affairs! How can you keep accusing me? I loved you; I wouldn't do that to you."

My laughter died. "Oh, get a life, Hugh. I knew the first time you did it, and I knew every time after that. How could you think I wouldn't?"

He glared at me, his eyes shooting green fire. "If you really thought I was seeing someone else, why the hell didn't you ever say anything?"

Well, he'd asked for it, and I was in just the right mood to give it to him. "Because your other women were doing me a favor," I said, voice low and angry. "As long as you were with them, I didn't have to put up with you. And since I'm being honest, I might as well tell you; for someone who's had so much practice, you suck in bed, Hugh. Do the women of the world a big favor. Take lessons!"

With that pronouncement, I slammed the door with all my strength, praying it would collide squarely with his nose. I stood there, panting like a racehorse who'd just finished the Arkansas Derby in record time, until someone cleared his throat behind me.

Oh, shit. I'd completely forgotten about Nick.

"Well, Peewee. Looks like you've gone from trying to catch wowzer cats to whipping your weight in them."

For the third time in less than an hour, I yanked the door open, then pointed with one outstretched arm. "Out! Now!"

"Okay, okay. I'm going." He sauntered to the door, then stopped to look down at me. "But I will see you later."

"Not if I see you first," I growled.

Chapter Fourteen

ഇ

Thursday, normally a slow day for Southern Supply, turned out to be a bumper day for the business. What was even more unusual was that the increase was due to the women of Morganville. It felt like every female in town found an excuse to stop by, and they all wanted me to wait on them.

I lost count of the times I heard, "bless her heart" flying around, all aimed at Piggy. A northerner walking in when this was going on would probably think there was something seriously wrong with Piggy and everyone was expressing sympathy. But we southerners know that you can insult someone as much as you want so long as you add that "bless her heart" to the end of your comment.

Everyone wanted to tell me exactly how they felt about Piggy and Gretchen, and thank me for doing what they'd wanted to do for years. A few women even urged me to run for mayor, which was about the silliest thing I'd ever heard. Not only did Southern Supply take up all my time, I hated politics.

Right before lunch, I called Jenna. "Hey, are you busy?"

"Nothing I can't put off. What's up?"

"I thought I'd buy you lunch. I need to get out of this madhouse for a while."

"Sure. I'll meet you at the Wagon Wheel in fifteen minutes. But be warned. I want the whole story straight from the horse's mouth."

The Wagon Wheel wasn't just the largest café in Morganville, it was the only decent place to eat. The food wasn't fancy, but they did have a great salad bar and down-home cooking. I got there before Jenna and grabbed a booth near the back.

Ten minutes later, she came through the door, paused until she saw me, and then walked back to the booth. She was wearing a blue-green business suit that set off her eyes and hair, and every male gaze in the room followed her progress across the cafe. Jenna didn't seem to notice, though, and that was another puzzle I'd never solved. She was gorgeous. She could have any man she wanted. But she never dated.

In the past when I'd asked her about it, she'd only said she was too busy, or she didn't need a man to make her complete, or she was happy the way she was with no one to tell her what to do. And yet I'd sensed she wasn't being quite honest about her feelings.

I waited until she sat down, and then reached for her hand. "Have I told you how much I love and appreciate you?"

She blinked. "What brought this on?"

"You. You're the only real friend I've got, Jenna. You don't judge me or tell me how to run my life, but you're always there for me, supporting everything I do. That's very precious to me."

Her grip tightened until I winced, and her gaze fell to the table. "I hope you always feel that way," she whispered.

"I will. That's a promise."

She shook her head. "Don't promise, Alix. You'll jinx us." Brushing a hand over her damp eyes, she smiled. "And stop trying to make me forget about Gretchen and Piggy. God, I wish I could have been there to see Gretchen's face."

By the time I repeated the tale, she was holding her sides, laughing and gasping for air. "Next time you decide to go off the deep end, make sure you have a video camera with you. I'm so proud of you. You've needed to let go for a long time now."

"Well, I'm not proud of me. I could have found a better way to put her in her place. It's not Gretchen's fault that Piggy is a whore, bless her heart."

That statement sent us both into gales of laughter. "Do you know, Sue Matthews actually wants me to run for mayor next fall?" I choked.

"Sounds like a good idea to me." The response was male and came from right beside me. "Mind if I join you?"

As my gaze met Nick's amused gray eyes, my laughter faded, replaced by a scowl.

"Yes."

"Of course not."

Jenna and I spoke at the same time. When I glared at her, she only smiled innocently. Naturally, it was her reply Nick chose to hear. When he sat down on my side of the booth, I moved over hurriedly, trying my best not to let his leg touch mine.

"I went by Southern Supply, but Kenny told me you had gone to lunch."

"Oh?" I took a sip from my soda. "A problem with your material?"

"No. I wanted to talk you. I heard the whole story about what happened yesterday at the IGA." His gaze held mine. "Still trying to save me, Alix?"

"Don't flatter yourself."

He crossed his arms on the table. "Then why did you do it?"

I sighed. "I did it because your son doesn't deserve to live with that kind of viciousness. Especially when the rumors aren't true."

"Daniel's a tough kid. He knew what to expect when we came back."

"That doesn't make it right," Jenna said. "I'm glad Alix put a stop to it." She gathered up her purse. "Well, got to run. You two enjoy yourselves."

Before I could protest, she was gone, leaving me with the suspicion that she was trying to push me at Nick. Maybe I'd thanked her for her loyalty a little too soon.

Nick made no effort to move to the other side of the booth. Instead, he stretched his legs out and put his arm across the back of the seat. "Are you doing anything this evening?"

"Filing my teeth," I snapped.

He grinned. "That sounds interesting. You do seem to have a thing for necks these days, don't you? First you go for Gretchen's jugular, then Hugh's. Who's next?"

"Look, Nick, how many times do I have to say it? I won't have dinner with you. I don't want to talk to you. Give it up."

Casually, he picked a fry up from my plate, stuck it in his mouth, and chewed. "The reason I asked is because Daniel has been bugging me to let him visit you. After the reception you gave me, I wasn't sure it was safe, but it looks like I made a mistake about that."

My breath caught in my chest. "Really?"

"If it's okay with you."

"It's fine." I could barely contain my excitement. For days, I'd tried to figure out a way to talk to Daniel without humiliating myself by going through Nick. Now he'd dumped the opportunity into my lap.

"Tell me about him?" I blurted the question eagerly, before I had time to think.

He straightened, a smile playing on his lips as though he'd discovered the master key to the Pearly Gates. "He's a great kid. Makes the honor roll every year without even trying. He likes to read and he's good at sports. And he's real outgoing. Never meets a stranger."

Exactly the way Katie would have been, I thought wistfully, pain curling in my chest.

Nick popped another fry in his mouth while he thought. "He's not a nerd, but he loves computers. He built his own from scratch last winter. I guess he's a little bored right now, though. He doesn't know any of the kids in town yet, and there's not a lot to do in Morganville. He spends most of his time following me or Bowie around, driving us crazy with questions."

"Who is Bowie?"

"Bowie Grant. I guess you could say he's a friend, but he's a lot more than that. He takes care of us."

I picked up my purse and the check. "Well, tell Daniel he's welcome to visit me any time he wants. Now, I have to get back to work."

* * * * *

The rest of the day dragged by in spite of the increase in business. I couldn't get my mind off Daniel, wondering when he'd be there, what we'd say to each other, terrified it would be awkward, praying it wouldn't.

It's hard to explain now, my feelings at the time were so confused, but I honestly felt like I had a small claim on Nick's son. The same blood that had flowed through my daughter's veins flowed through Daniel's. The same forces that had given Katie dark hair, gray eyes and dimples, had blessed Daniel in a similar fashion. Nick had fathered both children, and in my mind, that gave me a legitimate tie to Daniel, one that not even my anger at Nick would stop me from exploring.

And there's always the possibility that I had a darker motive, one I couldn't let myself acknowledge. Not then. Nick had left me. I had borne our daughter alone, loved her, and seen her die. All the hatred and anger I'd aimed at Nick still lived, buried inside those walls I'd built. He had nearly destroyed my life.

So if I couldn't have my daughter, I'd steal his son.

Oh, not physically. But mentally, emotionally? Since then, I've tried repeatedly to analyze my intentions, and the truth is, I simply don't know. While I hope not, maybe revenge *was* driving me. Maybe I thought Nick had no right to a healthy, happy child when mine had died. Maybe, God help me, I thought he owed me his son.

And Daniel made it so easy.

He was waiting on me when I pulled the Chevy to a stop in front of the barn, leaning against the wall, watching the kittens play. His eyes lit up at the sight of the old car, and he was talking by the time I got the door open.

"Wow! I can't believe you've still got the Chevy. Dad told me all about it. I didn't think it would be running anymore."

I smiled, then looked ruefully at the car. "It has its moments. I need to take it in and have a tune-up done. Sometimes it dies on me."

I'd kept the Chevy all these years over Hugh's protests. He hated it when I drove the old car, claiming people would think we couldn't afford better. Eventually I'd given in and let him buy me a BMW, one he traded in every year for a newer model. But I had refused to sell the Chevy, keeping it stored in the garage and starting it once a month to make sure it stayed in running order. When I left him, I left the fancy cars, too, and felt no urge to replace the Chevy with something better.

"Maybe I could do it for you." Daniel looked as though he was dying to get his hands on the car.

"You know all about engines, huh?"

"Well, not everything, but Dad taught me a lot. These old engines are simpler to work on than the new ones with all their electronic stuff."

"Tell you what." I smiled. "You give it a tune-up and I'll let you drive it sometimes."

"Awesome! You've got a deal."

"Only when I'm with you, though."

"Okay."

I didn't ask him if he had a learner's permit, or even if he knew how to drive. In the south, kids started driving before they were potty trained. I could still remember sitting on the Judge's lap, gripping the steering wheel tightly with both hands while he yelled encouragements and pretended I was scaring him half to death. I must have been all of three years old at the time.

"How do you like Morganville so far?" I asked, heading through the barn.

"It's okay, I guess. A lot different from Saudi Arabia."

A mild shock ran through me as I opened the door to my room. "That's where you've been living?"

"Yeah. For the last eleven years, anyway. I don't remember much about Kentucky. We left there as soon as Dad got out of the army."

"Why Saudi Arabia?"

He shrugged as I put my purse away. "A guy Dad met while he was in the army gave him a job with a big oil company. Dad ran the company's garages."

"It must have been interesting to live in place with a culture so different from ours."

"Not really." His attention was captured by the bookshelf against one wall and he moved closer, his gaze running over the books. "We lived in a compound the company provided for employees and their families. They even had a school. It was sort of like living in a small town. Are these the books my dad used when he stayed here?"

"Most of them. I've added a few in the last two months. Your Dad said you like to read."

He glanced at me over his shoulder, dimples popping out when he grinned. "It wasn't like I had much choice. Dad started reading to me about five minutes after I was born. Not kids' books, either. He read me novels."

"What about your Mom? Did she read to you, too?"

For a second he looked absolutely blank. "You mean Lindsey? No, she doesn't like to read. Besides, she wasn't around that much when I was little."

I wanted to ask why he called her by her first name, why she wasn't around, but from the way his gaze avoided mine when he mentioned her, I couldn't. There was something very wrong with this picture, something Daniel didn't want to talk about.

"Feel free to borrow any of the books you want. They should probably belong to you, anyway."

"Thanks. I'll check them out later." He turned and surveyed the room. "It looks just like Dad said."

I smiled. "There's not much you can do to fancy up a room in a barn."

He sat on the edge of the bed facing me. "Why do you live here? Everybody says you're rich, that you could live anywhere you want."

Taking a boxed pizza mix from the cabinet, I turned my back. "Hungry?"

"Sure."

I got a bowl down and dumped the flour mixture into it. "For the record, I'm not rich, just moderately well-off. And I guess I live here because it doesn't matter to me what it looks like. It's home."

He nodded, a curious wisdom filling his eyes. "It is for Dad, too. Whenever he talked about home, it was always about you and the Judge, or this room, or the Chevy. I think he stayed homesick a lot."

Moving like an old lady, I covered the bowl of dough with a towel and set it on the stove to rise, then took two sodas from the fridge and handed one to Daniel. I didn't want to talk about Nick, or even think about what his life had been like all this time, but I didn't know how to avoid it. He was Daniel's father and the one link we had in common. Of course the boy would want to talk about him.

I sat in the easy chair, my legs curled under me and sipped my soda. "If he was homesick, why didn't he come back?"

Daniel looked down at the can he was turning slowly in his hands. "He was trying to protect me. He didn't want me to know about what happened with his father."

I closed my eyes briefly. Christ, that sounded like Nick. Always the protector, always the guy responsible for everyone else. And now it was clear that Daniel felt guilty for keeping his father from coming home.

"I'm sure he only did it because he loves you, Daniel. And no matter what you hear from anyone else, your father is not the type of person who would do something like that deliberately. It happened because Frank gave him no choice."

"He told me. But that doesn't stop people from staring at us every time we go out, and none of the kids around here will talk to me."

"I don't think that has anything to do with your father. I think it's because they don't know you yet." I got up to check the dough and prepare the pizza pans. "I have an idea. How would you like to work for me part-time until school starts? Say in the evenings for a few hours? You could work in the electronics department with all the computers and video games. I bet you'll get to know the kids real fast that way. There's always a bunch hanging around."

"Honest?" His eyes lit up. "You'd do that?"

"You bet. And you'd be doing me a favor. Most of the people working for me don't know anything about computers except the basics. Why don't you drop by tomorrow and we'll get you started?"

"I'll have to ask Dad."

"Okay, but I'm sure he won't mind."

He got up and moved to where I was spreading the dough onto the pans. "You put your own toppings on?"

"Yes. They're better that way. Want to help? You can do one and I'll do the other."

While I listed the items, he took them from the fridge, and we spent the next few minutes piling ingredients on. Since my oven was so small, we had to cook them one at a time, and as we waited, Daniel regaled me with stories of the salvage yard, where, apparently, he'd been spending his days.

"You should see it. They've got this huge backhoe, the biggest one I've ever seen. It just scoops those old cars up and dumps them on a flatbed trailer as neat as anything."

Well, that would sure make a lot of people happy, I thought ruefully. The salvage yard was in worse shape now than it had been when Frank ran it. Waist-high weeds had taken over every available bare spot, with small trees growing in clumps that couldn't mask the rusty hulks of metal. The City Beautification Committee hated the salvage yard with an unstoppable passion. They had tried on several occasions to have the county confiscate it for nonpayment of taxes and plow it under, but there was a mystery surrounding the yard that no one could figure out.

Someone was paying the taxes on the place. According to the county tax assessor, every year when the taxes were due, someone would slip a plain white envelope into the night depository. All it contained was an untraceable money order and a typed note indicating that the money was to be used for taxes on the salvage yard. Foiled by this unknown person, the committee could only grit their mutual teeth and live with it. Now it looked like they were finally going to get what they wanted.

"What's your dad cleaning it up for?"

"He's going to build a garage. One that works on diesel and gasoline engines both. Bowie is going to help him run it after Lindsey leaves."

I was leaning over the oven, checking the pizza when he dropped that bombshell, and I jerked erect, burning my hand on the door in the process. I yelped, and instantly Daniel was by side, turning on the tap and shoving my hand under the cold water.

"If you get the temperature down fast, it won't blister," he said, sounding so much like Nick I could barely breathe. It wouldn't have surprised me in the least if he'd pulled out a tin of bee balm.

My teeth ground together, but the question I was fighting slipped out anyway. "Lindsey isn't going to live in Morganville?"

"No. She said there were some things she had to do here, but after that she's going to live near her mother."

Her mother? Liz had left a few years after Lindsey vanished, taking her brood with her. Rumor had it that she was living in Tunica now, working at one of the new casinos. In an odd sort of way, I missed her, although I knew Jenna had breathed a sigh of relief when she'd left.

What the hell was going on here? Nick and Lindsey had never married, Daniel acted like he barely knew his mother, Nick was building that huge house, and now Lindsey wasn't even going to live in it with him. I felt like I'd been dumped without warning into an alternate universe, one where reality was skewed beyond recognition.

I shook my head in confusion and realized Daniel was watching me, a concerned look on his face.

"Are you okay? Maybe I should get Dad."

"No!" I forced myself to regain control, and smiled. "It's fine, really." I turned the tap off and dried my hand. "See? It's not even red."

"Okay, but *I'll* get the pizza out," he said. He obviously no longer trusted my abilities around hot appliances. "It sure smells good."

It did, at that. The combined odors of mozzarella, tomato sauce, basil, and pepperoni filled the room as he carried the pan carefully to the table.

"Here." I took the cutter out of a drawer and handed it to him. "You do the honors while I get the plates."

"You use plates?" He was concentrating intently on cutting the pizzas.

I laughed. "You would too if you'd grown up with my aunt."

"Which one? Darla?"

Surprised, I stopped and glanced at him. "You know about Aunt Darla?"

"I know about your whole family."

My mouth opened, but nothing came out. It was almost a relief when someone knocked on the door, even though I was pretty sure I knew who it was.

I was right.

"I decided to see if my kid was holding you hostage," Nick said. "He's been here over an hour."

"You shouldn't have waited. I can take him home when he's ready to go."

"Hey, Dad. Look at this. I helped Alix make pizza."

Nick gave me a half-grin and squeezed through the door in spite of my arm partially blocking the entrance. "So that's what I smelled." He pulled a chair out and sat down next to Daniel. "Looks good, too. Are those pickled banana peppers on top?"

Daniel's brow wrinkled. "Yeah. I wasn't too sure about those, but Alix says she puts them on all the time. Want a soda?"

I sighed. It would seem Nick was staying for supper, whether I wanted him to or not. I couldn't throw him out on his ear with his son watching. "I'll get it." I motioned Daniel back to his seat. While I was getting the soda, I got another place setting and joined them, noting the way they were looking at the forks then at each other, amusement sparkling in their eyes.

"If you want to burn your fingers off, it's fine with me," I declared loftily. "But I'm eating in a civilized manner."

They shot me identical grins before they charged the pan like racehorses released from the starting gate.

"You'd think no one ever feeds you," I grumbled, using a spatula to slide a wedge-shaped slice onto my plate.

"Bowie does all the cooking at home," Daniel spoke around a full mouth.

"He used to be a mess hall sergeant," Nick added. "And it shows. No matter what he cooks, it all tastes the same. Like shoe leather covered in paste. I still have dreams about your Aunt Jane's fried chicken and your mother's cornbread."

"Guess what, Dad? Alix wants me to work for her. Is it okay?"

Nick frowned. "You're a little young to hold down a job, aren't you?"

I swallowed quickly. "It's won't be full-time. Just a few hours in the afternoon until school starts. It will give him a chance to meet some of the kids in town, and make a little money, too."

"He doesn't need the money."

"And I didn't imply he did." I bristled, glaring at Nick. "Anyone who works for me gets paid."

"Come on, Dad. She said I could work in the electronic department where all the kids hang out."

Nick's expression softened as he looked at his son. "Daniel, you don't know what the people in this town can be like."

"Yes, I do." His eyes, so much like Nick's, got a stubborn glint and his chin squared. "And I know they aren't ever going to change their minds about us if we don't make them. I'm not gonna hide, Dad."

Nick stayed silent while I looked at Daniel in amazement. I'd seen adults crumble under the weight of the town's disapproval. They could have taken lessons from this boy.

Finally, Nick nodded. "As long as you know what you're letting yourself in for."

"I do, and I'm not worried."

"Then I guess you've got yourself a job." Nick glanced at me. "I'll help you clean up."

"Thanks, but there's not that much. I can handle it."

"I insist. After all, you cooked."

Daniel stood. "Can I go check out the Chevy's motor?"

For once, I didn't mind being alone with Nick. "Help yourself." I smiled as Daniel hurried out the door.

Standing, I gathered the plates and carried them to the sink. "He's a great kid. You've done a good job with him."

Nick gave me a wry smile as he picked up the now empty pizza pans and followed me to the sink. "I don't think I had much to do with it. He's been that way since he was born. He's taught me more than I have him. It never occurred to me to stand up to the people in Morganville when I was growing up."

"It wouldn't have Daniel either, if he'd been raised the way you were. You gave him the confidence to stand up to them. And you were right. He's a tough kid."

"Maybe." He still looked troubled. "I just hope he's tough enough."

"If it will help, I'll keep an eye on him."

He picked up the drying towel and shook his head. "No. Let him handle it himself. It's what he wants."

My curiosity took control of my mouth as I watched him. "If you were so worried about what this would do to him, why did you come back?"

He stopped, the plate he was drying ridiculously tiny in his hands, and focused his gaze on mine. "Daniel and Lindsey talked me into it. I guess they know this is home to me, whether I like it or not. My roots are here, and always will be."

I tore my gaze away and continued washing the dishes. "Daniel feels guilty for keeping you away so long."

"I know." He went back to drying, putting the dishes away as he finished them. "I'm working on it."

"Good." I let the water out of the sink and rinsed the suds down the drain. "All done."

You can leave now, I added mentally. The way the small kitchenette was arranged, I was pinned between the stove, the sink, and Nick's body, and I wasn't enjoying it one bit. He was way too close for my liking.

He was aware of it, too. Before I could slide by him, he put one hand under my chin and forced me to look at him.

"Do you want to know the real reason I came back, Alix? It was because of you. You're my roots. Wherever you are would be home to me."

"Don't." I choked the word out, pushing with all my strength at his hand. "You can't make me believe your lies anymore, because I don't care. Do you understand me, Nick? I don't care."

He took a step back, his eyes puzzled and sad. "I don't know what's happened to you, Alix, but I never lied. Not once. And if it takes me the rest of my life, I'll *make* you care again. That's a promise."

Chapter Fifteen

ೲ

Daniel showed up at Southern Supply the next afternoon dressed for business in a white button-down shirt and khaki pants. I turned the store over to Kenny and spent the next two hours showing him around and outlining his duties, then worked with him awhile so he could get the general idea. He picked everything up so fast that I promised he could work alone the next day.

But even though I trusted him, my curiosity was killing me, and after an hour I strolled by the electronic department, doing my best to appear casual and unconcerned. Daniel was busily and enthusiastically singing the praises of a new video game to a boy who looked about his age, and two teenaged girls. The boy's attention was fixed solidly on the game, but the girls couldn't seem to take their eyes off Daniel, and I smiled.

I had hoped that since the kids his age were too young to remember Nick or Frank, they wouldn't have their parent's built-in prejudices. It looked like I was right. While naturally wary of strangers, as most kids that age are, Daniel's friendly, outgoing personality, combined with his good looks, was winning them over. Getting the kids on his side was half the battle.

After his parting shot the night I fixed pizza, I rather expected Nick to use picking Daniel up as an excuse to come by the store, but I didn't see him again for a few days. Instead, I finally got to meet Bowie Grant.

He was a bear of a man with a thick mop of steel gray hair. Only his warm, chocolate brown eyes kept his size from being intimidating. They smiled constantly, making the recipient of his gaze feel like they'd been blessed by an angel's kiss.

"It seems like I've known you and your family forever," he stated, with my hand engulfed in his. "Nick talked about all of you constantly."

I couldn't help but return his smile. Bowie was the kind of man who could coax a reaction from the sphinx. "I've heard a bit about you, too."

"Don't believe a word of it." He gave Daniel a mock scowl. "My cooking isn't nearly as bad they let on. I would like to learn how to fix southern style food, though. Maybe we can swap recipes sometime?"

"Sure. But I have to tell you, I'm not the real cook in the family. If you're serious, you need to talk to my Aunt Darla. She's the expert. There's nothing she doesn't know about cooking." I paused. "Come to think about it, there's nothing she doesn't know, period. Just be prepared to have your soul saved while she's teaching you."

I watched in fascination as he threw his head back and roared with laughter. "I've heard all about Darla," he said, wiping tears of merriment from his eyes. "I can't wait to meet her. She sounds like a hell of a woman."

Aunt Darla? *My* Aunt Darla? The man obviously enjoyed a challenge. Either that, or he was masochistic. But in spite of his apparent mental condition, I liked him.

Shortly after they left, it occurred to me that the only one in Nick's family I hadn't seen since their return was Lindsey, and if it were up to me, I'd never lay eyes on her again. My feelings toward her were so complicated that they resembled a ball of string, each emotion making up one strand, hundreds of strands twisted and knotted together until they were impossible to separate.

I suppose if I'm being honest, I have to admit there was some jealousy involved, but it was the least of what I felt. The hate was stronger. She had taken away the only man I'd ever really wanted at the time I needed him the most. She'd shared his life with him and given him a child. She'd taken the place that should have been mine.

But even the hate was overshadowed by the one thing I could never forget. She had made a fool of me. And there speaks the human ego, the voice inside us all that screams "Me! Me!" in a never-ending litany.

Because from the day I'd first met Nick in that dirty junkyard, Lindsey's hold on him was already bone deep. Because while I was happily dreaming about a life with him, she was pulling him inexorably back to her every time he left me. And I was too stupid, too innocent, to see what was happening when all the signs were right in front of me. Even if it was only in my own eyes, she had humiliated me, made me look and feel like an idiot. And while I hated Nick for what he'd done to me, it was Lindsey I truly blamed. With good reason, as I would discover before another month passed. I suspect if I had known what the next few weeks would bring, I would have packed my bags and left town right then and there.

The beginning of the end started the day after my family left for Hardy.

* * * * *

Aunt Darla and Aunt Jane had precooked enough food to last the Judge a month, but I was worried about him. Having the food available and getting him to eat it was two different things. I had checked on him Friday evening, and sure enough, he hadn't touched a thing.

"I'm not hungry." He glared at me from his easy chair in the living room.

Hands on my hips, I glared right back. "You'll eat if I have to sit on you."

"They never salt anything anymore, and they hide the shaker where I can't find it."

"You know what salt does to your blood pressure."

He rattled the newspaper and went back to reading, doing his best to hide the smile playing around his lips. "Don't know what good it does a man to live a few extra years if he can't enjoy them."

Sometimes I wondered if the Judge didn't act so cantankerous because he liked the extra attention it got him. I had to stand over him and argue down every bite he took. It made me even more determined that he was going to eat a good breakfast, so I set my alarm for dawn before I went to bed that night. I'd make him oatmeal, with raisins and brown sugar. It was his favorite, so I knew he wouldn't fight it.

The shrill clanging of my clock yanked me out of sleep Saturday morning, and I yawned while I fumbled for the green silk robe that matched my short gown. Both garments hit me mid-thigh, but I wasn't worried about dressing yet. There were no neighbors near enough to see me, and I didn't figure Nick's crew would work today.

It had rained the night before, thunder cracking so hard it shook the barn rafters. By the time I headed outside, the sun was already hot enough to make the moisture in the air feel like I'd stepped into a steam bath, and the silk gown instantly glued itself to my body.

There was a small mud hole right in front of the barn, and as I prepared to hop over it, a voice came from my left.

"Do you always run around outside like that in the mornings? Because if you do, I need to get here earlier *every* day."

I tried to stop, but my body had already gathered enough momentum to jump the puddle. I ended up wobbling on the edge a second before my foot landed squarely in the water, mud squishing between my toes.

"Damn," I muttered under my breath before glancing over my shoulder at Nick. He was standing next to the Chevy, the hood raised.

"What are you doing here?" I extracted my foot, accompanied by a sucking sound, then wiggled my toes as I tried to dislodge the mud. All I succeeded in doing was spreading it even more.

He shrugged. "I couldn't sleep, so I decided to come over and see what the Chevy needed to get it in good running order again."

The whole time he was talking, he was walking toward me. When he reached me, he took a shop towel from his back pocket, squatted, and picked up my foot. I had to grip his shoulder to keep from falling while he wiped the mud from my foot and leg.

He'd caught me at a vulnerable time, when I was still half asleep, unprepared, all my defenses down. And while I fought it, my traitorous body tingled from top to bottom at his touch, insisted on remembering what it was like to make love with him. His hands moved over my skin more like a caress than an attempt to clean, and the flesh under my palm was rock-hard with muscle. Heat radiated from him like a living thing bent on consuming me.

Mentally, I shook my head, trying to wipe away the stupor I'd fallen into. I had to clear my throat before I could speak. "I told Daniel he could work on the car. I don't remember including you in that offer."

He lifted his head, his gaze running over me until it met mine, and he made no effort to release my leg. His fingers curled just below my knee as though he intended to leave them there forever, his thumb moving in a slow circle against my skin. When he answered, his voice was husky and it scraped my nerves raw.

"Daniel is smart, but he won't be fifteen until the end of January. He can change the oil and the plugs, but there's still a lot he doesn't know about mechanics."

I pulled my leg from his grasp and he stood. In a way, that was even worse. Less than an inch separated his body from mine. "Why are you doing this?" I was getting desperate and it showed in my voice.

"You know why." His eyes were molten, a shade I understood very well, even though I denied the memories with all my strength.

"No, damn it, I don't! You've got Lindsey. Why can't you just leave me alone?"

His hands moved to my arms and he leaned closer. "I don't want Lindsey. I never have. I want you."

Finally–finally, my anger surged to the forefront, protecting me from the unwanted feelings that were stirring to life. I wrenched away from him, took a step back. "Do you really think I'm still that gullible, Nick? I can do the math as well as the next person. If Daniel's birthday is the end of January that means you were going straight from my bed to hers." My laugh was tinged with hysteria. "Do you know, I used to worry about you? I was afraid you weren't getting enough rest, working all day and then spending the nights with me. Looks like you had a lot more stamina than I gave you credit for."

His shoulders slumped. "Don't. Please. It wasn't like you think."

I took another step away from him. "Oh? Then what was it like?"

When he didn't answer, I turned toward the barn. "I guess that says it all. Stay away from me, Nick. I'm not playing your games anymore."

I marched to my room, back straight and head held high. No matter how my body might be protesting, he wasn't going to get to me again. I wouldn't allow it, wouldn't even permit myself to think about it. There was the Judge's breakfast to make, and now I had to shower and change before I went to the house.

Nick was still there when I finished dressing, leaning over the Chevy's motor, but I ignored him this time. That didn't stop me from feeling his gaze following my progress across the yard. It was a relief when I stepped into the kitchen and closed the door behind me.

Moving to the coffeemaker, I filled it with the decaf my aunts kept on hand for the Judge, then added water and hit the on button. It had made its first gurgle when I tilted my head, listening intently.

The Judge was an early riser, and I was late. I had expected him to be up and dressed by now, but the house was unnaturally silent. The hair on my arms popped erect and a shiver ran down my spine.

I tried to convince myself it was my imagination working overtime as I forced my feet to move. That it was only my worry about the Judge that sent an eerie feeling of emptiness through the house.

I was wrong.

He was sitting on the floor at the bottom of the stairs, slumped over against the first step. His eyes were closed, one side of his face twisted into an unrecognizable mask. His left hand was on his lap, curled until it looked like a claw.

I don't remember screaming or moving, but I must have done both. When Nick charged into the hall I was down on my knees, trying to lift the Judge's body, cradle it close.

"He's dead," I moaned. "Oh, God. I let him die."

Nick's hands were moving, touching the Judge's neck, his wrist. "He's not dead, he had a stroke. We have to get him to the hospital."

It took some effort, but he pried me away, then lifted the Judge in his arms as though he weighed little more than a child. "Alix!" His voice was sharp. "I need you to open the door for me."

His tone worked. Frantically, I scrambled to my feet and ran through the kitchen, holding the door wide while he carried the Judge out, my gaze locked on the pale, contorted face of the man who had raised me.

"We're taking my truck."

I was in no shape to argue. Pulling the passenger door open, I waited as he lowered the Judge to the seat, then climbed in after, putting my arms around my grandfather to steady and support his limp body.

"Hang on."

The trip seemed to take forever, even though we must have made it in less than fifteen minutes. There was a blurred sense of speed, of swaying as we dodged traffic, and I vaguely remember Nick talking to the hospital on his cell phone, letting them know we were coming. But all my attention was focused on the Judge.

"We're almost there," I whispered in his ear. "Don't you die, damn it. If you do, I'll never speak to you again." I was hanging on by a thread, in shock with fear. My body trembled continuously and I couldn't stop it.

They were waiting for us as the truck slid to a stop in front of the emergency room doors, waiting to take the Judge away from me. I chased them inside, into a small cubicle that was suddenly full of people.

Someone in blue scrubs stopped me, blocked my entrance. "How long has he been like this?"

It was Nick who answered. "Not too long, I don't think. He's dressed. It must have happened when he was coming downstairs."

"What kind of medication is he taking?"

"Alix?" Nick put his hand on my arm.

Absently, I told them the name of the blood pressure medication the Judge was on. I leaned to one side, trying to watch what the nurses were doing to my grandfather. "Is he going to be okay?"

"We'll know more later. There's a family room right around the corner. Why don't you wait in there?"

I shook my head. "I want to stay with him."

"You'll only be in the way." Nick put his arm around me, used it to guide me down the hall. "Come on. They'll let us know as soon they find out anything."

The waiting room was large and decorated in a style obviously meant to offer comfort, the furniture in warm beige tones, large and overstuffed. But I couldn't force myself to sit down. I simply stood in the middle of the room, unable to move once Nick released me.

"Should we call your family?" He gestured toward a courtesy phone on the end table near the couch.

In addition to shaking, my teeth were chattering. I ground them together fiercely and tried to think. "Cody. Call Cody. He'll know what to do. And Jenna. Tell her to run by the house and turn the coffeemaker off."

It seemed to take him a long time, but I still hadn't moved when he finished. "Everyone is on their way. Cody will try to reach your father before he heads in this direction."

I nodded. "Thank you. You don't have to stay. Cody can give me a ride home if I need it."

His jaw tightened. "I'm not leaving you here alone. Besides, I love the Judge, too. He's the closest thing to a real father I've ever had."

A sob welled up inside me, closed my throat until I couldn't breath. "Oh, God. I can't lose him. He's all I have left."

Instantly, Nick was beside me, leading me to the couch, pulling me down on his lap. His arms went around me and he rocked gently. "Ssh. He's going to be fine."

For the first time since he'd come home, I stopped fighting him. Instead, I buried my face in his neck and soaked him with my tears, let him soothe me, completely unaware that I'd just allowed him to put a huge chink in my defenses. A chink that would gradually widen until all the walls I'd built so carefully crumbled into dust. I'm not sure I would have cared even if I had known. At that moment, I would have snuggled up to the devil himself if he'd offered comfort.

"How can you love him after what he did to you?" My voice was quivery, punctuated by hiccups.

"What did he do to me?" His hands ran over my back.

"Oh, God, Nick. It was his fault they sent you away. He forced the sheriff to make you join the army. If you'd fought them, you could have stayed here, cleared your name. You wouldn't have had to leave."

"He did what he thought was right, Alix." His voice was low, soothing. "He was trying to keep me from getting hurt, maybe even going to jail. There was no guarantee that I'd have gotten off if it had come to a trial. He didn't want me to go through that. Besides, as it turned out, sending me away was one of the best things that could have happened to me. If he hadn't, I'd probably still be working at a gas station, barely making enough money to survive. Did you know he was paying the property taxes on the salvage yard?"

"The Judge?" I don't know why I hadn't realized it before. It made perfect sense.

"Yes. I came home expecting the salvage yard to be gone, confiscated because I hadn't paid the taxes on it. I think I *wanted* it to be gone, didn't want any reminders of my life there. Instead, it was still the same, waiting for me like the monster under my bed. The Judge knew I was going to have face it and deal with the past before I moved on. He was right, as usual, in more ways than one. I'd told Daniel about how I grew up, but I don't think he really understood everything that happened until he saw the place with his own eyes. Cleaning up the salvage yard and turning it into something good is just what I needed."

His chest lifted as he took a deep breath. "There's only one thing about that time I really regret."

"What?" I lifted a shaky hand to wipe the moisture from my cheeks, but I didn't move from his lap.

"Pushing you away," he said quietly. "That was the biggest mistake I've ever made. But I was just a kid and scared half to death. I was trying to be noble, to do the right thing, when all I really wanted was to die at the thought of never seeing you again."

I didn't believe him, of course. Couldn't believe him. Because if he were telling me the truth, why had he gotten Lindsey pregnant? Why had he sent for her instead of me? But I also couldn't deal with all the anger my questions would bring right now. Not while the Judge was fighting for his life. And I couldn't continue accepting Nick's comfort feeling the way I did.

Straightening, I pushed away from him and slid off his lap just as Cody rushed into the room. Nick's call must have gotten him out of bed. It looked like he'd jumped into the first clothes he'd came across and his hair was rumpled, as though he hadn't taken the time to comb it.

We hugged each other hard for a long second before he spoke.

"How is he?"

"I don't know. We're still waiting to hear something. Did you reach the rest of the family?"

"There was no answer at Dad's, but I left a message on his machine and told him to page me when they got home. I also called the local police. They know Dad and they're going to look for him."

He glanced over my shoulder, his expression wary in spite of his words. "Nick, thanks for handling everything and taking care of Alix. I owe you one."

"Don't worry about it. I'm glad I was there."

From the door, someone cleared his throat and we all turned toward the man standing there. He looked young to me, dressed in the dark blue ER uniform he wore, but his name tag indicated he was a doctor. Cody put his arm around me as though to protect me from any bad news we were about to hear.

"I'm Doctor Abbott. Are you the family of Mr. French?"

No one had ever called the Judge "Mr." before and it took me a moment to realize who he was talking about.

"We're his grandchildren," Cody said. "How is he?"

"Your grandfather is lucky to be alive. The stroke was a bad one, but we've got him stabilized for now. We're going to keep him in the emergency room a few more hours until we're sure it's safe to move him, then transfer him to ICU."

Relief left me limp. If it hadn't been for Cody's support I think my legs would have collapsed. "Then he's going to make it?"

"No promises, but I'd say his chances are looking pretty good. We did a CT scan and then started him on a new drug that can reduce the damage caused by strokes if the patient receives it fast enough. It's too soon to tell if it's working yet, but I have high hopes for his recovery."

"Can we see him?"

"Only for a minute, and one visitor at a time. He's pretty much out of it right now."

If I hadn't had the doctor's assurances, the sight of my grandfather would have driven me to panic. The Judge was the strongest man I'd ever known, but now he barely made a wrinkle under the sheet, and tubes and wires were everywhere. Half a dozen machines surrounded him with beeps and gurgles and hisses, and the smell of antiseptic stung my nose.

Trying not to disturb anything, I touched his cheek, needing desperately to feel his warm skin under my fingers.

The left side of his face was still distorted, drawn, but his right eye partially opened, focused on me, and the bewilderment reflected there broke my heart.

"You had a stroke," I told him, praying he'd understand. "You're in the hospital, but the doctor says you're going to be fine. Nick and Cody are here, and the rest of the family is on the way."

When his eye drifted shut again, I stayed another minute, telling myself he had heard me, that I really had seen the confusion leave his gaze.

Jenna was waiting in the hall as Cody slipped by me into the Judge's cubicle. "He's going to be fine," she whispered, hugging me. "You know he's too stubborn to die."

"I'm glad you're here." I wiped my eyes yet again, feeling a bit like a faucet that had sprung a leak. I didn't want to cry, but I couldn't seem to help myself. My emotions were too near the surface.

"Hey, you'd do the same for me." She dug in her purse and handed me a tissue. "Now, why don't we go to the waiting room and I'll buy you a cup of coffee."

"Okay." I blew my nose, then followed her, Nick walking next to me. When Cody joined us a few minutes later, he was quiet and shaken, his complexion two shades paler than normal.

"Christ," he said, rubbing his hands over his face. "You know it's bad, but it doesn't really hit you until you see him."

Perversely, seeing Cody so upset made me take a step back and pull myself together. Crying wasn't going to help the Judge, and my family needed me to be strong. Handing him the coffee Jenna had given me, I rubbed his back in a soothing motion. "The medication will work, Cody. It has to."

"God, I hope you're right. I don't know how he'll be able to stand it if it doesn't."

We were talking in low tones, Nick watching us from across the room, when Jenna suddenly stiffened. "What the hell is she doing here?"

I glanced toward the door and every muscle in my body tensed. Lindsey hovered in the entrance, her gaze going from me to Nick and back again.

She had changed. In spite of the baggy clothes that looked as though they came straight from a thrift store, she was one of the most beautiful women I'd ever seen. Unlike most people whose hair darkens as they reach adulthood, hers was still the same white-blonde it had been when we were children. She wore it up, twisted into a loose swirl from which strands escaped to frame her huge blue eyes, eyes that gave the impression of some indefinable sadness and vulnerability. Anger filled me, held me in an icy grip impossible to break.

I stood slowly, aware that Nick was frowning, moving to intercept her. But she was closer than he was, and she reached me first, a tentative smile on her lips.

"Alix. I heard about your grandfather. I'm so sorry. Is there anything I can do to help?"

Her voice was soft and hesitant, and I realized it was the first time I'd ever heard her speak. At the same time, I also realized Cody was staring at her with the dazed expression of a man who'd been hit in the head with a two-by-four. It scared me, fueled not only my anger but all my protective instincts. She already had her claws in Nick, I'd be damned if I let her do the same to my cousin.

"Yes, there is something you can do." My tone was as cold as the blood running through my veins. "Get out of my sight."

"Alix, please. I know this isn't the place, but sometime soon, we need to talk." Her expression was pleading with me, but I didn't care.

I turned on Nick furiously. "Get her away from me. Now. Maybe I couldn't stop you from coming back, and maybe I can't stop you from building a house where you are, but there's one thing I can do. If either of you ever come near me again, I'll press harassment charges. I'll do whatever it takes to get you thrown in jail. And that, Nick, is *my* promise to both of you."

Chapter Sixteen

Some of the greatest philosophers through the ages have said that through adversity springs courage and strength, but sometimes all it brings is more pain. I think that scene with Lindsey was when I first suspected just how badly Nick had damaged my armor. The sight of him and Lindsey, together in the same room, was almost more than I could bear. Now I know it was a deep hurt, a soul-searing pain that made me react the way I did, but at the time, I meant every single word.

Nick must have known that as well while his gaze held mine. His eyes reflected a multitude of emotions—sorrow, pain, regret, anger—and a quietly determined stubbornness. Without a word, he took Lindsey's arm and pulled her from the room, but I knew I hadn't seen the last of him. He would call my bluff.

"Are you out of your mind?" Cody was glaring at me. "How could you say something like that to Nick after he saved the Judge's life? Not to mention treating that woman so badly when she was only trying to be kind."

Jenna bristled, her glare heated as she put herself between Cody and me. "Until you know the whole story, stuff a sock in it, Cody. Alix has every right to treat them the way she did. And she showed a hell of a lot more restraint than I would have. If I'd been in her shoes, that hussy would have left here bald."

With a gesture of disgust, Cody left the room, and I could just picture him catching up with Nick and Lindsey, apologizing for my behavior. And making sure he was introduced to Lindsey while he was at it.

Wearily, I sank onto the couch and Jenna sat down next to me. "Hey, I know it doesn't seem like it now, but everything will work out."

"Will it?" I scrubbed at my forehead. "Christ, Jenna. It feels like I'm falling apart one piece at a time. I don't know what's wrong with me lately."

"I do." She took my hand. "You're ending a fifteen-year marriage, your mother barely speaks to you, your grandfather had a stroke, and you've never stopped loving Nick."

I yanked my hand from hers, the fingers automatically curling into a fist. "I do not love Nick. I hate him."

"No, you only think you do. Alix, the opposite of love isn't hate, it's indifference. And you couldn't be indifferent to him if your life depended on it."

"Damn it, Jenna. Stop analyzing me."

She held up her hands in surrender. "Okay, okay. But sooner or later you'll have to face the truth."

My chin went up stubbornly. "No, I won't."

"Has anyone ever told you you're a lot like your Aunt Darla?"

My lips twitched. I couldn't help it. "No, and if 'anyone' knows what's good for them, they won't tell me now."

"That's better." She grinned. "I was starting to think your face had frozen in a permanent frown. You know what you need?" She didn't give me a chance to answer. "You need to have some fun. Wednesday is ladies' night at the roadhouse. How about the two of us take a night off to howl?"

"I don't know...it depends on how the Judge is doing."

"He's going to be fine, and I won't take no for an answer. Besides, isn't your divorce final next week?"

I did some rapid calculations and felt a ripple of surprise go through me. "Thursday. It should be final Thursday."

"There 'ya go. A reason to celebrate." She hesitated. "You are glad it's over, aren't you? No second thoughts?"

"No second thoughts." I took a deep breath. "It just sort of slipped up on me, I guess. I'll have to let you know about Wednesday later."

Cody's reappearance put a stop to the conversation. He took a chair across the room from us, his expression thoughtful even through he didn't speak. Jenna stayed until they moved the Judge to ICU and got him settled, then left to keep an appointment.

When the doctor talked to us again, he was cautiously optimistic. It seemed the new drug was going to work after all, and I saw evidence of this myself when I visited the Judge later. His face had relaxed, looked more normal now, and his left hand was open, lying on the bed instead of curled tightly to his body.

Not long after that, my panicked family rushed in. It took a while to get them calmed down, and they each had to see the Judge before they believed he was going to make it. And then they took over. I sat in a corner of the large ICU waiting room, listening as they devised a rotating schedule of who would stay at the hospital with the Judge during the days to come, and who would stay home to receive sympathy calls from friends and neighbors.

I, of course, was not included in the duties. But that didn't mean Mama was going to ignore me. Maybe I had forgotten my divorce would be final next week, but she hadn't. It wasn't long before she joined me, a look of determination on her face, and a feeling of resignation swept over me when she spoke.

"Alix, you have to put a stop to this nonsense while there's still time. Hugh is a good man. He cares about you. It's insane to throw away fifteen years of marriage for no reason."

I forced myself to stay calm. "There is a reason. I don't love him. He doesn't love me."

"You've only hit a rocky patch, dear." She patted my knee. "It happens in all marriages. I'm sure you can work through it if you try."

"He's had one affair after the other since the day we married, Mama. Am I supposed to keep looking the other way?"

She hesitated. "He's a man, Alix. Sometimes they make mistakes. But I'm sure if you talked to him, let him know how you feel, he'd stop. You know I only want what's best for you."

"No, Mama." I stood. "You want what's best for you. You like having a daughter married to the richest, most prestigious family in the county. And if that means I have to be miserable the rest of my life, well, that's just too bad for me, isn't it? You've made it real clear that you care more about what Helena thinks than you care about me. You've turned your back on me when I needed you the most. So don't sit there and tell me you want what's best for me."

I was proud of myself. I hadn't raised my voice a single time. But I couldn't be sure I'd remain that calm if she pushed me. Head high, I walked out of the room and left her sitting there, face pale.

It wasn't until I was standing on the sidewalk in front of the hospital that I remembered I didn't have my car with me. I hadn't even stopped to grab my purse, so I didn't have the money for a cab or a phone call.

I was trying to figure out what to do when Cody came through the doors behind me. "Come on. I'll take you home."

Silently, I followed him down the hill to the parking lot and climbed into his truck. As soon as we were on the highway, he glanced at me.

"Sorry I came down so hard on you this morning. It's just that I've never seen you react that way to anyone before."

I nodded. "I supposed you apologized to them on my behalf."

"It seemed like the right thing to do. But you might be interested to know Nick was giving her holy hell when I caught up with them. I didn't hear the whole thing, but the gist of it was that he was pissed off because she'd hurt you. 'Again' was the word he used. Said all she'd done was make things worse, and that now wasn't the time for confessions. She looked like a little girl getting a scolding from her daddy."

"Stay away from her, Cody."

He took his attention off the road long enough to glance at me again, one brow arched in question. "What are you talking about?"

"Don't play innocent with me. I saw the expression on your face when she walked in. I'm telling you to stay away from her. You don't have any idea what she's really like."

"And you do?"

"Yes. She's so tangled up with Nick that neither of them will ever get lose."

"Funny, but I didn't get the impression they had that kind of relationship."

"They have a son. She's lived with Nick almost since the day he left." I twisted on the seat to face him. "Look, you warned me about getting involved with someone again before the ink was dry on my divorce decree. Now I'm returning the favor. Lindsey isn't what she seems to be, and I don't want you to get hurt."

He was silent for a long minute. "Are you going to tell me what really went on fifteen years ago?"

I straightened, turned to gaze out the window. "You know what happened."

"I thought I did, but I'm beginning to realize I don't even know half of it."

"Please, Cody. Stay out of it. This is my problem, not yours."

His jaw tightened, and I could almost see the sheriff emerge. "Just tell me one thing. Did Nick really kill his father in self-defense?"

"Yes. Frank abused him his whole life. There were plenty of witnesses that can testify to that much. I've never doubted that Frank went after him that night."

"Okay. I'll drop it. For now, anyway." He pulled up in front of the barn and stopped. "But if you need me for anything, anything at all, call me."

I leaned across the seat and kissed his cheek. "Thanks. I will."

Standing in front of the barn, I watched him leave, waving when he reached the end of the drive. After the day I'd gone through, my insides were coiled like a spring wound too tight. I needed to relax, and I needed something to take my mind off everything that had happened.

What I didn't need was to find Nick waiting in my room. He was sitting in the easy chair, ankle crossed over his knee, a book open on his lap. A bag sat on the table, and the odor of barbequed ribs drifting from it made my stomach growl in anticipation.

He looked up when I opened the door, one corner of his lips curving into a smile. "Before you start yelling for the cops, I think I should point out that it's not illegal to talk to someone."

"How about trespassing?" I slammed the door behind me. My voice may have been sarcastic, but I didn't have the energy to fight right now. All I wanted was some peace and quiet, a chance to settle my rattled nerves.

"That would work if the barn actually belonged to you. But since it doesn't, your family would have to press charges, and they aren't here." He closed the book and stood. "Even if they were, it wouldn't matter to me. Besides, if I know you, you haven't had a bite to eat all day."

He was right. I didn't have a legal leg to stand on. And as I watched him take the containers out of the bag, my resistance faded. There was coleslaw, fries, and baked beans to go with the ribs, along with warm, buttered Texas-style toast.

"You aren't fighting fair," I grumbled, moving closer to the table. He had even supplied the paper plates, napkins and sodas.

"I don't plan on fighting, period. You're doing enough of that for both of us." He filled a plate to overflowing and put it in front of me. "Sit."

Lowering myself to the chair, I took a bite and closed my eyes in bliss. "Still trying to take care of me, Nick?"

"I don't see anyone else doing the job. Why shouldn't it be me?"

My eyes snapped open, and I searched for the anger that should have been there, but wasn't. "I'm a big girl now. I don't need anyone to take care of me."

"There's a part of everyone that needs to be taken care of. Denying it exists doesn't change the truth, it only makes you very lonely."

Curiosity, always my downfall, overtook my common sense. "Even you?"

His smile was wry. "Especially me. I was so busy taking care of everyone else that it took me a while to realize what that big hole inside me was. No matter what I did or how many people I surrounded myself with, I still felt alone."

"Uh-huh." I didn't look at him. "And I'm sure there were plenty of women eager to help you out with that problem, even if Lindsey couldn't."

"Lindsey didn't live with me. And if that's your roundabout way of asking me if I dated, the answer is yes, occasionally." He stirred his coleslaw idly with a fork, thinking. "It was a waste of time and effort. Not that they weren't nice women, but they didn't have what I wanted, what I needed."

I took a sip of my soda, but it couldn't erase the sting of jealousy from my throat. "Do you even know what you want?

I seem to remember you had a little problem in that area once before."

He put his fork down and leaned back in the chair, his gaze holding mine. "Oh, I always knew what I wanted. I just didn't think I'd ever get it, didn't think I *deserved* to get it. I was the son of the town drunk, the guy who was raised in a junkyard. I was terrified the filth would rub off on the best thing that ever happened to me. And because of my own insecurity, I ended up hurting both of us. If I had it to do over again, I'd change a lot of things. But I don't, and you have every reason to hate me for leaving you. The only thing I can do is ask you to forgive me."

"Sorry, Nick. Too little, too late." With a calm I was far from feeling, I continued eating, forcing down food that had turned to sawdust. But suddenly there was a flurry of doubt in my mind. Was I wrong? Was it possible that Nick really had loved me?

The thought was more than I could bear. Because if it were true, then everything I'd forced myself to believe was a lie. And if I couldn't blame Katie's death on him, I would have to take on the responsibility, myself. Desperately, I slammed the door on that thought. It wasn't true. Hadn't I compiled the evidence against him, bit by bit?

"What the hell happened to you?" he murmured. "Why are you trying so damn hard to convince me that the Alix I knew doesn't exist anymore?"

"It's simply a fact. I'm not trying to convince you of anything." My voice was still calm, but my hands were shaking.

"Yes, you are. You have to work too hard at repairing these walls you've built for it to be real. I saw you with Daniel, remember. My Alix is still in there, and I *will* find a way to get her out."

"Don't bother." I pushed the food away and stood to clean off the table. I had to keep busy, keep myself from looking at him. "She died a long time ago and she's never coming back. That's the way I want it. She was a naïve child who thought love could solve anything, who believed in happily-ever-after endings, and that justice and honor always win out. She believed in the integrity of others and never questioned their motives. She didn't stand a chance and she's better off dead."

Nick's face went pale as I talked. "Christ, Alix. I knew I'd hurt you, but I didn't realize it would be this bad. I've got a lot to answer for, don't I?"

"More than you'll ever know." I tried to keep my smile chilly, but an image of Katie flashed through my mind and destroyed my equilibrium. The pain was worse than it had been in a long time, and I swayed. I had to be right about him. Dear God, I didn't know how I would go on living if I weren't.

He stood, caught my shoulders in his hands, and forced me to look at him. "I have to try, damn it. I've never stopped loving you. I won't give up that easily."

"Love?" The laugh that bubbled out of me verged on panic. "Once I would have given my life to hear you say that. But you don't even know the meaning of the word. People who love you don't tell you to get on with your life without them. People who love you don't sleep with someone else when they should be with you. People who love you don't leave you alone to have—" I stopped abruptly, horrified at how close I'd come to telling him about Katie after all the promises I'd made to myself.

He was staring down at me intently, his expression grim. "Leave you alone to what? Come on, Sweetheart. Scream at me, curse me, whatever it takes. You have to get it all out."

All my energy drained away and I closed my eyes, leaned my forehead against his chest. "I can't do this."

His arms closed around me, his lips moved over my hair. "It's okay," he whispered. "I understand. We've got lots of time to work it all out."

I didn't resist when his mouth traveled down my cheek, settled on mine. There was no passion in the kiss. It was sweet and gentle, and I could feel the ends of the frayed bonds that had once stretched between us begin a slow mending. It was a kiss that offered healing, if I could only give in to it. And for a second, I did. For that one brief second, I let go and returned the pressure, let myself pretend that nothing had changed.

But it had taken me fifteen long years to reach the point where I now stood. No kiss, not even one of Nick's, could change what I'd become. I wasn't a sleeping princess and he wasn't my prince. We were two ordinary people who had been shaped by the life we'd led.

It did, however, accomplish one thing I hadn't expected. Even as I stepped away from him, I knew I had to put an end to the anger. Keeping it bottled up was easy when I didn't have to see him every day, talk to him. But since he'd been back, I'd felt as though someone had thrown a match into a can of gasoline. If I didn't get it under control it would destroy me, burn me up from the inside out.

"Are you okay?" His hand trembled when he touched my face, ran his thumb over my lips, and again I was surprised. He didn't act like a man who'd been lying for his own ends. He acted like the old Nick, the one I'd loved with every ounce of my being.

I nodded, confusion making me weak. "I'll be fine, but I think you'd better go for now."

"Maybe you're right." He lowered his hand. "But I'm scared to death that if I leave, the next time I see you we'll be right back where we started."

I hesitated, then took the plunge. "How about if we call a truce for now?"

"Just for now?"

"It's the best I can do, Nick. I have a lot to think about."

"I guess you do." He walked to the door, then stopped with his hand on the knob. "But while you're at it, think about this. I love you. There hasn't been a single day in the last fifteen years that I haven't regretted not telling you when I had the chance. That house I'm working on next door? It's never been for me. I'm building it for you. Without you there to share it, it will never be anything but an empty pile of boards."

I don't know how long I stood there, staring at the spot where he'd been, my mind whirling like a wisp of straw caught in a wind devil. He'd told me the truth. I knew it on a level I couldn't explain. But there were so many unanswered questions, so much I didn't understand. And now I no longer trusted my own judgment. I needed someone to talk to, someone who could be objective and reasonable. I needed Jenna.

This had felt like the longest day of my life, but a glance at the clock showed me it was only eight-thirty, not even full dark yet. Jenna should be home by now.

Grabbing my keys, I climbed in the Chevy and headed across town.

* * * * *

A few years after she'd started working for Mid-Delta Real Estate, Jenna had a bought a little house on the outskirts of town. She'd gotten it dirt cheap because it needed a lot of repairs. But over the years, she'd turned it into what I laughingly called her "gingerbread" house. It looked like something out of a fairytale with its brightly painted, scalloped trim, its overflowing gardens complete with fountains and birdbaths, and its distinct air of femininity. And the inside was every bit as frilly as the outside. No doubt about it. The house had brought out a hidden streak of domesticity in Jenna that was the direct opposite of the cool businesswoman she became during the day.

Relief washed over me when I saw light spilling from the windows. She was home.

Parking the Chevy behind her Lincoln, I got out and followed the brick path around to the back. The kitchen door was open, the framed screen door keeping out mosquitoes and letting in fresh air. I rapped twice, then waited, head tilted, listening. From somewhere inside, I heard the low sound of her voice. She must be on the phone.

Not wanting to disturb her, I eased the door open and stepped into the kitchen, leaning against the counter until there was a lull in the conversation. Then I raised my voice. "Jenna?"

For a split second there was nothing but silence, then I heard a mad scrambling. "Alix? Is that you? Hang on. I'll be right there."

She was still belting a robe around her waist when she entered the kitchen, and her hair was in wild disarray. It was so different from her normal, impeccable appearance that I couldn't resist teasing her a little.

"Caught you, didn't I? All this time you've been having a wild fling right under my nose. Well, the game's up. You might as well confess."

"What?" The blood drained from her face, leaving her eyes nearly black in the surrounding whiteness. One hand clutched the robe together at her throat.

"Hey, I was only joking." I steadied her with one hand. "Are you okay? Has something happened?"

"No, of course not." Her smile was wan. "You just took me by surprise. I wasn't expecting anyone tonight."

"I should have called first." I was still a bit puzzled by her reaction.

"Don't be silly. I never call you before I come by." She walked to the sink and filled a pot with water. "Give me a second to put some tea on and then you can tell me what prompted this visit."

I sat down at her table, propped my elbow on the wooden surface and sighed. "Nick prompted this visit."

She glanced uneasily at the door leading to the living room, then closed it before joining me. "Nick?"

"Yes. He was waiting on me when I got home from the hospital this evening. God, Jenna, I'm so confused. I don't know what to believe anymore."

I paused at a muted noise from the other room. "I swear, that sounded like your front door closing. Are you sure I didn't interrupt something?"

"Positive. One of the shrubs thumps the house when the wind blows. Go ahead with what you were telling me." She was visibly more relaxed now, and I decided I'd imagined her earlier case of nerves.

"He told me he loves me, Jenna, that he's building the house for me. One minute I really think he means it, then the next I start remembering everything he did to me. I feel like I'm going crazy."

She crossed her arms on the table. "Why don't you talk to him, ask him about Lindsey and everything that happened? If he does love you, he'll tell you the truth."

"I tried. This morning before I found the Judge. He said I didn't understand about him and Lindsey, so I told him to explain it to me. He didn't answer."

"And you let him get away with that?" Her tone was disbelieving.

"I was upset."

"That's no excuse. Alix, the only way you're going to settle this, good or bad, is to force the issue. You can't keep going like you have been, shutting everyone out, barely existing."

Gloom settled over me like a shroud and I slumped in the chair. "It's useless. The fact is, he got Lindsey pregnant, then dumped me for her. Forcing him to talk about it isn't going to change a thing. So what if Lindsey didn't live with him? He still left me alone and pregnant."

"Whoa!" She held up one hand. "What makes you think Lindsey didn't live with him?"

"That's what he told me. And Daniel doesn't seem to think of her as his mother. He doesn't seem to care much about her at all. Not like he would if she'd lived with them. He even calls her by her first name."

"And Nick said you didn't understand." She looked thoughtful. "Is it possible that Nick isn't Daniel's father?"

The smile I gave her was wry. "You obviously haven't seen him. He's Nick's son, all right. Seeing him is like seeing Nick at that age. They even act alike."

"Okay, scratch that idea. But think about it like this. Even if he did sleep with Lindsey, maybe it only happened once. Anyone can make a mistake, right? Couldn't you forgive him?"

I shook my head. "Maybe. If that were all it was. But how can I ever forgive him for Katie, Jenna? How can I see him and not remember that my daughter would be alive if he hadn't left us?"

She reached across the table and took my hand firmly in hers. "Alix, you aren't going to like this, but it's not Nick's fault that Katie died. It's not anyone's fault. Blame him for leaving you, blame him for not being there when you needed him so desperately, but don't blame him for Katie."

"I have to." My voice was thick with grief. "He could have saved her."

"How? How could he have saved her?"

"I don't know!" I yanked my hand from her grasp and covered my eyes.

"Listen to me." She leaned forward and touched my arm. "You loved Katie so much because she *was* Nick's child. When she died it ripped you in half. Your family, bless their hearts, did what they thought was best for you, but they never gave you a chance to grieve. So you tucked it all away inside until it almost drove you crazy. Whether consciously or unconsciously, you protected yourself the only way you could. You tried to justify Katie's death by blaming Nick. But you know the truth, Alix. Even if he'd been standing in the room with her, Katie would have died."

"No." I was shaking so hard the table rattled.

"Yes." Her voice was gentle. "You'll never get over Katie's death until you can admit that it was only a senseless tragedy. Sometimes there just isn't a reason for the things that happen, no matter how much we search for one. You had her for six months, Alix. Would you rather have never known her, loved her?"

"No. God, no. Every minute I had with her was precious." Tears filled our eyes, spilled over until our visions blurred.

"Then concentrate on those minutes. Do you remember the first time she crawled? She had the most surprised look on her face."

And so, when I'd come to talk about Nick, I ended up talking about Katie. Talking about her for the first time since she'd died. For hours, we sat over tea gone cold and forgotten in our cups, and we laughed and cried as we talked about my daughter. And finally, after all those empty years, I began to heal.

Chapter Seventeen

ॐ

I was in a strange mood the next morning as I got ready for work; kind of numb and drained, and yet more at peace with myself than I could ever remember being. It was an odd combination, but one I welcomed. Nothing was going to ruffle me today, not even the call from my mother, asking me to stop by her house on my way home that evening. It was way past time for me to have a long talk with her.

Picking up the invoices I had neglected over the weekend, I walked out to the Chevy. As I went around to the passenger side of the car and put the paperwork on the front seat, I was aware of the sounds coming from next door. Circular saws buzzed, hammers pounded, and raucous male voices filled the air. And for the first time, I didn't ignore them.

I closed the car door and turned to study the progress they were making on the house. It was coming along nicely. The slab had been poured, and Southern Supply had delivered the first load of material Friday. One of the outside walls already stood erect, the bare bones of what would soon become a real house.

A smile curved my lips as a streak of pure possessiveness shot through me. It was all I could do not to go over there and start giving orders. Until I saw Nick and forgot all about the house.

He was standing on the slab, long legs braced apart, hands on his hips, a leather tool belt slung low around his waist. And he was watching me. In spite of the distance between us, I saw him wink, and my heart hit my ribs with a thunderous crash.

I hadn't reached the place yet where I was ready to confront him about the past, or to completely forgive him, but that didn't mean I was blind. He was the most gorgeous hunk of male it had ever been my privilege to stare at, and darn his hide, he knew exactly what I was thinking. His smile turned to a smug grin so full of satisfaction, that I couldn't help myself. I laughed. God, I'd missed him, missed having someone to flirt with, to laugh with, and to talk about everyday things with. All the things I'd never had with Hugh.

That wayward thought sobered me a bit, and with a final wave in Nick's direction, I climbed into the car and headed for the store. I felt too good to let thoughts of Hugh spoil it for me. As a matter of fact, I was going to call Jenna when I got to work and tell her I'd meet her at the roadhouse Wednesday night.

I also called the hospital to check on the Judge, and to my delight, he talked to me for a few seconds before Aunt Jane took the phone away from him. "How is he really?" I asked.

She laughed. "He's fine. They moved him out of ICU this morning into a private room, and he's already giving the nurses a hard time."

"Has the doctor been in?"

"He just left. He says there's still weakness in the Judge's arm, but they think with some occupational therapy he'll regain full use of it. If he keeps improving this way, they'll let him go home by the end of the week."

The rest of the day went by in a rush, and I spent it catching up on paperwork, skipping lunch so I could keep working. It was almost quitting time when Kenny thumped on the glass between my office and the customer service counter. When I looked up, he gestured toward the front and I saw Nick. He'd lost the tool belt, but otherwise he looked just as he had this morning.

I took the time to make one last entry in the books, then stood and walked to the counter.

"Do you always look so serious when you work?" he asked with a smile.

"Only when there's math involved." I returned his smile. "What are you doing here?"

Kenny had started edging toward the door as soon as I appeared, but when he realized I wasn't going to take Nick's head off, he hesitantly went back to work.

Nick gestured toward some boxes stacked beside him. "I had to pick up some nails for the nail gun, and since it's so close to quitting time, I thought I'd save Bowie a trip and give Daniel a ride home."

I glanced at the clock. "He should be here in a few minutes."

"How's he doing?"

"Wonderful." I grinned. "We've had more girls buying games since he started than ever before."

"There did seem to be a crowd when I went by that aisle earlier." He looked mildly disgruntled. "I hope all the attention doesn't go to his head."

"It won't. He's too much like you."

"Yeah, well, I don't remember hordes of girls chasing me around when I was his age."

"The only reason they didn't is because you ignored them."

He crossed his forearms on the counter and leaned forward. "I ignored them because there was only one girl I was interested in. And it's great to see her laugh again."

Before I realized what he was going to do, he kissed me, right there in front of God and everyone. Just a quick brush of lips, but it was enough to send confusion swirling over me.

"Welcome back, Peewee," he murmured. Heat flooded my face as a loud war whoop rang through the store.

"Way to go, Dad!" Daniel appeared beside Nick, grinning from ear to ear. And he wasn't the only one taking note. Kenny was laughing, too. Thank God, most of the customers had already left and the store was nearly empty.

"He thinks I'm over the hill," Nick said, giving Daniel a friendly shove.

"You act like it sometimes," the boy said. "But thanks to me, things are definitely starting to look up." He puffed his chest out. "I've been giving him advice."

"Oh, really?" I grinned. "Maybe I should take you to the roadhouse with me Wednesday night instead of Jenna. Can you dance?"

"Just call me Justin Timberlake." He executed a move that would have done N'Sync proud, and I blinked.

"Wow. You weren't kidding. You're hired."

Nick shook his head. "No way. He's only fourteen. He's not allowed to date unless I go along as a chaperone."

"You're just jealous because he can dance and you can't."

"Oh, Dad can dance. He took lessons."

Nick clamped his hand over Daniel's mouth, a dull flush creeping up his neck. "I think it's time for us to be leaving."

I widened my eyes in mock horror. "I don't believe this. Nick Anderson taking dance lessons? And the world didn't come to a screeching halt?"

"There's not a lot to do when you're stuck on a compound in the middle of Saudi Arabia," he muttered. "Besides, he didn't say I was any good at it."

Daniel forced Nick's hand away from his mouth. "He is, though. You should have seen him practicing with Bowie. They took the class together and both of them tried to lead."

"You and I are going to have a long talk when we get home." Nick glared at Daniel before turning to me again. "What to come with us? Bowie is cooking, so no promises on the state of your health after supper."

With Lindsey there? Not a chance in hell. Maybe I'd called a truce with Nick, but she was a different story entirely. "Sorry. I promised Mama I'd stop by after work."

"Well, guess I'll see you later then."

"Sure."

I watched them leave, then glanced at Kenny. "Wipe that grin off your face or I'll fire you for insubordination."

My words had no effect on him. "You can't fire me. You need me too much. Besides, it's nice to hear you laugh for a change."

"Have I really been that bad, Kenny?"

"Not bad." He hesitated. "It's just that you seem to take everything so seriously, like if you ever knew how to have fun, you've forgotten."

I thought about that for a second. "Maybe I did. And maybe it's time I started to remember."

He patted my shoulder. "Why don't you go on? I'll lock up for the night."

It surprised both of us when I kissed his cheek. "Thanks, Kenny. For everything."

That man was long overdue a raise, I decided as I gathered up my purse. He put in more hours than I did, never complained, and the whole staff looked up to him. I couldn't run the store without him.

* * * * *

Mama's new house was a small, single-story red brick. It sat at the end of a long lane, amidst a grove of towering pines that whispered in the wind like a hundred voices, murmuring secrets not meant for human ears. Since she was expecting me, I didn't bother to knock, just opened the door and stepped into the kitchen.

To my everlasting shock, she was at the counter putting the finishing touches on a mandarin orange cake, my all-time favorite since I was a little girl. "What's the occasion?" I asked when she glanced around.

Her smile had an edge of nervousness to it. "It's my way of saying I'm sorry." She got out two plates and carried them to the table, cutting the cake before she continued. "I stayed awake half the night last night, thinking about what you said at the hospital yesterday."

I watched as she bustled around the kitchen, getting forks, making coffee. "Alix, I never meant to hurt you, although I can see now that I did. You're still my baby and I really thought I knew what was best for you. I thought you were just hurt by the way Hugh had been carrying on, that given time, you could work it out. Maybe I'm getting old. I don't accept change so easily anymore, and Hugh has been part of your life since you were children. He's the only boy you ever dated."

"Sit down, Mama." I caught her arm and tugged her gently into a chair. "It's time we talked about this."

She twisted her hands together on the table and exhaled, the breath lifting a lock of hair on her forehead. "That's what your father kept telling me. I should have listened to him, should have known that you wouldn't divorce Hugh without a good reason. I'm so sorry I didn't trust your judgment."

A short bark of laughter left my lips. "I haven't exactly given you any reason to trust it. But I should have left Hugh a long time ago, Mama. He's actually a pretty nice guy, and I'm sure he'll make a wonderful husband for someone he loves. But we didn't love each other. Not the way a husband and wife should. We never did. I don't think he'd have married me if it weren't for Helena pushing him into it."

"And yet you stayed with him all this time. Why?" She looked confused and upset, and my heart ached over what I was about to do. Sometimes we forget that divorce doesn't only affect the two people involved. It's a rending of two entire families.

"I stayed with him because I didn't care what he was doing, Mama. After Katie died I didn't care about anything."

"But you married him. You must have had some feelings for him." Abruptly her face paled, her expression stricken. "It was my fault, wasn't it? I pushed you into marrying him."

Reaching across the table, I covered her hand with mine. "No, you didn't push me into it. I had my own reasons for marrying Hugh." I braced myself, then went on. "I married him because I was pregnant and scared. He offered me a way out, a way to give the baby and myself respectability." I hesitated. "Katie wasn't Hugh's child, Mama."

Her gaze locked on mine. "Nick," she whispered.

"Yes."

A second passed in silence, her shoulders slumped as she looked away to stare at the table in front of her. "I think I always knew; I just didn't want to admit it. She looked so much like him. Does he know?"

I shook my head. "I'm not sure I'll ever tell him. You have to understand. All this time I've blamed him for everything that happened, Mama. I blamed him for leaving me, for not caring enough to take me with him. And I blamed him for Katie's death. I know now that it wasn't his fault she died, but there's still a lot of other things I'm not sure I can ever forgive him for."

"How does he feel about you?"

"He says he loves me, that he always has. We've called a kind of truce for now, but it doesn't change the fact that Lindsey has been with him all these years, or that they have a son together. After fifteen years of hating him, I can't start trusting him again overnight. I don't know if I'll ever be able to trust him again."

"I did your father. It wasn't easy, but sometimes you have to take a chance."

"Daddy didn't have the baggage Nick has. He didn't lie to you."

She rubbed her forehead tiredly. "I wish I'd known all this a long time ago."

"So do I. Maybe if I'd tried to talk to you, made you understand, I never would have married Hugh. But I took the easy way out, and I paid for it. It's too late to change the past, but at least I can try to salvage the future."

"You're right, and I promise not to say another word about the divorce." Her lips twitched. "Did Hugh really have an affair with Peggy?"

"Yes. Among others. He does have appalling taste, doesn't he?" I grinned.

She laughed. "Helena hasn't called me since you confronted Gretchen in the store. I think she's dug herself a hole somewhere and crawled inside to hide from the embarrassment. She was so sure the problems between you and Hugh were all your fault."

"In a way, they were. It takes two people to make a marriage work and I wasn't interested in trying. If I had been, Hugh might not have felt the need to turn to other women. We might have learned to love each other."

"No." Her voice was quiet. "You and Nick were inseparable from the day you met. You never could have loved Hugh the way you did Nick, and it wouldn't be fair for either you or Hugh to settle for second best. You're doing the right thing." She picked up the knife, lifted out a huge slab of cake, and deposited it on my plate. "Now, eat up."

"Mama?"

She looked up at me.

"I love you."

We almost knocked the table over in our rush to hug each other, and both of us were soaked from our tears. We continued to sniff and smile while we devoured half the cake, and I figured both of us were going to be sick before the night was over. But it didn't matter if we were. We had regained something that was broken. Our trust and closeness. And I was going to make sure our relationship was never damaged again. I was finally starting to remember something I'd once known, but had forgotten. Lies and half-truths hurt not only the liar, but the people they love most.

Uneasily, I pushed thoughts of Nick aside. I suppose it was at that point when I understood he would have to be told the truth about Katie, something I wasn't prepared to consider just yet. I also knew I couldn't be honest with him until he granted me the same concession. Whether or not we had a future together was immaterial until we could untangle all the lies and pain from our past.

* * * * *

Tuesday evening I left Southern Supply and went straight to the hospital to visit the Judge. It was Aunt Darla's turn to sit with him, and from the looks the Judge was giving her when I walked in, I figured he'd about gone his limit. Taking pity on his inability to escape, I sent her down to the cafeteria to get something to eat.

When she was gone, the Judge breathed a sigh of relief. "That woman is gonna drive me to drink."

"She's worried about you." I couldn't help the smile I gave him.

"The only thing she's worried about is getting everybody else to do what she wants. How the hell I raised a daughter that thinks her way is the only way, I'll never understand. Come to think about it, she reminds me a lot of your Great-Grandma Hoskins."

Grandma Hoskins was the Judge's mother-in-law, and from all accounts she'd been a real tyrant. She was the bane of his existence before she died, ruling her husband and daughter with an iron fist. I'd heard the Judge say many times that it was nothing short of a miracle that he'd gotten my grandmother away from her long enough to elope.

We dropped the subject of Aunt Darla when an aide came in with his supper tray. I helped him get fixed in the bed, and took the covers off his food. I also noted that he ate without complaining about the lack of salt. The stroke must have really scared him.

"Have the doctors told you when you can come home yet?"

"Friday, maybe, if things keep looking good. Are you keeping an eye on my garden?"

"Yes, sir. Checked it last night after I got back from Mama's. Everything looks fine."

He eyed me for a second, the overhead light glinting off the lens of his glasses. "You and your mama talking to each other again?"

I nodded. "She understands now why I'm divorcing Hugh."

"It's about time. I was getting tired of seeing the two of you moping around. Besides, I never figured out why you married Hugh in the first place. You deserved someone better."

"Like who?" I held up a hand. "No, on second thought, don't answer that. I'm not sure I want to know."

But of course, I knew exactly who he was talking about. And as though the conversation had conjured him out of thin air, Nick came though the door, followed by Bowie. I could tell the Judge was delighted with his visitors.

Not long after the men arrived, Mama and Daddy showed up, and Mama had to hug Nick and fuss over him until it got downright embarrassing. When he finally escaped, he leaned against the wall next to my chair.

"She makes me feel like I'm still ten years old." He smiled down at me.

"That's Mama for you." From across the room, she was beaming at us happily. I nearly groaned. In spite of our talk last night, or maybe because of it, I could almost see the image of wedding bells forming above her head.

Trying to ignore her, I glanced back at Nick. "How's the house coming along?" I knew they had all the walls studded up this morning when I left for work, and I'd seen the delivery invoice for the roof trusses.

"Faster than I expected. We got all the trusses on today, and they'll start on the decking tomorrow if it doesn't rain. I could use some advice on a few things though, if you've got the time this evening."

A tingle ran over me. I was positively dying to take a closer look at the place. "Sure," I said nonchalantly. "I'm not doing anything after I leave here."

"Great." He appeared as cool as I was trying to be. "Bowie still has some errands to run and I left my truck out at the house. How about if I catch a ride home with you?"

"Okay. Now?"

"If you're ready."

Our exodus was interrupted briefly when Aunt Darla returned. I introduced her to Bowie and told her he wanted to swap recipes with her. Then I had the pleasure of watching her blush like a teenager and stammer out "Well, land's sakes" as she stared at Bowie, her hands busily smoothing imaginary wrinkles from her dress and tucking stray locks of hair back in place.

It was the first time in memory I'd ever seen Aunt Darla flustered, but from the way Bowie was looking at her, I didn't think it would be the last. By the time Nick and I left, they were huddled up in a corner talking each other's ears off.

"Where's Daniel tonight?" I asked as we walked out to the Chevy.

"Visiting one of his newfound buddies. I think they're both addicted to the same video game."

"I'm glad he's found some friends."

"Thanks to you."

"No." I smiled. "Thanks to Daniel. He's so outgoing and enthusiastic no one can resist him."

When we reached the car, Nick held out his hand. "Mind if I drive? It's been a long time since I've been behind the wheel of the Chevy."

I dropped the keys onto his palm. "Be my guest."

He opened the passenger door for me, then went around to the driver's side, pausing long enough to scoot the seat back to make room for his longer legs. "I'm glad you kept it. The only places you see cars this old and still in running order are in antique shows."

We stayed silent until he pulled out onto the highway, and I finally made up my mind to begin my quest for answers by easing into the subject through the back door. "Bowie and Aunt Darla seemed to be hitting it off."

He smiled. "There aren't many people Bowie can't get along with."

"You said you met him while you were both in the army?"

"Kind of." He glanced at me. "Bowie had retired, but he hung around the base a lot. I met him at the base hospital when he was having some minor tests done."

Well, so much for being subtle. His answer immediately raised ten more questions, none of which I wanted to veer off into. Things like, why was he at the hospital? And why had Bowie gone to work for him when Nick couldn't possibly have been making enough money to pay him?

I cleared my throat and got back on track. "Did you like the army?"

"Yes and no. One good thing about boot camp is that you don't have time to think about your problems. It's all you can do to crawl into bed every night and pass out. The army also made it possible for me to go through some schools that I couldn't have managed without them. That's how I got the job with the oil company in Saudi. But on the other hand, I don't do well taking orders. That's why I got out when my time was up."

"You could have come home."

His jaw tightened. "No I couldn't. I was still Nick Anderson, the guy who'd shot his father, the guy from the wrong side of town. I was still broke, still a nobody." He glanced at me again. "I promised you once that I'd make you proud of me someday, that I'd be somebody. I couldn't come home until I'd succeeded."

"And now you have?"

The smile playing around his lips was grim. "Well, I'm not broke anymore. The company paid well, and they gave large bonuses to get you to stay longer than a year. Since they also furnished housing, there wasn't much expense. I took what I saved and invested it. Maybe I'm not up to the Morgan's standards of rich, but I've got enough to live comfortably the rest of my life. So yes, I'd say I've at least partly succeeded. The rest of my goals are still up in the air."

I studied his profile. "Did you really think that's what I wanted? That I cared if you were rich or not?"

He pulled the car to a stop in the driveway and shut off the motor. His voice was quiet in the silence. "No, I knew it didn't matter to you. But it mattered to me, Alix. I couldn't stand the thought of you living in some dingy apartment, slaving away at a job you hated to help support us. It would have destroyed me. There was so much I wanted to give you, so much you deserved…" His voice trailed off, and I realized his hand was fisted on the steering wheel. He took a deep, shaky breath and pushed the door open abruptly. "Let's go look at the house."

Confused, I followed him across the grassy area that stretched under the trees between the barn and his house. It was almost as though he knew where the conversation was leading and wanted to stop me before I could ask the questions. A spark of anger curled inside me. I had a right to know, damn it. If he loved me as much as he said he did, then I deserved to know why he'd nearly destroyed me.

Strange, but even after everything I'd been through, I never doubted for an instant that he'd tell me the truth. He might refuse to talk about something, but lying was as foreign to Nick's nature as a sandstorm was to a rainforest. Somewhere along the way, I'd forgotten that.

I remembered it now and my anger faded as he helped me step up onto the foundation of the house, a distracted expression on his face. "What color shingles do you think I should get?"

In the last rays of the sun, I gaped at him. "That's what you wanted my advice on? Shingles?"

The thoughtful look faded from his eyes, and he grinned. "Among other things."

I crossed my arms over my chest and gazed up at him. Okay, if he wanted to play games, I'd go along with him for now. But we both knew this subject wasn't over.

"What kind of exterior were you planning?"

"Vinyl siding."

"Color?"

"What color would you use?"

"It's your house, Nick."

Even in the shadows cast by the upper floor, I saw his gray eyes go molten. "No, it's our house."

It felt like my insides were melting into a puddle on the cold concrete at my feet. "White," I whispered. "Make the outside white."

I don't know who moved first, or even if it mattered. I only know that I suddenly found myself in his arms, his mouth moving hungrily on mine. We were pressed together so tightly I could feel every inch of his hard body against me, feel the heat radiating from his skin. And nothing in my life had ever felt so right before. For that brief time, we weren't two people separated by fifteen years and a troubled past. We were one body, one soul that had been reunited across a seemingly unbridgeable chasm.

When it ended, we were both shaking, both gasping for air. But instead of releasing me, his arms tightened until they were almost painful and he buried his face in my hair.

"God, I can't lose you again." His whisper was harsh, filled with pain. "Not now, when I've waited so long to hold you. I think it would kill me. But I'm so damn scared you'll hate me when you find out the truth."

I rested my head against his chest, eyes closed. "And when will that be?"

"Soon. Too damn soon."

"But not tonight?"

He hesitated and I could feel the tension in his body. "No, not tonight. I know I don't have the right, but I'm asking you to trust me a little longer."

I leaned back and looked into his eyes for a second, then nodded. "Show me the rest of the house."

And so, for the next hour, we pretended to be nothing more than two people in love who were busily planning the home they would build together. We held hands, we laughed, and we argued over the layout of the kitchen. We discussed color schemes, shingles, and floor covering. We couldn't stop touching, or looking at each other, trying to memorize this forbidden moment.

When it was time to part, both of us were reluctant for the magic to end. We wound up necking like teenagers, standing in the front part of the barn after he walked me home, exchanging long, slow, drugging kisses that lasted forever, drove us both to the edge of our endurance, and left our bodies aching.

And then I stood in the open doorway and watched him drive away, unaware that this blissful peace would last only a few more days. Unaware that when I finally did learn the truth, the rage that erupted inside me would destroy the man I still loved with all my heart.

Chapter Eighteen

ร૭

I'd only been to the Roadhouse twice before, and both times were with Hugh. It had bored me out of my skull, sitting at a table with nothing to do except listen to Hugh joke and carry on with his friends. The music had been too loud, and the smoke stung my nose until I could barely breathe. I'd hated every minute of it.

But tonight felt different. The huge, barn-like building pulsed with excitement and laughter, shimmied to the rhythm of guitars, electric keyboard and drums that I could feel pounding from my chest to my toes. Anticipation shivered through me as I paused inside the door and scanned the dimly lit interior, looking for Jenna. At midnight tonight, I would officially be a free woman, a Cinderella in reverse, and I was more than ready.

The boot-stomping, swaying bodies on the dance floor blocked my view of the tables and any hope of spotting Jenna. Gingerly, I eased my way to the edge of the shiny wooden floor, trying not to get stepped on. I'd barely set out when Clifton Logan, one of my customers, grabbed me, let out a whoop, and two-stepped me effortlessly through the dancing mob.

Laughing, I thanked him for his gallant assistance. He swept off his ball cap and bowed. "Always my pleasure to help a damsel in distress. You looking for Jenna?"

"Yes. Have you seen her?"

He nodded toward my left. "I reckon that's her waving her arm off over there."

"Thanks, Cliff."

"No problem. Save me a dance for later?"

"Sure."

Jenna settled back in her seat when I reached her, and eyed my outfit enviously. "You've been shopping."

I had run home after work, swallowed a sandwich, and showered. Afterward, I put on my best black jeans, boots, and a new scarlet tank top, over which I'd added a black bolero jacket embroidered with red roses and trimmed in metallic gold thread. "I got them at that new South American boutique in the mall."

She sighed. "I wish I could wear red. Unfortunately, it looks horrible with my hair."

"Yeah, but you can wear green and I can't. It clashes with my eyes." I glanced up as a waitress stopped beside me. "White wine for me. Jenna?"

She gestured at her glass. "I'm fine." The waitress made a note on her pad, then left. Jenna waited until she was out of earshot, then leaned closer. "Listen, Alix. Hugh is here. I swear I didn't know until a few minutes ago. If I had, I never would have suggested coming to the roadhouse."

Instantly, I went tense and all my anticipation drained away. "Where is he?"

"Two tables to our left and back one."

"Is he alone?"

She grimaced. "If you're asking if he's with a woman, the answer is no. There are a couple of guys from the mill with him. Do you want to leave?"

My chin went up. "Absolutely not. This is supposed to be a celebration. I'm not going to let him ruin the night for me." I took a quick peek at his table and nearly groaned. He was rising from his chair, looking in our direction.

"Good for you," Jenna said. Her gaze was fixed on something behind me. "How about Nick?"

"Nick?" Puzzled, I jerked my gaze from Hugh in time to see Jenna point. Nick was crossing the dance floor, heading straight for us.

Oh, Christ. Both men were going to reach us at the same time, and I was terrified Hugh would spill the truth about Katie out of pure spite. "Stop Hugh!" I yelped at Jenna. "I'll stop Nick."

Neither of us hesitated. Like a well-trained football team, she dodged left and I sprinted to the right. Slightly out of breath, I skidded to a stop in front of Nick and smiled. "Hi. What are you doing here?"

His answering smile was rueful. "You're here. Where else would I be? Besides, Daniel pushed me out the door and ordered me to hurry. I think he's afraid someone will beat me to the punch."

I grabbed his hand and tugged him toward the dance floor. "Great. Dance with me?"

"Now?"

"No time like the present."

Once we were in position, I maneuvered him until his back was to the table, then peered around his arm. Jenna was standing in front of Hugh, one hand on her hip, the other on his chest. She was shaking her head, and I could tell she was talking fast. Hugh was staring down at her, lines of stubbornness etched on his face.

"It's a good thing I'm used to Bowie leading." Nick's voice broke my concentration. "What did you think I'd do, slug him?"

I should have known Nick would see right through me. Leaning back, I met his amused gaze. "Of course not. It was never you I was worried about, it was Hugh. It would be just like him to start a fight."

"Hugh Morgan? He never struck me as the type that would get physical."

I relaxed long enough to realize that Nick really was a good dancer. Our bodies seemed to fit together perfectly as we moved, and I suspected he'd had a lot more practice than what he'd got with Bowie. I squelched the tingle of jealousy that hit me. "Normally, you'd be right. But his ego is all tied up in this divorce, and I don't know how much he's had to drink."

"I think I can handle him."

"That's not the point."

"Then what is the point?"

With a sigh, I glanced back at Jenna and Hugh, then frowned. Jenna's hand was on his cheek and Hugh's expression had softened as he gazed down at her. "I don't want Hugh using you as the scapegoat for why our marriage didn't work. Right now, everyone knows about Hugh's cheating. He's lost the respect of some important people in town. If he can turn it around and put the blame on you and me, he'll do it. And all it will take for everyone to believe him is one good fight, in public."

He moved his hand to my neck and ran his thumb lightly over my lips. "Do you want me to leave?"

I fought off a shiver, fought off the need to feel his mouth on mine again. "No, but I don't want you or Daniel to get caught in the middle of this, either."

"I'm not worried about it." His arm tightened around my waist, pulling me closer against his body. "I don't care what anyone thinks about me."

He did care, though, deeply, whether he admitted it or not. But against my better judgment, I gave in and slid my arms around his neck. It simply felt too good, being with him this way, and I still ached with need from our passionate session in the barn last night. Even sleep had brought no ease, because I'd dreamed about making love with him. It had been so long since I'd felt any desire, felt anything, that now I was like a firecracker with a lit fuse, ready to explode at any second.

The song ended and another one started. I took the opportunity to check on Jenna and Hugh. To my surprise, they were on the dance floor, arms around each other in much the same position Nick and I were in. Once again, I frowned. Something about the way they looked at each other set off a niggling feeling in my head, but I couldn't figure out why. It was like a word that's right on the tip of your tongue, but you can't quite get it into the forefront of your memory.

"They sure look cozy," Nick said.

And his comment was all it took. Suddenly I was bombarded by memories. Jenna chasing Hugh in grade school, telling me how cute he was. Her laughing with him in junior high, and later, getting upset when she found out I was dating him to cover my relationship with Nick. Her reaction after graduation when she found out Hugh had married me. All the nights Hugh hadn't come home, nights when I hadn't been able to reach Jenna either. And most damning of all, the expression on her face Sunday evening when I'd jokingly accused her of having an affair without telling me. The same night I thought I'd heard someone sneaking out her front door.

I stumbled as the knowledge slammed into me, and came to an abrupt staggering halt. "Oh, my God."

"Alix? What's wrong?" Nick's voice sounded worried, but I couldn't tear my eyes off Hugh and Jenna.

"Oh, my God," I repeated, stunned. "It was Jenna. All this time, she was the other woman."

"You can't know that."

But I did. I knew it right down to my soul, couldn't understand how I'd missed it all those years. Instinctively, mindlessly, my feet took a step back. Almost as if my stare had drawn her attention, Jenna looked around and our eyes met. The blood drained from her face and she pushed Hugh away as though he'd burned her. I saw her lips form my name as she started toward me.

I took yet another step back, then another. "No," I whispered. Until then, I'd been in shock, but now equal measures of pain and anger hammered into me. If I had to confront her now, I didn't know what I'd do. So even as Nick moved to block her from reaching me, I turned and ran.

Someone called my name, but I didn't slow. I plowed through the crowd, pushing people out of my way with a strength born of desperation. I had to get out, get away from her, for both our sakes. I had to breathe.

Panting like a marathon runner at the end of a race, I jumped into the Chevy and tore out of the parking lot, slinging gravel behind me as the rear end fishtailed. I was pushing the old car harder than I ever had before, and if I'd been thinking straight I would have known better.

Ten minutes later, just as I reached the skeletal remains of the Star-Vu Drive-In, the Chevy hiccupped, stalled, caught again, and then died with a strangled wheeze. Cursing under my breath, tears streaming down my face, I wrestled the steering wheel around and let the car glide to a stop near the ancient screen. It was the last straw.

I was so far gone I didn't pay any attention to the lights from Nick's truck, illuminating the rows of headless metal stands, as he pulled into the lot. In a rage, I jumped out of the Chevy and kicked it as the headlights behind me went out. Then kicked it again and again, teeth clenched together to stop the screams that were fighting to get out. When I started beating the hood with my fists, Nick grabbed me from behind, pinned my arms to my sides and lifted me off my feet.

It only made things worse. "God damn it! Let me go," I screamed in fury, struggling with all my might.

"You're going to hurt yourself." He turned me to face him without releasing his hold. "If you need to hit something, hit me."

I lost control, totally and completely. Furiously, I pounded on his chest, sobs tearing my throat raw. He never even flinched, just stood there like a block of granite until I wore myself out. Slowly, my blows weakened, came farther apart. And then I was in his arms, my mouth on his.

"Make love to me," I whispered.

"Alix, you're too upset—"

I cut his words off with another kiss. "I need you, damn it. Now shut up and make love to me."

A low growl started in the back of his throat as I trailed hot kisses over his jaw, down his neck. Frantically, nearly tearing the material in my haste, I unbuttoned his shirt, desperate for the feel of his skin. His hands slid to my bottom, cradled and lifted me until I was pinned between his body and the car. When he reclaimed my mouth, took control, I wrapped my legs around his waist like a heat-seeking missile, doing my best to get closer to the flames.

I was vaguely aware of the sounds of traffic from the highway, but the old theater screen blocked us, hid us from the view of passersby. And even if it hadn't, I honestly don't think I would have cared. I was lost in Nick's scent, the feel of his body moving with agonizing friction against the material that separated us.

Mindless with the sensations coursing through me, I felt him shove my jacket down my arms, felt his hands move under my tank top as I arched my back. Then we were in the backseat of the Chevy, clothes flying in every direction as we strained to rediscover territory that had once been so familiar.

The night was hot and sweat slicked our bodies as we moved together, silk sliding on silk. With hands and lips we fought each other for dominance, wanting to be the first to torment, to please. My whimpers echoed in the night as Nick rasped a continuous stream of love words, expressions of desire so heated they served to inflame me even more.

Countless times we drove each other to the ragged edge of completion, only to pull back at the last second, wanting the sweet torture to last. When Nick finally joined our bodies together, we were both crazed from the erotic battle we'd waged, a battle in which each of us would be the winner.

With the heady odor of lovemaking surrounding us in the enclosed space, with Nick's mouth ravenous on mine, with his hardness filling me in a way I'd despaired of ever knowing again, I finally found release. It was so cataclysmic that I cried out, my body shaking with the rapture that consumed me. Nick captured my cries, held me and kept me safe as I convulsed. Then as my tremors began to ease, he stiffened, and I held him as he emptied his passion into my waiting body.

Joy like I'd never known before, as strong as the physical victory I'd found, settled around my heart like a warm blanket. I wanted to stay here forever, never let go of him again.

He must have been feeling something similar, because he made no effort to move away. Quietly, we clung to each other, a hand occasionally moving, soothing the tics and twitches of aftershocks as our breathing settled back to normal.

"Christ," he whispered, voice still husky with desire. "If this is another dream, I hope to God I never wake up."

"It's no dream." My hand slid down the long hard muscles of his back. "Do you realize the last time we made love was in this same place?"

"I know."

"But this time it's going to be different."

He levered his weight up on his elbows and threaded his fingers tenderly through my hair as he gazed down at me. "How?"

"This time, I'm not going to let you leave. I want you to stay with me tonight."

A smile curved his lips. "You don't hear me arguing, do you?"

It took us almost an hour to find all of our clothes, sort out what belonged to whom in the darkness, and then assist each other in dressing. The last was more hindrance than help, since we used it as an excuse to renew our teasing, touching, torment. All our inhibitions had vanished like a puff of smoke in a high wind. We positively wallowed in the pleasure brought on by the knowledge that we were free to do anything we desired to the other's body. And each action built the desire anew, rekindled the thirst we'd so recently slaked.

Back at my room in the barn, we made love again and again. Slower now that the first frenzy had been sated. And between times, we'd talk.

Once I asked him, "Does this make me an adulteress? My divorce isn't final until tomorrow, so technically, I'm still married to Hugh."

Nick had his head propped on one hand, the other tracing light patterns on my stomach, then between my breasts. We'd left a small lamp on, so I had no trouble seeing his gray eyes shift to mine.

"No."

"Are you sure?"

His hand stopped moving. "Do you feel married to him?"

"No. I haven't for a long time."

"Do you feel guilty?"

"Not in the least." I stretched. "I feel wonderful."

"So tell me, if we started making love at five minutes before midnight, and didn't finish until after, would that make it adultery for the first part and not the last?"

I tilted my head sideways and pretended to think about it for a second. "I don't know. Why don't we try it and find out?"

I'm happy to report that I felt no different before midnight than I felt afterward.

Yet another time he started the conversation. "Did you do this tonight just to get even with Hugh?"

We were lying spoon fashion, Nick's front pressed firmly to my back, legs twined together. "No." I didn't even hesitate.

"I didn't care enough about what he was doing to want revenge."

"But you were so damn upset earlier."

I turned over, pushed Nick onto his back, then lay across his chest so I could look at his face. "Yes, I was. I'd just found out that someone I loved and trusted has been using me all these years. I don't know. Maybe I used it as an excuse. But the truth is, I've wanted this from the second you walked into the store that first day. I just couldn't admit it to myself. Tonight, you were there when I needed someone the most, needed you the most."

His hand slid down my back. "I always will be." He hesitated. "But I don't think Jenna was using you, Peewee. I saw her face when she realized you'd figured it out. She was scared right down to her toes. She loves you, too."

With a sigh, I rested my cheek on his shoulder. "Maybe. I need time to think about it, sort it all out in my head. And I don't want to do it now."

I felt his lips curve in a smile against my hair. "What do you want to do?"

"Guess."

He got it right the first time.

After that we slept, curled together on the narrow bed, bodies tangled as though afraid the other would vanish if we let go for a single instant. Once, I woke up and just lay quietly, watching his face with a touch of awe. He was so damn beautiful that it set an ache burning in my middle, the same feeling I got from watching a glorious sunset, or seeing a work of art that touched me.

Even relaxed in sleep, his face was ruggedly male, the stubble of a night's growth of beard shading his jaw, raven hair tousled from hours of lovemaking. He was magical, a lone wolf that had chosen to subdue his strength, rest a while among mere mortals. And this magnificent creature wanted me. It was almost more than I could believe, and a streak of pure fear hit me at the thought of losing him again, a distinct possibility when the past dangled over us like the sword of Damocles.

I couldn't go on this way much longer. For the sake of my sanity, we had to get the past out into the open and deal with it. Until we did, I couldn't let myself love him completely, couldn't open myself to more pain. There was only so much one person could stand, and I'd reached my limit.

But for tonight, this one single night, I only wanted to be with Nick, to let go and love him unconditionally as I had before, no matter what tomorrow might bring. And so I snuggled down beside him, smiling when his arms came around me and pulled me closer.

When I next woke, it was to a slow-building heat and a sensation of delicious friction. I opened my eyes to find Nick watching my face intently as he made love to me. "Do you have any idea how many times I've dreamed about waking you up this way?" he whispered.

"How many?" I arched to accept him more completely.

"Every damned day of my life." A low groan rumbled in his chest. "Christ. I'd be in a room full of people, start thinking about making love to you in the morning, and then I'd spend the next half hour trying to hide the results."

"I kind of like the results," I murmured. "It would be a real shame to let it go to waste."

He threaded our fingers together, closed his eyes, and touched his forehead to mine. "You may regret saying that when I show up at Southern Supply this afternoon and drag you to bed."

"Not a chance," I whispered. By then, our breathing had quickened and any possibility of rational conversation fled, lost in pure desire. It was nearly dawn and we were both caught up in the realization that, all too soon, our night together would be over. And so we prolonged the moment as long as possible, until we couldn't deny our parting another minute.

"I have to get ready for work," I said quietly.

"I know. And I need to get out of here before the crew shows up next door."

Swinging my feet to the floor, I watched him pull his jeans on. He caught me staring and smiled.

"Can I see you again tonight?"

I took a deep breath and expelled it in one solid puff. "That depends."

He paused. "On what?"

Nervously, I clenched my hands in my lap, but I was determined to get this over with. "On whether or not you're ready to talk."

His gaze drifted away from me, and I saw the tension in his jaw. I sat there waiting while images only he could see flashed through his mind. Abruptly, he nodded. "Tonight."

I stood, rose on tiptoes and kissed him. "Thank you."

He put his hands on my shoulders and shook his head. "Don't thank me until you hear what I've got to tell you."

"There's something I have to tell you, too."

We were interrupted by a knock on the door. Hastily, I grabbed my robe and shoved my arms into the sleeves, belting it as I moved across the room.

To my surprise, Aunt Jane was standing on the other side. "Is something wrong with the Judge?"

"No, he's fine. But Jenna called. She said she's been trying to reach you all night and couldn't get through. I thought I'd better come over and check on you." Her gaze drifted past me to the phone that I'd taken off the hook last night and then onward to Nick. She smiled, her brown eyes crinkling at the corners.

"Nick. It's wonderful to have you home again. But next time, you might want to pull your truck inside the barn. I practically had to hogtie, gag, and stuff Darla in the hall closet to keep her from coming over here and flogging you with a broom."

He returned her smile as he buttoned his shirt. "I'll remember that. Do you have a ride to work this morning?" he asked me.

I'd almost forgotten about my car. "I can take the Judge's truck."

"Okay. I'll go by and see what I can do with the Chevy." He leaned down and gave me a long kiss. "See you tonight."

Aunt Jane and I stood and watched him walk to his truck, then she turned and studied me. "Are you sure you know what you're doing, Alix?"

"No." My gaze met hers. "I'm not sure about much of anything right now."

She reached over and brushed a strand of hair away from my cheek. "It almost destroyed you when he had to leave before. I don't want to see you hurt again."

"Neither do I. But if it's going to happen, I don't think I can stop it, Aunt Jane. I still love him."

Suddenly, she hugged me. "Then fight for him, Sweetheart. Don't let anything stand in your way or you'll regret it for the rest of your life."

Before I could respond, she headed back toward the house, but I caught the glimmer of moisture in her eyes and sighed.

* * * * *

For some reason, Southern Supply was a madhouse that morning. First, three semis full of material, two of which I hadn't ordered, all showed up at the same time. Then an entire pallet of concrete birdbaths toppled over without warning, shaking the walls until it felt like we were having an earthquake, and barely missing two of the dock workers. For the next hour, concrete dust from the pulverized baths filled the air. It was almost as if the powers-that-be had decided I didn't have enough chaos in my life and gleefully added more.

The one highlight was when Kenny came into my office and handed me a blue official-looking envelope. "Messenger just brought this over from your lawyer."

Gingerly, I opened it and pulled out the document inside. Relief and an exhilarating sense of happiness swept over me as I saw the words on top. Decree of Divorcement. Signed, sealed and delivered. It was finally over. Hugh no longer had any hold on me. I was free.

It took an effort to suppress my laughter as I wondered who had won the pool at the barbershop. I hoped it was someone who needed the money. From what I'd heard, it was a pretty sizable pot.

By noon, things had calmed down somewhat and I finally had a chance to think about Jenna. Oddly enough, my anger was gone as though it had never existed. The only thing remaining was a sense of loss. Not for me, but for her.

Because after thinking it over, I knew deep inside that Nick was right. She hadn't been using me. Jenna loved Hugh, and God knows, I understood what it was like to love a man you couldn't have. She must have been absolutely miserable all these years. But it hadn't stopped her from being there when I needed her, and she'd never shown me any resentment or jealousy. Which was more than I could say about my feelings for Lindsey.

I rubbed my forehead tiredly as depression settled over me like a wet blanket. As far as I knew, Lindsey was still living in the same house with Nick, although I made it a point to stay out of that area of town. Part of me wanted to confront him about it, but this time, things were going to be different. This time I wasn't going to demand he choose between us. I wasn't going to demand it for one simple reason. It had to be his choice, his decision. And if he couldn't decide, if he continued to live with Lindsey, then no matter how much I loved him, I didn't want him. It would hurt, but I'd lived without him for fifteen years. I could do it again if I had to.

How many times had I heard people say, that which doesn't kill you makes you stronger? More than I could count. But I didn't know how sorely I would be put to the test before the day was over, or that fate was rushing toward me at the speed of light. Fate in the form of Lindsey Swanner and my cousin, Cody.

Chapter Nineteen

🕉

After the brief hiatus around lunch, things started to go bad again at Southern Supply, and I started to wonder if the gods took dinner breaks. First, Kenny told me Jenna was on the phone. I hesitated. I really did want to talk to her, but not on the phone, and not when I knew we'd be interrupted every five seconds.

"Tell her you can't find me, that I'm out in the store somewhere."

Kenny arched an eyebrow, but went to do what I'd asked. Five minutes later, he was back. "Doug just called up from the dock. The cabinets for the Bergman job are here and he says they're a mess. All banged up, the doors are hung crooked, and they're even the wrong color."

"Christ. What next?" I mumbled. "Okay, tell him to pack them up and send them back. I'll call the cabinet people and tell them they just ran out of second chances. Do you remember the carpenter I talked to about a month ago? The guy that handcrafts cabinets in his workshop?" I shuffled through a drawer looking for the man's business card.

"Herman English?"

"Yeah." I shoved the drawer closed. "That's the one. See if you can find his number for me?"

One very heated argument later, I'd fired my old cabinet company and hired Mr. English, who was ecstatic over the chance to do our work. Then I took a couple of aspirin.

From there, the day went downhill. By quitting time, I was exhausted and my whole body ached, although I suspected that last had more to do with last night's activities than it did with the disastrous day I'd just been through. I'd reached the point where I dreaded seeing Kenny appear at my door. Which is why I frowned when he showed up again.

"Whatever is it, I don't want to hear it."

He grinned. "Look on the bright side. Tomorrow has to be better. You've got company."

"Who?" I prayed it wasn't Jenna because I was simply too tired to deal with her right now. All I wanted to do was soak in a tub of hot water for about an hour, and then get my talk with Nick over with.

"Your cousin."

"Cody?" I sat down in the chair I'd just vacated, more than a little curious. Cody called me occasionally, but he rarely paid unexpected visits. "Tell him to come on in."

"Okay. If you don't need me, I'm heading home. Want me to lock up on my way out?"

"Please."

I heard the murmur of voices as Kenny left, then glanced up at a sound from my door. And froze, my smile fading. Cody was standing there, still in uniform, and he wasn't alone. Lindsey was with him.

My gaze shifted between the two of them before coming to rest on my cousin. "What the hell do you think you're doing, bringing her here?" I managed to keep my voice cool even though inside I was seething with anger.

Cody put his hand on Lindsey's back and nearly pushed her toward the chairs across from my desk. "There are things you have to be told before the whole town finds out, Alix, and I knew you'd never agree to listen to Lindsey if we gave you a choice."

"Guess what? I still have a choice. Now get the hell out of my office."

"No. You're going to hear this out." He took the seat next to Lindsey and glanced at her, then took off his hat and balanced it on his knee. "It's time you found out what really happened fifteen years ago."

"Alix, please." Lindsey's voice was soft, hesitant. She looked much the same as she had that day at the hospital. Maybe a little more nervous, and a bit paler, but still beautiful. "I wanted to tell you as soon as we got back, but Nick wouldn't let me. He said I had to talk to the sheriff first."

Cody reached over and covered her hand with his. "And she did. Last Monday." He smiled encouragingly at Lindsey. "Go ahead. Start at the beginning."

Stiffly, I leaned back in my chair and folded my arms over my chest, a feeling of doom settling over me as I watched Lindsey. She cleared her throat, her gaze fastened on her and Cody's hands.

"The beginning." A tiny smile curved her lips. "Do you remember that day at the junkyard when you invited me to the church picnic? You scared me half to death. You were so strong, Alix. So friendly and outgoing. I'd never met anyone like you before."

She took a deep breath. "After that day, I watched every move you made. You were everything I wished I could be, and I wanted desperately to be your friend. But I didn't know how. There were so many people who loved you. The only one who cared about me was Nick. He was all I had, a brother and a father all rolled into one. I think I would probably have died if Nick hadn't been there. He was the one who saw to it that I ate, who got me ready for school every day. I suppose Mama loved me in her own way, but she had so many other things to worry about that I got lost in the shuffle."

Her gaze lifted to mine, and in spite of myself I was mesmerized. I didn't want to listen to her, didn't want to care about what she was telling me, but I couldn't stop the feeling of pity as I remembered the scared little girl she'd once been.

"But eventually we grew up," she continued. "And Nick started to change. He was spending most of his spare time at your family's farm. And when he was home, he talked about you constantly. I knew he was in love with you, and I was happy for him. At least, I was until that last year."

She looked at Cody beseechingly, and he nodded. "Keep going. You're doing fine."

Her hands were shaking and her chin trembled before she spoke again. "That fall my mother had Billy, my little brother. Frank hung around our house a lot, but when he wasn't there, other men were. Mama hated it, but it was the only way she could make any extra money. After she had Billy, Mr. Howard, Jenna's father, helped her get a job at the roadhouse waiting tables, and he gave her some money for the baby. But there wasn't enough to pay a babysitter, so I didn't go back to school. Instead, I stayed home to take care of my brother. I hated school so I really didn't mind. But then Frank started hanging around while Mama was at work. He scared me, the way he watched every move I made, the way he kept trying to get me alone."

Suddenly things were starting to click in my memory. "You told Nick. That's why he wanted everyone to think the two of you were dating."

Lindsey let out a sigh of relief. "Yes. We were both afraid of what would happen if Frank got me alone. Nick thought if his father believed we were a couple, it might slow him down a little. For a while, it did. But one night he came over after I put Billy to bed, so drunk he could hardly walk, and I barely got away from him by locking myself in the bedroom. If he'd been sober, the lock would never have stopped him."

She lifted a hand and tiredly rubbed her forehead. "That day you showed up at the gas station and saw Nick and me together, I'd just finished telling him what Frank had done. I knew what you thought, Alix, but I was terrified. Nick was furious and too ashamed of his father to tell you the truth. He went straight home and confronted Frank. They had a horrible fight, the worst I'd ever seen. Nick told him to stay away from me, but Frank wouldn't listen. He kept yelling that I was nothing but a two-bit whore, just like my mother, and that if I could spread my legs for Nick, I could damn well spread them for him. I thought they were going to hit each other, but by then Frank was a little afraid of Nick. Nick wasn't the little boy Frank used to beat anymore. He was younger and stronger than Frank, and he wasn't weakened from constant drinking."

Her gaze met mine again. "I wasn't sleeping with Nick, Alix, I swear. It would have been like incest to me. I loved Nick, yes, but not that way. He was my family."

My heart was pounding so hard I could hear the rush of blood in my ears. I was putting two and two together and not liking the answer I was coming up with. Because if she were telling the truth, if she really hadn't slept with Nick, then Daniel...oh, God. Pain stabbed through my stomach until I wanted to double over and clutch my middle, and nausea left a bitter taste in my throat.

Lindsey must have seen the realization in my eyes. Her free hand stopped its nervous movements and she became chillingly calm. "That's when Nick started spending his evenings with me. He'd come home as soon as he got off work, and stay until Mama got back. We both knew Frank was just waiting for the right moment, waiting until I was alone. Nick tried to talk me into leaving. He even offered to help me. He'd found out about this program they have in Little Rock, kind of like a job corps. They trained high school dropouts in different areas, and then helped them find a decent job."

Her voice dropped. "But God help me, I wouldn't listen to him. I was too weak, too afraid of leaving everything I knew and being alone. And I couldn't understand why I should have to. After all, Nick was there. I knew he'd protect me just like he always had."

She closed her eyes briefly before looking at me again. "And he did. Until you gave him an ultimatum. Me or you. He had to choose. And because he loved you, and couldn't stand the thought of losing you, he chose you."

A pained laugh escaped her lips while I gripped the chair arms until my knuckles turned white.

"I hated you for years after that, blamed you for everything that happened."

"Lindsey, I didn't know. If Nick had told me…"

She waved one hand vaguely in the air. "I know now that it wasn't your fault, although it took years of therapy for me to understand. You see, I didn't believe Nick when he told me he wasn't going to stay with me anymore. I thought it was some kind of joke. I sat there on the couch and watched him leave, waiting for the punch line. But there wasn't one."

She sucked in a breath of air that sounded more like a half-broken sob. "When I realized he was serious, that he wasn't coming back, I almost went crazy, I was so scared. Then, about an hour later, I heard a truck pull in at the salvage yard. It was Friday night. It never occurred to me that it might be Frank. I figured he'd be out drinking until all hours, like he usually did. I thought Nick had come back. So I checked on Billy and made sure he was asleep, then I ran to the trailer. But it wasn't Nick. Frank was there, and he wasn't drunk this time."

A single tear slipped down her cheek and she gripped Cody's hand tightly. "I tried to run, but it was too late. He caught me and pulled me back into the trailer. When I fought him, he beat me until I was nearly unconscious. And when I couldn't move anymore, he tore my clothes off and raped me. Not just once, but over and over again. It was like he wanted to punish me for escaping him as long as I had."

She reached up with her left hand and brushed the tear away. "Things are kind of blurry after that. I think he went into the bedroom for awhile. And when I heard him coming back, I knew it was going to happen all over again, that he wouldn't stop until he'd killed me. I snapped. I don't know where I got the gun, or the strength to use it, I only remember pulling the trigger. Even after the gun was empty, I kept pulling the trigger. That's what I was doing when Nick found me. He took the gun away from me and carried me home, then he called Mama and told her to get me to a hospital. As soon as she got there, he went back to the trailer, cleaned my fingerprints off the gun, and called the police."

"And told them he'd killed Frank," I whispered.

Lindsey glanced at Cody, and he nodded in answer to my statement. "Apparently, Lindsey wasn't in any shape to be questioned, and Nick knew it. She wasn't talking or moving, just staying wherever they put her, not even blinking. And Nick blamed himself for the whole thing. It almost destroyed him. I think part of him hoped he'd be punished."

Cody watched me intently as he talked, a worried expression on his face. "Everything she's told you is the truth, Alix. I've spent the last week checking all the details. Liz knew what had happened. I guess Nick told her. And because she didn't want Frank's murder pinned on Lindsey, she took her to the hospital in Paragould. The doctors there notified the Green County Sheriff, but they had no way of knowing about Frank, and probably wouldn't have connected his death with a rape if they had. Lindsey couldn't tell them what happened, and Liz wouldn't. They eventually chalked it up as an unsolvable rape and closed the case. I've talked to the doctors, and the sheriff, to Liz and even Nick. There's no doubt it was self-defense."

My head was spinning like I'd drunk a gallon of wine, waves of dizziness rolling over me until I could barely stay in the chair. I'd been braced to hear Frank raped her. What I hadn't expected was to discover that Nick had lied about killing his father.

That's when my feelings started to change. Up to that point, I was consumed with guilt and feelings of pity for Lindsey. No woman deserved to go through what she had, and it was partially my fault. But now, anger built slowly inside me, helping me get a grip on my emotions. I leaned forward and crossed my arms on the desk.

"You were pregnant. Daniel isn't Nick's son, he's his brother."

"Yes." Lindsey took over the story again. "Mama was the first to realize I was pregnant, but she didn't tell me. I think she was afraid of what I'd do. By then, I was finally starting to recover physically from the rape, but I still wasn't mentally stable. So she found out where they'd sent Nick and called him. Together, they decided that Nick would claim me as his stepsister on his army records. Mama couldn't afford a hospital for me, and the army had good ones. If Nick was my sole support, I could be treated for free as his dependant. They also decided it would be better not to tell me about the baby until I was safely admitted with people around who could watch me."

When Lindsey hesitated, Cody jumped in again. "They waited until Nick was almost done with basic training, then Liz put Lindsey on a bus for Kentucky. Liz was afraid people would start asking questions, so she reported Lindsey missing. Meanwhile, Nick had done all the paperwork and everything was ready. He picked her up at the bus station and took her straight to the hospital."

"And it's a good thing he did," Lindsey said. "When they told me I was pregnant, I really went off the deep end. I couldn't stand the thought of having part of Frank Anderson inside me. It was like being raped all over again, with no way to stop it this time."

She looked down at her hands, and I noticed she was once again wearing long sleeves.

"I tried to kill myself. Every time they left me alone for more than a minute, I'd try. I hated the baby. If the only way to get rid of it was to kill myself, then that's what I thought I had to do. Until the baby came, they put me on a twenty-four hour suicide watch. Then, when he was born, I refused to even look at him. I didn't care what happened to him."

Cody put his arm around her shoulders. "Nick took full responsibility for Daniel. When Lindsey signed away all her paternal rights, Nick adopted him. You've meet Bowie Grant?"

I nodded.

"Well, Nick met Bowie when he was visiting Lindsey at the hospital. Bowie was retired with no family, and he sort of took Nick under his wing. When Daniel arrived, Bowie moved in with them and took care of the baby while Nick was working. Lindsey stayed in the army hospital for the next four years, until Nick's service was up."

She nodded. "After the baby arrived, they were able to start me on a program of medication, and gradually I began to get better, although I was still a long way from being normal. By the time Nick took the job with the oil company, the doctors had decided I'd progressed enough to leave the hospital and live alone. So I went with them when they moved to Saudi. But I still could barely stand the sight of Daniel. I'm not proud of it, but I couldn't seem to help it. When I looked at him, I didn't see Daniel. I saw Frank."

My palms were slick with sweat, and I brushed them against my legs as I leaned back. "But you must have lived with them?"

"No. Nick made arrangements with the company so I'd have my own apartment. I was still seeing a psychiatrist, and once Daniel started school, Bowie kind of took over the job of taking care of me."

I tried to relax, but the longer we talked, the angrier I became, and the more I tensed. "Daniel said you had to talk Nick into coming home."

Her eyes got a faraway look in them and she smiled sadly. "Poor Nick. He was trying to protect both me and Daniel, even though he was miserable. We all knew he couldn't forget you, that he still loved you. I couldn't stand it anymore, couldn't bear to let it continue. Guilt was eating me alive. I knew that if any of us wanted a chance at a normal life, I had to come back and face the past. I had to put things right."

"What will you do now?" I forced my hands together in my lap.

Her gaze refocused and met mine. "I had planned to go live with my mother a while, but Cody convinced me to stay. You see, Daniel doesn't know the truth yet. He still thinks Nick shot Frank. I don't know how he'll react when he finds out what really happened, but he deserves to know why his mother has ignored him all this time. And I really do want the chance to try and get to know my son."

They didn't stay long after that. I walked them to the door and unlocked it to let them out, my anger barely contained. On the threshold, Lindsey stopped and put her hand on my arm. "Please forgive Nick. He loves you so much, and was so afraid that you'd hate him when you discovered the truth."

I didn't answer her, and her hand fell away, a look of sadness in her eyes.

"Are you going to be okay?" Cody asked.

"I'm fine." My calm tone hid the turmoil that boiled inside me.

"If you need me—"

"I'll call," I interrupted. I wanted them gone, out of my store, out of my sight.

I locked the door behind them and returned to my office, the rest of the store dark around me. Slowly, I sank onto my chair and buried my face in my hands. Time crawled by as I sat there, going over every detail of what I'd heard. And with every tick of the clock, my rage grew.

Any rational person would be thrilled that Nick had finally been exonerated. Any rational woman would be delirious with happiness to discover the man she loved hadn't cheated on her after all, that he really had loved her.

But I wasn't rational.

For fifteen years I'd worked hard to make myself hate Nick. For fifteen years I'd blamed him for Katie's death. For fifteen long, agonizing years I'd blamed him for not wanting me. The only thing I hadn't blamed him for was leaving. For leaving me, yes. But not for leaving. I'd thought he had no choice, that he'd been forced into it.

Now I knew better, and it was worse than I'd ever believed possible. All those old feelings swamped me, pulling me down until I was drowning in them.

Because he'd *had* a choice. He could have told the truth and stayed here, gotten help for Lindsey. No one would have subjected her to arrest after what she'd gone through. He could have trusted me enough to tell me what was going on from the beginning. If he had, I might have been able to help, to stop the chain of events that took place.

But he hadn't. He'd chosen to take the blame for Frank's death, and leave me all alone. He'd chosen to protect Lindsey and her child, a child of rape, while my child was left to die.

The pain and grief of Katie's death hit me as if it had happened only yesterday. It felt like someone had torn my chest open and pulled my heart out. And my rage grew. Out of all proportion, it grew until I was shaking with it.

I didn't leave the store until the sun was setting. If anyone had seen me, stopped to talk with me, I would have appeared calm. Unnaturally so. But it would have been the farthest thing from the truth. There was only one thing I could think about now, one thing I wanted.

I wanted to hurt Nick the way he'd hurt me. I wanted him to feel exactly what I was feeling, and know he'd done this to me. And then I never wanted to see him again.

His truck was the only one parked in front of the house he was building, but for the moment I paid no attention. There was something else I had to do before I confronted him.

I flipped on the lights in the front of the barn as I went through, then headed back to my room. Once inside, I grabbed a chair from the table and pulled it to the linen closet. Standing on the seat, I reached far into the darkness of the top shelf until my fingers closed around the box hidden there. I opened the lid and removed the contents, letting the empty box fall to the floor.

Over the years, one of the stalls had become a depository for various tools, things that were rarely used anymore. I rummaged though the pile until I found what I was looking for. A rusty old sledgehammer. Laying the heart-shaped pendant that bore both my name and Nick's on an anvil, I lifted the hammer over my head and brought it down with all my strength. Again and again, I pounded it, until the shape was unrecognizable. And then I picked up the misshapen lump of metal and turned.

Nick was standing behind me, his face pale in the overhead lights. "You know."

I wiped the sweat from my forehead with one hand. "Yes, I know."

"Damn Lindsey to hell." He took a step closer. "I wanted to tell you myself, to try and make you understand—"

"Stop right there." My voice was cold. "I don't want to hear any of your excuses."

"Alix, please—"

"You bastard," I whispered as fury shattered my icy demeanor. I threw the pendant at him, unable to stand its touch another second. It hit his arm and bounced to one side. "Did you know I went to your father's funeral? I went because I wanted to tell him that you were better than he was, that you could never be like him."

A laugh tore its way from deep inside me, a laugh born of anguish and anger. "You really had me fooled."

"Alix." It was a choked, desperate plea, but I wouldn't listen.

"Let me tell you exactly what happened after you decided your slimy nobility was more important to you than I was. Two weeks after you left, I discovered I was pregnant, Nick. Pregnant with your baby. And God, I was so scared, but I was happy too. Happy because I had a part of you no one could take away from me. Scared because I didn't know what to do, and I didn't want to hurt my family."

What little blood was left in his face drained away, leaving his eyes like two dark pits staring at me in shock. "Oh, God."

"You can forget about calling on God," I said furiously. "He never cared anymore than you did."

Only anger kept me going, kept me talking. A red haze of violence covered my eyes until it affected every thing I saw. Needing an outlet for the raw agony coursing through me, I paced up and down in front of him.

"Hugh found out I was pregnant, and asked me to marry him anyway. I didn't know what else to do so I said yes. I didn't love him, but I was willing to live with him to give your child a name. And he was willing to take on the responsibility you didn't want. He claimed the baby as his own, and in his way, he loved her as much as I did."

I whirled to face him. "That's right, Nick. We had a daughter. A beautiful little girl who was your mirror image. She was my life, the only thing I cared about after you left."

In a surge of outrage, I put my hand on his chest and shoved. "So tell me," I snarled. "Where were you when she died? Were you visiting Lindsey in the hospital? Were you busy changing Daniel's diapers, laughing with him? Loving him while Katie died alone without ever knowing her father? What were you doing when I needed you so desperately, when I went through the hell of her dying without you?"

It was the first time in my life I've ever seen a person crumble so completely, and I hope to God I never have to see it again. Right before my eyes Nick aged twenty years. His expression was one of such overwhelming horror and grief that it still haunts me, and his entire body seemed to fold in on itself.

Shoulders slumped, he lifted his hands and covered his face, his frame shaking in hard jerks. "I'm sorry," he whispered, voice ragged with pain. "Oh, God, I'm so sorry."

So I did what I'd set out to do that night. I destroyed Nick without a qualm or a single feeling of remorse. I crushed him like a bug under the heel of my torment. And when it was done, all I had left was emptiness.

Wearily, I gestured toward the door. "Just go. Get out of my sight."

Without another word, he turned and left, stumbling like an old man as he vanished into the night.

I don't know how long I stood there, staring blankly at the walls, drained of all emotion and tired down to my soul. The cats finally brought me back to myself, winding their way around my ankles, crying for attention.

Only then did I turn back to my room. I walked inside, took an overnight case from the closet and began to cram clothes in haphazardly. I didn't know where I was going; I only knew I couldn't stay here. Not in the room that held so many memories, the room where Nick and I had made love. Had it only been last night? It felt like centuries ago.

I ended up at my Uncle Vern's cabin in Hardy. One look at my face must have been enough for him. He opened the door and let me in, and never once questioned my arrival. I swore him to secrecy and spent the next week sleeping or sitting on the banks of Spring River, staring into the icy water. Occasionally, he'd put food in front of me, but I rarely touched it.

Who knows? If Jenna hadn't found me, I might still be there.

Chapter Twenty

ℬ

Mammoth Springs, the source of Spring River, was just across the Arkansas state line from Hardy, in Missouri. The water pouring from the underground springs was icy cold, and when mixed with the warmer air above, a night time fog was the usual results. It hung over the river eerily, seething like a living creature, until the sun burned it off, giving Uncle Vern's backyard a mystical, fairy tale appearance.

I woke early Saturday morning, before dawn, to the sound of my uncle rummaging in the hall closet for his fishing gear. Quietly, I listened to the front door close and the sound of his truck starting, than slid from the bed. Pulling on a pair of jeans and an old T-shirt, I padded barefoot to the kitchen.

The coffee was still hot, so I poured a cup, snagged one of Uncle Vern's flannel shirts to ward off the early morning chill, and walked down to the river. Sitting on the bank, sipping coffee, I watched the sun come up over the mountains and let the peace soak into me.

The gurgle of the river was soothing, almost hypnotic. The first rays of light broke through the fog, turning dew-drenched spider webs into jewelled delicacies of extraordinary beauty. Across the river, a doe stepped hesitantly to the water, a half-grown fawn by her side.

She froze when she saw me, head high, long ears flicking in my direction. For a moment we stared at each other, but when I didn't move she decided I wasn't a threat. Lowering her head to the water, she drank while a red fox squirrel scolded from a tree. Water dripped from her muzzle when she lifted her head again, and she kept an eye on me as the fawn, at some silent signal, took his turn at the river. Then they both vanished into the woods like ghosts, leaving me to wonder if I'd dreamed them.

I continued to sit there long after my coffee was gone, long after the fog had thinned away into nothingness. Sunlight glinted off the silvery scales of trout, leaping from the rapids in pursuit of the insects that hovered above the water, capturing my attention. And gradually, I became aware that I was feeling something.

Or maybe it was a lack of something I felt. Because for the first time since Katie died, the pain was gone. There was no anger left inside me. It was as if it had been burned away, leaving me clean and whole, like metal forged in a blast furnace.

I was pondering this amazing discovery when I heard the soft sounds of footsteps coming down the path from the cabin. They stopped behind me.

"Mind if I join you?"

Carefully, I put my cup on the ground beside me. "How did you find me?"

Jenna's flame-red hair came into view as she sat down, her gaze fixed on the river. "It hit me last night that this was the only place we hadn't looked. I figured if I called, your uncle wouldn't tell me the truth, so I drove up to see for myself."

I wrapped my arms around my knees. "I guess everyone is upset with me."

"They're scared. Cody told us what happened at the store. He blames himself for leaving you alone after that, but he said you seemed so calm that it didn't occur to him you might do something drastic."

When I didn't say anything, she assumed a pose identical to mine. "The Judge came home from the hospital a week ago Friday, and your Aunt Jane has been handling things at Southern Supply. Kenny says she's pretty good at it. You might want to consider keeping her on as an assistant when you get back."

She moved her head just enough to see me from the corner or her eyes. "Bowie brought your car back. He says it should run fine now."

I lowered my forehead to my knees. "And Nick?" I was sure feeling something now. Horror at what I'd done to him, to us, and the realization that I could never take those words back.

"I don't know. No one has seen him. He's even stopped work on the house."

We fell quiet for a few minutes, each of us lost in our own thoughts. Jenna was the one who broke the silence.

"Do you hate me? I know what you're thinking, but I swear, Alix, I wasn't using you."

"I know."

She finally looked at me, surprised. "You do?"

I raised my head and nodded. "After I had time to think about it, I realized I was more shocked and upset because I hadn't figured it out sooner, than because of what you did." Shifting slightly, I faced her. "You love him."

"Since we were kids." Her chin lifted. "And he loves me." Her defiance collapsed like a leaky balloon. "God, it was so hard, loving him and loving you, too. I hated myself, and I hated Hugh for not having the guts to stand up to his family. Helena made it real clear that I wasn't 'suitable' wife material for a Morgan, and Hugh always did what she told him."

"I wish you'd told me. I never would have married him."

"I know. I wish I had, too. But I knew you loved Nick, so it never occurred to me that things would get so out of hand. I couldn't believe it when I found out you'd gotten married." She glanced at me. "Hugh was the first guy I slept with, and the whole time he was dating you, he'd come to me after he dropped you off."

I couldn't help it, I laughed. "Lord, what a mess we were. The whole time I was sneaking around sleeping with Nick, feeling guilty as hell about using Hugh, he was doing the same thing with you." I put my hand on her arm. "I'm so sorry, Jenna. You're probably the only innocent in this fiasco."

"No, don't." She shook her head, red curls bouncing. "I'm not innocent. No one twisted my arm and made me keep seeing Hugh. And for a while after you married him, I didn't. I told him it was over. But then Katie died. He was hurting too, Alix, and you'd simply shut down. When he came to me for comfort, I loved him too much to refuse him."

"Poor Hugh," I murmured. "He was as miserable as I was. So all those times I thought there were other women, it was always you."

This time her laugh was bitter. "Oh, there were others. The irony is that he wasn't doing it to hurt you; he was doing it to hurt me. Every time my conscience started bothering me and I'd tell him not to come back, he'd find someone else to torment me with. And it always worked. After a few weeks he'd show up at my door and tell me how sorry he was, how much he loved me, and I'd take him back. It was like being addicted to a drug. I knew I shouldn't, but I just couldn't help myself."

"Well, he's free now. If you want him, he's all yours."

Her grin was wry. "Thanks, but I'm not sure I *do* want him. I've been doing some thinking of my own lately, and I've decided that I deserve someone better, someone who loves me enough to tell the whole world about it, and who's willing to fight for me if that's what it takes. Maybe I'm the one who's too good for Hugh. Unless he does a lot of changing and growing up, I'm writing him off as a lost cause."

We shared a look of understanding before she asked, "What about you and Nick?"

My gaze went back to the river. "It's over. There is no Nick and me anymore." The ache that surrounded my heart as

I finally put my thoughts into words was nearly unbearable. And I had no one to blame but myself.

"I don't believe that. He's crazy about you."

"Maybe he was, but he's not now. Not after what I did to him. No one could forgive that. Not in a million years."

"You told him about Katie?"

I blinked, trying to expel the moisture that gathered in my eyes. "I didn't just tell him, Jenna. I tore him to shreds with it, very cruelly and deliberately. I wanted to hurt him, and I succeeded beyond anything I could have imagined. He's never going to speak to me again."

"You can't know that."

"And you didn't see him. He was destroyed, and it's my fault. You said he'd stopped working on the house. Since he was building it for me, that should tell you something."

"I see." She took a deep breath and gave me a wry smile. "Do you think they have a twelve-step program for men we could both join?"

"Somehow, I don't think it would work for either of us," I said miserably.

"You're probably right. But, you can't hide here forever. Sooner or later you'll have to go home."

"I can't," I whispered. "I can't go back to the barn, and I refuse to move in with my family like I'm ten years old."

She thought for a second, her head tilted to one side. "You don't have to. I've got a house you can move into. It's small, only two bedrooms, but it's completely furnished and only a couple of blocks from Southern Supply. The owners wanted to sell it, but with the market sluggish like it is, they're willing to rent it out. All we'd have to do is move your clothes and you could be settled in by nightfall."

Maybe it was time for some changes. My life sure hadn't been anything to shout about so far. Abruptly, I made up my mind and stood. "Let me grab my things and leave a note for Uncle Vern."

I suppose part of me hoped that when Nick discovered I was back, he'd call. It was a small, futile hope, but there nonetheless. I sure couldn't call him. Not when deep down I figured he'd give a warmer welcome to Beelzebub rising from the flames of hell than he would to me.

Of course, moving into the little house took a bit more effort than Jenna had implied, and first I had to deal with my family.

Everyone was at the farm when we arrived, and listened quietly while I apologized for scaring them, and gave them the news that I was moving. Once again, they tiptoed around me like they had after Katie died.

Afterward, Jenna helped me pack my things into the boxes we'd picked up on our way through town. Not only did I have my clothes, I had all my personal items and dishes to pack. As each box was filled, one of us would carry it out to the Chevy.

Strangely enough, I discovered I didn't like the car anymore. Like the room in the barn, I had clung to it all these years because it was familiar, because it was a part of Nick I couldn't let go of, even though I hadn't realized that's what I was doing. But for now the Chevy was all I had, so I'd drive it until I could buy a new car.

When the last box was packed, Jenna brushed the hair away from her face, gave me a meaningful glance, and then headed for the door. "I'll go unlock the house and turn on the air conditioner. See you in a few minutes." She was giving me time to say goodbye to my old life, and I took it.

Alone, I stood in the middle of the empty room, my gaze moving over the rickety bed, the lumpy old easy chair, and the small window. There was a feeling of abandonment about the room now, an air of infinite sadness. It was almost as though the room knew its usefulness had come to an end, that no one would ever rest within its sturdy walls again.

With tears in my eyes, I went out and closed the door softly behind me. I was halfway through the front part of the barn when my foot hit something, sent it skittering across the floor ahead of me with a tinkle of metal.

A sob caught in my throat, I leaned down and picked up the remnants of the pendant. Clutching it in my fist, I leaned weakly against a stall, tears streaming down my cheeks. "What have I done?" I whispered, my heart breaking into a million pieces. "Oh, God, what have I done?"

* * * * *

The next week was odd, unreal. I spent Sunday unpacking and arranging my things in the cozy little house I'd leased. It had been remodeled recently and had every convenience I could possibly want, including a flowerbed off the back porch overflowing with roses in every color imaginable. And yet, for me, who had never had close neighbors before, it was strange being able to hear children playing so near. Traffic was a constant background murmur that kept me awake most of those first nights.

Monday morning, I had the utilities switched over into my name, and my phone moved. When I got to work, I discovered Aunt Jane there before me. Neither of us said a word, she just continued as though she'd been working at Southern Supply forever. And Jenna had been right. The woman was a marvel of efficiency. For the first time in ages, I found myself with time on my hands.

I spent it wandering through the store, staring at the merchandise as though I'd never seen it before, and chatting with employees I'd barely spoken with since the day I'd hired them.

Not once during that week did I see or hear from Nick, although I jumped every time the phone rang. Daniel still came to work each afternoon, but I made it a point to keep my distance from him. He looked so much like Nick that it was painful for me. If he found my behavior strange, he didn't show it.

Thursday morning I took the Chevy to the farm, parked it under the shed, and climbed into Jenna's Lincoln. We drove to Jonesboro, and when we came back I was driving a brand new, bright red Isuzu Trooper, a vehicle about as unlike the Chevy as I could find.

It was late that evening when my doorbell rang. I wasn't surprised. Cody had stopped by for a few minutes almost every night. I knew he still felt guilty about leaving me alone at the store that night, even though we were both very careful not to mention the incident again. I think he believed I'd go into screaming fits if he said anything, and being male, he was pretty helpless around crying women, sheriff or not.

I put the last dirty dish in the dishwasher, and went to answer the door. To my surprise, it wasn't Cody, it was Hugh.

"Hi."

"Hello." Puzzled, I simply stood there, frowning.

He shifted his weight from his right foot to his left. "Mind if I come in for a while?"

Well, why not? This entire week had a surreal quality about it. Finding Hugh on my doorstep was just the latest in a long string of weirdness. I pushed the door open and led the way to the kitchen.

"Tea? I just made a fresh pitcher."

"That would be great."

I dumped some ice into glasses, poured the tea, and carried it to the table.

Hugh took it, staring at it like he'd never seen tea before. "I guess you're wondering why I'm here."

"It did cross my mind." I took a sip from my glass.

"Would you believe I miss you?"

"Sure you do. Like a plague victim misses the rat that carried the fleas."

He looked up, smiling. "You weren't that bad."

"Well, that's certainly a load off *my* mind."

His smile dimmed. "I really do miss you, Alix. In spite of everything I did to hurt you, I loved you. Part of me always will."

"Just not the right way," I said quietly.

"No, not the right way." His gaze shifted down again. "Being with you was like being married to my sister."

I reached across the table and took his hand. "Hugh, it wasn't your fault any more than it was mine. We were too young when we got married, and we did it for all the wrong reasons. It's a miracle we stayed together as long as we did. And if it's any consolation, you really weren't that bad either."

"Not even in bed?" He laughed at the expression on my face, and I returned his grin.

"Well, let's just say it's hard to start a fire when all you have to work with are two broken sticks. I don't think either of us put our heart into the effort."

"Maybe if we'd tried harder…"

I released his hand and leaned back. "No. It still wouldn't have worked. We both loved someone else."

"I guess you're right."

"So, how's it going with Jenna?"

He grimaced. "It's not. She won't talk to me anymore. I haven't seen her since that night at the roadhouse. I wish I knew what she wanted."

"That's easy enough," I said softly. "What she wants is someone who'll be proud of her, someone who puts her first."

With a sigh, he lifted a hand to rub his eyes. "I've been a real asshole, haven't I? To you and her both."

"We're only human, and we all make mistakes. I've made some real dillies so don't think you've cornered the market."

"Do you think she'll ever forgive me?"

"You'll have to ask her that."

"What about you?" His gaze met mine. "If it's not too late, I'd like to have my friend back."

Tears filled my eyes and I could barely answer him. "You've got her."

We hugged for a long moment before Hugh gave a shaky laugh. "I better get out of here before they reopen the betting pool at the barbershop."

I released him, took a step back and wiped my eyes. "Who won the first one?"

"Mooney Orr."

My mouth dropped open. "The slimy little shit who beat me up in fourth grade?"

He grinned. "That would be the one. He said after Nick broke his nose and knocked out two of his teeth defending you, he knew you and I didn't stand a chance."

"Well, I'll be damned."

When we reached the front door, he paused and looked down at me. "Can I call you some time, just to talk?"

I smiled. "You can call me any time."

"Thank you." He dropped a kiss on my forehead. "I'll see you later." He was whistling as he went down the sidewalk and I hoped he was on his way to see Jenna. In spite of all we'd been through, or maybe because of it, I knew what a nice guy Hugh could be.

The next day, Friday, went pretty much like the rest of the week had gone. I drifted through it in a semi-daze, opening new accounts for several customers, doing what little paperwork Aunt Jane left me, and generally feeling useless. I even ordered more of those blasted birdbaths just to stay busy.

It was something of a relief when everyone went home that evening, leaving me to gather the receipts and lock up. I piddled for a while, delaying my departure, but there really wasn't much reason to be there. I thought briefly about taking my Trooper for a long drive, but I wasn't in the mood for that either.

In the end, I stopped at the store to pick up some groceries and headed home, knowing tonight would be no different than any other in the last week. I'd watch some boring show on TV until I could barely hold my eyes open, then go to bed and stare at the dark ceiling for the rest of the night, thinking about Nick.

What I didn't expect was to find Daniel sitting on my front porch waiting for me.

I parked the Trooper, got out my bags, and was halfway across the yard before I saw him. Suddenly, my heart was lodged in my throat and my pulse was hammering until I could barely breathe. I realized I'd come to an abrupt halt and forced my awkward feet to move forward until I was standing at the bottom of the steps.

"Daniel?"

When he glanced up, he looked as haggard as I'd been feeling.

"Daniel, what's wrong?"

"It's Dad." His throat moved as he swallowed, and fear shot through me.

"What's wrong? What happened?"

"I don't know what's wrong!" He sounded so desperate that I closed my eyes for a second against the pain.

"Come inside. We can talk there."

Taking one of the bags from my arms, he followed me to the kitchen. I gestured toward a chair. "Sit down."

He slumped onto a chair and I took the one next to him, the groceries forgotten in my worry. "Tell me," I said quietly.

"I think he's trying to kill himself."

"What?" The words hit me like a fist, sent me reeling dizzily, and I knew the blood had drained from my face.

"I don't mean he's got a gun or anything like that, but I don't know what else to call it. He stays locked up in the house all the time, and he won't let Bowie work on the garage or the house. He won't eat, or shave, or anything. He just sits there. We've tried to talk to him, to find out what's wrong, but he doesn't listen and he won't answer. And I know he's not sleeping because I hear him walking around at night after he gets home. I've never seen him like this before."

I was shaking so hard it was a miracle I didn't fall off the chair. "Wait, I thought you said he stays home all the time?"

"During the day he does. But every evening for the last two weeks, he leaves at the same time and doesn't come home until after dark. We didn't know where he was going until yesterday."

A feeling of dread swept over me. I didn't want to ask the next question, but I had to know. "What happened yesterday?"

Daniel looked up, his gray eyes, so much like Nick's, meeting mine. "I followed him. He went to that cemetery near the Baptist church. Do you think that's where his father is buried?"

"Oh, God." I covered my face with my hands. "No. No, it's not where his father's buried." It was where our daughter was buried.

"Alix, you've got to help him. He's been in love with you forever. We all know it. If anyone can get through to him, it's you." His voice dropped to a scared whisper. "If you don't, he's going to die. I don't know what else to do anymore."

I dropped my hands and did my best to pull my shattered heart back together. "You said he leaves at the same time every evening?"

"Yes. At seven." Hope lit his eyes. "Does this mean you'll talk to him?"

I glanced at the clock. It was already six-thirty. "I can't promise it will do any good, Daniel, but I'm going to try. I'm going to try real hard."

"Should I wait here?"

"No. I don't have any idea how long this will take. You might as well go home. I'll call you later."

He stood and hugged me tightly, and I prayed he would never find out that his father's condition was all my fault.

Moving like a robot, I put the groceries away and then went to change out of my business suit. I wanted to give Nick time to get there ahead of me, because I was afraid if he saw me, he'd leave before I had a chance to talk to him. I didn't have any idea how I was going to get through to him; I only knew I had to find a way. And who better than I? If anyone knew about grief and shutting down your emotions, I was that person. Even if the only reaction I got from him was hatred, it was better than nothing.

I waited until fifteen minutes after seven, then climbed in the Trooper and drove slowly across town, and parked in the church's lot. The house Nick had rented wasn't too far away, and I realized he must have walked the distance. His truck was nowhere to be found.

I saw him immediately. Katie's grave was near the back of the cemetery, under a big sweet gum tree, not far from where my Grandmother French was buried. And if I hadn't been expecting him, I'm not sure I would have recognized him.

He was standing there, staring at her headstone, hands in the pockets of his faded jeans. His T-shirt was wrinkled and hung on him loosely, as though he'd lost weight. A beard covered his jaw and his hair looked like it hadn't been combed in days. And my heart broke all over again. I was responsible for this. I had done this to him, and now I had to make it right.

I stopped behind him and he was so oblivious, so lost in his own thoughts, that he didn't know I was there until I touched his arm. When I did, he jumped, then spun to stare at me from red-rimmed eyes. But only for a second.

Before I could form a word, he jerked his gaze away and started to turn. "I'm sorry," he mumbled. "I didn't know you'd be here. I'll go."

"Nick, wait. Please."

He stopped, his head lowered, still refusing to look at me.

"I don't want you to go," I whispered. "I came here to talk to you."

"Talk to me? How can you stand to even look at me after what I did to you?"

I moved until I was in front of him, forced him to meet my eyes. "Listen to me, Nick. You didn't do anything to me. I did it to myself. No one forced me to marry Hugh. No one forced me to turn my grief over Katie's death into anger and hate. Do you understand? I did it to myself."

"You were right to hate me. I left you. You were carrying my baby and I left you." His tone was flat, unemotional.

"I don't hate you!" I was desperate, yelling in my fear for him. "I wanted to hate you. I even convinced myself that I did. But no matter how hard I tried, I couldn't stop loving you. I love you, damn it!"

"Don't. There's no way you could love me, and I don't need your pity." He backed up a step, but his attention was caught by Katie's headstone again, and he stopped. "I never got to see her." His voice was raw with bottled-up pain. "I never got to hold her."

And suddenly I knew how to get through to him. I had to force him to let go of those emotions choking him. Get them out so they could stop poisoning him. It was something my family should have done for me a long time ago, something that Jenna had finally managed that night we sat in her kitchen and cried together.

Frantically, I dug through my purse until I found my wallet. Once I had it open, I took out the picture of Katie I kept with me and handed it to Nick. He took it like a man in a trance, his gaze fastened hungrily on her tiny face.

"Let me tell you about Katie," I said quietly.

And for the next hour, that's exactly what I did. At some point I became aware that tears were running down his cheeks, and silent sobs shaking his body, but I swallowed my own pain and kept going. When I finished, I took the step that separated us and put my arms around him, knowing that his attention was focused on me intently.

"You were only twenty when you left, Nick. Not much more than a boy. You did what you thought you had to, and that's the best any of us can do. Katie died from SIDS. Even if you'd been here, there was nothing you or anyone could have done to stop it. But you saved the child you could. You saved Daniel, and he's wonderful. I wouldn't blame you if you hated me for the way I told you about Katie, but for Daniel's sake, don't keep doing this to yourself. He loves and needs you, and he's scared to death for you."

Almost reflexively, his arms lifted, went around me so tightly I could hardly breathe. With his face buried in my hair, we both cried. We cried for our child, for the hurt we'd caused each other, and for all the time we'd lost. And when there were no tears left, Nick lifted his head and looked down at me.

"I love you," he whispered.

"Then come home with me," I answered.

And he did.

When we reached the tiny house I was renting, he asked where the bathroom was. I pointed him in the right direction and then went to the kitchen. While he showered and shaved, I called Daniel and told him his father was going to be late and not to wait up for him. And then I held the phone away from my ear, smiling at the deafening yell coming across the line.

By the time Nick showed up in the kitchen, cleaner and minus the beard, I had a stack of sandwiches ready. He dug in like he was starved, polishing off almost the entire pile by himself.

Pushing the plate aside, he leaned back in the chair. He still looked tired, but the haggard appearance was fading and his gray eyes were alive again when he looked at me. "Do you have any more pictures?"

Luckily, I did. One of the first things I'd moved were the albums full of Katie's pictures. Together, we sat on my bed, backs against the headboard, shoulders touching, as we went through it and talked, just like we'd done when we were kids. When we'd turned the last page, we held each other for a long time, until our need for another kind of solace became overpowering, and then we made love, slowly and sweetly.

It was dawn when Nick turned to me and clasped my hand. "I swear, I'll never leave you again," he whispered.

I lifted my other hand to his face, fingers caressing his skin. "It wouldn't do you any good if you did," I said. "Because the next time, I'd come after you."

Epilogue

I wish I could tell you that Nick and I were married a week later and lived happily ever after, but I can't. We loved each other, there's no doubt about that, but sometimes love isn't enough. We were two people who had hurt each other beyond words, and things like that aren't easily fixed. It was a long time before the pain began to ease and we learned to trust each other again, a lot of hard work and even harder talks.

There were other problems, too. All the mistakes we'd made hadn't only affected us, they had been like a stone thrown into a pool, the ripples continuing long after the rock reached the bottom.

Daniel finally had to be told about the circumstances of his birth before he discovered them from the local gossips. As painful as it was for them, Nick and Lindsey sat him down and told him everything while I waited at home, chewing my nails with fear for all their sakes.

It was late that night when Daniel showed up at my house with a suitcase full of his clothes. I ushered him to the spare room, tucked him in, and then called Nick to let him know his son was safe. For the next month, Daniel lived with me, a silent, pale ghost that took up space but wasn't really there. I didn't pressure him to snap out of it because I knew this was something he had to work out on his own. Having gone through something similar with my own father, I could understand what he was feeling.

But Daniel was a smart kid. Eventually he realized that sperm does not a father make. It's the unconditional love and caring shown by the person who raises you that makes a parent. For me it was the Judge. For Daniel, it was Nick, and the love they had for each other finally overcame the hurt.

With Lindsey, it wasn't so easy. I think Daniel finally understood why she'd denied him all those years, and even came to forgive her. But part of him could never really accept her as his mother. The best she could hope for was his friendship, and it was slow in coming.

Cody helped somewhat because Daniel liked and respected him. Cody and Lindsey were married six months after they first met, and you can see how much they love each other just by looking at their faces when they're in the same room together.

I will admit it's rather strange knowing she's a member of the family now, but I, too, have learned to forgive and forget. We'll never be best friends after all the years I hated her, and yet I've discovered that Lindsey can be a very sweet, caring person when given the opportunity.

Nick eventually finished building his house, but he didn't move into it. I continued to live in the little house I'd rented, and for the first time in our lives, Nick and I attempted a normal relationship. We went out to dinner, to the movies and plays, and to all the town celebrations. And together, we began to attend church, something I'd thought I would never do again. Aunt Darla was nearly beside herself with excitement.

Speaking of Aunt Darla, lately she's been flashing a diamond engagement ring the size of a hen's egg. And if flashing it doesn't get your attention, she's not above shoving it under your nose. She's still leading Bowie on a merry chase as far as the date of the wedding goes, but the man doesn't know the meaning of giving up. According to Nick, one side benefit of Bowie's association with Aunt Darla was that his cooking improved.

I think they'll have a good, happy life together. Bowie is a vibrant, healthy man who loves working in the garage with Nick and shows no sign of slowing down. And, of course, the only way Aunt Darla will slow down is when they shove her in a box and bury her.

The Judge is fit and fine, still putting out his garden every year. He recovered from the stroke with no lasting damage and takes much better care of himself now. I figure he'll outlive all of us.

Once I heard him regaling Daniel with tales of the wowzer cat who lived under the trestle at the railroad tracks. I had to smile at the look of disbelief on Daniel's face.

Not long ago, my family underwent some shuffling in the arrangement of their living quarters. With Aunt Darla soon to be married and moving in with Bowie, and Aunt Jane practically running Southern Supply single-handedly, it would leave the Judge alone too often. So Mama and Daddy moved back to the farm, and Aunt Jane took over their small brick house. She really likes having a place of her own.

Aunt Jane seems to be happier with her life than I've ever seen her. She positively glories in running Southern Supply. I can understand why. After all, I did the same thing. For a long time the business gave me a reason for living, for going on. Now I have other things that furnish me with those reasons, and I'm thrilled to leave most of the business to Aunt Jane. It allows me the time to fulfill a childhood dream. My writing.

Sometimes the words flow smoothly, like water over slick stones. At other times, my fingers slow on the keyboard, memories swamping my senses until all I can see is the past. Occasionally, the tears still come, but it's funny how I seem to be remembering more of the good things lately than the bad. I credit Nick with this miracle.

A year and a half after that evening in the cemetery, almost to the day, Nick called and asked me to meet him at the house he'd built. Since it was already after dark, I was puzzled, but agreed anyway. Any excuse to see Nick was a good one.

I climbed out of the Trooper and paused to let my eyes adjust to the moon's glow. It was big and round that night, and cast the yard in a silvery-blue sheen of light. I was still standing there when Nick appeared from beneath the dark shadow of a tree.

"Hi," I said, voice low to keep it from carrying on the cool night air. "What's up?"

"There's something I want to show you on the back porch."

I arched a brow as he took my hand and led me across the yard. I'd been to the house hundreds of times, and I couldn't imagine anything on the porch I hadn't seen countless times before.

The yard at the side of the house was pitch-black, but I could see a flickering glow of light coming from the corner of the building. More mystified by the second, I stepped into the backyard and came to an abrupt halt.

Candles lined the rail surrounding the porch, the flames casting a golden glow over the area. Even more light adorned a table set carefully with fresh-cut flowers in a silver urn, and a bottle of champagne with two stemmed glasses.

And in front of the bottle sat a shape I would have recognized if I were blind as a bat. It was a tin of bee balm.

I looked up at Nick, my knees suddenly wobbly, and he smiled before leading me up the stairs. "Open it," he said quietly.

With hands shaking and tears blurring my vision, I lifted the top off the small round can and stared down at the ring nestled on a bed of blue velvet.

His hand moved to my chin, lifted until our gazes met. "Congratulations," he whispered. "Twenty-six years ago, a feisty little girl, armed only with a tin of bee balm, set out to save a ragged, lonely boy. She succeeded so well there's only one thing left to do. Marry me, Alix. It's time we filled this house up with love, laughter and a family."

"Yes," I choked. Crying and laughing at the same time, I threw myself into his arms. "Oh, yes. It's way past time."

Mama was in hog heaven. She finally got to plan that big wedding and took full advantage of the situation, nearly driving everyone crazy with her frantic pace and elaborate schemes. You'd have thought the Queen of England herself was about to tie the knot in Morganville.

I think I finally believed it was really going to happen when Nick slipped away from his bachelor party the night before the wedding and showed up at my door. Smiling, I let him in.

"What are you doing here?" I asked. "You're supposed to be with the good old boys, watching naked girls jump out of cakes and getting sloshed out of your mind."

"There's only one naked girl I want to see," he said putting his arms around me. "Besides, I have something for you, and I didn't figure Darla would let me anywhere near you tomorrow morning."

Reaching into his pocket, he pulled out a box. "I'd like you to wear it for the wedding."

Curious, I opened the box and immediately started crying. Inside lay half of a heart pendant on a golden chain. Nick's name and our wedding date were engraved on the back. Soaking his jacket with my weeping, I reached inside his shirt and tugged out the other half.

"Hey, if I'd known we were going to have to man the lifeboats, I wouldn't have given it to you," he said, holding me tightly. "Want me to take it back?"

"Over my dead body," I sobbed as my mouth found his.

The next day, Mama got to see me walk down the aisle in a fancy white dress to become one with the most handsome groom in the world, one whose love and pride shone from his eyes as he took my hand in front of the whole town. And we both knew that this time there would be no betting pools. This time was forever.

Our wedding was magical. Jenna, of course, was my maid of honor, and she also caught the bouquet after the ceremony. To my surprise, when it came time for Nick to toss my garter, he aimed it right at Hugh. Maybe he was hoping Hugh wouldn't stay single much longer.

I checked to see if Jenna had noticed, but she was pointedly ignoring my ex-husband, and I grinned. Hugh had done a lot of changing, but Jenna wasn't giving an inch until he shook off Helena's hold on him. From the way he was looking at my best friend, I didn't think she'd have much longer to wait.

For our honeymoon, Nick and I spent two wonderful weeks in a secluded cabin high in the mountains. On our return, we moved straight into the house he'd built for us, the house he'd built for me.

Two nights later, during a ferocious storm, lightning struck the old barn. Nick and I stood together on the back porch, leaning against each other for support, as we watched the futile attempts of the fire department to put it out. By dawn, there was nothing left but a blackened square filled with partially burnt timber, acrid smoke rising lazily from the ruins.

"We don't need it anymore," Nick told me softly. "We have each other."

"I know," I replied. But I think both of us felt a deep sense of loss, as though a well-loved old friend had died.

The next day, Daniel moved in with us, and he's one of my greatest joys. He calls me Mom, hits me up for money and asks my advice about girls. I thank God for him every day.

On his sixteenth birthday, I gave him the keys and title to the old Chevy, happy to have a place for it again. Daniel was ecstatic. Gleefully, and with a raw enthusiasm that made me tired to watch, he tore it apart and rebuilt it from the ground up, adding things that were never meant to be on a car that old. But he was happy, so I was happy. But I laid awake nights praying he wouldn't wrap it around a tree.

Nick laughed at my fears and called me a mother hen, but I noticed a few worry lines on his face, too, every time Daniel left in the car.

That was almost a year ago. It doesn't seem possible that Daniel is sending off for college brochures now. Nick appears resigned to our son's leaving the nest, and is looking forward to having the house to ourselves. I hope he's not counting on it too heavily.

Tonight, I sat in the audience at the country club's banquet room and watched my husband stride confidently to the podium to accept the presidency of the Morganville Chamber of Commerce. Amidst thunderous applause, his gaze met mine across the room and I could almost hear his thoughts.

He'd finally kept his promise to me. Frank Anderson's son had become somebody, someone I could be proud of.

Now, as I lie in our bed making this last entry in my journal, one hand cradles my stomach where our child grows. I know exactly what I'm going to say to him when he comes upstairs to join me.

He always was someone. Because the core of the sweet gum tree never changes. Like Nick, the deep red wood stays true to its nature. Strong, and steady, and pure.

Why an electronic book?

We live in the Information Age — an exciting time in the history of human civilization, in which technology rules supreme and continues to progress in leaps and bounds every minute of every day. For a multitude of reasons, more and more avid literary fans are opting to purchase e-books instead of paper books. The question from those not yet initiated into the world of electronic reading is simply: *Why?*

1. ***Price.*** An electronic title at Ellora's Cave Publishing and Cerridwen Press runs anywhere from 40% to 75% less than the cover price of the exact same title in paperback format. Why? Basic mathematics and cost. It is less expensive to publish an e-book (no paper and printing, no warehousing and shipping) than it is to publish a paperback, so the savings are passed along to the consumer.

2. ***Space.*** Running out of room in your house for your books? That is one worry you will never have with electronic books. For a low one-time cost, you can purchase a handheld device specifically designed for e-reading. Many e-readers have large, convenient screens for viewing. Better yet, hundreds of titles can be stored within your new library — on a single microchip. There are a variety of e-readers from different manufacturers. You can also read e-books on your PC or laptop computer. (Please note that

Ellora's Cave does not endorse any specific brands. You can check our websites at www.ellorascave.com or www.cerridwenpress.com for information we make available to new consumers.)

3. *Mobility.* Because your new e-library consists of only a microchip within a small, easily transportable e-reader, your entire cache of books can be taken with you wherever you go.

4. *Personal Viewing Preferences.* Are the words you are currently reading too small? Too large? Too… ANNOYING? Paperback books cannot be modified according to personal preferences, but e-books can.

5. *Instant Gratification.* Is it the middle of the night and all the bookstores near you are closed? Are you tired of waiting days, sometimes weeks, for bookstores to ship the novels you bought? Ellora's Cave Publishing sells instantaneous downloads twenty-four hours a day, seven days a week, every day of the year. Our webstore is never closed. Our e-book delivery system is 100% automated, meaning your order is filled as soon as you pay for it.

Those are a few of the top reasons why electronic books are replacing paperbacks for many avid readers.

As always, Ellora's Cave and Cerridwen Press welcome your questions and comments. We invite you to email us at Comments@ellorascave.com or write to us directly at Ellora's Cave Publishing Inc., 1056 Home Avenue, Akron, OH 44310-3502.

Cerridwen Press

Cerridwen, the Celtic goddess of wisdom, was the muse who brought inspiration to storytellers and those in the creative arts.

Cerridwen Press encompasses the best and most innovative stories in all genres of today's fiction.

Visit our website and discover the newest titles by talented authors who still get inspired—much like the ancient storytellers did...

once upon a time.

www.cerridwenpress.com